DISCARDED

THE ONE TRUE LOVE
OF ALICE-ANN

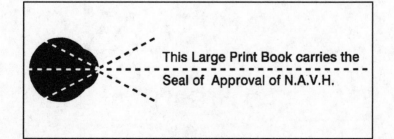

This Large Print Book carries the
Seal of Approval of N.A.V.H.

THE ONE TRUE LOVE OF ALICE-ANN

EVA MARIE EVERSON

THORNDIKE PRESS
A part of Gale, a Cengage Company

Farmington Hills, Mich • San Francisco • New York • Waterville, Maine
Meriden, Conn • Mason, Ohio • Chicago

LIBRARY OF CONGRESS CATALOGING-IN-PUBLICATION DATA

Names: Everson, Eva Marie, author.
Title: The one true love of Alice-Ann / by Eva Marie Everson.
Description: Large print edition. | Waterville, Maine : Thorndike Press, a part of Gale, a Cengage Company, 2017. | Series: Thorndike Press large print Christian romance
Identifiers: LCCN 2017028783| ISBN 9781432843205 (hardcover) | ISBN 1432843206 (hardcover)
Subjects: LCSH: Large type books. | Christian fiction. gsafd | BISAC: FICTION / Christian / Romance.
Classification: LCC PS3605.V47 O54 2017b | DDC 813/.6—dc23
LC record available at https://lccn.loc.gov/2017028783

Published in 2017 by arrangement with Tyndale House Publishers, Inc.

Printed in the United States of America
1 2 3 4 5 6 7 21 20 19 18 17

To the heroes and heroines of World War II, those who fought abroad and those who fought at home. You truly are "the greatest generation."

ACKNOWLEDGMENTS

Books are never written alone, although writing can be a solitary life. Novels that take place in a bygone era are *certainly* not written alone.

And so I say thank you to all those who were instrumental in helping me create what has become one of my favorite stories to date.

To my brother, Van Purvis, who shared with me about WWII POWs in Georgia and the stories our grandmother told him. Thank you to my aunt Audrey Purvis Deloach, who shared about her life as a farmer's daughter in the 1940s. Thank you to my old classmates Craig Evans, a sixth-generation Southern farmer who explained so much about farming, both *now* and during WWII (and thank you to our classmate Marty Robinson, for suggesting I speak to him!), and Ron Evans, whose service to our country is beyond appreciated. The moments I spent with you and Jan Gay in the hallway of Veterans' Victory House as the WWII soldier "graduated to glory" will forever stay with me.

Aunt Mary Beth Kicklighter Branch, thank you for the brief story you shared with me many, many years ago about marrying Uncle Warner and then not seeing him again for so long because of the war. This brief exchange has resonated within my heart all these years. Huge thank-yous to my uncles Jerry and Bobby Kicklighter — Mother's big brothers — who also shared so much with me about life at home during the war, about my great-grandfather losing much of his land for Camp (Fort) Stewart, and about how life in the South changed during those years. Uncle Jerry, your story about the cow and the bell made it into the book!

Allison Bottke, you helped me understand issues of cattle enough that I felt secure in what I wrote about cows on a farm. Cynthia Howerter, thank you so much for sharing your uncle's story, which was so much like the story I heard years ago of the WWII soldier shot down in the Pacific. A very special thank-you to my uncle Vondes Purvis, whose "bacon and eggs" line has stayed with me my whole life. (I love and miss you, still . . .)

Thank you, Jonathan Clements, agent extraordinaire, for this and so much more.

Tyndale! I love my Tyndale family and especially my editors, Jan Stob and Kathy Olson.

Thank you!!!! Sandie Bricker. As my critique partner you kept me going when I wanted to quit (somehow, always around chapter 5). You cried and laughed in all the right places. And you trust me enough to give your honest opinion.

A GIANT THX to Word Weavers International, my precious, hardworking weavers of words. Thank you for allowing me to be a part of your tapestry.

Thank you, Lord God. Your goodness toward me amazes me daily.

CHAPTER 1

Bynum, Georgia
December 7, 1941
2:20 P.M.

Alice-Ann Branch stood in front of her bedroom dresser, eyes focused on her reflection in the large oval mirror hanging before her. Her foot tapped to the rhythm of a Glenn Miller tune that played in her head as her slender fingers wound frizzy light-brown hair, first from the right side of her face, then from the left. She secured both sides — as best she could — with the new tortoiseshell combs she'd purchased the day before at Hillis's Five & Dime with money Grandmother Branch had sent for her birthday.

She blinked hazel eyes, large and plain, then frowned at the overall vision looking back at her. "Silly ole freckles," she said, leaning closer. "I bet Shirley Temple doesn't have to put up with these things." Or if she did, they were covered by stage makeup. Oh, if only she lived in Hollywood, California, instead of stinky ole Bynum, Georgia.

Or if she could only have skin like Claudette's, all peaches and cream and naturally blushed. Or a shapely figure like Maeve's. Even at sixteen, Maeve's curves put Rita Hayworth's to shame.

Alas, what God had given her two best friends he'd somehow managed to skip right over when the doling-out time came for her.

In her case, the time hadn't come. It simply *went*.

Maybe, she reckoned, when elements of grace were being passed out, God hadn't been able to locate the farmhouse where her mother — God rest her soul — had brought her only daughter into the world. Oh, sure, the Almighty had done quite well when it came to her older brother, Nelson. He'd grown up to be tall and lanky like their father, with the olive complexion of their mother. Why, even his eyelashes were long and naturally curled. He was all Cary Grant with a dollop of Clark Gable. Or maybe a dash of that new radio star, Frank . . . what was his name?

Alice-Ann dashed out of the bathroom and down the stairs to where her family — Papa, Nelson, Nelson's bride Irene, and

12

Papa's older sister Aunt Bess — sat around the living room Zenith, listening to a Sunday afternoon football game. The shouts of the fans nearly drowned out the announcers, not that she could make much out of what they were saying anyway.

Football had never been of much interest to her.

Well, except when Mack played for the high school team, back when he and Nelson and Maeve's brother, Carlton, had been in school.

"Hey, Irene," Alice-Ann said, stopping just inside the wide opening between the expansive shotgun hallway and the living room. "What's the name of that — ?"

"Hush now, Alice-Ann. Can't hear with you blabbering on," her father scolded. He scooted up in his chair, his pipe clutched tight between his teeth, and rested his elbows on his knees. He still wore his Sunday-go-to-meeting slacks, but he'd changed out of his one good shirt, replacing it with a long-sleeved flannel.

"Sorry, Papa."

"*. . . on the twenty-yard line . . .*" Alice-Ann managed to catch the announcer's words from the crackling of the radio her father had purchased only a year before during an after-Christmas sale in town at Smitty's

Department Store.

Alice-Ann scooted over to where Irene sat next to Nelson, flipping absentmindedly through the latest *Ladies' Home Journal* magazine. Irene didn't bother looking up, even as Alice-Ann squatted beside her. "Hey, Irene," she whispered. "What's the name of that new singer with the Tommy Dorsey band? Frank somebody? The one you showed me in that magazine?"

Irene sighed heavily. "Sinatra."

"Alice," Aunt Bess said from the chair angled in the far corner of the room, away from the clamor of the radio and others. She held knitting needles in her hands and worked gold yarn furiously between them.

Alice-Ann stood. "Yes, ma'am?"

Aunt Bess jerked her head in a "come here" motion.

Alice-Ann sighed. Here she was, all of sixteen as of today, and still she felt like a child in the presence of her family. "Yes, ma'am," she said, skirting around the sofa to the chintz chair.

That chair. It had been a favorite of her mother's, and Alice-Ann could still see her sitting in it. Feet shed of shoes and curled up under her, hidden by the folds of a floral-print dress. In spite of the six years that had passed since her death, whenever Alice-Ann walked past it, she smelled hints of the gardenia perfume that wafted from the lotion Mama always wore. Still saw the beautiful Earlene Branch, with her soft waves of blonde hair and her oh-so-perfect smile framed by bubble gum–colored lips. And whenever she dared sit there — typically in the earliest hours of morning when everyone else slept — she felt her mother's arms, heard her voice singing along to her favorite songs and speaking of long-ago stories.

"Tell me again, Mama. Tell me about meeting Papa and falling in love . . ."

"Your papa was such a handsome man. And funny! Oh, so funny."

"Really, Mama? Papa was funny?"

Even as old as nine and ten years of age, Alice-Ann could hardly imagine her no-nonsense father as being anything but crotchety.

"So funny, Alice-Ann. He always made me laugh. Still does, when it's just him and me. Alone."

"And he asked you to the dance and . . ."

"He and my brother Joe were good friends. They had come up to the church one day while I was practicing my solo for the next morning — that was shortly before the Spring Fling. I remember how he looked at me that day, there in the church. Like he was seeing

me for the first time. And when the dance came around, and — hmm. Well, there was another little complication, but he asked Joe if he could take me along as his date anyway."

"And Uncle Joe didn't like it one bit."

"No, he didn't. But your papa was relentless —"

"What's relentless?"

"Relentless means he wouldn't give up. Said he couldn't give up on the idea of holding me in his arms and swinging me all around the dance floor. Maybe stealing a kiss or two."

"And then one day he asked you to marry him."

"That's right. Said he only had this old farm of his daddy's to bring me to, but one day it would yield a right nice crop. It has, too. We survived hardships because your papa's worked hard."

"Because he loves you?"

"Because he loves all of us. You and Nelson and me . . ."

"Alice," Aunt Bess said, her piercing brown eyes never leaving her handwork. "We've managed to eat a cold lunch, and Irene and I have gotten the kitchen cleaned up, and all so your party can start on time without a hitch. Your friends will arrive within the next two hours." Only then did she glance up and cock a brow. "So why

16

don't you go check the back room and make sure everything is set up like you want for your party and stop worrying your daddy. Least you could do, considering how much Brother hates cold cuts for lunch especially on a day as nippy as this one."

"Yes, ma'am." Alice-Ann stepped back, pulled the sides of the plum-colored dress Aunt Bess had made special for her celebration, and spun around. "But before I do, what do you think, Aunt Bess?" she asked, keeping her voice down. "Do I look all grown-up like you said I would?"

Aunt Bess had returned her attention to her knitting but stopped long enough to size her up. She gave Alice-Ann a generous wink. "You'll do in a pinch," she said with a smile.

"Oh, Aunt Bess." Alice-Ann leaned over to give her maiden aunt a tight squeeze, but not without protest from the family's matriarch. "I'm absolutely about to burst with excitement about my party." She kissed Aunt Bess's dry cheek, which with Aunt Bess's size, also tended to be fleshy. "Thank you for convincing Papa."

"Stop this foolishness now," Aunt Bess said, her voice filled with a lilt. "You'll ruin this afghan I'm working on."

Alice-Ann pulled herself away. "Yes'm. I'll

17

go check on things." Not only because her aunt had asked, but more because she wanted everything to be perfect. Better than perfect. Because tonight — oh, *tonight.* Tonight, when everyone was laughing and dancing and drinking punch and eating Aunt Bess's cake, she'd tell Mack — Boyd MacKay to be exact, the most handsome man alive and one of her brother's best friends — that she'd loved him since she'd been a girl of twelve and that, if he'd only give her a chance, she'd devote herself to loving him for eternity. And if he turned her down, she'd . . . she'd . . . well, she'd be *relentless.*

Her thoughts were nearly drowned out by her father and brother, both of whom had drawn upright, staring at the large radio against the wall and in front of the sofa. "Come on, now," Nelson hollered, his fist in the air. "Run, now. Run!"

"He's gonna do it," Papa added. "That son of a gun's gonna make it."

Even as little as Alice-Ann knew about the game, the wild cheers from the spectators — those thousands of voices that rose from across the miles of wire and somehow managed to infiltrate their Sunday afternoon living room — told her something spectacular and exciting had happened. She looked over her shoulder and winked at Aunt Bess, who shook her head at what she called "tomfoolery."

Alice-Ann reached the opening to the hallway and foyer when the tone of the broadcast changed. She turned instinctively, resting her hand on one of the spindles that rose from the half wall between the living room and foyer.

"We interrupt this broadcast to bring you this important bulletin from the United Press —"

"What in the world?" Papa asked, clearly agitated. Sunday afternoon sports were one of the few things in life he looked forward to.

Even Irene glanced up, and Aunt Bess stopped her knitting.

"Flash: Washington. The White House announces Japanese attack on Pearl Harbor —"

Alice-Ann looked at her father as he and Nelson locked eyes. "Sweet Lord, have mercy," he said. "Well, Son. No doubt about it. We'll be going to war now."

Alice-Ann ran the near mile between the farmhouse she called home and the next farmhouse over, the one belonging to Mr. George James, his wife Miss Josephine, and their two sons, George Junior and Pete. She and Pete were in the same class at Bynum

High School.

As soon as she passed through the squeaking gate of the unpainted picket fence separating the yard from Miss Josephine's winter garden, the family's mutt dog scampered off the porch to meet her, tail wagging as if there were nothing wrong in the whole wide world.

Alice-Ann reached down to pet the hound between his ears. "Hey there, Sniffer," she said, her voice strained from the knot in her throat. She took several deep breaths. "You may not know it, but we've got a mess on our hands."

The front door rattled open and Alice-Ann looked up to see Pete — all six feet and big ears of him — standing in the opening behind the screen door. "Hey, Alice-Ann," he drawled. "You heard, I guess?"

Alice-Ann nodded. "I've come to use your phone, if you don't mind."

He pushed the screen open. "Sure thing."

She gave Sniffer a final pat and started up the front porch steps, the dog at her heels.

"Go lay on down, dawg," Pete said.

"He's not bothering —" Alice-Ann started, but Sniffer had already found his spot on a pile of blankets thrown onto the gray-painted planks of the wide porch.

She entered the house to the scents of

20

fried chicken and pumpkin pie. As in the home she'd left minutes before, the family sat around the living room radio. Mister George looked as if he'd topple off the edge of his chair at the slightest breeze. At the sight of a visitor — even a neighborly one — Miss Josephine stood, wringing her hands in her bib apron. "Alice-Ann," she said. "It's awful. Just awful."

Alice-Ann nodded. She tried — truly, ever since she heard the announcer breaking into the football game — to think about the men and women who had undoubtedly lost their lives way over there in Hawaii. But right then something else weighed heavy on her heart, not that she could easily share it with any of the adults in her life. One word from her torn heart would send her from the "you're nearly grown" ranks and right back to "you're still just a child."

"Miss Josephine," she said, "I need to use your phone, if you don't mind. I was — I was to have my birthday party this evening —"

Josephine James brushed imaginary wisps of hair from her high forehead as she crossed the room. "Where's your coat, hon? I can't believe Bess let you out of the house without a coat."

Alice-Ann looked down at herself, still

dressed in her party attire. "I ran out in such a hurry."

Pete had joined George Junior on the worn floral-print sofa. He cracked his knuckles and declared, "I'm signing up, Daddy. I'll go get them Japs."

Alice-Ann gasped. Only then did it dawn on her . . . *Nelson.* Would he be required to sign up? To go to war? *If* they went to war? And surely they would. Papa had said so.

Her brother hadn't been required to register the year before when President Roosevelt signed the Selective Training and Service Act. At twenty, he'd been too young, though he'd be twenty-one soon enough. But what about now? And what about — *Mack?*

Mack, whose father and mother — Mister Lance and Miss Myrtle — ran MacKay's Pharmacy, Mr. MacKay being the pharmacist. Only a few years ago, he'd wanted nothing more than for Mack to follow in his footsteps, and while Mack had toyed with the idea — even going to school for a while — he'd never really settled in.

"Come on, Alice-Ann," Miss Josephine said, startling her. The doe-eyed woman placed her hand on Alice-Ann's arm. "I know, hon. This has put me in a terrible state too."

Alice-Ann nodded, saying nothing, and followed along behind like old Sniffer had trailed her only moments earlier. "Miss Josephine," she whispered as they entered the bright kitchen at the back of the house. The room remained warm from Sunday dinner; still, Alice-Ann shivered as she crossed her arms. "Do you think — ?"

Miss Josephine turned to look at her. "Something to drink, Alice-Ann? Some hot tea perhaps?"

"No, ma'am." She swallowed. "Miss Josephine, do you think that — that we'll go to war?"

"I don't know," Miss Josephine answered, looking down at her sensible brown shoes. The woman who had always been a paragon of fortitude in Alice-Ann's eyes now seemed frail and unsure. "My George said we would, soon as he heard the news."

"So did Papa. He said there's no avoiding it now. No pretending the rest of the world isn't falling down around us." She glanced over her shoulder. "But what about — do you think — anyone from *Bynum* will have to go?"

Miss Josephine's lips, still tinted red from fixing herself up for church that morning, drew into a thin line. "I don't know, hon," she said. "But if I had to guess, I'd say probably so. We certainly lost enough young men back in the Big One. What's to keep it from happening again, I wonder."

Alice-Ann's hands flew to her mouth. George Junior, having turned twenty-one recently, had been required to enlist. That meant —

The older woman pulled a chair out from the kitchen table and sat. "My George says Mr. Roosevelt will probably drop the age down to eighteen, what with all this. Pete will be spared, but George Junior will — if we go — George Junior will for sure now —" Her eyes filled with tears. "Eighteen or twenty-one won't matter for him."

Alice-Ann rushed to sit next to the woman who'd been as much like a mother to her as Aunt Bess, and she grabbed her hands. "Don't worry, Miss Josephine," she said. "If our boys have to go, this war will be over before they have time to get their boots dirty. They don't know who they're messing with over there. You'll see."

Miss Josephine gave a weak smile as tears slipped down her cheeks. "Such hope and optimism in someone so young."

So young. Sixteen wasn't young. Sixteen *that day.* How could those Japanese do something like this on *her* day? And what about her party? Ruined. Her night of declaration of love for Mack. Destroyed. All because people over there in a faraway country wanted more than God had given them by rights. "Miss Josephine." Alice-Ann's voice returned in a whisper. "I have to use your phone now. Aunt Bess says there's no sense in trying to celebrate anything tonight, and if I don't make some calls right away, everyone will show up at the house before too long."

"No." Miss Josephine shook her head. "No sense at all." She jerked her head toward the back of the kitchen. "You know where the phone is, hon. Go make your calls."

Alice-Ann stood, her hands slipping from Miss Josephine's. "Thank you, ma'am."

Miss Josephine looked up as she brushed the last of her tears away. "What an awful thing to have happen on your birthday," she said as though the notion suddenly struck her. "And your party spoiled too. Who will you call first?"

Alice-Ann didn't have to think long. "Boyd MacKay," she said, then felt heat rush to her cheeks. "Because he has a phone, what with his daddy being the pharmacist and all, and he can make some calls for me." She spoke the words too fast, even by her own estimation.

Miss Josephine smiled, and Alice-Ann wondered if the woman had gone wise to her motives. "That's true," she said graciously. "Then I daresay you should call your friend Claudette after you hang up with Boyd. With her gift of gab, that girl won't *need* a phone to let the others know."

CHAPTER 2

To Alice-Ann's way of thinking, Tucker's
Soda & Ice Cream Shoppe — which doubled as a hamburger joint and magazine
stand — seemed both eerily silent and
bursting at the seams with conversation. On
Monday after school — where they'd all
been ushered into the auditorium to hear
the president's speech — she sat in a high-
backed booth alongside the left wall, opposite the stretch of counter and chrome
barstools, each occupied. The aroma of
burgers sizzling in the kitchen reached
across the room, stirring Alice-Ann's stomach. Across the table, Claudette Evans
leaned over an ice cream soda, pulling on
the straw with crimson-painted lips. "So
what did Aunt Bess say, exactly?" she asked
between sips. "Can you or can't you have
your party this coming weekend?"

"She only said, 'We'll see.' Papa is pretty
sure the world as we know it is coming to

27

an end. He says that if ever the farmers would be needed, it's now." Alice-Ann took a sip of her own soda. "All Aunt Bess will really say is, 'Emmitt, don't upset the kids so.' "

"Meaning *you.*"

Alice-Ann frowned. "Yeah. It's not like Nelson and Irene are children, and I guess my sixteenth birthday meant nothing at all when it comes to thinking of me as a grown-up instead of a child."

"Did you at least get to eat your cake?" Claudette tilted her head. The overhead light reflected on her blonde hair, causing it to shimmer. Once again, Alice-Ann felt the pang of having mousy do-nothing hair, and she grabbed a handful of it and tugged.

"No one felt like eating anything, much less cake."

The jukebox tune changed from "When You Wish upon a Star" to "Blue Skies" as the front door opened, momentarily filling the room with afternoon sunlight. Alice-Ann looked up to see Maeve practically sliding toward them, her skirt swaying as she darted between the patron-filled tables. "Hey, Ernie," she called to the soda jerk at the counter as she reached the booth.

Ernie Tucker smiled a toothy grin, the first ray of sunshine in an otherwise-somber restaurant. Alice-Ann supposed no one felt like smiling, even though their appetites hadn't changed. "Hey, Maeve," he called back.

Claudette leaned over the table. "Ernie's so smitten he can't see his root beer from his Coke floats." She winked and Alice-Ann giggled.

"How about a dish of vanilla?" Maeve called over the music and conversation.

"Coming right up," he said, then nearly fell over himself getting to the ice cream freezer at the far end of the fountain.

Claudette and Alice-Ann laughed all the harder as Maeve slid in beside Claudette. "Wait till you girls hear the buzz on the street," she said, her voice conspiratorial.

The hair on the back of Alice-Ann's neck prickled. Something in Maeve's face told her this wasn't about a new Bing Crosby film coming to town. "What?" she all but whispered.

"We all heard the speech the president made today at noon, right? Well, after school I went home and Daddy says it was on the radio in every house in America. That *no* self-respecting American would have missed it."

Maeve's father owned the five-and-dime. She, her older brother Carlton, and their parents lived in the spacious apartment overhead. Often were the times Alice-Ann and Claudette had spent the night with Maeve, sneaking downstairs, once the upstairs lights had gone down, to rummage through the goods and snag a chocolate bar or two. As long as business hours were in effect — Monday, Tuesday, Thursday, Friday, and Saturday from nine until five, and Wednesday from nine to noon — Anson and Mary Catherine Hillis, Maeve's parents, kept a radio playing behind the cash register counter. Getting the news before anyone else in town was of paramount importance to Mr. Hillis, Papa had remarked a time or two at the dinner table. But, Alice-Ann supposed, this time the town had been right on time with him.

"It's what this entire soda shop is talking about," Claudette muttered. "If you listen carefully, the only thing you hear is 'war' and 'Japs' and 'Axis powers' and —" Claudette ducked her chin to lower her voice — " 'a date which will live in infamy.' "

"I don't even know what *infamy* means," Alice-Ann retorted. "But I have a feeling it's going to affect me one way or the other."

Ernie appeared then and placed the ice cream dish in front of Maeve. "Here you go, M.," he said.

"Thank you, E."

He slid into the booth in the vacant spot next to Alice-Ann, forcing her to slide closer to the wall. "Are y'all talking about the war? About us going into it?"

Alice-Ann sighed. Didn't he have work to do?

"Are you sure, Ernie?" Maeve asked, batting her lashes at him as he pulled the starched white soda jerk cap off his head and placed it on her own. "About us going into the war?"

Gracious, the way that girl flirted one would think she was Ginger Rogers or somebody.

"Yeah, I'm sure. You heard what President Roosevelt said today good as I did. And I'll tell you one thing, boy. I'd sign up tomorrow, if I could." He reached across the table and grabbed Maeve's hand. "Would you like that, Maeve? Would you be proud of me if I went over there and kicked those Japs right between the teeth?"

Maeve frowned, her thick brows forming a V between her dark eyes. "No, I wouldn't like that. I wouldn't like that at all, Ernie Tucker. I don't want anyone I know going off to war. What if you never come back, huh? What if you end up six feet under some foreign soil or in the middle of the

31

Pacific Ocean?"

Alice-Ann kept her focus on her ice cream soda. Like Ernie could go even if he wanted to. That boy's asthma had kept him off of every sports team since they'd been in elementary school.

"Ah, no, M.," he said, and Alice-Ann cut her eyes over to the two of them. "You watch. With boys like your brother and Mack and the others signing up —"

"Mack?" Alice-Ann jumped in her seat. "Surely you don't mean Boyd MacKay."

"What are you talking about, Ernie?" Maeve cut in, sliding her hand out from under Ernie's bony one. "*My* brother? Carlton's not going off to war. You're full of beans."

"Sure he is." Ernie reached across the table to rescue his cap from Maeve's head, then placed it on his. "I gotta get back behind the counter." He slid partially out. "But just so you know, Dad said Carlton and Mack were in here earlier. Them and a few others. All of 'em talking about taking the bus to Camp Stewart to enlist over there." He stood. "Can't believe your daddy didn't tell you, M." He winked. "Enjoy your ice cream."

Maeve pouted as she pushed the bowl

away. "Enjoy your ice cream, my great-aunt Agnes."

Alice-Ann sank against the wall, feeling the cold of it seeping into her back, turning her spine to stone. "Mack," she whispered. "This can't be true. *Can't* be happening." Not now. Not when she was so close to telling him how she felt.

Claudette grabbed her hand. "It's gonna be all right, kiddo," she said. "Don't worry. I bet if you tell Mack how you feel, how you *really* feel, he'll stay." She looked around the room as if she'd lost someone. "I mean," she said, her eyes returning to Alice-Ann's, "*all* the men in town can't leave for the war, can they?"

Maeve stood. "I gotta go." She reached into the side pocket of her dress and brought out a dime, which she laid on the table. "I gotta go," she said again, then turned and left.

Alice-Ann and Claudette watched her until the glass door had closed behind her, then looked again at each other. "Breathe, Alice-Ann," Claudette said.

"I don't know if I can."

"Listen, all you have to do is tell him. Beg Aunt Bess on your knees if you have to, but be sure you have that party." Her eyes softened. "Tell him. He won't go. I'm sure of it."

But Alice-Ann didn't feel the same confidence as her friend. Instead, she buried her face in her hands and said, "Now I think I know what *infamy* means."

By the time Alice-Ann neared home — taking the five o'clock bus to the remote crossroad, one-fourth of which doubled as the long stretch of driveway leading to the farmhouse — she'd devised a plan. She knew exactly what needed to happen to ensure her happiness. Hers and Mack's.

All she had to do, really, was talk him into marrying her. Now. Before he left Bynum and headed to wherever men who joined up to fight the Japanese went to train for such things. She could go with him, perhaps. Surely the military had a place for married couples to live. Probably drab, colorless square rooms without personality, but Aunt Bess could teach her how to make curtains and throw pillows and . . .

Or, if going with Mack was out of the question, she could at least stay in the States and dutifully wait for him.

Alice-Ann stepped off the bus alone, saying a hurried good-bye to the driver, old Ben Brown — who wasn't old at all, to tell the truth. She clutched her schoolbooks to her chest, her imitation lizard leather purse dangling from her wrist.

The sky had grown darker than expected. By now, she would have usually made it home, typically been hard at work helping Aunt Bess with supper. But the distressing news about so many boys leaving for Savannah — Mack in particular — had kept her in town a little later.

Aunt Bess would be somewhere between worried and mad. And Irene? Well, Irene would be simply furious because she'd had to carry the load of helping without Alice-Ann's assistance.

Alice-Ann frowned. The relationship she'd hoped for when Nelson announced his betrothal to Irene Marks had become anything but. She'd always wanted an older sister, someone to show her how to put on lipstick and rouge and to talk with about clothes and boys. Someone she would have had automatically, maybe, had her mother not died.

Aunt Bess certainly didn't fill that role. Aunt Bess was a *maiden* aunt who'd put on too much weight in her thirties and allowed herself to grow old before her time, Papa always said. Aunt Bess wore her graying hair up in a "puffy bun," wisps of it curling around her face. She never wore makeup, not even the tiniest bit of lipstick on Sunday.

And the last thing she did was gab about Hollywood and clothes. Certainly not boys.

But Aunt Bess had, once upon a time, been young and vibrant. Alice-Ann had seen the pictures. For years they'd hung in the living room along with other family photos. So Alice-Ann knew . . . Aunt Bess had hardly been a beauty — Alice-Ann looked remarkably like her, a point which distressed her greatly — but she'd always had remarkable spirit and godly character.

She'd been engaged to be married once but lost her fiancé in the Great War. Romantic as that had always seemed to be, Alice-Ann found it hard to believe her aunt, even back in those vivacious days, had so much as dated. The notion didn't seem to fit, which scared Alice-Ann even more about her own life's fate, if God chose that she follow the path of her doppelgänger.

On the upside of having Irene as a sister-in-law, she sure could be dandy at talking about Hollywood and movie stars and who dated whom or had been seen out with this one or that one at movie premieres and expensive restaurants. But she couldn't have been further from the sister Alice-Ann had hoped for. Sometimes, in fact, Alice-Ann felt that Irene only tolerated Nelson's family, waiting for the day when the two of them could either have the farmhouse to themselves or build their own place.

Alice-Ann increased her speed and prepared her "why I'm late" speech as she ran up the front porch steps and along the side of the wraparound porch to the back door. She opened the screen, balancing it on her elbow as she rattled the old brass knob and pushed the door open to the warmth of the kitchen.

Aunt Bess stood at the gas stove Papa had bought not too long after Nelson and Irene had married back in the summer, stirring a wooden spoon in a pot of, from the smell of it, either turnip or collard greens. "Where have you been?" she demanded. Then, before Alice-Ann could answer, she added, "Never mind. I'm sure you've got a story spun and ready to tell. Get your coat off, Alice, and help Irene set the table."

Alice-Ann dropped her books on the white laminate countertop beside her, aware of the scowl on Irene's face. She held a stack of plates and placed them, one at a time, around the old kitchen table Aunt Bess had painted pale yellow before the wedding. "To go with the curtains," she'd said, then proceeded to whip out material accented in tiny yellow flowers she soon enough made into ruffled curtains for the windows along the back wall. Aunt Bess had wanted, if nothing else, the girl from town marrying her nephew to feel as much at home as possible in the old farmhouse. Not that Irene ever uttered a thank-you so far as Alice-Ann knew.

"Sorry, Aunt Bess," Alice-Ann said, hurrying to the silverware drawer. "Everyone in town is buzzing like bees about the boys going to Camp Stewart to sign up. You know —" she jerked the drawer under the drainboard sink open and pulled out the necessary utensils — "for the war."

"What are you talking about?" Aunt Bess asked, turning back to the stove.

Irene nearly dropped the last of the plates onto the table, her face pale and her mouth gaped. "What?"

"Don't worry, Irene," Alice-Ann said, placing the silverware on the table. "I'm sure this won't have anything to do with Nelson. The men in town were saying the same thing Papa says — the farmers will be needed here now, more than ever. People have got to have food and food comes from crops and crops come from farmers. Like Papa and Nelson."

But Irene's angst didn't seem soothed. "I

know where crops come from, Alice-Ann."

Aunt Bess came to the table, her wide girth pushing Alice-Ann out of the way. She slid one of the wooden chairs — painted the same shade of baby parakeet as the table — from underneath and ordered Irene to sit.

She did.

No one, not even Irene, *didn't* do what Aunt Bess said to do, right when she said to do it.

"Alice, get Irene some water, please." Aunt Bess took the chair next to Irene's. "You're concerned about your brother, I 'spect."

Of course. Irene's twin brother, Frank, would be among those who went. He'd always been a feisty one. Always gung ho. Knowing Frank Marks, he'd be the first on the bus. First to enlist. First to go fight. First to —

Alice-Ann took a glass from the cabinet and ran water from the faucet into it, then took it back to the table. Aunt Bess gave her another of her looks as she shook her head. "Not from the faucet. I've got some with sliced lemons in the icebox."

Alice-Ann returned to the sink to empty the glass of its contents.

"And then go get your daddy," Aunt Bess said as Irene sobbed. "And your brother.

39

They're in the living room listening to the news."

Alice-Ann looked back at the table in time to see Irene's face fall into her slender hands, adorned only with the tiny ruby and gold ring Nelson had slid onto her finger at their wedding.

"It's as delicate as she is," he'd said when he first showed it to Alice-Ann.

Alice-Ann poured a fresh glass of water and took it to Irene, then left her aunt and sister-in-law to find her father and brother. As expected, Papa sat next to the Zenith, his eyes locked on the rug, his face grim with worry. He'd already cleaned up after a day's work, but Nelson was nowhere to be seen.

Papa looked her way as a news reporter declared, *"And today the United States has declared war on Japan. . . ."*

"What took you so long, young lady?" Papa pulled his pipe from between his teeth. "It's all well and good to stay a little while after school, but you've got chores, you know."

"Yes, sir," Alice-Ann said. "Papa? Did you hear that some of the boys from Bynum are signing up? Volunteering?"

He nodded. "I heard. But don't worry.

Nelson and me, we'll be needed here on the farm."

"Yes, sir." Alice-Ann's stomach turned sour. Her father and brother had been the last ones on her mind, and she chastised herself for not having thought of them sooner. "Papa, Aunt Bess wants you in the kitchen."

Papa stood and adjusted the thin belt over his narrow hips. "Go get your brother then. He's upstairs washing up."

Alice-Ann nodded, then left the room and trotted up the stairs. She walked the narrow hallway to the closed door of the newly installed indoor bath Nelson had insisted upon for Irene's sake. "No wife of mine is going to the outhouse, Pops," he'd told their father. "She's from town, after all." If for no other reason, that made Irene's addition into their family worth her moodiness. Alice-Ann had grown tired of traipsing to the outhouse or using a chamber pot in the middle of the night.

Alice-Ann rapped on the door. "Nelson?"

The sound of water spilling into the sink stopped. "Yeah."

"Aunt Bess wants you now. And Papa said come on." She took a deep breath, deciding not to tell him that his wife sat downstairs crying into her palms. "And I need to ask

41

you something."

The painted-white wooden door opened. Her brother, handsome with his hair spiked from a face washing, the natural twinkle that always resided in his eyes shimmering. "What's that, Priss?"

Alice-Ann crossed her arms as she took a step closer. "Did you hear some of the boys are going to Camp Stewart to enlist?"

Nelson blew out a breath. "Yeah, 'fraid so."

"Do you know if — if — do you know if Mack and Carlton are signing up?" Adding Carlton's name, she hoped, would keep her brother from being suspicious about her feelings toward his friend.

Nelson nodded. "Talked to Mack today. He said he and a few others are heading over there tomorrow."

"Irene didn't seem to know yet. She's worried about Frank, I reckon."

"She has good reason to worry. We all do."

Alice-Ann felt her knees go numb. She drew in a ragged breath. "Do you think he'll — they'll — go to war?"

Nelson smiled. "I suppose you're grateful your daddy and brother will stay home, but Mack and Carlton are like two more big brothers to you, huh?" His hand cupped her chin and brought her eyes to his. "I never had to worry about you as long as I knew they were somewhere around."

She swallowed hard, unable to answer.

"Don't worry, Priss," he said, releasing her and then dipping his hand into his back pocket for the comb he kept there. "Our boys will go in, take care of business, and be home before you turn seventeen." He ran the comb through his thick locks. "You'll see."

CHAPTER 3

It had taken days, but Alice-Ann finally convinced Aunt Bess that the only proper thing to do during "this incredibly solemn time" was host a party. Partly, she said, in honor of her birthday and, in greater part, for the boys leaving town, ready to win the war. Especially now that the entire world, it seemed, had turned around and declared war on the United States.

Aunt Bess set the date for Friday, December 19, because, she said, once the twentieth hit, "we may as well be celebrating Christmas as your birthday."

This wasn't the first year Alice-Ann's December birthday had gotten all mixed up with that of the Savior, but it sure was the most inconvenient.

Friday afternoon, Claudette and Maeve rode the rattling school bus home with Alice-Ann, small pieces of luggage at their feet, each filled with a party dress and shoes and, Alice-Ann hoped, a small gift for her. The three friends had set a rule years back that they would exchange Christmas cards rather than gifts, concentrating more on their birthdays when it came to gift exchanges.

Maeve, of course, purchased something from her parents' five-and-dime. Being the daughter of the town's only doctor — his only child, in fact — Claudette upstaged them all with her gifts, which sometimes shot a tinge of regret through Alice-Ann at the meagerness of her own offerings. But she was a farmer's daughter, and homemade gifts were the usual fare, even among family members. A monogrammed handkerchief, a knit scarf and cap, a cross-stitched sampler . . .

Although next year, she'd decided, she'd present them both with tatted doilies for their dressing tables. Aunt Bess had promised to show her how. As soon as the New Year rolled around, she'd said.

The girls entered the house and shed their coats, hanging them on the hall tree inside the front door.

"Aunt Bess is probably in the kitchen," Alice-Ann said, leading the way to the back of the house.

Sure enough, Aunt Bess stood at the

45

counter, one hand fisted and planted on a hip, the other slathering frosting on a perfectly formed cake.

"Mmm," Claudette said, smiling. Even her hazel eyes lit up. "Looks divine, Aunt Bess."

"It *is* divine," Aunt Bess told her. "I only make *divine* cakes."

"What can we do, Aunt Bess?" Alice-Ann asked. She opened the icebox and pulled out a half-filled pitcher of milk. She held it out for her friends. "Milk?"

"I'll get the glasses," Maeve said first, moving to the cabinet where they were kept as if the kitchen were her own. One thing Maeve had always adored about coming to the farm was drinking truly fresh-from-the-cow milk. Living in town, she and Claudette both only enjoyed milk brought by a dairy farmer.

"We'll have an early supper," Aunt Bess said, dropping the frosting knife into the deep porcelain sink. "So don't go spoiling your appetites." Maeve placed three glasses on the oilcloth-covered table, which Aunt Bess had already set for the evening meal. "Drink your milk," Aunt Bess continued, "and go on upstairs and get ready."

The girls gulped down the sweet milk, then grabbed the cases they'd left with their coats and ran up the stairs.

"I wonder where Irene is," Maeve said when they'd reached the landing.

"No telling, knowing her," Claudette answered as Alice-Ann shushed them both.

"Be careful. These walls have ears, you know."

"No worries, doll. She's not here," Claudette said.

The friends flew into the bedroom and Alice-Ann closed the door. "How do you know?" she asked.

"Because. I saw her walking into Smitty's when the bus drove us through town."

Alice-Ann nearly dropped her books onto her narrow desk near the window. "You did? Wonder what she's doing there."

"If you saw her, Claudette," Maeve put in, her voice holding doubt, "why did you say you didn't know where she was at?"

Claudette placed her books and suitcase on the chenille-covered bed, which wobbled beneath the weight. "Because, Maeve . . ." Claudette rolled her eyes playfully. "I don't know where she *is;* I only know where she *isn't.*"

Alice-Ann crossed her arms. "I only wish she liked me better. Or even a little."

"Maybe," Maeve pondered, "she was at Smitty's to buy you something for your birthday."

"No. She and Nelson gave me my present the night of — well, on the night of my birthday." Nelson, who'd always been gifted with woodwork, had made five clothes hangers for her, each one monogrammed with her initials.

"Maybe she's Christmas shopping," Maeve added. "Only a few days left, you know."

Claudette tossed her hands into the air. "Who knows and who cares? Come on, girls. We've got to come up with a plan of action to make sure our Alice-Ann here has loads of time with one Boyd MacKay before the night's over."

Alice-Ann tingled at the thought. "Well, one thing's for sure, it's too cold to meander outside."

Maeve sat on the bed. "Maybe you could offer him a glass of punch and he'll walk over to the table with you and *then* you can tell him."

"With Aunt Bess not a foot away?" Claudette said. "No. What you need to do, Alice-Ann, is offer him a cup of coffee. He's going off to the war soon. He's a man who drinks coffee now." She cut her eyes toward the ceiling. "Probably black. No milk. No sugar."

"Because he's sweet enough," Maeve said

with a giggle, which brought a smile to Alice-Ann's lips as well.

Claudette wasn't to be deterred. "Can you please be serious for one minute, Maeve?" She focused her attention on Alice-Ann. "Now, here's what you do. Ask Aunt Bess if you can go to the kitchen to prepare it. . . . He'll follow you . . . and . . ." Her eyes lit up as she raised her arms, pretending to wrap them around a man's shoulders. "You'll say, 'Mack, my darling —' "

Alice-Ann and Maeve giggled again. "You watch too many movies, Claudette," Maeve said.

"A hopeless romantic is what I am," she said, then fell across the bed on her back, her arms crossed over herself as if she were in a passionate embrace. She quickly raised herself up on her elbows. "Hey. Speaking of gorgeous, have either of you gotten a gander at the new manager of the old Walker's Inn?"

Both girls shook their heads.

"He and his mama came to church last Sunday. Dreamy, I tell you. Positively dreamy." She fell against the bed again with a sigh. "A living doll and the living end."

"I'm a Baptist," Maeve said, opening her suitcase and bringing out her dress, which she fluffed in the air. "We don't sit in church

49

dreaming about men, no matter how good-looking they are, when we're supposed to be listening to the preacher."

"Well, I'm Methodist, Maeve Hillis, and *we* are freethinkers."

Alice-Ann moved to the bed, anxious to change the subject. The way people carried on — especially the in-town Baptists and Methodists — one would think they were of different faiths entirely. Like the Lewens, who ran the finer of the two clothing stores in town, but who had to drive all the way to Savannah each and every Saturday to worship, leaving their store in the care of their employees.

"Gracious," she said to her two friends, "to hear you two talk, we're not even playing on the same team. Bottom line is, we all love Jesus, right?"

Maeve and Claudette shared a sheepish glance. "Right," they both mumbled, followed by two sincere apologies.

Alice-Ann smiled, content at her peace-making abilities. "Come on, city girls," she said, changing her tone. "Show me your dresses, and then I'll show you mine."

The words were barely out of her mouth when the sound of a car rolling up the dirt driveway stopped her from walking to the closet. Instead, she moved to the window, pushed back the thick muslin curtains, and peered out. "Irene's back."

"Lucky her, having a car," Claudette said, coming up behind her. "Daddy says he'll buy one for me; he just won't say *when*."

With Maeve joining them, the three friends watched in silence as Irene swung out of the car, two small parcels in one hand, her red purse in the other. She bopped the door shut with her slender but curvaceous hip and then meandered toward the front door.

A moment later, she called out to Aunt Bess from the front hall that she'd arrived home.

Alice-Ann held up a hand. "You two hang up your dresses." She glanced at her narrow closet door. "And while you're at it, check out the hangers Nelson made for my birthday." She'd made it halfway across the room. "And the little sachets hanging from them are from Aunt Bess."

"Where are you off to?" Claudette asked.

Alice-Ann's hand clasped the doorknob as she turned and whispered, "To see where the queen of Bynum has been."

She met Irene halfway on the staircase. "Well, hey there, princess," Irene said to her, stopping. She held up one of the parcels, wrapped in white paper and tied

51

with a tiny pink ribbon. "Your brother insisted I go to town and pick this up for you."

Alice-Ann couldn't help but be a little curious. "For me? Something store-bought?"

Irene smiled, although Alice-Ann couldn't tell if it was for real or for show. "I suppose at sixteen, you deserve it." She took a step up and Alice-Ann took three down, realizing if she were on the staircase, she at least had to look like she'd been heading somewhere other than to be nosy. "Oh, by the way," Irene added, and Alice-Ann turned. "I ran into Mack at the soda shop. He says he's real excited about coming out tonight and celebrating with us."

Heat rose from somewhere deep in Alice-Ann's chest, settling along the flesh of her cheeks.

Irene's eyes widened and her smile grew lopsided. "Oh, so *that's* how it goes."

Alice-Ann shrugged. "How *what* goes? I don't know what you're talking about, Irene Branch. He's Nelson's friend after all, and he's like a big brother to me. Always has been, so why shouldn't he come to my party?"

" 'The lady doth protest too much, methinks.' "

Alice-Ann huffed in reply. Irene, of all people, quoting Shakespeare. "Now I *really* have no idea what you're talking about."

Irene's chin lifted a fraction. "I also ran into Carlton Hillis. He's excited about coming too."

"Carlton's also a very nice young man, and I'm glad he's coming as well."

Being Maeve's brother, Carlton had been as much a part of her life as Nelson. Over the years, while Nelson had taught Maeve and her how to bait a hook, Carlton had taught them how to ride bikes and roller-skate and even how to do the jitterbug and the Big Apple. He'd also served as a chaperone and chauffeur a time or two when they'd needed to go somewhere. Kind and soft-spoken, smart beyond the grading system at Bynum High School, Carlton had always been the type of boy one couldn't help liking. And he rarely spoke to Alice-Ann without calling her "doodlebug."

"But no blush from the young Miss Branch?"

Alice-Ann turned to descend the rest of the stairs, choosing to ignore her sister-in-law.

"He's bringing a date," Irene said from behind her and Alice-Ann whirled around, nearly falling to the landing.

"Who is?"

Irene's brow rose, taunting her. "Well, if what you say is true, and both Carlton and Mack are just like brothers to you, does it matter?"

Of course it mattered. But if Irene really knew the way Alice-Ann felt about Mack, she'd tell Nelson — and he'd lecture Alice-Ann until she begged for mercy — or she'd hound her mercilessly for the rest of her life. Either way, the options were enough to give Alice-Ann the shudders.

No doubt about it. She *had* to convince Mack to marry her before the night was over.

"It doesn't," she said. "Both can bring two dates for all I care."

Irene laughed easily. "Ease up, will you? Carlton is the one bringing a date. Darling *brotherly* Mack MacKay will be free for the taking."

CHAPTER 4

The party began at seven and was in full swing by half past the hour. Aunt Bess kept the food and punch table in the hallway fully stocked. Papa made sure there were plenty of tunes coming from the Zenith in the living room while Nelson kept a moderate blaze going in the fireplace.

A small table in the corner near the bay window held the few token gifts for Alice-Ann that some of her guests had brought. An hour had passed since the last person arrived — for a time, Alice-Ann felt like the whole town of Bynum and the farming community had come — and she'd not opened any of them yet. Her eye, of course, had been mostly on the long, narrow box Mack had placed there, and her heart fluttered every time she thought about what might be inside.

"A bracelet, no doubt," Claudette had whispered in her ear. "Jeepers, I hope it's not a watch," she added. "That would be so provincial." She gave a wink before sashaying across the room to join Maeve and Ernie, who — out of his soda jerk and school attire — looked surprisingly handsome.

Most of the conversation that evening centered on the number of boys who'd gone off to register — some who were hardly old enough to shave — and Alice-Ann did her best to sway it back to a subject more festive, like the holiday of the following week. For the most part, it worked. Somehow, though, it always seemed to steer back to the ominous.

Worse still, for the majority of the night, Nelson and Irene monopolized Mack's time, the two men leaning against the wall facing each other, speaking in hushed tones. Irene's body practically melted into her husband's, their arms laced around the other's waist. Familiar and slightly brazen, in Alice-Ann's way of thinking. Although she imagined herself, or at least she tried, leaning into Mack in the same way. Feeling so at ease next to another human being that she'd cease to know where he ended and she began.

And vice versa.

"Great party, doodlebug."

Alice-Ann turned to see Carlton standing behind her. "Hey, Carlton," she said. "Thank you."

His brows — shades darker than the light brown of his thick hair — knit together in the way they always did when he had something to say. "Happy birthday. Hard to believe you and Maeve are sixteen already."

Alice-Ann looked around. "Where's your date?"

Carlton smiled slowly and Alice-Ann relaxed, realizing for the first time that her whole body had been tense from watching Mack with her brother and Irene. "Betty Jo? She's around here somewhere," he answered, keeping his tone vague as his eyes briefly scanned the crowd before coming back to Alice-Ann.

"She certainly is pretty, Carlton. I mean, I don't know her well, but I always thought she was a real pretty girl."

Carlton pulled a piece of gum from a pack in his shirt pocket, then put it back as though he'd changed his mind. "She's a nice girl, all right." He leaned forward, bending his six-foot-two frame so as to be closer to Alice-Ann's ear. "I'll let you in on a little secret, though."

The warmth of his breath, blended with the faint hint of recently consumed punch

57

and peppermint, gave her the slightest of shivers. She wasn't accustomed to having a man — even one who felt more like a brother than a *real* man — speak so close to her ear. "Oh?"

He winked. "Can you keep it?"

"Sure."

"Even from Maeve?"

Alice-Ann bit her bottom lip, feeling even more grown-up than ever before. "Even from Maeve," she said, although she wasn't sure how she'd manage. Maybe if she told Claudette, then Claudette could tell Maeve, and . . .

"I think Betty Jo's expecting more than just a friendship or casual dating between the two of us."

Alice-Ann's breath caught in her throat. "Like marriage?"

"I think so. She's hinted enough."

"Are you going to ask her to marry you? Before Uncle Sam calls you up, I mean?"

When Carlton grinned, Alice-Ann could see more clearly why Betty Jo Shannon would be so taken with him. Sea-blue eyes, wide brow, straight nose, and full lips. He even smelled good. Beyond the peppermint and the punch, he carried an earthy scent, spicy and fresh.

"Thinking about it," he said, straightening. "Do you think she'll wait for me while I'm gone?"

"You won't marry before you leave?"

Carlton crossed his arms. "No. That wouldn't be fair, I don't think." He scanned the room again as though looking for her. "A girl like Betty Jo should have a wedding with all the fixings, don't you think?"

"Big white dress and a church full of flowers," Alice-Ann remarked.

"Exactly."

Fleetingly Alice-Ann pictured her own wedding — the way she'd always imagined it — her little church full of familiar faces, the scent of roses rising to the rafters. In her mind's eye she could see Mack standing at the altar, beaming with both pride and love as she floated toward him on her father's arm. He wore a smart suit of dark blue and she . . . she would have finally arrived at the day when she could slip on the wedding dress she always hoped would be hers.

In truth, the dress belonged to Aunt Bess. Like the photos of her aunt and other family members that once hung on the living room wall, the creamy satin-and-lace gown had been placed in her aunt's hope chest, having never been worn. Such a romantic tragedy — her one true love dying before

Aunt Bess could wear it on her own special day, leaving Alice-Ann to wonder what could possibly be worse: never wearing the gown or never knowing the love of a husband.

"Alice-Ann?" Carlton now asked, and she sighed.

"What?"

He smiled and she felt heat drain from the top of her head to her chest. Surely he could read her mind.

"Um," she said, hoping to redeem the situation. "Why don't you want Maeve to know?"

Carlton chuckled. "Because. If I tell Maeve, she'll tell Mama, and Mama will insist on me marrying right away." He grinned again. "Mama is worried to death I'm going over to Europe or some exotic place, and I'll come back with a foreign bride."

Alice-Ann's heart stopped. "Come back with — is that *possible*?" And if it were, would Mack do something like that? Come back with some brunette from England or a delicious little number from France? One who spoke French, the language of *love*?

"Sure it is," Carlton said. A new look came to his eyes, full of tenderness and . . . *something more.* Just what it was, Alice-Ann

60

couldn't quite put her finger on. "There she is now," he said, one hand reaching beyond Alice-Ann's shoulder.

As the opening measures of " 'S Wonderful" came from the Zenith, Alice-Ann turned to see Betty Jo gliding across the room. She wore a gray wool skirt, complemented by a red-and-white reindeer sweater — the latest thing, not that Alice-Ann could ever afford one. Betty Jo had pulled her hair, the perfect shade of wheat, back into a low ponytail and tied it off with a red scarf. She looked for all the world like an ad in one of Irene's magazines.

Alice-Ann pulled at her own hair, wishing she could get it to stay back like Betty Jo's — slick and stylish and without all the wispy curls around her face, which were exactly like Aunt Bess's.

"Happy birthday, Alice-Ann," Betty Jo said, reaching her with a wide smile from red-painted lips. "I wanted to say so earlier, but you had a mob around you when we came in."

"And a merry Christmas to you," Alice-Ann added with a grin.

Betty Jo slipped her arm into Carlton's, and for a moment, Alice-Ann's breath caught. Oh, why couldn't she have Mack to do such a simple thing with? Why hadn't she been able to tell him two weeks earlier how she'd felt, allowing him time to see that she was truly the girl for him?

No. The *woman* for him. Then the two of them would, tonight, be like Nelson and Irene, and Carlton and Betty Jo. Or Maeve and Ernie, even, though they hadn't quite reached the body-molding stage.

Oh, that stupid ole war and those horrible bombers! Alice-Ann wished she could stomp her foot right then and there, but —

She shook her head to free it of all such thoughts. "So how do you feel, Betty Jo, about Carlton enlisting?"

Betty Jo pouted. "Miserable." She looked up at him as her arm squeezed his. "But I understand. It's what our brave men have to do, really. Now that the war has come to our own shores."

"It's true," Carlton said. "We thought that if we just kept doing what we do here in America, eventually the Allies would win over the Axis powers and we could all go on with our day to day." His thick eyelashes lowered as he added, "But we can't turn a blind eye anymore. We have to do something." He kissed the top of Betty Jo's head and said, "Don't you worry though, Betty Jo. We'll take care of them."

"What about your studies, Carlton?"

Alice-Ann asked as she felt the presence of another person near her. She glanced up and back to see Mack standing behind her, and her whole body tingled.

"I can finish those when I come back," Carlton answered. "Georgia Teachers College isn't going anywhere, I'm sure."

"War," Mack said with a tease, "will give us more education than that college of yours, my boy." He slapped Carlton on the shoulder and they laughed. "No telling what we're going to get into over there."

Alice-Ann opened her mouth to protest, but Aunt Bess called out over the music and conversation. "All right, young and old. Let's have Alice-Ann open a few gifts and then we'll cut the cake."

Whatever she had to say would have to wait. Finally the time had come to see what nestled in the narrow box from Mack.

She deliberately put off opening the gift, waiting until all the others had been unwrapped and the givers properly thanked. Finally, with only two left — the one Irene had brought home earlier and Mack's — she opened the one from her brother and sister-in-law.

Inside, a lovely pink-and-white powder tin held heavenly scented Cashmere Bouquet talc. She thanked them both, meaning it, knowing this meant her brother truly saw her as a young woman now and no longer as a little girl in want or need of paper dolls.

Then the big moment came. Alice-Ann pulled back the paper from the slender box slowly, opening it with ease. Her breath caught in her throat as she stared at a sterling silver charm bracelet, graced by a single cross dangling from one of its links. A precious gift. So much so, she hardly knew how to respond. Even with all her planning — her countless hours of plotting exactly what she'd say on the evening of her party — she was left speechless by the thought that had gone behind it, never mind what it might have cost him.

Mack took it out of the box without her asking, unclasped it with his lovely masculine fingers, and secured it around her wrist. "Just a little something to remember me by," he said.

As if she'd forget him.

"I know how much your faith means to you," he added.

"Thank you, Mack," she managed around the knot in her throat, forcing herself by sheer will not to throw her arms around his shoulders, screaming for the whole world to hear: *Please don't go!*

Mack leaned over and kissed her on the

cheek, his full lips soft and moist. "Happy birthday, Alice-Ann," he said.

She closed her eyes, and when she opened them again — praying she'd not been dreaming all along — she spied Irene standing nearby, a faint smile on her lips. Not the sneering kind, either. The understanding-between-women kind.

Maybe she understood, after all. Maybe her sister-in-law wasn't half-bad.

With her gifts opened and exclaimed over, Aunt Bess marched into the living room with the cake all aflame, singing at the top of her lungs. " 'Happy birthday, dear Alice . . .' " as everyone else — Alice-Ann's family, school chums, and church friends — sang along.

Including Mack, who put his arm around her shoulder and squeezed.

"Make a wish, Alice-Ann," he said. "And if you can't blow the candles out by yourself, let me know. I'm full of enough hot air for both of us."

Words which brought a round of laughter from the crowd.

"Maybe," Alice-Ann said low enough for only him to hear, "you *should* help me." After all, she wasn't sure if she had enough air in her lungs for the next necessary breath, much less to blow out sixteen candles.

Mack drew up straight and tall. "Stand back, folks. Miss Branch has asked her *other brother* to help blow out the candles."

And with that, Alice-Ann's hopes fell, and her wishes deflated.

By the end of the evening, when everyone had gone except Mack, Irene gathered a few plates together and eased up next to her. "Look, kiddo. I don't think he's the guy for you, but if *you* think he is, you'd best tell him soon. Come the first of the year, he'll be gone and all you'll be left with is a box full of wondering."

Alice-Ann fiddled with the cross charm. "He only thinks of me as his kid sister."

Irene shifted her weight and lowered her chin. "Listen up. Your brother only saw in me some knobby-kneed girl who — well, that's another story. But let's just say it takes the right moment and the right words and then suddenly you're looking at a mess of fish for supper."

"What? What does *that* mean?"

"Never mind. Like I said, that's another story for another time. Bottom line is this — once you know what you want, go for it."

Alice-Ann held her sister-in-law's eyes with her own. "Really, Irene?"

"Once I knew that your brother was the man for me, I pulled out all the stops. I made sure he knew how I felt. Then with the selective service and all, I decided I wasn't taking any chances, which is why I'm your sister-in-law and not just your brother's girlfriend." She shook her head. "I'll get rid of the family long enough for you to talk to Mack, got it?"

Flurries of excitement built up inside her. "But what do I say?"

Irene rolled her eyes. "Do I have to do it for you? Just tell him how you feel."

Alice-Ann exhaled with a rumble. "Okay." She nodded once, then once more for good measure. "Okay. I can do this."

"Nelson?" Irene called out as she walked toward the entryway. "Will you help me with all these dishes, please?"

Nelson pointed to Mack. "I was about to walk Mack here out to his truck."

Irene turned and looked back at Alice-Ann with a wink. "Alice-Ann? Why don't *you* walk Mack out while your brother helps me with the dishes?" She turned again to face her husband. "Or sleeps in the dog-house tonight if he doesn't?"

Mack laughed as Nelson blushed. "So *this*

is what it's like, being married? Go on, Nelson." His gaze crossed into the living room and he crooked his arm. "Miss Branch? Do you mind walking me out?"

Alice-Ann squared her shoulders and smiled. "Not at all, Mr. MacKay." She was halfway across the room, her own arm extended to slip into his — like Betty Jo's had with Carlton's — before she had a chance to take in another breath.

CHAPTER 5

Like the gentleman he'd always been, Mack helped Alice-Ann into her winter coat, then shoved his arms into his own before opening the front door and topping his head with his hat. They stepped onto the front porch, met by a shock of cold air and the strong scent of firewood smoke in the air. Without much thought, she dipped her hands into her coat pockets and pulled out a pair of knit gloves.

"Good idea," Mack said. He paused at the top of the steps as he retrieved a scarf and a pair of gloves from his own coat. "Do you have a cap or a hat?" He jutted his chin outward an inch or two. "I had to park practically in the next county. Don't want that little head of yours getting too cold."

Alice-Ann pulled out the cap that matched the handmade gloves from the opposite pocket and shoved it onto her head, grateful that — at the very least — it kept her frizzy hair from making such a spectacle of itself. She looked up at Mack for approval and received a broad smile in return.

"Good thing there's a moon tonight," Alice-Ann said as they started down the steps. She clasped her hands in front of her, the heaviness of the bracelet warm and lovely against her skin, and wished on the stars that she could hold Mack's hand. Or that he would reach for hers.

Mack looked up too. "It's a nice one. So full and round. And I believe I see *the man.*"

Alice-Ann searched for the fictitious resident of the moon as she often did when it hung full and bright in the ink-black country sky. "My mother used to sing a song about the moon." She grinned at him, slowing her steps, wanting all the time in the world before they reached his truck.

"Can you sing it?"

She nodded. " 'Moon, moon . . . so full and round,' " she sang, her voice a soft soprano. " 'Moon, moon . . . don't fall down. Stay where you are, right by that star, until moon, moon . . . my love is found.' "

Mack stayed silent for a moment, then breathed in and out, sending a puff of his breath into the night air. "I forgot how pretty your voice is."

"Mama could sing too. Better than me,

for sure." And if the world grew quiet enough, sometimes she could still hear it.

"You're a good piano player too, as I recall." He nudged her with his elbow and she giggled.

"I'll do in a pinch, but it's not really a passion or anything."

"Nah. You're better than that."

"Mama," Alice-Ann said, growing somber, "had the prettiest reading voice too. I still remember the way she'd put on the voices of the characters from the fairy-tale book Papa bought me when I was maybe three or four." She smiled, thinking of its dog-eared pages and the pretty pinks of the cover. They'd faded over time.

"Do you like to read?"

"I love reading, when I have time. Seems like lately, what with school getting harder and harder, and more chores around the house than ever, and helping Papa when I can with the farm, there hasn't been much of that. But if I can get a book a week at the school library or from the bookmobile when it comes out this way, I'm happy."

They drew closer to the truck, which looked newly washed. The Army-green color deepened in the dark and the moonlight. "Do you like to write? I mean, letters and such?"

Alice-Ann nodded, unable to speak. They were here now, and she had yet to tell him . . .

"Will you write me while I'm gone?" he asked. "I know Mama will and maybe Daddy — he's still pretty bent out of shape about all this and my life choices in general — but I'd like to get a few letters from others, you know. Keep me informed as to what's going on around town." He rested against the rounded hood of the truck, where chrome letters spelled out *DODGE* against a red background, and he chuckled. "Alice-Ann Branch."

She looked up at him. He'd spoken her name like a word in one of the sonnets Mrs. Tankersley made them read in English literature class. *Oh, please . . . please . . . take me in your arms. Tell me that you love me.*

"I cannot believe you're sixteen years old now," he said. "Where has the time gone? One minute you're a little girl tagging along behind your brother and Carlton and me, and the next you're walking me out to my truck, nearly grown, and I'm asking you to write me when I go off to war."

Alice-Ann swallowed. "Can I tell you something?" she blurted, sounding nothing like she'd hoped she would.

"What's that?" He burrowed his hands into his coat pockets.

She shuffled up beside him, resting herself against the truck's hood as well. The chill of it went down into her bones and she shivered, pressing her knees together. "Do you remember when I was twelve and I had my birthday party?"

"When you were twelve?" he asked, as though it were so long ago — a lifetime maybe. He looked as if he was hard-pressed to recall it at all.

"Remember, we all went out on that scavenger hunt through the woods and into some of Papa's empty fields?"

Mack didn't answer this time, but from what Alice-Ann could see of his face, his mind had begun to search for the exact year.

"You were sixteen," Alice-Ann said. "You and Carlton and Nelson. And you —"

Mack laughed easily. "Oh yeah. That was the year I brought Annabeth Sowell to the party."

"And I —"

Mack drew out a hand and pointed to her with one finger. "And you caught us kissing behind the barn." He shook his head as his hand returned to the pocket and he stared at his shoes. "I remember being so mad with you."

"That's because . . ." Alice-Ann turned her head away from him, looking out over the dark field beside them, a field that, come summer, would be ripe with tall stalks of corn. Oh, the memory of that night. Seeing them pressed into the shadows, Mack's arms around the skinny Annabeth, his full lips against her thin ones. "I deliberately followed you back there, you know. I meant to catch you. To break you two up."

"Break us up?" He winked. "Now why in the world would you want to do a thing like that?"

She smiled up at him, sheepishly enough, she hoped. "I didn't like you seeing Annabeth. I didn't like you seeing *anyone.* Ever. I guess, fortunately for me, you never really dated one girl long enough for them to even wear your letter jacket."

"Well . . . I guess — wait a minute." His voice held the same lilt as always. "What are you telling me, silly girl? Surely you didn't pull this kind of stuff when our Nelson fell head over heels in love with the alluring Irene."

Alice-Ann crossed her arms. This wasn't going as planned. Didn't the man have a brain in his head? He'd always been fun-loving, hardly serious Mack. But now, with only a few weeks left before he went for his physical and then another few before he left for good, she needed him to focus on her. On her words.

"Mack, you're not paying attention." She turned to face him, resting her hip against the frigid cold of the hood. "I'm trying to tell you that since I was twelve years old and you were sixteen that I — I — well, I've loved you. *Love* you, actually."

The typical quizzical stance of his brow turned downward. "Of course, kiddo. I love you too."

"No, Mack." The wind whipped around them and her nose grew icy in protest. She prayed it didn't start running; that would be the absolute worst thing to happen. "I'm trying to say — I *am* saying — I am *in* love with you, Boyd MacKay." As soon as the words were out of her mouth, she threw her face into her hands. "Oh, you must think I'm a ninny. A little girl ninny."

She half expected him to jump into his truck and leave, speeding away, leaving her standing alone on the side of the Georgia dirt driveway. What had she been thinking, making such a declaration? And to a man four years older than herself? Why, he could have anyone. *Anyone.* Why should he want a frizzy-haired, plain-faced child who stood out in the freezing cold with a knit cap pulled low over her ears? And the gloves on her trembling hands were not the elegant style worn by the likes of Miss Norma Shearer or Miss Ginger Rogers either. No. These were practically *mittens.*

Instead, his arms came around her, protective and strong. He pulled her to his chest, and for a moment, she stopped breathing. "Alice-Ann," he murmured, "that's about the sweetest thing anyone has ever said to me."

"I didn't mean it to be," she said, her words muffled by his coat.

She'd hoped it to be endearing. Provocative, maybe. But not sweet. Surely not that.

She pulled away from him. "You're making fun of me," she said, looking at the new shoes Aunt Bess had purchased for her in town — black perforated leather wedges adorned with a bow. Aunt Bess had paid $1.98 for them, never noticing the sign near the display declaring them a beau bewitcher.

Some bewitching.

Mack crooked his index finger and, using it, raised her chin. His brow remained furrowed and she wondered if he might just possibly kiss her. "What *did* you mean?"

Alice-Ann felt tears forming. "Never mind," she said, taking another step back.

Mack seeing her cry and her nose all runny was the last thing she wanted. She started back toward the house, but Mack caught her hand and drew her back.

"Don't do this, Alice-Ann. I can't bear to have you mad at me."

"I'm not mad."

"But you're not happy." He released her hand.

"I'd hoped —" Mack chuckled then, and because he had that way with her, she laughed too. "You really *do* think I'm a ninny," she said.

"Nah, Alice-Ann. I don't think that at all. But I *do* believe you've probably got stardust in your eyes when it comes to me."

"I don't."

"What do you want with an old boy like me, anyway? Especially me. I'm hardly beau material. Besides, aren't there plenty of boys your own age who keep you awake at night?"

She pouted. "Like who?"

Mack leaned against the truck again, bringing her with him. "How about Pete James? I saw him bring you a glass of punch tonight."

"Pete," she all but huffed. "He's such a child. And a glass of punch isn't a promise ring, you know." Then again, neither was a cross charm on a bracelet.

"All right then. What about someone else?" He appeared to ponder every male in Bynum. "How about Rodney Fisher?"

Mack obviously didn't understand a woman of sixteen. When you loved someone, you loved them. Period. "Hardly," she said.

He grinned at her. "Well, if you're bent on an old guy, how about Pete's brother, George Junior?"

Alice-Ann shook her head. "He looks too much like his father."

Mack laughed. "He does do that, doesn't he?"

"It'd be like kissing *Mister* George."

Mack nudged her. "Kissing, huh?"

Alice-Ann crossed her arms again. "Stop that." How could she possibly explain to Mack that she never wanted to kiss anyone but him, anyhow? What were the right words to say when trying to express that she wanted him to be the first? The last? The only.

Mack remained silent until, a few moments later, the front door opened and Irene stuck her head out. "Alice-Ann," she called in the night air. "Aunt Bess says it's too cold for you to be out here another minute."

"Can't you just hear Aunt Bess saying

that?" Mack teased. *"Irene, go tell Alice right now that it's much too cold out there for her to be standing out in the middle of the world in the freezing cold."*

Alice-Ann giggled as she straightened, keeping her eyes on the house. "Tell her I'm coming," she hollered back. She waited a moment before facing Mack. "Well, Boyd MacKay, now you know. And I guess that's that." She stuck her thumb out and jabbed it toward the porch. "I'll be going on back in the house now."

But Mack caught her hands. "Tell you what let's do, Alice-Ann. You mean the world to me, you know that, right?"

Alice-Ann nodded, wondering where his words might be heading.

"I can't promise you anything. Not now. Not with us at war and me leaving soon." He grinned at her. "If it weren't for the Japs and Hitler and all the rest, I'd be staying right here in Bynum and — if you'd told me how you felt, maybe . . . well, maybe we'd go out as friends and —"

"As *friends*? Mack, I don't want to —"

"Hey, now. I'm the guy, remember? Let *me* drive the tractor, okay?"

Alice-Ann felt a blush all the way down to her toes.

"Write me? Like I asked earlier?"

Write him? Of course she'd *write* him. But she wanted more. So much more. She wanted to *marry* him. "Yes," she said. "If you'll write me back." And even if he didn't . . .

"I can absolutely promise you that."

A thought came to her. "Oh. Maybe you'd better not — maybe you'd better write me at Maeve's address instead of here."

"Why's that?"

"If Papa or Aunt Bess or, Lord forbid, *Nelson* ever got ahold of how I feel . . ." How she hoped *he* would feel one day too. "It's just best."

"What about Irene?"

Alice-Ann shrugged. "She's all right."

Mack nodded. "Yes. Yes, she is. Okay, then. I'll write to you at Maeve's." He dipped his head playfully. "It'll kind of be like we're spies, huh? War spies?"

Alice-Ann giggled. "Yeah. Espionage agents." She liked the idea of it. Very much so. The whole idea gave their new relationship — if it could be called that — a mysterious hint of intrigue.

Mack kissed the top of her head, near the rim of her cap, close to her forehead. His lips were cold and moist.

And perfect.

"Go on inside," he said. "I'll see you

Christmas Day for sure."

Her hands fell from his and she shoved them back into her pockets. "All right." She walked backward, watching as he climbed into his truck and started the engine. The front lights illuminated everything around her. She turned, holding her breath to keep from running inside like a child who'd just been given a lollipop.

Determined instead to walk like the young woman she was now. Straight and tall.

And filled with hope.

CHAPTER 6

Two Years Later
Friday, December 10, 1943
At precisely four thirty in the afternoon, Alice-Ann stepped to the employee time clock in the narrow back hallway of Bynum Bank & Trust, slipped her card in, and waited for the resounding *thunk.* She removed the card and stared at it.

"Yep," she said to her fellow employee — and the only other teller — Nancy Thorpe. "Exact as always."

Nancy giggled lightly. "When Mister Dooley says he doesn't like overtime, he means it."

"And when we say we don't like it on a Friday, *we* mean it," Alice-Ann concluded as she slid her arms into the sleeves of her wool coat, careful not to catch the bracelet from Mack on the hem. She shivered as the cold satin lining penetrated her skin.

"Got plans for tonight?" Nancy asked,

inserting her time card, then removing it and staring at it briefly before returning it to the metal holder hanging nearby.

Alice-Ann nodded. "I'm going to the movies with Maeve."

"Oh? I saw that *The North Star* is starting at the theater tonight." Nancy extended her purse for Alice-Ann to hold while she put on her coat. "That Dana Andrews makes any movie worth the price of admission."

"He's handsome all right," Alice-Ann agreed. But he wasn't Mack.

Together, they walked down the hallway of the small white-brick building located on the corner of Main and Cooper in downtown Bynum.

"What about Claudette?" Nancy asked as they neared the door. "Or is she still too *gone* over Johnny Dailey?" She turned her chin and hollered over her shoulder before Alice-Ann could answer. "Bye, Mister Dooley! Bye, Miss Portia! See y'all on Monday."

Alice-Ann did the same, keeping the volume of her good-byes to a minimum. "Good-bye," she said, loud enough to be heard without sounding quite like a fishwife.

Not that Nancy did. But Nancy had not been reared by Aunt Bess, who insisted that a lady never raises her voice except to call her family in to dinner. "And even for that, God gave us back-porch bells."

Alice-Ann sighed as they stepped out the back door and into the chill of the alleyway. "Claudette's all there and *all* gone, as the saying goes."

"Do you think they'll get married? Her and Johnny? This town sure could use a wedding to cheer it up." Unlike so many other small towns across America, Bynum had — so far — been spared the death of any of her sons. But being so close to Camp Stewart meant a constant reminder of the war — jeeps full of the enlisted driving through town, their wives and family members often renting the front rooms and bedrooms of Bynum's in-town citizens.

Seven dollars a week, Alice-Ann heard some were charging. Of course, that included meals.

During weekend furloughs the enlisted men came to town for a visit with their loved ones, taking in a movie or going to one of the dances on the outskirts of town, but mostly just holding on to each other for all it was worth.

Those were the scenes Alice-Ann tried to avoid; they only reminded her of who *wasn't* in town.

"Oh," she now said with a toss of her

frizzy curls, "they're certainly talking about it. I wouldn't be surprised if the 'King of Walker's Inn' doesn't give her a ring for Christmas this year." They rounded the building and were met by a strong breeze.

"Gets colder every year around Christmas," Nancy said as she wrapped her arms around herself.

Alice-Ann did the same. "What about you? Do you have plans for tonight?"

"Of course. It's Friday, and on Friday Harry likes corned-beef hash." She laughed easily. "So I go home, cook it up, and we eat in front of the fireplace and listen to the Frank Sinatra show."

Alice-Ann smiled, remembering only two years earlier when she couldn't remember the star's name. "He sure can sing."

"And he's *dreamy.*"

They came to a stop on the front sidewalk. "Nancy!" Alice-Ann nudged her workmate. "You're married," she added with a laugh.

"But not dead," she said. "And even though I'm old enough to be his older sister, I've still got eyes in my head and they still work just fine."

Alice-Ann laughed again. "Nancy, I don't think I could possibly be happier that I get to work with someone like you. You've brought a true spark to my life, you know."

The day Alice-Ann had decided to try for a job at the bank had been a blessed one indeed. It had been a Monday, shortly after the first of 1942, when so many of Bynum's men had gone off to serve their country. That afternoon, after school, Alice-Ann marched into Bynum Bank & Trust. Mr. Douglas Reddick — the bank's president and a man affectionately known as Mister Dooley — sat at his desk near the back of the oversize room. Even more blessedly for Alice-Ann, without his secretary Miss Portia Ivey to guard him.

To Alice-Ann, Miss Portia had always been a study in contrasts. Now a woman in her early forties with a creamy complexion and soft, sad eyes that rarely blinked behind her specs, she'd always looked at Alice-Ann as though she were missing an arm. As culture dictated, Alice-Ann was polite to the woman the few times their paths crossed over the years. While she couldn't say Miss Portia was unkind, the woman never seemed happy enough to offer so much as a smile in return.

"Well, well . . ." Mister Dooley heaved his round form from the chair and came around the desk to offer Alice-Ann a warm hug. "To what do I owe this unexpected plea-sure?"

Alice-Ann asked if she could sit in the chair opposite his desk, and he'd all but insisted she do just that. "How's your aunt Bess?" he asked, returning to his chair. Then, not waiting for a reply, he added, "And your daddy? He came in the other day, you know. Worried about the farm. And about what was going to happen in general now that we've entered the war."

"Yes, sir. I overheard him talking about it with Nelson the other night. Said he had to borrow a little money from you."

Mister Dooley leaned over his desk, reached for a half-chewed cigar, and shoved it between his back teeth. "Nothing your daddy isn't good for," he said. "Now, don't you go worrying."

"I'm not worried," Alice-Ann lied. "But I would like to do my part." She glanced over her shoulder to where Nancy Thorpe waited on a customer from the other side of the teller's partition. Returning her attention to Mister Dooley, she added, "With Gus Sanders having signed up, that leaves Miss Nancy working by herself as your one and only teller. So I wondered if I could work after school and all day during my Easter vacation days. Maybe full-time once school is out in June? Unless, of course, the war is over by then and Gus comes back."

Mister Dooley puffed on the foul-smelling cigar before answering. "You any good with your arithmetic?"

She pushed back her shoulders. "I've made all A's in every subject since I started at Bynum High, Mister Dooley."

He slapped his hands together. "Well, I don't see any reason why we can't at least try. Salary is thirty cents an hour. Sound doable?" The bells on the front door chimed, letting her know that either the customer had left or another had entered.

Thirty cents. Why, it was practically a fortune. She couldn't wait to tell Aunt Bess.

"Yes, sir."

"You come back tomorrow. Portia'll have some papers for you to fill out." He stood, and Alice-Ann did the same. "Nancy," he bellowed, his words echoing in the cavernous room. "How'd you like Miss Alice-Ann Branch to work alongside you?"

The round-faced woman with short dark-blonde hair and crystal-blue eyes made all the brighter behind large-framed glasses smiled at her as though she were a long-lost friend. "Why, I'd adore it," she answered.

Since that day, she and Alice-Ann had become good friends. Not *best* friends like Maeve and Claudette — after all, Nancy was in her late thirties. But good friends nonetheless.

Now, standing on the sidewalk in the cold, Alice-Ann glanced at the petite Timex watch gracing her right wrist, turning the face toward her with the fingertips of her left hand. The cross charm dangled over it, and as she always did, she whispered a prayer for the one who had given it to her. "Well, I'm going to walk over to the five-and-dime. Maeve said she'd be there waiting on me."

Since graduation, Maeve had gone to work for her father, filling Carlton's part-time position until he returned. After that, she intended to join her brother in college. "If all goes well enough," she'd clarified.

Nancy thumbed away from the center of downtown. "I'm heading home." She smiled, her teeth white against the red of her lipstick. "Corned-beef hash, you know."

"And Harry," Alice-Ann said with a wink.

"That's right." Nancy gave a low whistle as she turned and walked away, leaving Alice-Ann to watch for a few moments. Watch and wonder what it might be like to have married someone like Harry Thorpe.

As a young man, he'd been drafted into World War I. During the summer, shortly before the war's end, he'd been sent to France, where he'd served on the front line.

He'd returned at the war's end, wounded by shrapnel to his back, rendering his legs useless.

But Harry Thorpe had proven himself to be greater than the enemy's attacks. After a long convalescence in the hospital, he'd learned to get around with the help of a wheelchair. He went to school, received his teaching degree, then returned to Bynum to teach history at the high school.

He'd been one of Alice-Ann's favorite teachers, and now his wife had become one of her favorite people.

"Goodness," Alice-Ann said aloud at the memory, then turned and crossed Cooper Street, her eyes glancing at a window facing the road, where a red-bordered flag hung with three blue stars in front of pulled blackout curtains.

She winced. Having one son fighting in the war was bad enough; having *three* sons away seemed beyond comprehension.

Alice-Ann hurried along the sidewalk and into one of the two double wood-framed glass doors of Hillis's Five & Dime. It rattled as the overhead bell rang, signaling her entry. The scent of cedar pencils and rubbery erasers met her, and she looked toward the counter to see Miss Mary Catherine slamming the register shut and dropping change into Nola Whitney's upturned palm.

Miss Nola looked her way as her gloved hand folded over the money. "Well, hello, Alice-Ann," she said.

"Miss Nola," Alice-Ann returned with a smile as she unbuttoned her coat. "How are you and Mister Hoke?" Miss Nola and Mister Hoke owned and operated Whitney's A&P grocery store two doors down.

"We're all right, I suppose," she said, the words holding not an ounce of truth in them. She opened her purse and dropped the money inside, then grabbed the brown paper bag on the counter and held it to her chest. "Just ready for Washington to bring us some good news for a change."

Alice-Ann glanced over Miss Mary Catherine's shoulder where the flag with a single blue star hung in the large window. "I'm sure this will all be over soon enough," she said, shrugging out of her coat in spite of the chill running through her bones. "Is Maeve in the back?" she asked, hoping the subject could be easily changed.

"She ran down to the post office to drop something off. Nola, tell Hoke if that's not what he's looking for, to let me know. We'll be happy to exchange it."

Miss Nola had stepped closer to Alice-

Ann, who moved aside and farther into the store to avoid the gust of cold air sure to hit her when the door opened. "I'm sure it'll do just fine," she said. Then, stopped at Alice-Ann, she added, "Tell your aunt Bess I said hello, will ya?"

Alice-Ann nodded. "Yes, ma'am."

As soon as the woman had closed the door behind her, Miss Mary Catherine sighed so deeply, Alice-Ann wondered if she might have expelled all of her oxygen. But when she looked her way, the older woman's face held such sadness that fear slid over Alice-Ann. "Miss Mary Catherine? Is everything okay?" She crossed the distance between them.

Maeve's mother raised a trembling hand to her thin lips. "I'm just worried about Carlton and . . ." She rested her hip against the counter as the tremor seemed to radiate through her entire body.

Alice-Ann threw her coat over the counter, walked around to where the woman stood, wrapped her arms around her, and felt her exhale until she fell nearly limp against her. "Are you — are you sure you're okay?"

She pulled herself out of Alice-Ann's arms. "You know, darlin' . . . Miss Nola and Mister Hoke never had children, so she can't know — she can't understand how fearful it is. She comes in here talking about what all she's heard going on in Europe — the things they're showing on the newsreels over at the theater . . ."

Carlton had joined the US Army Signal Corps and was serving his country as a motion picture combat cameraman.

"The most frightening thing of all," Miss Mary Catherine continued, "is that all the awful fighting is going on right in front of *my* son's camera!"

She stepped around Alice-Ann, opened a narrow drawer beneath the countertop, and pulled out a linen handkerchief. "I told Maeve and I'm telling you — from now on, I think it best if you girls didn't go in to see the show until after the newsreels are done." She blew her nose and Alice-Ann blinked rapidly. "Y'all don't need to see anything like what my boy is having to film."

"All right, Miss Mary Catherine. If you think that's best."

The door opened and the two women turned toward it.

Maeve stopped short, the door ajar. "What's — what's happened?" she asked. "Is it Carlton?" She closed the door quickly. "Mama?"

"No," her mother replied. "No. I'm just being silly."

"Another weepy spell?"

Miss Mary Catherine nodded. "You girls go on upstairs now and get some supper. I'm going to close up." She opened the cash register drawer and pulled out a stack of one-dollar bills. "But lock up before you do."

Maeve did as she was told, then grabbed Alice-Ann by the sleeve and pulled her toward the back of the store, where a staircase led to their apartment. "Come on," she whispered. "I've got something for you."

Alice-Ann's heart skipped. A letter from Mack! It had to be.

CHAPTER 7

"A letter from Mack?" Alice-Ann asked, rushing up the stairs behind Maeve.

"Shhh," Maeve said.

As soon as the girls reached the pink- and white-accented bedroom and Maeve had closed the door, she pulled open the center drawer from her vanity and retrieved the envelope. "For you," she said, beaming, handing it over as though it were a prize.

When Mack's handwriting met her eyes, they filled with tears. "Finally." She dropped into an occasional chair near the window, kicked off her shoes, and tucked her feet beneath her as she ripped one side of the envelope where Mack had so beautifully penned her name and some other had stamped next to it: *Opened By Censor*. She frowned. Was nothing sacred?

Alice-Ann blew into the envelope, puffing the paper wide enough for her to extend her fingers and slide out the folded paper.

"I'll go get us some Co-Colas while you read," Maeve said. "And maybe a couple of sandwiches?"

Alice-Ann looked up and nodded. "Sounds good."

"I won't be long."

She glanced down at the letter, then back up to her friend. "Take your time."

As soon as the door closed, she began to read:

Dear Alice-Ann,

How are you, kiddo? I'm sorry I haven't written in so long. There are a lot of things happening here in the Pacific. More than I can talk about. But what I can, I will.

I have to be honest here because I know I can talk to you about these things. Things I cannot say to my mother or father. Things they would never understand. Especially my father with his feelings about what makes a man a man. Don't get me wrong. I know what he does there in Bynum is important. If someone has a toothache or a severe stomachache, they're awful happy to see him standing behind the counter. But I'd like to think what I'm doing right now is even bigger than that. If the Axis powers take over, a toothache or a stomach cramp will be the least of our worries.

Alice-Ann, there are times when I wonder if what I'm seeing and hearing, what I'm smelling and tasting — all of it — sometimes I wonder if these things will ever fade from my memory. I don't want to upset you, but war is not at all what I thought it would be. I have to be open with you, Alice-Ann. There are times when we fight for our country, but most times we fight just to stay alive. This isn't Americans fighting the Japs or the Allies fighting the Axis powers. Sometimes this is just good ole Boyd MacKay from Bynum, Georgia, trying to get back home in one piece. This is about my survival as well as yours. I hate to admit it, but sometimes more so.

Okay. I've written it. You've read it. Now I want you to promise me, little girl, that you'll forget I said it. You won't tell Nelson. You won't tell Irene. You won't tell Maeve, who is probably only a few feet from you right now, watching you read this.

Alice-Ann shook her head. *No, Mack . . . she gives me my privacy. She understands how I feel. That when I read your words, I can barely breathe. That I, too, live for the day you return to Bynum, Georgia. And although I cannot say the words to you in a letter — not yet, anyway — I have dreams that on that day when you return home, I will run into your arms, hold on to you, and never, ever let go.*

You won't breathe a word of this to a single soul.

Now on to better things. I want to tell you about a dream I had.

Alice-Ann's breath caught and she fingered his bracelet. He, too, had dreams?

Last night I dreamed I was at your kitchen table. Your daddy and Aunt Bess sat at the ends. Nelson and Irene sat on one side and you and I sat on the other. And do you know what Aunt Bess had made me? Special, just for me? One of her pecan pies. Lord have mercy, girl. What I wouldn't do for one of her pies . . .

The door opened and Maeve entered, carrying two glasses — one in each hand — filled with Coke, both balancing a small sandwich-topped plate on the rim. "Did I give you enough time?"

Alice-Ann folded the letter and shoved it into the envelope. She would read the rest later. After the movie. After returning home and getting ready for bed and drawing the bedcovers up under her arms. "Sure," she said, standing. She met Maeve halfway across the room.

"Did he report anything important?"

Alice-Ann shook her head as she took her drink and sandwich, then returned to the chair. "Just the usual."

Maeve set her glass and plate on the bedside table before removing her shoes and sitting cross-legged on the bed. "No undying words of love?"

Alice-Ann felt heat rush to her face. "No." She bit into the sandwich, choosing not to talk about it, but thinking that Mack had, at least and at best, trusted her with his deepest feelings. And secrets.

And that alone was *something* to dream upon.

The following morning Alice-Ann slept in later than usual. When her eyes fluttered open, she peered around the room, dabbed in light that had escaped around the corners of the blackout curtains. She knew without looking at the clock on her bedside table that she'd missed breakfast with the family.

Papa would be none too happy; that much was for certain. And she could just imagine Aunt Bess's sarcasm when she finally went downstairs. "Well, good afternoon," she'd say, in spite of the fact that the sun still hung in the morning sky. The cows would have been milked, food prepared and eaten, and the dishes would have already been washed and put away.

She'd offer to gather the eggs for penitence, and not only for sleeping in.

Alice-Ann stretched beneath the thick melon blossoms quilt Aunt Bess had finished for her only that month, and the dried-in-the-fresh-air linens, smiling. Then, flipping onto her stomach, she retrieved the letter kept in hiding beneath her pillow. *This* was her reason for sleeping in so late. After she'd returned home, she'd read Mack's letter again and again until the wee hours of the morning, searching for clues . . . for hidden meanings . . . for the lines within the lines, wondering what Mack might write if every letter wasn't read by the censors before finding its way to her.

Opening it again, she squinted against the shadows to read the words for the umpteenth time since receiving the letter a day earlier, her breath catching as it had the night before when she'd come to the final

100

paragraphs.

Alice-Ann, we're being moved to the island of Emirau here in the South Pacific within the next little while. Not sure exactly when, but soon. My squadron will be made up of ████████████ ███████████████████████, both land based and seaplanes, and I'll ████████ ███████████████, little girl.

Alice-Ann squeezed her eyes shut as a chill ran down her arms. One she knew hadn't come from the icy air of her bedroom. Something about this place called Emirau, about words sliced out by the censors, didn't sit well with her.

A light tap came to the door. "Alice?" her aunt called from the other side.

Alice-Ann shoved the letter under her pillow and turned onto her back. "Yes'm?"

The door creaked open and natural light from the hallway fully illuminated her bedroom. "Are you planning to sleep the day away?" Not exactly the line she'd expected, but . . .

Alice-Ann glanced at the clock for the first time that morning. *Eight thirty.* She sat up and reached for the bathrobe draped across the foot of her bed. "Gracious. I had no idea." She shoved her arms into the sleeves. "I guess I was more tired than I realized. I know I've missed breakfast."

"You've missed quite a bit more than that." Aunt Bess walked into the room, jerked back the blackout curtains, and then sat at the foot of the bed, her hip pressed against the wrought-iron footboard, which formed indentations in the floral housedress and flesh.

Alice-Ann remained still, hoping Aunt Bess wouldn't realize she was concealing a letter from Mack. One move . . . or one crinkle of the paper . . . "Oh?" she said, her voice a little louder than she'd intended it to be. "What did I miss exactly?"

"Nelson and Irene told your papa and me this morning that another Branch will be entering this home soon enough."

A moment passed before Alice-Ann fully understood. "Irene is — she's —"

"Mm-hmm. Expecting sometime in June. Lord help us when this house is filled with a baby crying and cooing and toddling about." Aunt Bess's words sounded harsh, but Alice-Ann could hear the excitement binding them together.

She smiled. The idea of a baby in the house came as a thrilling bit of news, one she couldn't wait to tell Mack about. She'd write to him that very afternoon.

And maybe one day . . . *one day* . . . she and Mack would have such an announcement to share with Aunt Bess and Papa themselves.

Sunday morning the family gathered around the breakfast table, each dressed in their Sunday best. Alice-Ann couldn't help but notice that her father had a new glow about him, an excitement that a new life would come into the family soon. His happiness was exceeded only by Nelson's, but Irene looked a little green around the gills. Alice-Ann had heard tell of morning sickness, and for sure, Irene had not been up for breakfast over the past few weeks, but that hadn't been so unusual either.

"Roberta Kerr is singing a solo in church this morning," Aunt Bess reported over the rim of her coffee cup. She inhaled before taking a sip, something she'd done since July when coffee had been released from the rationing list.

Alice-Ann crooked her finger in the handle of her own cup and brought it to her lips, then blew across the creamy surface. "I sure do love to hear Miss Roberta sing."

Irene moaned. "Oh, my gracious, Nelson . . . the smell of the coffee . . ." And

103

with that she shoved her chair back, the legs of it scraping against the hardwood floor, and darted from the room.

Alice-Ann's mouth gaped open as she returned the cup to its saucer, choosing not to take so much as a sip. "I'm sorry, Nelson. I —"

"Nelson," Papa interrupted, "if you know what's good for you, Son, you'll hightail it on up those steps and see what you can do to help."

Nelson sighed deeply enough that Alice-Ann had to bite back a smile, even as she contemplated the fact that bringing a child into the world might not be worth it if even the aroma of fresh-brewed coffee caused a woman to throw up. Especially considering those long months of rationing.

After her brother left the room, she dared to ask, "Papa, when Mama was expecting Nelson and me, did *she* get sick?"

At first her father seemed put out by the question. His eye rested on his plate filled with fluffy scrambled eggs, a slab of ham, and slices of buttered toast topped with Aunt Bess's homemade peach preserves. But then he chuckled as he shoveled his fork beneath the eggs. "With Nelson she did. That woman swore up and down she was go'n die." He looked across the table at his sister. "Remember that, Bess?"

"I remember. Made me glad I'd never married."

Alice-Ann frowned. How could *not* having a baby make a difference when it came to living without the love of a man?

"But with you," her father continued before she had much time to think about her aunt's words, "she never had a moment of what some folks call morning sickness or pain in her back or nothing."

Her father's memory brought a smile to Alice-Ann. She looped her finger in the cup's handle again and, this time, took a hearty swallow. If her mother hadn't been sick with her, then it stood to reason that she wouldn't be sick either, when her time came.

Of course this was not the kind of thing she would likely write Mack about. But rather something to keep for another day.

Irene had to forgo church, which Alice-Ann thought to be too bad. The one place she enjoyed being the most — other than with her friends — was in the small sanctuary at Oak Grove Baptist Church — nestled, appropriately, in a grove of giant live oaks. The simple wooden structure had been built at the turn of the century by the area's farming families, erected in the white sand beneath the shade of branches dripping with Spanish moss and bushy dark-green leaves. Oftentimes, in the middle of preaching, the wind caught hold between them and moaned as the reverend spoke from behind the pine pulpit. Alice-Ann had always thought it gave the whole service an even greater spiritual element.

But mostly, during the hot summer months, those shade trees kept the nearly intolerable temperatures tolerable. Even with the windows wide-open and the women giving the handheld fans from Willis Funeral Home a workout, the air inside the church could become both stale and suffocating. Especially during those long, rainless summers that drove the farmers nearly mad with worry and drove their wives to their knees.

Alice-Ann's memories were filled with those times when drought had struck. Every night of the week she and her family — along with the other members of Oak Grove — drove the dusty path to the church. There they had prayer service, the congregation collectively begging God for the rains to come. A single rumble of thunder, typically a result of the heat, caused tears to fall and *amen*s to rise. But when the rains finally came, the good people gathered again to offer praise.

Praise and long tables of covered dishes. As the prayer and worship filled the soul, the fried chicken and potato salad filled the stomach. But for Alice-Ann — food notwithstanding — she'd always come away from the experience more deeply in love with the Lord, not only for having heard their pleas, but for having placed her in such a community of believers.

Today, on this particular Sunday, Alice-Ann rode in Nelson's truck as it rambled behind their father's. Beyond the windshield, the sky had turned dark gray in anticipation of a cold snap Nelson commented on with a frown.

"Pop's gonna bust something if we have a freeze like they're expecting."

Alice-Ann felt a new foreboding, much like the one she'd experienced on Friday evening and all day Saturday when she read Mack's letter. She wrapped her arms around her middle and pressed her gloved hands to her sides. "Nelson," she ventured, hoping to change the subject.

"Huh?"

"Are you excited about the baby?"

"Yeah, of course," he said, casting half a smile her way. "Sure I am."

"Even though it's making Irene awful sick?"

"Well, I don't like that part, of course. I've never liked seeing Irene sad or sick or any of those things." Nelson hit a series of ruts along the sides of the narrow Georgia red clay road leading to the church, rattling Alice-Ann even more than she already was.

She looked out the window and watched the tangled and naked tree limbs as they passed them by. "Nelson?" she said his name again without looking at him. "Do you think Mack and Carlton and Irene's brother Frank and all the rest of the folks from Bynum serving in the war will make it back okay?"

Nelson shifted the truck as his foot eased onto the brake. "I reckon. I mean, only God knows for sure, Alice-Ann. Now, what's made you go and ask a question like that?"

"I'm just wondering. We've been pretty lucky here in Bynum, haven't we."

She glanced over to see him turning the large steering wheel as he guided the truck to park alongside their daddy's.

He cut off the engine. "Better not let Aunt Bess hear you talk like that," he said. "You know how she feels about luck."

Alice-Ann nodded. Aunt Bess didn't believe in luck. She believed fully in God's

108

grace, whether times were good or bad. "Yeah, I know."

Nelson pulled on the chrome handle and the door popped open. "But I guess I'd have to say we've been blessed so far. Two years and no one from Bynum's had to wear the black armband. I know every night before Irene and me go to sleep, we pray that God will keep smiling down on us, so I guess he is."

They exited the truck and joined their father and Aunt Bess at the back of the open-style beds. Alice-Ann linked her arm with Aunt Bess's and pulled her close. "Awful cold," she said.

Aunt Bess glanced skyward. "Getting that way," she said, then peered at her watch. "I thought we were a mite late, but I don't hear the organ music yet, so we must be all right on time."

"Must be," Papa said from behind her.

The red-painted front church door opened and Shirley Davis stepped out, handkerchief pressed to her mouth.

"What in the world?" Aunt Bess muttered as the wife of Jesse Davis, owner of the town's only feed and seed store, strode carefully down the brick steps and then toward them. Miss Shirley was also the chief telephone operator, her voice being the one most folks heard when they picked up the receiver. Aunt Bess had always said that if a secret was to be kept in this town, Miss Shirley was the one to keep it. She made sure the other operators followed the same rule.

"Oh, Bess," she said, her eyes wet with tears. "Emmitt." She reached for them with her free hand, coming first to grasp Aunt Bess's, then Papa's.

"Woman, what's got you in such a tizzy?" her father asked, even as Alice-Ann's breath caught in her throat.

"Philip and LuAnn's boy — darlin' Marty —" she said, drawing the words together in such a way, they sounded as though he'd been given the name "Darlin' Marty" at birth.

"What about him?" Nelson asked, coming around them.

Alice-Ann looked his way, seeing the concern etched in fragmented lines along the face that usually smiled without reason. Both Marty Dibble and his twin sister, Genice, had joined up — Marty with the Navy and Genice with the WAVES — and both had been school chums of Nelson's. And if memory served her correctly, Genice and Mack had dated a time or two.

"He's been killed, hon," she said, blowing

her nose as daintily as possible. "Over in the Pacific."

"Dear Lord," Aunt Bess whispered, her hand pressing against her heart. "And we'd come so far without a death here in Bynum."

Nelson took a step back. Then another.

"Everyone's inside. Of course Philip and LuAnn aren't here today. They got the news late yesterday afternoon via telegraph. Reverend Parker informed us straightaway this morning." She shook her head as though repeating the information to anyone who hadn't heard yet had become her painful duty. "They're having a moment of prayer, but I felt like I had to come outside . . . get some air . . . ." She gasped dramatically. "And then I saw you walking up."

Alice-Ann's arm slipped from the warmth of Aunt Bess's. She joined her brother where he stood on the other side of the truck, leaning against the closed door, one heel on the footboard, smoking a cigarette.

Something he rarely did, except at the end of a hard day or when in distress.

And right now, with all the emotion swarming inside her, Alice-Ann wished she could join him.

"Nelson," she whispered, her eyes filling

with tears, which caused her brother's handsome face to blur in the staring.

He swallowed hard, his Adam's apple bobbing in his throat. "Yeah," he said, his voice barely a croak. He extended his arm, crooked, inviting her to step closer, and she did.

"Mack's in the Pacific," she said, her lips pressed against the fraying material of his winter coat. Somehow, even as she said the words, the bracelet felt heavier against her wrist.

"Yeah," he repeated, his jaws clenched. "I know, Alice-Ann. I know."

CHAPTER 8

Silent anguish had come to Bynum. Misery rolled in with a telegram, strong enough that, to Alice-Ann, it seemed it would never leave. Even more so, Alice-Ann believed the town itself mourned as it laid her martyred son to rest, the first since that day a little over two years ago when her special day had turned pear-shaped. Upside down, like a sand-filled hourglass, spilling its contents much too quickly.

There were times when Alice-Ann thought the sands would never reverse. Living under the oppression of rationing books — even though farmers had it easier than most — and the fear brought about by pulled blackout curtains. Aunt Bess fussing about trying to help her friends in town by sharing things like sugar, Papa stressing about overworking his mules and tearing up the plows, Irene complaining about everything, Nelson trying to keep everyone's spirits up, and herself, riding a bus to work and back, driven by a bus driver who, in keeping with the gas restrictions, wasn't allowed to go over thirty-five miles an hour. There were days when she thought she'd die on that bus, whether heading to town or back home again.

Now that thought had practically taken shape, breathing in and out, like a living thing.

It had been too easy, she'd told Mack in her next letter to him, to believe that one day — someday soon — life would simply return to the way it had been before that awful day when the Japanese chose to fly their planes into American skies.

But in reality, she'd penned the night after receiving the news about the handsome redhead with a spray of freckles across his upturned nose,

I am old enough now, Mack, to know that this can never be. I'm no longer the child you watched walk toward the front porch of the farmhouse. The girl who declared her undying love for you.

My love has not changed other than it has rooted more deeply. I cannot ever see myself loving anyone but you, ever. I know you haven't given me much encouragement — except those few times when you shared with me private thoughts you have always carried so deep within your heart. All I have are my dreams and a prayer for you that I speak every night. I ask the Lord to keep you all safe, Mack, but you most of all.

I'm not sure I could bear a life without you in it.

Please don't laugh at my words. Please don't pass them off as continuing to be some silly high school crush. I'm not in high school any longer, Mack. I'm a grown woman now. I have a job and I help with the household finances. And with this war, I see things through the eyes of an adult, not a child.

In case you've wondered, I only go out with my friends.

Not that there were many young men knocking on her door, asking her out. Young women with fuzz for hair, pale eyes, and even paler skin . . . young women with a mouth full of teeth, two of which crossed slightly in the middle of too-generous lips . . . didn't have a beau calling every Friday night and Saturday afternoon. Young women like herself, she knew, were more than grateful for the men who might look beyond the book's cover and want to know about the story inside.

Men like Mack, who had known her for her entire life.

I wait for you. I told you once that I want you to be the first man I ever kiss. The last. The only.

Nothing has changed, except that there is a sudden sadness hanging over us now. A dark cloud that rains and rains.

I beg you, Mack. Stay safe.

More than that, she begged God.

On the following Friday after work, Alice-Ann said good-bye to Nancy at the corner, then crossed the street as she did every afternoon. She nearly trotted in the cold to the five-and-dime, her hand holding the skull-fitting beret she'd squirreled money away for. The one she'd hoped would make her look more like Miss Gene Tierney, the way she looked in one of Irene's magazines.

The store's doors had been decorated with green wreaths wrapped in red velvet ribbon, and the windows had been made to look as though the town had experienced a dusting of snow. Above it, a large sign encouraged Bynum's citizens to come inside and buy

116

war bonds and stamps.

Maeve stood behind the counter, handing change to Ernie's kid sister, Mary Etta, a pretty fifteen-year-old who stood with her saddle oxfords pressed together as though a tension cord had pulled her erect.

"Hey there," Maeve said with a smile. "Got something for you."

Alice-Ann ignored her. The last thing she needed was for Mary Etta to hear that she'd received a letter from Mack. Knowing bobby-soxers as she did, Alice-Ann reckoned Mary Etta would waste no time in telling her best friend and then probably mention it again at dinner, which meant that Ernie would hear, and then —

She smiled at Mary Etta. "How's school, Mary Etta?" she asked, hoping Maeve got the subtle hint.

Mary Etta fastened the oversize buttons on her coat, then grabbed the small brown paper bag and held it up. "I'm out of erasers." She frowned. "Well, I was. Now I'm not."

"Only a few more days until Christmas break, I imagine?"

"We're out now, Alice-Ann," she said, pulling a knit cap from the recesses of her coat pocket and sliding it onto her head, pressing the dark-blonde curls to a scarf around her throat. "Christmas is only a week away, you know."

With that, she walked out, leaving Alice-Ann and Maeve to gawk at one another.

Alice-Ann shrugged. "Honestly," she said, walking to the counter. "What with Irene throwing her guts up every ten minutes and Marty Dibble getting himself killed and the whole town mourning and Mack getting ready to —" She stopped herself.

"Mack getting ready to what?"

Alice-Ann shook her head. She'd chosen not to tell Maeve or Claudette — and who'd seen much of *her* lately? — what Mack had told her about going to Emirau. She'd somehow managed to find time to go to the library during her lunch break on Monday, skipping the opportunity to eat her sandwich and drink from the thermos of coffee Aunt Bess had packed for her earlier that morning. Avoiding the librarian's eagle eyes, she looked up the location of the island, along with some photographs in an oversize and heavy encyclopedia. What she'd learned had kept her from being hungry again until the next day's breakfast.

"Nothing," she said. She smiled. "Do you have a letter from Mack for me?"

Maeve shook her head, her brown curls barely moving under the layers of home-

118

made setting lotion she'd taken to using of late. "Uh-uh." She pulled an envelope from her smock. "But you *did* get a letter from my brother." She grinned as she handed it over. "And so did I. Wait till you read it." She walked around the counter to lock the door. "He probably tells you pretty much what he tells me, without the 'Give Mama and Daddy a hug for me' stuff."

Alice-Ann stared down at the chicken-scratch handwriting of Maeve's older brother — her name on the envelope, but addressed to Maeve's post office box. "What does he have to say?" she asked, flipping it over, then back again, choosing not to open it right then.

"He told me about how the people over there in England talk. They sure have some funny ways," she said, turning the key and dropping it into the same pocket she'd pulled the letter from. She crossed her arms as she stepped over to Alice-Ann. "Hey, Ernie and I are going to the Methodist church tonight to hear their cantata. Want to join us?"

Alice-Ann offered the best smile she had to give. "No, but thank you. It's been a hard week and I'm sort of beat. I also think Aunt Bess wants to try to find a Christmas tree tonight."

Maeve glanced over her shoulder, out the window to the heart of Bynum, where streetlamps had begun to flicker. They wouldn't stay on long; once darkness fell, the whole town faded to black. "Getting dark, already," she said. "I bet she won't go out in those woods tonight to cut down a tree." She bounced on the balls of her feet. "Come on, Alice-Ann. Come with Ernie and me. It'll be fun."

Alice-Ann slid Carlton's letter into her coat pocket as she shook her head again. "No. I wouldn't have any way of letting Aunt Bess know and if I just didn't show up, Papa would cut a switch for sure."

Maeve's mouth gaped open and Alice-Ann laughed.

"I'm kidding, Maeve," she said, walking toward the door, hoping she was right. Since Marty Dibble's death, Papa had been anything but easy to live with. "Thanks for the letter from Carlton."

"You *do* write him, too, don't you?" Maeve asked, coming up behind her to lock the door again.

Alice-Ann nodded halfheartedly. Of course she *wrote* to Carlton. Short, kind letters telling him of the weather and the latest book she'd read or a movie she'd seen. She figured he got enough heartfelt sentiments from Betty Jo Shannon.

"Of course I do," she said. "Doesn't he tell you these things too?"

Maeve shrugged. "Not really, no."

"Oh," she said. "Well, I do write to him. At least once a week." *Or so . . .*

Maeve smiled. "Good. You've got such a way with words, Alice-Ann. And I imagine he's seeing some awful things over there. I just want him to have something to smile about."

Well, of course she did. Alice-Ann would want the same for her own brother. She gave her best friend a hug before walking out, returning to the corner in front of the bank, and then crossing the street to the bus stop. Only when she made it to her usual seat — four from the back, left side — did she pull Carlton's letter from her pocket.

Dear Alice-Ann,

I wish you could see the way the boys flurry around when the words "mail call" are shouted out. You'd think no one had ever received so much as a postcard before. But these are more than just letters from home and from our loved ones. They help us forget what we're seeing, what we're doing, and maybe even a little of who we've become, which isn't all bad. Especially now with Christmas coming.

I also wish you could hear the people over here talking. Ha-ha. Some of the Yankees I'm stationed with think I talk funny, but then we heard these British. They say things like "Bob's your uncle," which means "and that's that." Isn't that the funniest thing you've ever heard? So, if you were telling me how to get from your farm over to our place, you might say, "You walk down the drive, take the bus to town, get off across from the bank, cross two streets into the center of town, and Bob's your uncle!"

You can use that sometime on Maeve and Claudette. I haven't told Maeve (I told her about the "roundabouts") and I don't write to Claudette, so have at it.

We have to leave out again early in the morning, so I guess I'd better stop writing for now and turn in. Most of the boys already have — I'm the lone wolf. Keep Maeve out of trouble, will you? When she writes, she goes on and on about Ernie and I think it's beginning to worry Mama and Daddy. (Oh! Another thing. Over here, they call their mama "Mum" and their daddy "Dad.")

All right, then. Bob's your uncle!

Take care,

Carlton

Alice-Ann couldn't help it: she smiled. Then, as the bus neared her stop, she read it again, this time imagining Carlton sitting up on his cot, one knee bent, the foot flat against the sheets, his stationery splayed across a book that rested on the other outstretched leg. She pictured him as she had so often seen him, the fingers of one hand combed through his thick hair.

For sure, Carlton Hillis was a catch for Betty Jo Shannon. She was one lucky girl.

Later, before she turned off her light and said her final prayers, Alice-Ann pulled two random letters from Mack from the stack she kept hidden in her closet in an old handkerchief box under her straw hat and tied off with a red ribbon she'd once worn in her hair. She marked their place by pulling the letters beneath them out a fraction of an inch, then climbed into her bed, sitting cross-legged beneath the covers as she read.

August 15, 1942

Dear Alice-Ann,

Have I written to you yet about all the walking we do every day? Sometimes I think I put in more miles each day than Nelson does out there on the farm. If we're not marching, we're walking to mess (that's where we eat), and if we're not walking to mess, we're walking to where we shower, and that's not even where we go to the bathroom. (Sorry to talk about such as this. I think I've grown a little calloused to it all.)

I know some people think the farmers are the lucky ones because they stayed behind to work the land, but sometimes I think we are. I don't mind telling you that I'm not at all keen on fighting and maybe dying, but at the same time, this is what I want to do for my country. Whenever I get afraid, I think of my folks and you and Nelson and Irene. I think of Aunt Bess and your daddy. I think of everyone in Bynum, doing their part. And I know you are all worth dying for.

I know this letter is a little morose, but when you're stationed here and when you see the leftovers of December 7, you

start to think about things like that.
Send news from home, will you?

Love ya,
Mack

November 12, 1942

Dear Alice-Ann,

How's life on the farm? I have to tell you, little gal, it's not too shabby over here in "paradise," as they call it. Of course, that doesn't mean it's all fun and games. We're up early, we work hard, and then most nights we collapse on hard bunks and we don't get much sleep in between. I've really bonded with these boys. One in particular. His name is Horace. He's from Idaho, where they grow the potatoes. Ha-ha.

What's Nelson and Irene up to? Any little ones coming along? Wouldn't that be something? You tell ole Nelson that if he and Irene have a baby, I want them to name him Mack, after his wonderful uncle. Of course, if it's a girl, they'll have to name her Mackenzie or something like that.

All right then. Lights out and up and at 'em before the sun barely peeks its eyes over the Pacific. Take care.

Love ya,
Mack

She read the first letter again, her eyes focusing on one particular line: *"I don't mind telling you that I'm not at all keen on fighting and maybe dying, but at the same time, this is what I want to do for my country."*

Alice-Ann folded the pages, sliding them back into their envelopes and tucking them both under her pillow. Maybe with his words so close she'd dream of him that night. Maybe.

For a while, as her eyes fought hard-earned sleep, she allowed her mind to venture back to other words in other letters. Over their two years of correspondence, Mack had shared so much with her. Surely he would fall in love with her. Love her like she loved him. And if not, she felt certain she could love him enough for the both of them.

But surely he would. Perhaps he already did but had chosen to wait until he could say the words to her face. Whisper them in her ear . . .

After all, he'd already shared such private things with her. Things men only said to the women they loved. Things he said he'd never revealed to another living soul. Like about the problems he'd had with his father — not only in the days and weeks as he prepared to leave for training, but before that. He'd shared them all with her, asked her to keep them tied in a bow and in her heart. And she'd told him she would. Of course she would. Always.

Forever.

CHAPTER 9

Four Months Later
April 1944

"Somebody want to tell me *how* I'm supposed to run this farm without *workers*?" Papa's voice carried up the stairs, and Alice-Ann's shoulders hunched against the anger, even though not directed at her.

"Pop," Nelson's voice followed. "*You* are not running this farm without workers. *We* are not running this farm without workers. Not entirely anyway. Didn't Harry Thorpe organize some of his high school boys to come out and work with the farmers one day a week?"

He surely had. Nancy had told Alice-Ann all about it. And, she said, while the boys worked the fields, the girls in home ec learned to knit warm socks and scarves for the soldiers.

Papa's footsteps were heavy against the rugs and hardwood floor as Alice-Ann crept to her bedroom door, opening it enough to hear more clearly but without causing it to creak and give her eavesdropping away.

"A day a week is a help but it's not always enough. Even migrant labor is getting more difficult to find. And half the women in this town — women I'm sure I could put on a tractor and show them how to drive it and how to harvest — they're off working in factories."

"Pop, come on, now. The women are only trying to make up for the lack of men on all fronts. Good men who are off fighting for us. Besides, Alice-Ann and Aunt Bess have been pitching in."

That they had. Growing up on a farm — as both she and Aunt Bess had and both right here in this house — meant knowing how to harvest vegetables by hand, walking row by row in the early mornings of summer, trying to get it done before the sun blistered. Before "the bear," as her father called it, got you. That moment when all the life nearly drained out and a person could no longer see or think straight. It also meant knowing how to pick worms off the tobacco and learning — even at an early age — how to drive a tractor (if you were blessed enough to own one) while your daddy yelled out orders, his work boots covered in caked dirt and dusted with sand. And at the end of the day, it meant knowing how to can and freeze and dry and, when all was said and done, thank the good Lord for his provisions.

"There's crops out there that'll need harvesting soon, Nelson," Papa now bellowed, drawing Alice-Ann one step back into the room, though she kept the door ajar. "What do you suppose we do about that? Not to mention we got a full moon coming up soon. Gotta plant by the full moon and we've got to get it done *right then.*"

"We've got some workers. Why are you acting like we don't? Every morning I go and pick up day labor and not a single one of 'em minds walking behind a plow and a mule. What more do you want, Pop?"

Alice-Ann pictured her brother standing with his arms stretched out, palms up. His usual pleasant expression soured by the stress their father had increasingly put on him since the war. She closed her eyes and shook her head at the moment. When she heard the door across the hall ease open, Alice-Ann looked up to see Irene peek out, her eyes filled with a mixture of stress and sadness. A jazzy Duke Ellington tune wafted out past her, and Alice-Ann waved her hand in warning. "Turn it down," she mouthed.

Irene closed the door as quietly as she'd opened it. A moment later, it reopened, this time surrounded by silence. Irene's lips were pressed together and her hand covered the rounding of her stomach as though she were trying to keep her baby from hearing the argument.

"And I guess you know," Papa continued, followed by a creaking that told Alice-Ann he'd made his way to his chair. A relief, somehow. Sitting, Papa tended to exert less anger. He might not have *lost* his fury and it might not have quelled one iota, but at least he doled it out in easier-to-digest doses.

"Know what?" Nelson finally asked, his voice also a tad less anxious.

"About George James's boy."

Alice-Ann exchanged a glance with Irene, who shrugged her shoulders.

"No, sir. What about 'im?"

"Now they've both signed up. Both had deferment and they know the labor's hard to come by, but Pete's followed his brother, thinking war is so much easier than working the land. What kind of son leaves his daddy and mama to try to go it alone in times like these?"

Alice-Ann shook her head. Even as far

131

back as December 1941 she knew George would go — he seemed the type. But *Pete?* Pete loved the land. Always had. And for a boy with such big ears, he ought to be grateful for what offered him a good living, although hard-earned. If nothing else, he could say to some half-blind girl someday, "Look here . . . I got five hundred acres of God's best dirt . . . Lucky, too, out here. We got electricity and a phone. Farm next to ours? The Branches'? They got electricity but no phone. And we both have indoor plumbing. My daddy and Mr. Branch saw to that when Nelson married that uppity Irene . . ."

She shook her head again, wondering how it was her brain sometimes went off in such directions.

"Maybe he just —"

"That ain't all. Butterwick's boys have done the same." Papa's sigh traveled up the staircase.

"I'm sure they'll work it out, Pop. All of 'em."

"If we lived closer to Camp Stewart, we'd have the POWs. Of course, the farmers out west have the Japanese from the internment camps to help in the fields. Don't know why we don't rate high enough." He paused and Alice-Ann waited for her brother to com-

132

ment. She supposed Papa waited too, but when he didn't, Papa added, "I've heard tell there's a POW camp coming soon to Bulloch County."

"Would you want that? The Germans and Italians working alongside us? So close to Alice-Ann and Aunt Bess? To Irene and the baby?"

"I reckon the only thing keeping *you* here is Irene and that baby coming."

Again, eyes met from opposite sides of the hallway, in time for Alice-Ann to see Irene simmering with fury and hurt. Alice-Ann raised her hands and mouthed, "He doesn't mean it."

But Irene turned and closed the door. Loudly enough, this time, to be heard.

Alice-Ann took a step back, her hand gripping the cut-glass doorknob as she readied herself to close the door and dash to the bed. It'd be easy enough to pretend she'd been lying there all along, reading from one of the books she'd recently checked out from the library.

A pause from the first floor clued her in that both Papa and Nelson had heard Irene's protest. She waited a breath without moving. Then, "No, sir," her brother said, loudly enough and as though nothing had happened one floor up. "That's not the only

133

reason I'm here and you know it. We're in this thing together, Pops. I may not be fighting a war over there like Mack and Carlton and the rest of 'em, but I'm surefire pulling my weight on our own soil, making sure everyone left over here's got food in their gut and tobacco to roll. That stands for something too."

The chair creaked again, but no footsteps followed. "Well, sir," Papa added. "I did hear some good news today down at the feed and seed."

"What's that?" Nelson asked, his voice calmer.

"Heard tell John Deere has been working to get us some better tractors and the implements we've been needin' all along. What we can't find the manpower to do, we'll get out of oil and grease. Come summer when the tobacco's high, we'll see what shakes out. 'Tween now and then, I reckon we'll make do."

As a springtime thunderstorm pelted the sidewalks of Bynum beneath a gray-blue sky, Alice-Ann stood at her teller's window, counting her drawer, doing her best to concentrate — *five, ten, fifteen, twenty*. All the while, her mind pored over the letter she'd dropped into the mailbox outside the post office earlier in the day, making the otherwise-simple task difficult.

Truth is, Mack, I often wonder if Papa would be so cantankerous if Mama were still alive. Would he carry on so? I picture Mama soothing him, talking to him sweetly to bring down his feverish pitch.

And then she wondered, would Mack stop right there in his letter reading to consider that Alice-Ann might calm and soothe him one day, were he to come home from work, upset at something, stomping around their living room? Would he picture the two of them as she dreamed they'd be — him sitting in an easy chair much like Papa's and her draped across his lap, her legs crossed over the extra padding of the armrest? He'd lay his head back, close his eyes, and she'd sing to him, planting kisses along his brow between the stanzas —

Fifty-five, sixty-five . . .

"Oh, dear."

"What is it?" Nancy asked from beside her as she wrapped a thick band around a stack of bills.

Alice-Ann winced. "I got off in my counting."

"Daydreaming, no doubt."

If the heat in her cheeks wasn't a giveaway, Alice-Ann didn't know what would be.

Nancy had guessed some time ago that Alice-Ann's letter writing to Mack and her refusal to remove his bracelet meant more than pure friendship. Like Claudette and Maeve and — she hoped — Irene, Nancy was good for secret keeping.

"Just start over," Nancy said. "And think about fives and not ones."

Alice-Ann giggled, then looked across the room to make sure they hadn't raised any suspicion in Miss Portia. But the older woman seemed immersed in her own end-of-the-day routine. "You mean like the one and only?" she asked Nancy, her voice whisper-soft.

"Exactly." Nancy nodded toward the stack of bills. "Now, concentrate. If your drawer is off, it means we both have to stay and —"

The front door opened, the torrential rain increasing in volume.

"I'm sorry," Miss Portia began, her voice no-nonsense as always. "We're closed." She stood, muttering, "I thought I'd locked —"

"Maeve?" Alice-Ann said, now recognizing her best friend, framed by the open door, silhouetted by the miserable exterior. She dropped her cash on the counter and came out from behind the windows, her heart pounding as rapidly as Maeve's gulps for air. "Maeve?" she said again, this time running across the terrazzo floor, her black-and-white pumps tapping in rhythm.

Maeve's hands cupped her mouth, her round eyes filled with tears that spilled over without restraint. Alice-Ann grabbed her shoulders where the drenched material of her dress clung. Her hair — always coiffed — plastered itself against her head as a puddle formed at her feet as though she'd had an accident of nature.

"Is it — ?" Alice-Ann wanted to ask if something had happened to Mack, but before she could, Miss Portia, Mister Dooley, and Nancy had joined them.

"Here," Miss Portia said, wrapping her own raincoat over Maeve's shoulders and pulling her close. "Nancy, close the door and then run to the back and get some of the old towels Etta-Sue uses to clean."

Nancy shut the door, turned the key, and then darted to the back.

"Sit over here, child." Mister Dooley motioned to one of the chairs that lined a half wall separating the main room from the offices. "I'll get a glass of water."

Miss Portia sat next to Maeve, and Alice-Ann knelt at her feet, wrapping her arms around Maeve's legs to keep her shivering — from the cold or whatever news she bore,

Alice-Ann couldn't be sure — at a minimum. "Maeve, what is it?"

Maeve gasped. Once. Twice.

"Let her catch her breath," Miss Portia said.

Mister Dooley returned with one of the crystal glasses from his wet bar, which Maeve took in her hands but did not drink from. Startled by movement, Alice-Ann glanced over her shoulder long enough to see Nancy drop several towels onto the polished terrazzo floor, then mop up the water with her foot.

"Maeve." Alice-Ann said the name again. "Please. Tell me. What is it?"

"Carlton," she finally breathed out.

Alice-Ann gasped. "No." Dear God in heaven, how could it be? How could a young man so full of life, so vibrant and funny — ?

"He's not — he's not —" She shook her head as she swallowed. "He's been hurt bad, Alice-Ann. Blind, they say. Can't walk." The glass in her hand shook so, and water splashed onto the skirt of her already-soaked dress.

Alice-Ann rose up on her knees, the harsh reality of the floor pressing against them. "When?" she asked, taking the glass and handing it to Miss Portia, who in turn handed it back to Mister Dooley.

"I don't know," Maeve whispered. "We just got the telegram." She looked out the front window as though she expected to see herself running from the five-and-dime to the bank. "I came here. Mama — Mama is screaming. Can't be controlled. Threw me away from her. Daddy is crying — so, so hard — I've never seen him like this, Alice-Ann." Her sobs broke through then, and her backside bounced on the hard surface of the chair as though someone had goosed her. "I don't know what to do!"

Miss Portia stood. "Sit here, Alice-Ann." She looked at Mister Dooley. "Come, Doo. Grab a couple of umbrellas and let's go see what we can do." Next she turned to Nancy. "Lock up behind us, you hear?"

"Yes, ma'am."

"Don't know how the door wasn't locked in the first place, but I suppose the good Lord knew . . ." She paused. "No one leave until you've finished up, but don't rush. When you can, bring this child home so she can get out of these wet clothes. If she's not careful, she'll catch her death . . ." The words trailed off as she reached for the umbrella Mister Dooley brought her.

As soon as the front door had closed behind them and Nancy had locked it,

Alice-Ann pulled Maeve closer still and said, "Tell me exactly what you know."

"I only know he was injured while filming, but I don't know what. Hit in the head, the telegram said. Knocked off of something and fell. Fell far and hard." Her breath shuddered, and she sighed. "I think it happened several weeks ago."

"And you're just now hearing about it?"

Maeve's chin dropped to her chest. "I don't know. I don't know."

Nancy put her hand on Alice-Ann's shoulder. "I'm going to count your drawer and mine. You stay here."

Alice-Ann nodded without looking up, wondering if Nancy's thoughts had gone to her husband. To Harry, who'd returned after the Big One, leaving his ability to walk on some foreign soil. "Thank you, Nance."

"I'm so sorry." Maeve rested her head on Alice-Ann's shoulder, the crown nuzzling into her neck. A shiver from the dampness passed through Alice-Ann and she inhaled against it. "I'm so sorry," Maeve whispered, though about what Alice-Ann wasn't sure.

"Don't be. No. I'm the one who's sorry, Maeve. I mean . . . Carlton. Blind and unable to walk." She couldn't imagine it.

"He's been in the hospital in London, it said."

"London."

Her head nodded. "But they're sending him home. He'll be in another hospital for a while — I don't know where — and then he'll come home to recuperate further."

Alice-Ann pulled back and Maeve sat straight. "Then he'll be okay? Eventually, I mean? And he and Betty Jo can —"

"I don't know, Alice-Ann. The telegram didn't say."

"If he's coming home, then there must be hope."

Maeve returned her head to Alice-Ann's shoulder. She took in a deep breath and released it, one tiny puff of air at a time. "No," she said. "If they're sending him back to the States, then all hope must be lost."

Alice-Ann hugged her friend closer. "Don't say that, Maeve. Don't think like that. We'll pray for him. Every single day." She turned her face toward the teller windows. "Won't we, Nancy?"

"You bet we will," Nancy said without looking up.

And every day, Alice-Ann thought, *I'll ask God to watch over Mack with a little more attention than usual.*

Because if something like that happened to Mack . . .

Well, she'd love him anyway. Just as she

was certain Betty Jo would look past Carlton's injuries. Like Nancy had with Harry. The men they loved were more than eyes and legs, after all.

So much more.

CHAPTER 10

Carlton returned on a Thursday in early May.

May 4, to be exact.

At noon that day, Alice-Ann met Claudette for a prearranged lunch at Tucker's. They hadn't seen each other in weeks — in fact, Alice-Ann mused during the walk over, she'd not seen Claudette in nearly as long as it had been since she'd heard from Mack.

The thought penetrated her, chilling her bones in the warm sunshine of near summer. Knowing what she knew — that he'd taken on this mission, this going to some exotic island she'd never heard of before — she couldn't help but worry. Then again, she told herself, perhaps her letters to him and his to her were not being delivered *because* of the importance of the work. The secrecy.

Alice-Ann smiled at the thought. Mack, in some clandestine work to bring down the

Japanese. Well, then. Maybe the lack of correspondence wasn't due to mail service, but
more to Mack having been so busy he didn't
have time to write. Perhaps all he did, day
in and day out, was fight the Japs, then eat
and sleep what little he could, then fight the
Japs some more.

Of course. That was it.

She crossed the street, lightly running on
the balls of her feet, already feeling better
about things.

Claudette had arrived before her and had
saved a booth, hard to come by with the
lunch crowd. She waved furiously as soon
as Alice-Ann entered, the bells over the door
alerting the room to her arrival. Alice-Ann
waved back, then worked her way around
the tables and to her friend, who, dressed in
pink, looked more like cotton candy than a
girl simply going out for lunch.

As a budding young woman, Alice-Ann
had managed to accept her more-than-
mousy appearance around Maeve and,
especially, Claudette. But over the past two
years, the friendship between Maeve and
Alice-Ann had grown deeper. Claudette, on
the other hand, spent more time with
Johnny Dailey and, in the process, seemed
to have grown even more glamorous and, in
many ways, distant. They saw each other at

the few dances Bynum threw for the soldiers and citizens from time to time, but otherwise, the time Alice-Ann spent with Claudette was more miss than hit.

Alice-Ann slid into the booth. "I hope you weren't waiting too long."

"Not at all." Claudette smiled, nearly grinning. "How have you been?"

"I've been okay." Alice-Ann looked toward the counter, wondering where their server might be.

"I've ordered for us," Claudette said.

Alice-Ann felt heat rush to her cheeks. Unlike most young women in town, Claudette hadn't gone to work. How she spent her days, exactly, Alice-Ann could only guess. She often imagined her, lounging in her princess-perfect bedroom, a book in one hand and a tall glass of Coke poured over crushed ice in another. Or strolling along some leaf-scattered path, humming a little tune. Claudette didn't understand the value of a nickel hard-earned, or that sometimes a meal — even in a soda shop — could only be a bowl of tomato soup with *perhaps* a cheese sandwich on the side if it happened to be payday.

"Don't worry," Claudette continued as though she'd read Alice-Ann's mind. "This is my treat."

"You don't have to do that," Alice-Ann said.

"I want to." She sat up straight. "Cheese-burgers, fries, and icy glasses of Co-Cola — just like old times before this awful war came to town."

Alice-Ann could only smile in response.

"Besides," Claudette went on, "we're celebrating."

Celebrating. How could they celebrate on such a day? "Carlton is being brought home today," she muttered.

Claudette reached her right hand across the table and grabbed Alice-Ann's left. "I know. I went by earlier and talked to Maeve. I invited her to lunch too, actually, but she — well . . . They've got his room all set up. Of course, they're going to have to get him up those stairs first and I daresay he won't be coming down them any time soon."

"No." The thought gave cause to wince, and momentarily she pictured Nancy's Main Street home with the ramp built over the front porch steps. "Do you know what time he's expected?"

"Maeve said around three and I overhead Daddy telling Mama he'd be there then to check on things. Are you going by after work?"

She hadn't considered it, in all honesty.

146

Of course she'd go to see if she'd received anything from Mack, but the idea of visiting with Carlton hadn't so much as tickled her brain. "I — I don't know."

"You should. Maeve said Carlton wrote to you from time to time. It'd be a nice gesture." She looked up then as Mr. Tucker approached their table, a lunch plate in each hand.

"Two cheeseburgers," he said. "Fries and —" He frowned as he looked down at the table. "Where are your drinks?"

"Not here yet," Claudette said, her voice filled with humor. "I say fire the help."

"Hard enough *getting* help these days, little missy," he said with a wink. "Much less firing it." He shook his head. "I'll have the drinks sent right over."

Alice-Ann's stomach rumbled. "Smells wonderful," she said. "I can't remember when I had a juicy burger last."

Claudette bowed her head and Alice-Ann did the same. "Thank you, Lord, for your bounty and goodness. We pray for the men and women fighting for our country and for all those still here. We pray for Maeve and her family today, Lord, and ask that you be with them. Amen."

"Amen," Alice-Ann added. She plucked a fry from the platter and blew on it, watching the steam rise in front of her nose. "So what are we celebrating?" she asked.

Claudette waited as Tucker's head cook, Lurline Reynolds, placed their drinks on the table. "Here ya go, ladies. Y'all just holler if you need anything else."

"Thank you, Lurline," she said, then watched her retreat. "Gracious, Mr. Tucker has her running the back *and* serving drinks? Where is Ernie?"

Alice-Ann shrugged. "Maybe he's over at Maeve's. Helping."

"Could be. Would make sense, though his going over there during a hectic lunch hour is — well . . ." She smiled. "None of my concern." She slid her left hand across the table. "This. *This* is what we're celebrating."

Alice-Ann looked down to see Claudette's ring finger sporting a cluster of sapphires circling a small diamond. She returned the fry to the plate as she breathed out, "Claudette."

"I know," her friend giggled. "Isn't it lovely?"

"When?" she asked, looking up.

"Saturday night. Can you believe it? It seems like only yesterday we were schoolgirls in your bedroom and I was all starry-eyed, talking about how dreamy Johnny is."

Claudette eyed the ring, turning it under the overhead lights. "This ring belonged to his mother."

"Miss Nell?"

Claudette nodded. "I'm hoping that her giving him the ring his father proposed with means she and I will get along okay."

"Do you get along now?"

Claudette nibbled on the end of a fry and shrugged. "She thinks I'm spoiled."

Alice-Ann wrapped her fingers around the burger. "You *are* spoiled," she said truthfully, but she smiled to lessen the words.

Maeve met Alice-Ann at the front of the store, closing and locking the door behind them. "We've only allowed Doc Evans in and, of course, Betty Jo since Carlton got home."

Alice-Ann tilted her head at her friend, whose eyes were red-rimmed and swollen. "How is he? How does he look?"

"Just awful," Maeve whispered. "You'll see, but . . ." A fresh set of tears spilled from her eyes and she dabbed at them with a lavender handkerchief.

Alice-Ann recoiled at the thought. "Maybe I should wait a day or so."

Maeve's lips parted in a tiny O as she shook her head. "Oh, you must come up and say something to him. He'd be devastated. It's bad enough that . . ."

"What?"

Maeve took a step closer. "I don't know, Alice-Ann. Betty Jo acts like he's some sort of stranger." She shook her head again. "Or worse, a monster."

Alice-Ann's heart pounded as she wondered exactly what Maeve meant. Did he *look* like a monster? And if so, what kind? "Well, I —"

Maeve slid her arm into Alice-Ann's. "Come on up. We won't stay in there long." She started toward the back, nearly dragging Alice-Ann with her. "Mama's fluttering around the room, trying her best to act like everything's just fine and dandy." They came to the end of the sewing notions aisle. "But I just know," she said, stopping, "that when she and Daddy go to bed tonight, she'll cry herself to sleep in his arms."

Alice-Ann tried to picture the scene but couldn't. Instead, her eyes focused on each individual step of the back staircase, listening to the muffled voices coming from upstairs.

"Mama, I'm fine . . ."

Alice-Ann squeezed Maeve's arm with her own. "He *sounds* strong."

"He's a rock," she said, her voice low. "I

know in time he'll be okay. It's just that right now —"

"Maeve? Did I get a letter today?"

Maeve stopped at the top of the staircase. "No. I'm sorry, Alice-Ann. But I can tell you that Mr. MacKay was here yesterday buying some cornstarch and I heard Daddy ask him what they'd heard from Mack."

Alice-Ann's heart quickened again. "What'd he say?"

"He said not a word for weeks now, but that maybe no news was good news."

"Maybe so," Alice-Ann said, though something in her heart kept telling her otherwise.

Maeve pulled her into the bedroom across from the one Alice-Ann had slept in many a night when they'd been girls. The air inside was thick and still and smelled of a man's cologne trying desperately to mask the odor of injury.

"Carlton," Maeve said as she drew in a shuddering breath and turned toward the bed, where a pajama-clad man who looked only vaguely familiar lay propped up on a mound of linen-covered pillows. "Look who's here to see you."

"Oh, Maeve, *really.*" Betty Jo, who sat in a corner chair on the far side of the room, crossed her legs and pursed her lips. "He can't *see* who's here."

Blessedly, Alice-Ann's intake of breath couldn't be heard over Carlton's sigh. "It's only an expression, Betty Jo." Then, turning his face toward the door, he added, "Tell me who."

Alice-Ann took a step forward. "Hello, Carlton."

A crooked smile crossed his face, still shaded with yellow and green from the bruising. His eyes, once full of fire and mischief, were shielded by dark, oversize sunglasses. The arms were wide and equally as dark, as if they'd been designed to keep light out from all angles. The lips that had always been ready with a quick comeback were now puffy and red and chapped in places. "Why, if it isn't little Alice-Ann Branch. How're ya doin' there, doodlebug?"

She took a step, aware of Betty Jo's disapproval by the way she folded her arms across her middle as she took in a harsh breath. "I'm all right . . . but I'm not so little anymore, I reckon."

She smiled at Maeve's mother, who stood at the head of the bed, her arm resting along the headboard. "Hello, Mrs. Hillis."

"Alice-Ann," she said. She took a step closer to Maeve, who stood alongside the closet wall. "I'm going to go check on your father. Carlton?"

His face moved gingerly toward her voice. "Yes'm?"

"Need anything?"

Carlton reached for his mother's hand and she readily gave it, their arms stretching toward each other. "Mama, I *promise*. If I need anything, I'll call."

Mrs. Hillis seemed unconvinced, but she kissed her son's hand anyway and left the room.

Carlton craned his neck. "I hear you've been writing back and forth with Mack, too, Alice-Ann." He said it almost as if it were a question, as though he'd been surprised by it. But why should he be? After all, she'd written to Carlton, hadn't she? Wouldn't he consider it perfectly normal that she would write to *two* of her brother's best friends?

Her toes curled, cracking in the silence as she realized Betty Jo now knew of her correspondence with Mack. Would she tell anyone? Would it somehow get back to Nelson or Papa? Or what about Aunt Bess, who'd always been somewhat friendly with Betty Jo's grandmother?

"Off and on," she finally said, hoping her words sounded casual enough.

Carlton's fingers laced together, resting atop the covers pulled over his legs and lower body. "So how's he doing? Do you

153

know where he's stationed?"

"He said —" She stopped herself before revealing too much, then reconsidered. What would Betty Jo or Maeve know about all this anyway? Wouldn't one island in the South Pacific sound pretty much like another? But Carlton . . . why, Carlton could know something important. They might have been on separate continents, but they fought the same war, didn't they?

She decided to take a chance. "Do you know anything about Emirau?"

"Emirau?" he asked as what little bit of pale was left on his face became patched with red.

CHAPTER 11

After news of Marty Dibble's death on foreign shores had come to Bynum months before, his mother — Miss LuAnn — had taken to her bed. Most folks thought her melancholy would fade with time. But from what Alice-Ann could reason, her depression had only grown worse.

A few weeks after the town grieved for the first time, Aunt Bess had served a simple meal for supper, and — as the mashed potatoes were passed from one hand to another — she'd cleared her throat and pointed her eyes at Alice-Ann.

"LuAnn Dibble is not returning to her position at the church," she said. "Teaching the three- to five-year-olds during the Sunday school hour."

Alice-Ann reached for a serving bowl rounded by snap peas Aunt Bess had canned back in the summer. Instinctively she knew Miss LuAnn's decision was somehow about to affect her. "Somebody taking her place?" she asked, her hand gripping the spoon shoved beneath the mound of green.

"Reverend Parker came round this morning, asking if you'd be interested in taking the role."

Alice-Ann spooned the peas onto her plate, then passed the bowl, never once taking her eyes from Aunt Bess's.

"Quite an honor to be asked," Aunt Bess continued.

Alice-Ann took the bowl of potatoes from her father. "What'd you say?" she asked, even though she knew the answer.

"Well, of course, I told him you'd do it."

Papa coughed a little. "Maybe LuAnn won't stay down too long," he said.

"Well, let's hope not, Brother," Aunt Bess said. "But not because this might mean Alice has to help out on Sundays."

"Alice-Ann has enough to do," he retorted, "what with working five days a week and being out in the fields most Saturdays with her brother and me."

Aunt Bess bristled. "How hard can it be, Emmitt? Teaching little ones?" she asked, using his given name. The rarity of it caught Alice-Ann off guard.

Truth be told, Alice-Ann took to her new role like pats of butter on hotcakes. She'd come to look forward to those Sunday mornings when she sat with the little ones around her, all dressed in their Sunday best. And being the sons and daughters of hard-working farmers and their equally-as-hardworking wives, their Sunday best was the same, every Sunday. Not that anyone cared. Folks weren't making too much of a fuss about what the big people wore, much less the children. Besides, freshly scrubbed and eager, they all looked adorable.

The little girls wore simple flour sack frocks and frilly white socks, the lace lying gently against black patent shoes. Most wore their hair in long braids tied off by wide ribbons. The boys — a few donning clean overalls, but most wearing pressed black slacks, white shirts, and their older brothers' cast-off suspenders — had washed behind their ears the night before, some for the first time since the previous Saturday. Alice-Ann often thought they smelled like their fathers' aftershave, leaving her to speculate on how such things played out.

Would her sons — hers and Mack's — stand next to their daddy as he shaved, pretending to do the same, rewarded by a slapping on chubby cheeks with aftershave that lingered on his fingers and palms?

Her favorite part of the Sunday school

hour was when, after singing an a cappella hymn or two, she told the children to take their seats. Then, opening her *Bible Story Time for Young Readers* book — the same one her mother had read from so very long ago — she brought the stories to life, using the same voice techniques her mother had.

"Miss Alice-Ann?" The children practically sang her name as they spoke it, requesting her attention. "You're the best teacher *ever.*"

Of course she wasted no time writing Mack about her experiences with the children each and every Sunday afternoon. Though, in recent weeks, she wondered if he'd read her words at all.

The Sunday afternoon after Carlton returned home, Alice-Ann begged Nelson to take her into town.

Irene — who'd grown more miserable as the days added up to forty weeks — lay stretched across the living room sofa, her back to Alice-Ann. Her feet were bare — for who could find nylons anymore — and propped up on a stack of throw pillows Aunt Bess had brought in for her.

"What do you need to go into town for?" she whined, her chin resting on her shoulder as she peered toward the foyer, where Alice-

Ann stood in the archway.

Lately, whining had been about the only way Irene talked. Whiny and so high-pitched only ole Sniffer next door could make out her words. But that day, she had to manage to raise her voice over the music coming from the stereo — the Andrews Sisters singing "Shoo Shoo Baby" — to make her point, loud and clear.

Alice-Ann entered the room fully, walked over to the Zenith, and turned the volume down enough to keep from shouting. Without looking at her sister-in-law, she directed her answer to her brother. "There's a matinee Maeve and Ernie and I want to go see." She gave him her best little-sister smile. "Cary Grant and Janet Blair in *Once upon a Time.*"

Irene moaned. "Maeve and Ernie . . . you'd think those two would be married by now the way they goo-goo-eye each other all the time." Then, without missing a beat, she added, "Have Claudette and Johnny Dailey set a date yet?"

"Later this year," Alice-Ann answered, her face still pointed at Nelson. "Please?" she asked. "You know how much I love Cary Grant, and I promise Ernie will bring me back."

He glanced at his wife. "Why doesn't

Ernie come get you?"

"Come on, Nelson. Ernie's not a farmer. His gas is rationed and you know it. Besides, he's trying to save his money." She shot a look at Irene. "Maybe he is *saving up* for a ring or something."

Nelson ran his hand along the back of his neck. "Yeah, well . . . What if Irene needs me and I'm not here?"

Alice-Ann tapped her foot. "She's a month out, Nelson. Besides, if anything happens, she's going to be wanting Aunt Bess and Doc Evans. *Not* you."

"Oh, how would you know?" Irene all but barked. "You've never been in my shoes, Alice-Ann. Fat and round and perfectly miserable."

Her father walked in about that time, stopping just inside the doorway, his hands shoved into his pants pockets. He looked worn-out. Beat, really. And his brows had come together in the middle — a sure sign that he wasn't to be messed with. "What's all this about?" he asked in such a way that let everyone in the room know there was no option when it came to answering.

"Papa, I —"

"Alice-Ann asked for a ride into town to see a matinee," Nelson intervened.

"I'll take you," he said, his voice a staccato. "Get your purse and gloves and I'll meet you in the truck."

Alice-Ann knew her eyes had grown large. She certainly didn't want to look a gift horse in the mouth, but . . . "You, Papa?"

Nelson rested his hands on his hips. "Pops? You feeling all right?"

Papa had already started to leave the room. "I feel just fine." He stopped, turned, and looked at both Nelson and Irene. "She pulls her weight around here," he said. "I figure one good turn deserves another."

Alice-Ann wasn't about to argue. "I'll go get my things," she said, darting out of the room, up the stairs, and into her room before he had a chance to change his mind. She returned so quickly, her shoes tapping down the stairs at such a rate, she nearly lost her balance. She grabbed the banister to right herself, took in a deep breath, and finished the flight like the lady she hoped she had become.

Papa already had the truck running when she climbed into the passenger side. "Thank you, Papa. Really."

He shoved the gearshift to first and eased on the gas. "Figured it would give us some time to catch up. We rarely get to."

Alice-Ann looked out the window as her hands clasped each other. She shook her

161

head at the reflection she saw in the glass. In all her life, she'd *never* known her father to want to talk to her about anything, much less "catch up." The thought of such a conversation sent a wave of both fear and shock through her. Had he guessed about Mack? Had someone told him? Maybe Mack's father had mentioned it in passing. But . . . did Mr. MacKay *know* she wrote to his son? She couldn't imagine.

"Work is good," she said finally, hoping to steer the conversation in a general direction.

"What do you do with yourself there all day?"

She turned and smiled at her father. Had he grown genuinely interested? The few times he'd come in on banking business, he never said a word to her. Whether she had a customer in front of her or not. He simply came in, conducted business with the bank's president, and walked out. "Oh, you know. People come in and put money in and I log it. People come in and take money out, and I log that too. It's not very exciting, but I'm not complaining. I enjoy working with Nancy and Mister Dooley."

He gave her a half grin. "Not Portia?"

Alice-Ann turned a little more fully in her father's direction. "Oh no. I didn't mean that. I guess — I, um — well, you see, Papa, Miss Portia more or less keeps to herself. Does her work and leaves us to ours as long as our figures come out right." Alice-Ann giggled, thinking how distant Mister Dooley's secretary remained, even while keeping a maternal air about her. "Barks out her orders, but in a motherly fashion. Nancy says that if we were in a private girls' school, she'd be our schoolmarm."

He shifted gears as the truck rambled along toward town, then reached up and flipped the radio switch. Tommy Dorsey's band singer crooned the lyrics to an old standard. Papa bobbed his head to the beat, which caused Alice-Ann's to tilt in bewilderment.

Who was this man?

"She ever tell you we was sweet on each other once upon a time?"

Alice-Ann blinked. "Who?"

"Portia." He spoke the name so matter-of-factly, Alice-Ann forced herself to say it back.

"Miss Portia?"

He chuckled again. "She and your mama got real close at a summer camp way back when. Used to be, when you saw one, you saw t'other. She ever tell you that?"

Alice-Ann felt her frown clear to her toes.

Mama had told her there'd been a little complication when Papa asked her to the Spring Fling. Had the complication been Miss Portia? "No, sir."

"Portia and I went out a time or two. A little sweet on each other, but then . . . That day I saw Earlene — really saw her — and then the dance I finally got to take her to. Oh, boy. And of course, Portia was there. I felt sort of sorry for her, but by then your mama had caught my attention and my heart."

"You saw her at the church, practicing."

Papa's face softened as though he was reliving the moment, right there in the truck. "Didn't want to hurt Portia, but after that day, I wasn't about to give up in my quest to get your mama to go out with me." He took his eyes off the road momentarily. "She was something else, your mama."

"I know, Papa. I remember."

He rested his wrist against the hard steering wheel, allowing his hand to flop down on the other side. "You remind me of her sometimes."

"Me?" She looked at her reflection in the window again in wonder. Earlene Branch had been soft and fair. Even as Alice-Ann had grown into womanhood, and as she'd tried every way possible to fix herself up a little, she'd not been able to quite capture a semblance of beauty. "I sure don't see that, Papa," she said. "I mean," she added, looking at him, "I don't think I'm an ogre or anything, but . . . well . . . don't you think I look more like Aunt Bess than Mama?"

Papa squared his shoulders; his left hand slid down the steering wheel as the right reached for the gearshift. They neared town. "I didn't say you *look* like her, Alice-Ann. I said you remind me of her. You're good and kind. You have a caring nature. You're a hard worker." He slowed the truck to a stop at the edge of town. "I went to the feed and seed the other day. Saw Anson Hillis in there. He told me about you coming over to see his boy after work on Thursday."

Alice-Ann took in a breath. "He looks pretty beat up, Papa. I felt sorry for him."

Papa nodded. "Well, I think that was right nice of you to do that."

Alice-Ann opened her mouth to speak, but only air came out.

"Think you can walk the rest of the way in?" He glanced out the dust-splattered windshield.

Alice-Ann opened her door. "Thank you, Papa."

"See you after the movie," he said as she closed the door behind her.

165

She hurried across the street and onto the sidewalk leading to the theater, hoping she'd easily find Maeve and Ernie inside. She took deliberate steps, her thoughts whirling. Portia Ivey had once been smitten with Papa. But Papa had been crazy about Mama.

Poor Miss Portia. Before she'd gone to work at the bank, Alice-Ann thought Miss Portia looked at her as though she were missing an appendage. Perhaps not. Perhaps she looked at Alice-Ann, wondering, if things had gone differently . . . if Papa hadn't heard Mama singing in the church that day . . . they would be mother and daughter instead.

"The heart loves who it loves and no one else," she remembered Aunt Bess saying. *"And it makes no excuses for it."*

Alice-Ann reached the ticket window of the theater, opened her purse, and pulled out her quarter. "Have you seen Maeve and Ernie?" she asked the attendant.

"Got here about five minutes ago."

She nodded as he handed her the ticket through the tiny opening at the base of the glass.

Alice-Ann stepped into the carpeted lobby, and as she inhaled the aroma of buttery popcorn, she made a decision that

166

surprised her. The ride with Papa had been a special one. A rare treat. She wouldn't divulge the conversation they'd had to anyone.

Not even Mack.

CHAPTER 12

Alice-Ann stretched her arms as she stepped out of the theater and onto the sidewalk. The movie had been an excellent choice for a Saturday afternoon matinee. She said as much to Maeve and Ernie, who walked out behind her.

"That Cary Grant," Maeve said. She rolled her eyes toward Ernie, who feigned a look of hurt. "Not that he has *anything* on you, E."

Ernie grinned, nodding. "You think you're fooling me, M., but I know if Mr. Cary Grant walked up right now and said, 'Come away with me, dear Maeve . . .' " Ernie's imitation of the actor left his audience of two in giggles. He sighed. ". . . you'd do it."

Maeve placed her hand over her heart and said, "I admit . . . I'd have to think about it."

Alice-Ann swatted at them both. "Stop it, you two." Turning to Ernie, she said, "Come on. Papa said for you to bring me home straight after the movie."

Ernie groaned, looking first to Maeve, then back to Alice-Ann.

"What?" she asked. "Please don't tell me something is wrong with your daddy's car. Because if that's so, Ernie Tucker, you'll have to *borrow* somebody's."

Maeve pulled Alice-Ann farther down the sidewalk toward Smitty's Department Store and away from the small crowd coming out of the theater. "Listen, Alice-Ann," she said, her voice secretive. "We were going to dash over to see Carlton real quick. Mama'll have supper ready soon and — you see, after he eats, he usually goes right to sleep, so . . . if Ernie is going to see him, it'll need to be before he takes you."

Alice-Ann felt her stomach flop. If Maeve and Ernie were going to see Carlton, that meant she'd have to do the same. Quite frankly, she wasn't sure she was up to the visit. Seeing Carlton had been painful enough before, and in spite of her father thinking her to be so wonderful for her act of kindness, truth told, she hadn't found it so pleasant an experience. "Well, I — I told Papa I'd — and you know we don't have a phone, so I can't call — and . . ."

Maeve stopped, dipped her head as she

169

crossed her arms and said, "Betty Jo broke up with Carlton last night."

"Yesterday afternoon, really," Ernie added.

"It doesn't matter, E."

"What?" Alice-Ann asked. *"Why?"*

Maeve shook her head, her dark curls catching the light of the afternoon sun, even as her face fell. "I'm so sad for him, Alice-Ann."

Alice-Ann swallowed. "But I don't understand . . . He said he —" She stopped herself, tore her eyes away from the pained expression on her friend's face to look across the street to the floor above the five-and-dime, where she knew a blind and lame man lay. Heartbroken. Hadn't it been enough that he'd lost his sight and the use of his legs? Even temporarily?

"What were you going to say?" Maeve asked.

Alice-Ann looked again at her friend, remembering Carlton standing in her living room during her belated birthday party, leaning over her and whispering, *"I'll let you in on a little secret. . . . Can you keep it?"*

"I — uh — sure, we can go see Carlton first. We *should* in fact and I — I think Papa will understand."

"We'll only stay a minute or two," Ernie added. "I said I'd get you home if you

170

joined us today for the show and that's exactly what I'm going to do."

They started for the street, stopped at the curb for oncoming traffic, then darted to the other side. When they stepped up on the sidewalk in front of Maeve's family's store, Alice-Ann grabbed her friend's hand. "Did she say why? Betty Jo?"

Maeve's eyes filled with tears, which she blinked back as she shook her head. "She *said* she felt they'd grown apart since he'd left, but Carlton said he knew the truth. I could hear them — what with the bedroom door being left open and all. Even though they were talking about something so personal, Carlton asked her to leave it open out of respect for Mama."

Alice-Ann waved away the notion, respectable though it might be. "What'd *he* say? What does he think is the truth?"

"He said — and I quote — 'Don't lie to me, Betty Jo. Tell it to me straight. Just say it. You don't want to be saddled with a man who can't see and who can't walk.'"

"Didn't he remind her that the doctors said this isn't forever? That his vision should return and that he can have physical therapy and — and . . . ?"

"No."

"But why not?"

171

"I don't know, Alice-Ann." She looked up at the second-story apartment. "Why don't you ask him?"

"I —"

"Guys aren't like that," Ernie interjected. "Guys don't *think* and *talk* like that. If Betty Jo can't love him through this, then what if he doesn't get his sight back? What if he doesn't walk again? I mean, does he really have to ask? *Everyone* should know love is supposed to be stronger than all this. Stronger than blindness and being unable to walk."

Alice-Ann nodded. "Like Nancy and Harry. Nancy loves Harry, no matter what. In fact, I think she loves him more, sometimes."

Maeve took a deep breath and Ernie slid his long hands into his pants pockets, clearing his throat before muttering, "Let's go, girls. We're not going to change the course of their love story by standing out here."

Maeve entered the bank on Monday at precisely 11:58.

She called out to Mister Dooley and Miss Portia as she walked purposefully toward the tellers' windows. They nodded in unison in reply but said nothing.

Alice-Ann sat up straight, hoping to see

an envelope in her hand. Something — anything — from Mack.

"Hey, Nancy," Maeve said, her soft curls bouncing as her steps slowed near Alice-Ann's window.

"How's your brother, Maeve?"

Maeve nodded. "He said he saw a flash of light this morning. It didn't last long, but it happened." She looked at Alice-Ann. "Don't you think that's good news?"

"That's wonderful, Maeve."

"*And* Doc Evans came over this morning. Carlton is moving his legs a little on his own. Again, not much, but Doc Evans said this means the swelling around his spine is going down."

"That's marvelous," Alice-Ann said. "Truly."

She slid over to fully face Alice-Ann. "I have a favor to ask."

"What?"

Maeve glanced at the wall clock. "Are y'all about to close for lunch?"

"Well, yeah . . ."

"Have lunch with me?"

Alice-Ann had brought a cheese sandwich, two of Aunt Bess's homemade bread and butter pickles, and a thermos of sweet tea, which she'd planned to devour after running down Cooper Street to the library. *If*

she were lucky, the book she'd been await-
ing since putting her name on the list would
be there, sitting on the holding table.

"Well, I —"

"Mama's made her famous beef stew —
it's Carlton's favorite."

Alice-Ann took in a breath, savoring the
imaginary aroma. How long had it been
since she'd eaten Maeve's mama's beef
stew? "With biscuits?"

"What do you think?"

Alice-Ann swirled around. "Nancy, I
believe it's time to clock out for lunch."

Nancy laughed behind her. "I'll stay here
and enjoy my soup."

Warm air encircled them as soon as they
stepped outside. Alice-Ann turned her face
toward the sun and breathed in, hoping for
a whiff of what would soon be her lunch.
But the only thing her lungs drew in was
the scent of oil from an oversize Buick
rambling past.

Before they stepped into the store, Alice-
Ann tapped Maeve on the shoulder. "All
right, Maeve. Come clean. *Why* am I here?
And don't say for beef stew."

Maeve sighed as she opened the door.
"How well you know me."

"Almost as well as I know myself."

They closed the door behind them and

Maeve locked it to keep customers out during the noon hour. Ceiling fans spun in lazy circles overhead, stirring up more warm air than providing cool.

Alice-Ann pulled the lightweight orange scarf she'd donned earlier in the day from around her neck. "It's going to be a hot summer. That much is for sure already."

"You can say that again," Maeve agreed. She turned after they'd made it halfway to the back staircase. "Now listen. I know you know I've asked you here for more than just stew."

"And biscuits."

Maeve smiled, and it looked to Alice-Ann like she was grateful that her friend appeared open to the real reason she'd been asked for lunch. "I was thinking that . . . because you read to the children on Sundays . . . and you know how you told me you read in character and how much the children love it . . . well, I was thinking that maybe you could do the same for Carlton." Her eyes widened as her face lit up.

"Read to him? Like he's a child?"

"Yeah." Maeve sported a tiny pout. "Come on, Alice-Ann. He'd do it for you and you know it."

"But, Maeve, I —"

"Look, I know you're pining away for

Mack and just waiting for the day he returns home —"

"Or at the very least, when I finally get a letter from him."

Maeve's hand found Alice-Ann's. "I know. I'm sorry and you know we're all just worried sick. But in the meantime, there's a young man upstairs who spends nearly his entire day just staring at nothing. Mama and Daddy and I have to work, so it's not like we can babysit him."

Alice-Ann opened her mouth to protest further, to remind Maeve that she, too, worked, and that soon enough she'd need to help even more at home, once the baby arrived. But before she could utter so much as a peep, Maeve continued in what Alice-Ann suspected to be a rehearsed speech. "I'd do it for you, Alice-Ann, if it were Nelson."

Alice-Ann closed her mouth. She inhaled deeply; the rich aroma of stew and buttery biscuits caused her stomach to growl.

Both young women giggled.

"You're right," Alice-Ann said. "You would." She nodded once, then twice for good measure. "Let me talk to Papa and Aunt Bess," she said, although she knew exactly what Papa would say. "And if they okay my coming home a tad later than usual, I'll do it."

"When can you start?"

Alice-Ann laughed. "*If* I start . . . I'll come tomorrow."

"Right after work?"

"The same as I've done for over two years now."

The following afternoon, Alice-Ann clocked out of work, walked to the five-and-dime, greeted Mrs. Hillis, who stood behind the counter, waved at Mr. Hillis and Maeve stocking shelves in the center of the store, and then made her way up the staircase to the Hillises' apartment. She took a deep breath at the top of the stairs, then walked to the kitchen, tucked the book she carried under her arm, retrieved two bottles of Coke, opened them, and — with one in each hand — carried them into Carlton's room.

A plain occasional chair had been placed near the bed facing Carlton, who sat up straight, looking toward the door as though he could see who stood there.

"Hi there," she said.

The smile broke easily. "Hey yourself, doodlebug."

"Care for some company?" She raised one hand. "I brought two Co-Colas — one for me and one for you — and a book I got from the library yesterday. Maeve said you might like to have me read to you."

"I'd love that." He extended a hand toward the chair. "Have a seat."

Alice-Ann placed one of the sweating bottles on the bedside table, where a small plate had been left for such things, then eased herself down into the chair. "I placed your drink on the table."

He grinned. "I heard."

"Would you prefer I hand it to you?"

"No," he said, slowly reaching for it as his fingers walked along the edge of the table. "I've got it."

Alice-Ann placed the book in her lap and her own bottle on the floor. Sitting upright again, she gripped the curved wood of the armrests, keeping her feet planted flat on the floor. When she took in a breath, she became more aware of the staleness in the room and she sighed. An injured man lived there. Day in. Day out. He hadn't been outside in days, and though Alice-Ann felt certain Carlton had been *bathed,* a musky aroma lingered.

"It's a nice day out," she said. "Warm, but nice." He turned his face away from her and toward the sunlight streaming in. "Maybe I could open the window for you?"

"That'd be nice," he admitted. "I think Mama's afraid a little breeze will give me a cold or something."

Alice-Ann stood, placing the book on the floor, walked to the window, pushed the old blackout curtains back as far as they would go, and then turned the crank until the panes separated and spread outward. A late spring breeze eased in, bringing with it the freshness of midafternoon and a light floral scent. Alice-Ann peered down at the tiny patch of garden Mrs. Hillis had managed to plant and had been tending behind the store for as long as she could remember.

"Your mother's roses are starting to bloom," she said.

"The Confederate roses or the knock-outs?"

Alice-Ann smiled. "Both." She returned to the chair. "How wonderful that you know the difference."

"Doesn't everyone?" He laughed as she sat, this time crossing her legs. Carlton blinked. Once. Twice. He took a sip of his drink and returned it to the table. "You're getting more comfortable. Not as bothered by being in an injured man's bedroom, even one you've thought of as a big brother since you were a pup."

"What?" She uncrossed her legs.

179

"Uh-oh. I've made you nervous again."

Alice-Ann leaned forward. "I don't know what —"

"When you came in and you first sat in the chair, you were tense. Once you opened the window and returned to the chair, you were relaxed." He smiled again, the deep dimples cutting into the sides of his face. "Until I said something."

Alice-Ann chuckled. "You're right. But how did you — ?"

"When you're blind — even temporarily — you learn to lean on your ears to *see* things. When you first sat, you kept both feet on the floor. After you opened the window, you crossed your legs." He paused long enough to adjust the linens folded neatly at his hips. "Not to mention that tension is *felt,* not seen."

Alice-Ann slid back in the chair and crossed her legs again. She studied Carlton's face for a reaction, her eyes slanting in his direction. Sure enough, his smile widened.

"Now you're just testing me."

Alice-Ann laughed. "I was."

"Did I pass?"

"You did." She bit her bottom lip. "With flying colors."

"Mmm," he said. "Colors."

Alice-Ann prickled. Had she said the wrong thing? Used the wrong words? "So, um . . ."

"Tell me about your day today," he interjected.

She welcomed the change in topic. "Well, I worked of course. Oh, but Papa's getting some new farm implements. Compliments of the government. He and Nelson are all excited about it. You'd think it was Christmas or something."

"How are the crops?"

"Soon to be ripe for pickin'. We've got farmhands, of course, to do the bigger jobs, and a few of the POWs now that the camp is up in Bulloch, but it won't be long before Aunt Bess and I will be up early on Saturdays, picking a mess of peas and snaps from her garden." She looked down at her hands. "And I'll be forced to cut okra, which, if you must know, is my *least* favorite thing to do."

"I never did that," he said. "What's it like?"

"They're prickly," she told him. "Like little needles that stick just under the skin." She wiggled a little. "Makes me itchy just talking about it."

Carlton's brow shot up. "I'm suddenly very glad I'm a city kid."

181

"City? Ha-ha."

A light blush kissed his cheeks. "All right. Bynum's a mite of a town, I grant you, but it's still not the country."

"The country's not so bad."

"I know . . ."

"But if I *could* . . ." Her words had come too easily, she realized, so she allowed the hidden wish to slip into the sunshine and fresh air that had now filled the room.

"You'd?"

She giggled. "It's silly. I can't even believe I almost said it."

Carlton grinned. "Tell me."

"You know," she drawled while reaching for the book on the floor, "I'm supposed to be reading to you."

"Tell me," he coaxed.

She opened the book, the paper sighing as she turned to the first page. Alice-Ann cleared her throat, preparing her voice for the words.

"Alice-Ann."

She looked up. "*A Tree Grows in Brooklyn*," she said. "It came out last year and I had to get on a waiting list at the library. Picked it up yesterday afternoon —"

"Alice-Ann," he repeated her name, his voice rising in a question. "Tell. Me."

She closed the book. "All right, but you'll

think I'm silly."

"I promise not to make fun of you."

"Well . . . all right." She sighed. "If you promise."

"Cross my heart," he said, imitating the words, "and hope to die."

"All right, then. See, there's this . . . house. A cottage, really."

Carlton used the strength of his arms and fists to shift in the bed, to face her better. "Where?"

"Near Nancy and Harry's. You remember them, right?"

He chuckled. "I lost my sight, not my memory."

"I'm sorry."

"Don't be. Go on. Nancy and Harry. Cottage."

He wanted to hear. Carlton Hillis truly *desired* to know her thoughts. Her dreams. A first, for sure. Not even Mack had. Not really. Not ever. Alice-Ann had written to him, she'd shared, but he'd never come out and asked. Or even coaxed her as Carlton seemed to do now. "It's in disrepair. Slight, but still, it's in disrepair. No one's lived in it — Nancy says — for ten years or more. But it's so . . . *cute.*"

"Cute?"

She laughed again. "It *is.*"

"A house that's *cute.*"

"A cottage, really," she reiterated, hoping that the words *cottage* and *cute* used together kept her from sounding completely idiotic. After all, Carlton had been in college when his sense of American pride had taken over and he'd enlisted. "He's so smart, that Carlton," she'd heard a thousand times or more, followed by the typical "Always has been."

"What's so *cute* about it?" he asked. The tone of his voice made her feel more girl than woman, but somehow less silly.

"Well, I've only seen it from the sidewalk. Maeve and I used to ride our bicycles up and down Main Street and —" She felt herself grow warm. "I'd always hop off my bike and say to Maeve that I thought it was . . ." She smiled. "Cute."

"And what did Maeve think?"

Alice-Ann laughed. "She thought it was haunted. Said that's why no one ever bought it . . . because someone was murdered in there."

Carlton chuckled. "The old Burkhalter place. Ah, yeah."

She narrowed her eyes. "Do you think it's true? About the murder?"

He shook his head. "Only in the minds of little boys sitting around a campfire." He chuckled again, low and steady. "So have you ever gone inside?"

"No. I went up *to* the house. Peered in a few windows."

"But?"

"But, nothing. Sometimes girls daydream. You know, about their lives when they're all grown-up. I picture myself in a house like that one." And of course, she pictured a life there — all too often — that included Mack.

A wave of inspiration came over her, one that pushed Mack to the back of her thoughts and brought Carlton front and center. "How about I make a deal with you."

His brow now furrowed. "What kind of deal?"

"Doc Evans says you're getting better. Swelling is going down."

"That's true."

"And Maeve said you saw a little light yesterday."

"Also a fact."

"So then how about you work a little harder to walk again, and one day we can walk down there and see it together."

He barked out laughter. "*See* it? I only experienced one shaft of light. Like a bolt of lightning. Lickety-split."

"Well, it's a start. Besides, you're the one always saying your blindness is temporary.

Once your sight comes back, what will you do? Sit up here and smell your mama's roses all day?"

He gave her a half grin. "All right, doodle-bug." He extended his hand toward her. "Shake on it."

She leaned over, took his hand in her own, felt the rough calluses against the softness of her skin. "Deal?"

"Deal."

CHAPTER 13

After a week's time, the familiarity of her new role settled over her like a well-worn sweater. The May days grew warmer and warmer, promising a typically scorching Bynum summer.

Each morning, Alice-Ann woke up, got dressed and ready for the day, then went downstairs to eat breakfast. Aunt Bess had, weeks earlier, opened all the windows; now she'd placed oscillating fans at two of them. Those same fans would be moved upstairs at some point during the day — one for Nelson and Irene's bedroom, one for Papa's. Two others — the ones from Aunt Bess's room and the one from Alice-Ann's — went from the bedrooms to the living room and dining room sometime after Alice-Ann left for work. She wasn't sure exactly when, but she imagined that as soon as she left the house, Aunt Bess shuffled up the stairs and back down again, her mission nearly complete.

When the camp started driving the prisoners over to Bynum every morning for work details, Nelson began rising earlier than usual so he could make a run to pick up workers. This meant she no longer took the bus but caught a ride with her brother. Then each evening, she waited outside the five-and-dime for Nelson to return after a long day in the fields. He'd drop the prisoners and their guard off and then pick her up and they'd drive back to the farm. Slowly, so they could talk and — as Nelson often said — "allow the day to settle down a little."

Work continued to be that: work. Alice-Ann couldn't help but wonder from time to time if she'd keep her job after the war was over, if it ever were. She also couldn't help but remember the lines from the boys who'd signed up so quickly in December of 1941. *"We'll get those Nazis and Japs,"* as if the mission would be — start to finish — fought and won in a month's time.

She kept two books with her now — the one she read quietly during her lunch break and the one she read to Carlton after work. They were nearing the end of Betty Smith's novel, a fact Alice-Ann hated. They both enjoyed it immensely.

After work, she said good-bye to her coworkers and boss, and Alice-Ann collected her purse and scarf. She walked out of the bank, crossed the street, and entered the five-and-dime, the doors now left open, front and back, likely in the hope of catching a breeze. She greeted Mr. and Mrs. Hillis, then gave Maeve *the look.*

A letter? it asked.

Maeve never once nodded.

The creaks in the staircase had become familiar beneath her feet, like a phonograph record that had been set to play at the same time, every day. When she reached the apartment upstairs, she called out to Carlton with the same question.

"Co-Cola?"

"Over ice, please," he called back.

Alice-Ann now knew Carlton preferred his drinks from a glass rather than a bottle. She prepared their refreshment, then went into his room. They always talked a while before she read, mostly about her day . . . about Nelson . . . and Irene's miserable condition . . . about the German POWs working on the farm . . . and about the weather and how it affected the crops. Occasionally he asked her more personal questions. What did she think of Claudette's upcoming wedding? Did she think Johnny's mother would *really* let Claudette live at the hotel as the woman of the house or would she always be second fiddle in Johnny's life?

What did she think of Maeve and Ernie?

And each day, Alice-Ann found herself answering in greater detail. At first, she'd been unable to — so rarely did anyone ask her what she *thought*. Then, as time went on, she spoke more freely. Sometimes, Alice-Ann thought, she found herself looking more forward to their chats than she did reading to him.

She also looked forward to hearing how he'd progressed in the twenty-four hours that had passed since she'd visited. She laughed at the notion that the wiggling of ten toes could mean so much or that a single flash of light could bring such celebration.

That day — a Wednesday — he'd seen more than one. Several, in fact, he told her as soon as she sat. "I think you're my healer, Dr. Doodlebug," he said. "My good luck charm."

Alice-Ann felt herself blush under the compliment. "You'd have seen them whether I came up here every day or not."

"Maybe so," he said. "Guess we won't ever really know, though, will we?"

Alice-Ann opened the book, no longer comfortable. "Ready to hear the end?"

Carlton made a show of straightening the pillows bunched at the small of his back. "Ready."

Alice-Ann caught the last bus heading out of Bynum that afternoon, as she did each weekday, working hard at keeping her mind away from the obvious.

Where was Mack?

As soon as she arrived home, she walked into the kitchen, where Aunt Bess pulled a plate out of the fridge, having kept it for her. "How is he doing today?" she asked, placing the plate on the table and removing the covering.

Alice-Ann set her purse on the counter and slipped out of her shoes. "He saw several flashes of light today."

"Well, that's something, isn't it?" Aunt Bess reopened the fridge and brought out a bottle of milk. "Sit down and I'll pour you some milk to go with your supper."

Alice-Ann pulled the chair out from under the table. "Anything new on Irene?" Not that she heard the cries of a newborn or anything.

"Not a single cramp, much less a contraction." Aunt Bess put the glass to the right of

Alice-Ann's plate, then returned the milk to the icebox before joining her at the table. "But the way that girl carries on these last couple of weeks, you'd think she was the first and last woman on God's good green earth to ever be in the family way."

Alice-Ann nearly choked on the sliced tomato she'd just then bitten down on, its luscious juice squirting along the side of her tongue. "Aunt Bess," she said around it.

"Well, my word. Can you imagine when she gives birth? That girl won't know what hit her." Aunt Bess leaned over the table. "All I've got to say is, I sure hope Nelson goes to get her mama when the time comes."

Using her fork, Alice-Ann cut into the deviled egg that wiggled alongside the tomato. "I'm sure he will." She sighed as she brought the bite of egg to her mouth. "Where are they?"

"Your daddy suggested they walk a little. Said it used to help your mama when she got to this point. They went out the back path toward the pond." Her eyes traveled to the back window. "I don't 'spect they'll be gone much longer. If the walk doesn't throw her into labor, the mosquitoes will carry them both away."

Alice-Ann nodded, then finished up the cold supper and glass of milk. "Well," she said, rising to take her plate to the sink, "if it's okay with you, Aunt Bess, I'm going to my room. I'm pretty beat tonight."

"You go on. I've got this."

Alice-Ann reached for her purse when Aunt Bess added, "Oh. Your daddy's in the living room. Be sure to say good night to him before you go up."

"I will." She had to stop in to steal away the fan, anyway.

She started out, then stopped and turned back into the room. "Aunt Bess?" she said to the woman clearing the rest of the table.

"Hmm?"

"Did you know that Miss Portia had a . . . well, a thing for Papa back long ago?" Since Papa had told her, she'd had a monstrous time looking at her coworker without squinting her eyes and tilting her head, trying to imagine the older woman younger . . . and in pursuit.

Aunt Bess ran water in the sink and threw in a little dish detergent. "I did."

She stepped closer. "Why do you think Papa never . . . after Mama . . . why didn't Papa go out with anyone? Think about getting married again? Maybe to Miss Portia?"

"Your daddy," she said, swishing the soap into a froth with her hand, "could never see himself with anyone but Earlene." Aunt

Bess stopped her bubble making long enough to look at Alice-Ann with complete and utter tenderness. "A love like theirs doesn't come along every day of the week, Alice-Ann. That boy thought your mama hung the moon and the stars." She shook her head. "No. There could only be one love for my brother, and Earlene was it."

Alice-Ann kissed her aunt's cheek, then left the room fully this time. She walked into the living room, where her father read the newspaper by a dim light. "Hey, Papa," she said, keeping her voice low. Nothing in the room stirred, which told her the fan had already been moved into her bedroom.

He looked up, lowering the paper from in front of his face. "Got home, did you?"

"Yes, sir."

"How's our boy?"

Alice-Ann smiled. Funny how all it took was an injury — severe as it was — for a young man to become the son of every father in the county. "He's getting better. He can wiggle his toes, and today he saw several flashes of light."

"Don't worry. He'll get it all back," he said, then raised the paper up again.

"I'm not worr—" She stopped. Sighed. "Well, I'm going to bed, Papa. I'm pretty tired already."

"Moon's not full up yet," he said, "but I can't say as I blame you. Once Nelson and Irene get back in, I'll be right behind you."

"Good night then, Papa." She trudged up the stairs, retrieved her nightclothes, then went into the bathroom. She ran water in the sink, lathered up a washcloth, and gave herself a sink bath. After brushing her teeth — which she did with her eyes closed — and tidying up, she crossed the hall to her bedroom. Along the way, she heard her brother's and sister-in-law's voices, mingled with Aunt Bess's.

Hearing no anxiety or hope in their tones, she closed the door behind her.

When she was sure no one had started up the staircase, she opened her closet door and rifled around until she found the box where she kept Mack's letters. She pulled one randomly from the middle, sat on the floor in front of the closet door, and read it. Once more. Pretending she'd only received it that afternoon. That she'd devoured it on the bus ride home. That she'd hidden it in the confines of her purse so none of the family — not even Irene — knew about it. Still pretending that, she now read it again, before going to bed and dreaming of her one true love, so as to dream of the words he'd penned. With love . . . she hoped.

Alice-Ann returned the letter to its envelope, the envelope to the stack, and the stack back to its hiding place. Soundless, she crept to her bed and eased in, willing the springs not to creak beneath her light weight. She drew the cotton sheet up over her — completely — then turned onto her stomach.

"Oh, Mack," she cried into her pillow, hoping it could somehow absorb the agony. "Where are you?"

The following day was nearly a carbon copy of the previous. Up, to work, to Maeve's — this time reading to Carlton from a new book — then home as dusk settled around the farm. Still, no baby's cries filled the night. Still, no news from Mack.

And then Friday's sun rose in the east as it always did. Alice-Ann went to work, ate her lunch, and read her book.

As always.

But by midafternoon, time stood still as the awful news pulsated through Bynum like a telegraph that the sender hadn't meant to release but now couldn't stop. The words — brief, choked, and unbearable — had to be repeated. From one store to the next. From one mouth to another's ears.

Boyd MacKay and his crew had been shot

down several weeks earlier, somewhere over the Pacific.

None of the American soldiers survived.

Chapter 14

The bank closed early that day.

Alice-Ann caught the first bus out, took the last seat on the right, and stared out the window — recently washed to a sheen. Familiar landmarks and signs came and went, and as Alice-Ann counted them — three patches of farmland before her own, five signs for Mason's Seafood Restaurant in Savannah (*World's Biggest Shrimp*) — she contemplated how she'd enter the house with such grief washing over her and yet keep her deep love for Boyd MacKay secret.

Ben Brown rolled the bus in front of the long driveway to the farmhouse where she'd grown up and yet which, at that very moment, seemed a stranger. Foreign. Like the Pacific.

When the bus stopped, she gathered her purse and gloves and the hat she hadn't bothered to don, and walked up the aisle between the seats. There was no one else on the bus, their farm being the one farthest from town. Halfway down the aisle, she paused.

When had the other passengers gotten off?

Had there *been* other passengers?

Ben Brown grabbed the lever to open the door, clearing his throat and looking back at her. "Shame about the MacKay boy," he said. "Always liked him."

Alice-Ann swallowed. Nodded as she fingered the bracelet.

"I hear tell," he went on as though he couldn't see the mounting grief bubbling up inside her, "that the plane got shot down sometime back, but until the government could confirm it, they didn't bother to let the family know." Alice-Ann gripped the back of the seat nearest her and squeezed. "Can you imagine such a thing?"

"No," she said. Then, catching herself, "No, sir."

He slid his beefy hand along the back of his neck and massaged the muscles with nubby fingers. "Makes me glad I never married," he added. "Never had children." His eyes caught hers and he winced. "Ah, I'm sorry, girl. He and your brother were good friends, if I remember correctly."

Alice-Ann looked at her shoes. The same ones she'd worn on the night of her party.

Aunt Bess had purchased them for her . . . she'd so hoped they'd make her look grown-up and that Mack would see her as a woman that night, all dressed up and ready to be kissed.

But he hadn't kissed her. He'd left her only to dream of the day he would. The day he could. But he'd never —

She pressed her lips together, imagining his taste. Wondering at the feel of it. What it might be like if — "I'd best get on home," she said. She rushed up the remainder of the aisle and thundered down the steps.

She'd made it halfway to the house, the heat wrapping around her like death, squeezing air out of her lungs. Each step forward came on legs of lead, and her skin and scalp glistened and prickled with sweat. Not that Alice-Ann cared. For once, the humidity caused no distress. At least she could feel it. Mack . . . he felt nothing. Mack, his body somewhere at the bottom of the Pacific Ocean, assuming there had been anything left to drop into its deep recesses.

Alice-Ann gasped at the thought and blinked back her tears as a scream — high-pitched and distressful — came from the house. She jumped. *Irene.*

She ran the rest of the way to the house,

kicking up dust, the strain pulling at her calf muscles. When she reached the oaks stretching near and shading the house, she hollered out her aunt's name, grateful to be out of the sun but unsure as to whether or not to enter the house.

She'd seen many an animal being born — calves and piglets, kids and foals — but never a human being. Even though she fairly understood the logistics, she wasn't altogether certain she wanted to be a part of what was taking place inside her home at this very moment.

She contemplated calling for Aunt Bess again when Nelson popped out of the open front door, pushing the screen with the ball of his hand. "Alice-Ann," he said, panting, rubbing his neck in the same way Ben Brown had done only minutes before.

Her eyes widened and she blurted, "Did you hear about Mack?"

Her brother swallowed, his Adam's apple bobbing. "Yeah," he said, looking down at his dusty work boots. Or maybe the boards in the porch; she wasn't sure. "Pops heard at the feed and seed and — when he told me . . ." His eyes returned to hers. "That's when Irene —"

Another cry came from upstairs and they both looked upward to the painted-blue porch ceiling.

"Did her mama get here?"

Nelson placed his hands on his hips, splayed his fingers, and nodded. "Maybe ten minutes or so ago, I reckon." He walked over to the swing at the far end of the porch and sat. His feet pushed back and his knees locked, holding the swing up and out. "Aunt Bess said to come on out here. To stay out of her way."

Alice-Ann moved closer. "Where's Papa?"

Nelson walked the swing back to its original position. "Next door, I reckon. He went to call Doc Evans." He rested his elbows on his knees. "But he hasn't got back yet and . . . you probably ought to go on in there and see if you can help."

"Me?"

"Well, you're a woman, aren't you?"

Alice-Ann blinked. "That hardly gives me a degree in —" Another cry broke the heated stillness and again they looked up briefly. But then, seeing her father lumbering across the cornfield, she said, "There's Papa." The stalks nearly reached his shoulders; soon, they'd tower his full height.

Alice-Ann left the porch to meet him, aware that Nelson had followed but stopped at the bottom of the steps. "Papa," she said, hearing the strain in her voice, wishing she

202

could throw her arms around him. Wanting so badly to tell him that the love of her life had died and, because he knew how that felt, asking if he would please hold her . . . and tell her everything would be okay. Surely one day. One day.

But today — today of all days — Irene had chosen to go into labor and Papa appeared occupied with only that.

He wiped his mouth with a semi-clean bandanna he pulled from the pocket of his bib overalls. "Nelson," he shouted, all but ignoring his daughter.

Nelson reached them before Alice-Ann could fully turn. "Is he coming?" her brother asked. "The doc?"

Their father shook his head. "Claudette answered when I called. Said her daddy was out there at the MacKays'."

"Well —" Nelson breathed out. "I — Pops, what are we supposed to do? Aunt Bess says she only helped once or twice when she was a young girl and Irene's mama —"

The screen door squeaked open and the three turned to see Aunt Bess sauntering toward them. "Where's Doc Evans?" she demanded.

Papa repeated the news. She sighed as she cupped Alice-Ann's chin. "You all right,

203

little thing? What with this terrible news from town?"

Alice-Ann bit her bottom lip to ward off the tears as she nodded.

"I know you'll grieve later, but right now we've got bigger fish to fry." She looked at her brother. "Brother, you're just gonna have to go get him. I think the baby may be coming out backside first."

Nelson kicked at the dirt with his shoe, one eye squinted as the other studied their aunt. "What does *that* mean?"

"Think and you'll figure it out," she told him.

Realization dawned and he looked at their father. "What are we gonna do, Pops?"

Papa scratched his forehead with grimy fingernails, then looked out over the corn-field. "Maybe one of the colored ladies out in the county farther on — maybe one of them knows how —"

"They'd all be out in their own fields, Papa," Alice-Ann interjected. "We'd have to find one of them; they'd have to go home and get cleaned up . . ."

Papa nodded. "You're right. You're right."

"Then what, Pops?"

"Well, look here," he said, then shook his head. "No . . ."

Alice-Ann swatted at a mosquito that she

thought more likely in need of her salty sweat than her blood. "What, Papa?"

"Pops?"

"Whatcha got on your mind, Emmitt?" Aunt Bess asked.

He stuffed the bandanna back into his pocket. "One of the Germans right here in our own fields . . . he speaks pretty good English. . . . He told me out there the other day that in Germany he worked with his daddy — you know, before the war got started over there — and that his daddy was a doctor. Maybe he —"

"Pop," Nelson said, his voice incredulous, "no piece of German scum is going to touch my wife."

Papa opened his mouth to speak as another cry tore out from the open upstairs window. The foursome looked up to see Irene's mother at the screen. "What are you *doing*?" she shouted. "Somebody's got to *do* something here! *Bess?* Where is that doctor?"

Aunt Bess turned a stern eye to Nelson. "I don't care if that man is German or Japanese or *Pekingese,* you hear me? That girl up there is in trouble. She's your wife. Now go find the man and don't give me any grief over it." She made three long strides toward the house before turning again. "And if I were you, I'd be praying he knows something about these kinds of things instead of worrying about his lineage."

When Aunt Bess made it back into the house, Nelson turned to their father. "Pops?"

If Nelson had expected empathy, he didn't get it. "I've not seen Bess like this too many times in my life, boy," he said. "I 'spect we'd best go find that German."

How could she, Alice-Ann wondered later, survive the night without Mack to write to about the events of that evening? Who else would she tell about the German man who'd come in from the fields covered in dust and grime, about how he'd washed up in their indoor bath and that when he'd come out, he looked as much like a human being as the rest of them? His blond hair spiked from the water, his blue eyes clear and intense like a summer's day.

Every fiber of her being cried out to sit at her desk, paper angled just so in front of her. *Dearest Mack,* she'd write, her pen scratching against the paper, and then go on to tell him how she'd noted the German's hands. His fingers. That after seeing Ben Brown's fat ones, and Nelson's splayed at his hips, and Papa's nails edged in grime, this man had exited the bath wiping his hands on one of Aunt Bess's hand-stitched towels, pulling his long, slender, and pale fingers one at a time. So hard she wondered why they hadn't popped out of their sockets.

And then, she'd write,

he walked into Nelson and Irene's bedroom as though he'd been within its floral-papered walls a thousand times or more — or even only a few — and closed the door behind him. I heard him, Mack. I heard him telling Aunt Bess and Irene's mother what to do, every step of the way, because I stayed upstairs, sitting on the top step, where I could see the door if I looked one way, and Papa and Nelson in the living room if I looked through the slats of the railing.

Papa practically had to sit on Nelson to let the German touch Irene, but I stayed calm and I listened, Mack, and I heard. The German knew what he was doing. He turned my little nephew around only moments before Irene pushed him out into the world.

Alice-Ann wasn't sure who'd cried louder, the baby or Irene.

Of course, Aunt Bess sobbed into her handkerchief. So did Irene's mother — into her own — and declared the baby beyond perfect.

Papa grinned a lot, chuckling a time or two, and Nelson knelt next to the bed, kissed his wife, and examined his son beneath the folds of the blanket Aunt Bess had crocheted for the occasion.

But I, she would write, if only she could, *I stayed at the door and watched . . . and wondered why today of all days this baby had to be born. How can we go on now, from this day forward, celebrating his birthday year after year, knowing the day also marks the anniversary Bynum heard of your death?*

She had thanked the German and offered him a glass of iced tea when the ordeal was over and the adults continued to ogle. He'd readily accepted, following her down the stairs and into the kitchen.

"Do you have a name?" she asked as she handed him the glass.

"Danke," he said. "Thank you." He swallowed the tea down in quick gulps and she realized he'd come in from the fields and that he'd probably been parched the entire time and that someone should have realized this fact sooner.

"Your name is Danke?" she asked, mainly to cover her shame for not offering the drink before.

His chuckle caught her off guard — his teeth pearly white and even, which caused her to press her lips over her crooked ones. "*Nein . . .* um, no. My name is Adler. *Danke* is German for 'thank you.' "

Alice-Ann smiled without warning. "Oh," she said, feeling the blush that pinked her cheeks. "How do you say, 'You're welcome'?"

"*Bitte.*"

"*Bitte,*" she repeated.

Adler handed her the glass. "That is good."

"*Danke,*" she said, then laughed easily, wondering if he meant her attempt at speaking his language or the tea.

"May I — may I have a little more?" he asked. "I am thirsty still."

"Of course," she said, embarrassed that he'd had to inquire of something she should have offered when he'd finished the first glass. Alice-Ann poured the tea as close to the top as she dared. "You can sit at the table if you'd like."

Adler looked at the table, then back at her as he took the refilled glass. "No. This is fine."

"Do you mind?" she began. "May I ask . . . ?"

"Of course. Anything." He drank the second glass down more slowly, but still within one long swallow.

"How old are you?"

"I am twenty-five. And you?"

"I'll be nineteen in December."

He grinned. "Then you are eighteen."

Feeling both childish and foolish, she took the glass and asked, "More?"

"No. *Danke.* I am good now."

Hearing footsteps overhead, she glanced up, then said, "Truly. Thank you — *danke* — for what you did to help my sister-in-law and my new nephew."

Adler stood with his feet placed wide apart. A soldier at attention. "You have all been very kind to me. Your *Vater* — um — your father — he looks at me and I think he sees a man, not a Nazi."

Alice-Ann placed the glass on the countertop and the ice rattled as it settled in the bottom. "Are you? A Nazi, I mean?"

"No," he said without hesitating. "Not here," he added, pointing to his chest. "In the heart." Adler blinked. "You must understand, your American men and women joined because they wanted to defend what was theirs. I didn't ask to — Hitler's war is not my war." He sighed. Blinked again as if he were pushing back a memory, then said, "My best friend was a Jew."

And then, she would write to Mack if only she could, *he wiped a tear from the corner of his eye. I've heard that Hitler has done terrible things to the Jews, but I don't know what. Aunt Bess and Mrs. Hillis tell Maeve and me not to go into the movies until after the newsreels are finished. To protect us, I know, but it keeps me in the dark about something I think I should know.*

But I realized right then, Mack, that not every German is heartless and maybe not even all the Japanese are either. In fact, Papa reminded me later, some part of our family somewhere had come from Germany back in the early 1800s.

But I don't know any Japanese. Still, I'm sure . . .

Nelson came into the kitchen then and offered his hand to the German without hesitation. "Thank you. I — I wish I could do something for you. Pay you or . . ."

"Your family has been very kind. That is enough."

"His best friend was Jewish," Alice-Ann added as though she had suddenly become the German man's best friend.

"We have a Jewish family here in Bynum,"

211

Nelson said, then shook his head in a way that told Alice-Ann he'd realized the shallowness of his words. But he continued on anyway. "They own Lewen's Department Store."

Adler nodded like the news mattered to him. "What will you name your son, then?" he asked.

Nelson looked at Alice-Ann. "Irene and I decided . . ." He smiled. Or perhaps he winced. "We're going to call him Mack." He returned his gaze to Adler. "For my best friend, who . . . died . . . in the war."

"Mack," Alice-Ann whispered, realizing in her heart that, for the first time since he'd heard the news of his friend's death, her brother actually felt the sting of it too.

Well, I suppose that's something, she would write to Mack later, if she could.

You will no longer be with us, but he will grow up and folks will say his name and they will remember.

Love always,
Alice-Ann

CHAPTER 15

Saturday morning broke with a baby's cry, loud and shrill. Alice-Ann sat up straight in the semidarkness, the sheet bunched around her waist, one hand clutching the hem.

Should she get out of bed? See if Irene and Nelson needed help? Or was this their issue to deal with?

The door across the hallway opened. Closed. Footsteps — Nelson's — hurried down the stairs as the crying ceased. A minute later, the footsteps returned, this time coming up the stairs and toward the bedroom. The door opened. Closed.

Alice-Ann lay back down, grateful. And then . . .

Mack is dead.

She closed her eyes against any memory of him, then allowed them to wash over her. The way he'd teased her when she'd been a child. His easy smile. The laughter in his eyes. Birds outside her window welcomed the day in song, but she willed them to silence so she could hear his voice. Keep him as close to her heart and memory as though he spoke to her in that very room.

"Tell you what let's do, Alice-Ann. You mean the world to me, you know that, right?"

Lying in her bed, Alice-Ann nodded in the same way she'd done that night. That last, wonderful night.

"I can't promise you anything. Not now. Not with us at war and me leaving soon. . . . If it weren't for the Japs and Hitler and all the rest, I'd be staying right here in Bynum and — if you'd told me how you felt, maybe . . . well, maybe we'd go out as friends and —"

The Japs and Hitler . . .

"My best friend was a Jew . . ." Adler's voice interrupted. *"I didn't ask to — Hitler's war is not my war."*

Alice-Ann shook her head, squeezing her eyes tighter still. *No, no, no. Mack. Only Mack's voice.* Adler's she could hear anytime she wanted. All she had to do was walk out into the fields. But Mack's . . .

"You're getting more comfortable."

Her eyes opened and she blinked in the milky light of her room, the sun having filtered in around the curtains arranged across her window, billowing from the fan.

Carlton? Had Carlton been told of Mack's death?

"I think you're my healer, Dr. Doodlebug. . . . My good luck charm."

Alice-Ann sat up again. She didn't *want* to be his healer. She only wanted —

She drew her knees up, wrapped her arms around her bent legs, and pressed her eyes into the bones there. A kaleidoscope of colors swirled. *Please, God . . . please, please, please. Let me hear his voice one more time.* Her fingers instinctively reached for the comfort of the bracelet.

Crying from across the hall resumed, then subsided almost within the same breath. Alice-Ann took a deep breath, raised her head, and blinked away the black and gray that remained.

"Let me drive the tractor, okay?"

Claudette found her later that morning in the tobacco field, where she walked among the hip-high thick green leaves searching for predatory worms that might have decided to feast among them.

Her friend said nothing. She didn't have to. She walked straight up the row, her bangles announcing her arrival, her eyes full of emotion. Alice-Ann stood, motionless, waiting. When Claudette reached her, their arms slid around each other naturally, and even in the blistering heat, they held on as though gasping for breath. For a moment, Alice-Ann wondered — ridiculously — if somehow the love and nuptial hope within Claudette could transfer, chest to chest.

But then Claudette squeezed. Let go. And Alice-Ann took a step back.

"I had to come," she said.

Alice-Ann nodded as Claudette looked toward the house. "Daddy said Irene had the baby."

"Yesterday. Sometime early evening." She shook her head. "I'm not sure of the exact time."

"He said one of the POWs helped."

Alice-Ann wiped beads of sweat from her brow with her fingertips. "Adler. His name is Adler." She started to say his full name, then realized she'd not learned it. How rude of her . . .

"Have y'all heard anything from Irene's brother?"

"She gets a letter once a week." Alice-Ann gave a shrug. "I think he's doing okay, which is — at least — one blessing we can thank God for."

Claudette looked up. "Horribly hot out here," she said, gazing upward. "Not a cloud in the sky."

"No," Alice-Ann said, her own eyes searching for at least one. Finding none.

"Alice-Ann," Claudette said, and their eyes met again. "I'm so, so sorry about Mack." Her tiny fingers fiddled with a gold locket nestled in the hollow of her throat, and Alice-Ann wondered if perhaps it had been a gift from her fiancé. From Johnny.

"No one knows," she said. "I mean, no one in my family. Well, Irene does, in a way, I guess. But I think she's probably a little more than busy with other worries right now." Alice-Ann shrugged. "I have no one, really. To talk to."

Claudette grabbed her hand, something Alice-Ann nearly regretted, Claudette's being so clean. So dainty and lovely. And her own being dusty and dry. Thick in the skin. She tried to break free, but Claudette hung on. "I'm here," she said. "Anytime you need to talk."

"Thank you, Claudette. Truly."

A light chuckle came from inside her friend as she said, "You know, I just bet your aunt Bess has some *cold* lemonade in the icebox."

Alice-Ann nodded. "She does. And it's sweetened to perfection."

"Good." She smiled. "I'm parched, I tell you."

"You know the way. I'll be right behind you."

Claudette stepped between two of the tobacco plants, wrapping her dress skirt against her. "Tell you what. How about we walk side by side."

Alice-Ann nodded. "Come on, then."

"Have you talked to Maeve?" Claudette asked when they'd taken several steps. "Since the news about Mack came out?"

"No." Then, realizing she'd answered forcibly, she smiled and added, "I haven't really had a chance. What with the baby . . ."

"I'm just wondering how Carlton took it. They were good friends — him and Mack and your brother."

She knew that.

A moment later they reached the path leading to the house and turned toward the refreshment inside. "Maeve said you've been coming over and reading to Carlton."

"I have. Yes." But she couldn't imagine continuing. Not now. Before yesterday, reading to Carlton had been something to pass the time. To check off the days until Mack returned. But now . . .

"You've always had such a wonderful way of doing that, Alice-Ann. I remember when you were called on in school to read out loud. Do you remember?"

"Yes. Of course." Alice-Ann pulled her hair, which in the humidity had frizzed more than usual, into a ponytail at the nape of her neck and hoped for a breeze to blow across the wetness there. They were only a few yards from the house. The windows were open; a Count Basie tune drifted from beyond the screens. Outside, the cicadas attempted to keep rhythm but failed.

"Mrs. Sindersine called on you more than anyone else in the American lit class," Claudette droned on. "She said you had the gift."

Mercifully, before Alice-Ann felt compelled to respond, they reached the house and, as in years past, headed straight for the back door, where a half-dozen laying hens scratched in the dirt.

Tuesday afternoon, as they prepared to clock out, Nancy asked Alice-Ann the question she'd dreaded for days. "Will you continue to read to Carlton?"

Alice-Ann pushed her card into the machine and waited for the *thunk*. She shrugged. "I don't have it in me right now."

Nancy pushed her own card in, retrieved it, and slid it back into its holder. "You know," she said with a laugh, "I can't help but wonder, day in and day out, why in the world Mister Dooley has a time clock for three employees."

Alice-Ann, hoping that Nancy had lost interest in her previous question, chuckled. "I think it makes him feel like one of those fancy bankers over in Savannah or up in Atlanta."

"Oh." Nancy giggled easily, then sobered. "Now, about Carlton?"

"Why should I?" Alice-Ann asked, then winced, hating her own words. Hating herself in the midst of them.

"Why *shouldn't* you? Mack's dying — no matter how awful — doesn't erase the fact that you've deepened a friendship with a man who waits to hear your voice every afternoon after work and sometimes even on the weekend. A man who has — according to his sister — been working even harder with Doc Evans on his exercises, trying to get the use of his legs back." Her brow rose. "From what I hear, he's doing this because you challenged him."

Alice-Ann smiled. "I told him I'd show him the house next to yours if he'd get better."

"The house next to mine?"

"It's a lovely little cottage, don't you think?"

Nancy's eyes widened. "If you like the

scene of a murder."

Alice-Ann shook her head. "That's folk-lore."

Nancy looked skeptical.

"Carlton told me and I believe him."

"Murder or no, it could use some work. A *lot* of work, in my way of thinking. I wouldn't want to be the poor soul who tackled it."

"Maybe not, but when I look at it, I see it as it will be. Or at the very least, as it *could* be. Not as it is now, all wallpaper peeling and boards in need of nails."

Nancy slipped a cupped hand under Alice-Ann's elbow and squeezed. "Then answer me this, Miss Branch. How could a young woman with so much compassion for a *house* not have as much for a man who's been injured in the war?"

Alice-Ann sighed. "Papa's sure to be after me soon enough. He thinks I'm some sort of hometown hero, reading to Carlton for a half hour or so in the afternoons."

Nancy reached into her purse and retrieved her gloves. "Then let's hope you won't let him down."

Alice-Ann walked into the five-and-dime as though nothing had transpired in the days since her last visit. She greeted Mr. and

Mrs. Hillis — both standing behind the cash register counter, deep in conversation. She caught sight of Maeve straightening a display of laundry detergent. Her friend turned at the sound of her footsteps, opened her mouth to speak, but quickly closed it.

"Is he up?" Alice-Ann asked, keeping her voice nonchalant.

Maeve nodded.

Alice-Ann took the steps lightly, her fingertips only grazing the round banister hung on brass hoops. When she reached the landing, she paused. Took a breath. Sighed.

"Co-Cola?" she called out.

Her question was met by silence. Then, "Over ice, please."

She smiled as she went into the kitchen and prepared their drinks. When she entered his room, she found him as always. Sitting up. A sheet drawn up to his hips. He wore powder-blue pajamas, the top buttoned to his throat, which she thought looked horribly uncomfortable.

"I'm placing the glass on the table," she said as she put it on the small plate near the corner.

"I know."

Her chair — usually angled near the side of the bed — had been pushed against the wall. She set her glass next to his, then retrieved the chair, placed it where it belonged, and sat.

Alice-Ann raised her eyes slowly to his face, waiting for the obvious. But he said nothing. He only sat, staring toward her, his breath coming in an easy tempo. Finally he cleared his throat and said, "You left your glass on the table."

She jumped. "Oh. Sorry." She reached for it.

"Mama will have a fit if she sees a water ring."

Alice-Ann gripped the glass. "Aunt Bess would too."

"Sometimes I think mamas just like to throw a fit every so often."

She nodded. Took a sip of the drink, the liquid burning her throat, which she hadn't realized had gone so bone-dry. Then she smiled. "You look kind of like you were expecting the general or somebody."

Carlton tilted his head. Blinked. "What do you mean?"

"You've got your shirt buttoned all the way to your Adam's apple," she said.

He reached up, unfastened the top button. "Doc was here earlier. I think I got carried away with the buttons while he was talking to Mama and me. Well, more Mama than me." He shook his head. "Sometimes I

223

suspect he thinks I'm still a boy."

Alice-Ann peered around the room. "Do you still have the book I left last week?"

"Are we going to read or are we going to talk about it?"

"About what?"

"Don't do that. Not with me."

Not with him? Coming over to read to him a handful of times hardly qualified them as confidants.

"I can't."

"Why not?" He reached for the glass of cola with precision, the backs of his fingertips tapping the condensation-laced front, then sliding around so that his fingers wrapped around it. He took several swallows before returning his drink to the plate, then brought his eyes back in her direction.

They were clearer today, she realized. The swelling had gone down, the black and blue, the green and yellow giving way to the natural tan of his skin.

"Can you see me?" The words blurted out of her.

He shook his head. "Not quite. Not altogether clearly, I should say. But I know you're wearing blue."

She looked down at her belted dress, a simple frock that buttoned down the front and fell to just below her knees. "If you can't see, then how'd you — ?"

"The colors. I'm starting to see more of the colors." Carlton turned his face toward the window. "I think it has to do with the sun coming in from the window because I tend to see them more this time of day."

"When did this start?"

"The day we found out about Mack. Friday."

Alice-Ann placed her glass on the floor next to the chair, then worked her thumbnails together. "Have you — have you heard anything more?"

"Daddy and Mama went over to the Mac-Kays' on Saturday. They're going to have a memorial, but they don't know when just yet." He paused. "How's Nelson doing with the news?"

"He's — he's been a little preoccupied since Friday."

"I heard. A boy. Named him after Mack."

She shook her head. "You can't keep a secret in this town."

"No, ma'am, you can*not.*"

If he could see the blue of her dress, could he also see the red she knew blistered her face? "What do you mean?"

Carlton crooked a finger. "Scoot the chair closer."

Alice-Ann inched it forward.

"All the way to the side of the bed."

She dragged it until the armrest pushed against the mattress. When she'd settled again, he reached for her left hand. His fingertips ran along the silver of the charm bracelet. "He was special to you, no?"

"Did Maeve say — ?"

"No. Betty Jo figured it. The night of your party." He waited a beat, perhaps for her to say something. Perhaps to gather his own thoughts at the memories of that night. "Said she'd never seen anyone so taken."

Alice-Ann bent at the middle until her face pressed into the mattress near his hip. If she'd been that transparent to Betty Jo, whom she hardly knew, then surely everyone there had been able to tell. "Oh no . . ." She breathed out, then inhaled the scent of washing powder and some sort of spice. Familiar, somehow . . .

His hand came to rest on the back of her head. "It's okay."

She shook her head. "Nooooooo," she whispered.

Oh yes. Yes. The night of her party. Carlton had smelled of peppermint and spice. She remembered now.

His fingers wove through the mass of curls, massaging her scalp, and she broke. Bringing her hands under her face, she allowed her fingertips to catch the tears she'd held at bay for days. For months, perhaps. For years. "He's not coming back," she whimpered.

The rubbing continued, encouraging her to let it go. Let it all go. "No," he said. "He's not." Finally, when nothing remained except an eerie silence between them, she raised her head and he cupped her chin. Empathy flickered in the blue of his eyes and the wide brow wrinkled with worry.

"I'm sorry," she said, not moving out of the odd embrace, afraid he'd think her not appreciative of his compassion.

Using his thumb pads, Carlton swept the moisture from her face. "Don't be." Then he smiled. Faintly, but a smile nonetheless. "Now we both have secrets to hold on to for each other."

"I don't —"

"You kept my secret about wanting to marry Betty Jo, right?"

Alice-Ann nodded.

"Then I'll keep your secret, doodlebug." He released her. Laid his hands on his chest. "You're completely safe with me."

CHAPTER 16

Days slipped by. One, then two. Another one and another one. Alice-Ann lived each day — each moment of the day — as she thought expected of her. The dutiful daughter, heading off to work, Monday through Friday, putting in the hours. Her paycheck would go mostly to Papa, to help with the farm, which continued to struggle in spite of government help.

"I reckon we're all in a mess," Papa said one night over a cold supper.

Nelson, who looked plumb worn-out and weary — both from work and from a new baby keeping him up all hours — nodded. Beside him, Irene nestled their son in her arms, cooing to him in the way of mothers. "We'll get through it, Pops. When the war is over, the country and the tide will turn. You'll see."

Aunt Bess pushed her chair from the table, rose, and retrieved a plate of sliced tomatoes she'd forgotten on the countertop. "Let's just pray to the good Lord that we don't have another depression like the last one. Don't think we could handle another one."

Depression.

If Alice-Ann had time, she might consider her own sadness. But work — at the bank, at the unyielding farm — never gave her a moment to rest, much less to think for too long. Only at night did she allow herself the privilege of weeping. After she'd bathed, gone into her room, and closed the door. After she'd read one of Mack's old letters (sometimes two), never touching the ones near the top of the stack. The ones where he talked about what would be his last mission.

Reading the letters kept him alive and coming home. To his parents. To Bynum. To her. She imagined him entering the house. Reaching for the baby who bore his name. Holding him as he'd one day hold one of their own.

And then kissing her.

The kiss she'd hoped — *believed* — would only be his. She always and only had wanted her first and last kiss to belong to Mack. The first, the last, the only.

On the weekdays, after work, she walked

to the five-and-dime to read to Carlton. Though it seemed, with each passing day, they spent more time talking — him about losing Betty Jo and her about losing Mack — than delving into the words of Carroll and Wilder and, most recently, Travers.

Some days, she read to him from the *Savannah Morning News.* On Thursday afternoon, she regaled him with articles and letters to the editor from the *Bynum Telegraph,* their local paper, which turned a blind eye to world events, focusing more on who had dinner with whom after church on Sunday, who had visitors from out of town, and recent births and nuptial announcements. And of course, what was going on in the schoolhouse.

On the first Saturday morning in June, the third Saturday since hearing of Mack's death, she worked alongside Aunt Bess in the gardens and on the back porch, where they washed a load of linens and hung them out on the line. After a simple lunch of tomato and cucumber sandwiches — her favorite when slathered in mayonnaise — she took a hurried bath, then dressed for town. Lately, she'd forgone the matinee with Maeve and Ernie to spend time as her papa's new heroine, reading to a man who grew somewhat stronger with each passing day, his vision clearer.

Alice-Ann got off the bus in town, but instead of going to the Hillises' apartment straight off, she walked beneath the store-front awnings to MacKay's Pharmacy. The door, held open to allow the air to circulate, had been draped in black.

Alice-Ann's breath caught in her throat and she paused a moment before going inside.

Janie Wren, a young woman who'd graduated with Alice-Ann but whom she'd never been particularly close to, stood behind the front counter, flipping the pages of a glossy magazine she'd no doubt snagged from the nearby rotating wire stand. She looked up, blew a bubble of gum as she did, then popped it with her tongue. Her hand flew over her mouth, apologetically. "Hi there, Alice-Ann," she said, smiling around her fingertips.

Alice-Ann gripped her purse with both hands. Janie had always been a pretty girl, but since high school she'd grown more so. Mature and almost sultry. Her hair, silky smooth and perfectly coiffed, a peaches-and-cream complexion, and her intense green eyes made her Hollywood-star perfect, which only made Alice-Ann more uncomfortable in her own skin. "Hey,

Janie," she managed.

Her old classmate straightened, squared her shoulders, then spit her gum into a tissue she retrieved out of a box on the counter. "How've you been? It's been a long time since I've seen you. You've been good?"

"Things are . . . things are okay."

"I heard about Nelson and Irene having a boy. I think that's just keen of them to name the baby after Mack."

Alice-Ann forced a smile and stepped closer to the counter. "He — ah — he cries a lot."

"Don't they all," Janie said with a laugh. "When my sister Patricia had her daughter — never have I *ever* heard such a pair of lungs on something so tiny." She flipped the magazine closed, then leaned over and returned it to the rack.

Alice-Ann now stood close enough to catch the scent of Janie's perfume, light and flowery. A thought washed over her, that if Mack had stayed, or even returned, if he'd gone to work for his father as Mr. MacKay had always wanted, he'd be here, day in and day out, *with Janie.*

The thought left her nearly nauseous and most definitely envious.

Why couldn't *she* have been blessed with looks like Janie's? Like Maeve's and Claudette's and Irene's? All of them so naturally —

She stopped as reality struck her. Janie, as lovely as she'd always been, now wore light touches of makeup. She looked to the back of the store, past the lotions and potions, the shampoos and cosmetics, to the pharmacy.

"Mr. MacKay is in the back, if you've got a pharmaceutical need."

Pharmaceutical . . . Even her words sounded all grown-up.

"Um . . . no."

She'd only come in to offer condolences to the family, something she should have done before now but had been unable to rouse herself to do. She'd hoped to step in, say her piece, and then cross the street to the five-and-dime. To the Hillises' apartment and to Carlton's room. On Saturdays, they read the newspaper and from the Bible. It should have all been simple enough. But then . . . "I — I only wanted to —" She breathed in Janie's scent again. "Janie, what is that perfume you're wearing?"

Janie's green eyes dazzled. "Isn't it something?" She came around the counter in a flurry. "Follow me, Alice-Ann. It's body lotion, actually. And quite reasonably priced." Janie walked Alice-Ann down an aisle between the lotions and cosmetics. "Look at this," she said, pointing to an ad featuring actress Elyse Knox for Jergens.

" 'Object Romance,' " Alice-Ann read, then chuckled. " '. . . say Elyse Knox's Hands.' "

"Smell," Janie said, opening a half-filled square-shaped bottle displayed on the shelf.

Alice-Ann leaned her nose closer to the open bottle. "Mmm . . ."

"Here. Try it." She squeezed a dollop into Alice-Ann's cupped hand. "This bottle is what we call a 'tester.' " She leaned closer. "Trust me. I *test* it several times a day."

Alice-Ann rubbed the silky lotion into her hands, then up and down her arms. The scent of it caught the stirring breeze from the ceiling fan overhead and tickled her nostrils. "It's lovely."

"And see this?" Janie nodded at the advertisement, then peered over her shoulder to the back, where Mr. MacKay, one arm wrapped in a black band, busied himself behind the high-rise pharmacy counter. "See how they have her with a pilot in the ad?"

Alice-Ann studied the ad, then nodded.

"You know, she's getting married to Tom Harmon, the football player and war hero?"

Alice-Ann shook her head. She'd hardly

had free time to devour magazines as Janie apparently had. "No, I — Tom *who*?"

"Harmon. He's a *pilot,* you see?" Janie had lowered her voice and she looked over her shoulder again. "He's in the United States Army Air Corps —"

"Like Mack," Alice-Ann sighed.

"Yes. But listen to this. Last spring — a year ago — he crashed his plane in South America."

"South America?"

"In the jungle. I read an article that said after he ordered his men to bail out, he parachuted fifteen hundred feet from his plane." Her perfectly arched and penciled brows shot up. "He landed in a tree."

"Alive, obviously . . ." Unlike Mack, at the bottom of an ocean.

"The *sole* survivor. None of his men made it. Not a single one."

Like Mack. "That's . . . awful, Janie."

"He worked his way through the jungle for days, Alice-Ann. *Days.*"

Alice-Ann reached for the bottle of lotion, thinking to buy two — one for herself and one for Irene. Since the baby's birth, she'd been nicer. More tolerable.

Janie's hand touched hers. "Wait." For the third time, she looked toward the back. Alice-Ann glanced up. Mr. MacKay watched them briefly, then went back to work. "Six months later, after all that, he got shot down *again* in China, but he was rescued by some anti-Japanese group — I don't know what they're called." She tossed her head as though it didn't matter for her purpose in telling the story.

Alice-Ann grabbed the two bottles as pressure filled her chest; then she grabbed a third. Where in the world was Janie headed with this story? "So that's why there's a pilot in the ad?"

Janie grabbed Alice-Ann by the short sleeve of her dress and all but dragged her to the front. "No," she said, still keeping her voice low. "I mean, yes, but that's not the point." She sighed. "Don't you see? If Tom Harmon could survive all that, then maybe *Mack* survived too." Her green eyes sparkled in the afternoon sunlight that spilled through the large storefront windows. "And wouldn't that be wonderful if he did?"

"I —" Her mind whirled and her ears rang. Had Janie been *in love* with Mack? All this time? Was she still? Had she expressed those feelings to him? Had he done the same? "Did you — ? How well did you — ?" She couldn't bring herself to finish the question.

"Know Mack?"

"Yes." Had she spoken the answer or only imagined it?

Janie took the bottles of lotion from Alice-Ann's grip, then stepped back behind the counter and set them down with a gentle thud as she shook her head. "Not as well as I wanted to," she admitted. Brazenly, in Alice-Ann's point of view. She pushed the keys on the cash register. "But I've been writing to him. I have so dreamed and . . ." She leaned over the counter to whisper the rest of the sentence. "Why do you think I took the job here?" Janie looked past Alice-Ann's shoulder. "The MacKays have come to mean an awful lot to me."

"I . . . see."

"Alice-Ann, I'm *not* giving up. If some football player from Michigan can survive the war, then so can *our* Mack. He may not have gotten his picture on the cover of *Life* magazine like 'Old 98,' but he *is* a survivor. Anyone who knows him knows that." Janie looked back at the register. "That'll be seventy-three cents."

Carlton tilted his chin and wiggled his nose. "What's that smell?"

Alice-Ann brought her forearm to her nose, her hands wrapped around two sweating glasses of cola. "Body lotion. I — went over to the drugstore and . . ."

Carlton eased his legs to the floor.

"Carlton," she exclaimed, crossing over to the bedside table, where she placed the glasses of Coke. "Look at you."

He grinned. "I can't walk. I can't even stand, really, but how's *this* for progress?" He reached for her hand and she willingly gave it, then sat in the chair angled toward his knees. "And you're wearing something light on the top and . . . *plaid*? On the bottom."

Alice-Ann crossed her legs and squeezed his hand. "Pedal pushers. They're kind of a new thing. Comfortable in this heat, I can tell you." She squeezed again, then released and brought her hands together in her lap. "I'm so thrilled, Carlton, that you are healing so well."

He nodded. "Me too. I'm ready to get out of this room."

"What does Doc Evans say about that?"

Carlton pressed his fists into the foam mattress and pushed, bringing his shoulders up around his ears. "He's bringing some kind of contraption on Monday that's supposed to help strengthen my legs. Help me to walk again."

"That's — wonderful."

He sniffed again. "And you really do smell good."

She giggled. "Jergens lotion. I got it over at — at the drugstore." She took a breath. "Elyse Knox advertises for it."

"The woman marrying Tom Harmon?"

"How do you know that?" she asked, grateful he'd not inquired further about her going to the MacKays' place of business.

"It's *Tom Harmon,* Alice-Ann."

She shook her head and leaned back in the chair. "Until today I'd never heard his name."

Carlton laughed easily. "You're such a girl." He squinted toward her lap. "Even in . . . what did you call them?"

"Pedal pushers."

"Girls in pants." He shook his head. "My, how the war has changed the world."

"I've worn bib overalls my whole life and you know it."

He leaned forward. Slowly. "In a pea patch." He chuckled. "I don't believe I ever saw you in them uptown."

"Aunt Bess would tan my bib-overalled hide."

Carlton laughed hard, then winced. Alice-Ann stood, put her arms on his shoulders, and pressed. "Sit back; sit back."

He eased himself into the nearly flat pillows at the bed's headboard, which she pulled out and fluffed, then replaced. "Here you go."

"Sorry," he said.

"No. Don't apologize, Carlton. For pity's sake . . ."

After a few deep breaths, his body relaxed. "Okay. Okay." He looked up at her. "Did you bring the newspaper up?"

She'd snagged it from Mr. Hillis downstairs but had left it in the kitchen. "I did. Hold on and I'll go get it."

Alice-Ann dashed into the kitchen, then returned with the slightly askew *Savannah Morning News*. She sat, unfolded the paper, and snapped it as she'd seen her father and brother do time and again. "Now then," she said. "What would you like to hear first? World news or local?"

"Give me two to choose from off the front page."

She dropped one corner of the paper to peer at him. A smile crossed her lips without her willing it. He looked so boyish and yet so grown-up, all at once. "All right." She returned her attention to the paper. " 'Allies Smash Rome Defenses.' " She dropped the corner of the paper again. "That's one."

"And two?"

" 'US Urged to Join French Talks.' "

"Hmmm . . ." He paused. "What are you looking at now?"

"How did you — ? Never mind." She frowned. "I'm looking at an ad for natural gas and our need to conserve it at home so it can be used for warplanes."

"Got to."

"We've conserved everything else. We girls are even cutting our skirts shorter to save on material."

He grinned. "I can live with that."

Alice-Ann shook her head in amusement. "Carlton . . . pick an article and hush."

He pretended to straighten up. "Yes, ma'am. I'll take the first one and then the second one."

She popped the paper back into place. "All right," she said, then took a deep breath and prepared her voice to sound as though it came straight from the radio. From Washington or some other faraway place she'd probably never visit. "Here's the first news article for June 3, 1944. . . ."

CHAPTER 17

During the few days that followed, Alice-Ann kept her fears — that Mack might have been writing to both her *and* Janie Wren — hidden under the surface of what had become *normal.* But at night, she pored over his letters, looking for clues that he might have been corresponding with more than her . . . or his parents.

She found not a single hint. Either Janie had only expressed her own fantasies, or Boyd MacKay was as suave and slick as Hollywood heartthrob Joseph Cotten. Still, each and every night as she said her prayers, Alice-Ann asked God that, if it *could* be so — if Mack *could* still be alive — then *make* it so. "I'll do anything," she whispered into the thick darkness of her bedroom, placing her plea like a gambler's deal. "I'll be a better Christian. I'll work more at the church, if you want me to. I'll do *anything,* God. Anything."

She knew better, of course. She could all but hear Aunt Bess's stern warning against such prayers. *"You should be a better Christian,"* Aunt Bess would surely say, *"because that's what Christ expects of you. Not for love, Alice. Those kinds of prayers will get you nowhere."*

But she prayed them anyway, hoping God knew the intent of her heart, as surely he did.

" 'I the Lord search the heart, I try the reins, even to give every man according to his ways, and according to the fruit of his doings,' " she said, taking her imaginary argument with her aunt a step further by quoting from Jeremiah. Then she added, "Jesus, please search my heart . . ."

The agony of her prayer tore at her, leaving her to cry herself to sleep and wrestle with herself in her dreams until morning came.

Then, on the evening of June 6, as one bit of bad news seemed to be in need of worse news to ride coattails on, their family radio crackled with breaking devastation. *"We are continuing in our coverage of the invasion, which, as you know . . ."*

Alice-Ann listened with her ears but kept her eyes on her father's face. *Grim* hardly began to describe it. For too long, she'd focused only on how the war affected her — the rationing, the long days at work, the blackouts. How it worked all of them — with the exception of maybe Irene — to the bone. There were nights, too many to count, when she'd been too tired to sleep. Others when she'd been too worn-out to wash her face and brush her teeth.

And this war — this awful thing — had taken Mack and Marty Dibble from both the town and the people who loved them, and returned Carlton Hillis with severe trauma to his nervous system. Now this.

". . . what we have reported thus far has come to us from England — not London — but somewhere in England . . . This is being referred to as 'The Invasion.' There are still no Allied confirmations . . . only what the unreliable Germans have reported . . ."

Alice-Ann stood on shaky legs, walked around the sofa to her mother's chair, where Aunt Bess held a darning needle in one hand and a sock in the other, not touching, merely being held. Alice-Ann sat on the thick armrest, then felt her aunt's arm slide around her hips. "It's going to be all right, Alice," she whispered. But to convince herself or her niece, Alice-Ann wasn't sure. "In the end, I'm quite certain this will move us toward the war's end. Our boys coming on home."

"But what does it mean for *now*?" she asked, her voice perhaps too loud. Papa shot a look at her — one she hadn't seen in a while — and shushed her.

"Early Tuesday morning, landing craft and light warships were observed in the area between the mouth of the Somme and the eastern coast of Normandy . . ."

Irene stood, her sleeping baby cradled against her, nuzzling at the bodice of her dress. "I'm going to put him down." She took two steps from her husband before turning back. "And get a map." Words that relieved Alice-Ann. At least she wasn't the only one in the room completely ignorant of where "The Invasion" had taken place.

"The long-expected Anglo-American invasion appears to have begun . . ."

Her father's jaw worked back and forth.

"Papa?" she dared ask. "Please? What does this mean?"

But it was her brother who turned to look at her, his face pasty white. "This is *big*, Alice-Ann," he said, his words soft-spoken.

"How big?"

Nelson shook his head. "I don't know, little sister. Just . . . big."

"Are any of *our* boys over there?"

He turned back to the radio. "No way to

know for sure, Alice-Ann. No way to know." He sighed deeply. "Not for a few days, anyhow."

Several long days and many news reports later, Bynum had her confirmation.

Pete James — like so many others — had died on Omaha Beach in northern France. Funny-looking Pete, with his too-big ears and lanky bones. Pete James, who'd sworn with the crack of his knuckles on his mother's living room sofa that he'd "get them Japs."

But the Japs were only a fragment of the enemy. In the end, Pete James never had a chance — a real chance — at getting anyone.

"I feel so shallow," Alice-Ann admitted to Carlton on a warm Saturday afternoon a few days later, as they sat for the first time in the Hillises' living room. With Carlton's daily improvements, Doc Evans had managed to find a wheelchair for him, on the promise that he would get out of bed every day, get dressed, and — soon enough — get out of the house.

"Why's that?" he asked.

Alice-Ann studied his eyes, now completely void of bruising and swelling. They were also clear as glass, as they'd always been, but she'd never fully noticed. "I — I didn't tell you before . . . because I —"

Outside the open window, from the sidewalk below, a child called to his mother and the mother responded, "Well, come on then."

"Tell me now," Carlton coaxed, tilting his head and pulling her back into the room. He smiled and echoed the mother's words. "Well, come on then."

She chuckled. "Okay. Remember the day I came here smelling like body lotion?"

"The *first* day, you mean?" he teased.

Alice-Ann nodded. Since the day she'd smelled Jergens on Janie Wren, she'd reveled in the scent of it on her own body, not to mention having appreciated the way it lent itself to making her feel more like a woman with each application. "Yes. The *first* day."

"I remember."

"I told you I had gone to the drugstore that day — to MacKay's, really. I hadn't intended to shop. I only wanted to tell them how sorry I was. You know, about Mack." She paused, not sure where to go from there with her explanation.

"And?"

"I saw Janie Wren. She's working there

now. Do you remember her?"

"Pretty girl? Graduated with your class?"

"Mine and Maeve's. Mm-hmm."

He grinned, then brought his hands up in the air to form a curvaceous figure. "I remember." He whistled between his teeth and she swatted at him.

"Oh, stop it."

Carlton had the good decency to blush. "Well, she *is* pretty. Or at least she was the last time I saw her."

Alice-Ann grimaced, feeling the old self-consciousness fly over her. "Ugh. She still is."

His eyes squinted. "Do I sense the green-eyed monster?"

"Maybe."

"And Janie's beauty bothers you because . . . ?"

"Because I'm *not* — truth be told — beautiful. Not by the longest stretch of the word. I can't even be considered *attractive.*"

He shook his head. "Alice-Ann, you're a beautiful girl in your own right."

Alice-Ann couldn't be sure which bothered her most, that Carlton had called her a "girl" or that he'd declared her beautiful "in her own right."

He raised both hands. "Wait. No. That didn't sound right." He leaned forward and rested his elbows on the arms of the chair. "What I meant to say was —"

She waved her hand in the air to stop him. "Carlton Hillis. If you and I are going to be friends, then the least we can do is be honest with each other."

"Ah . . . then. What is this honesty you speak of?"

"First of all, my hair is like a — a — Brillo pad."

"Hyperbole doesn't look good on you, Miss Branch."

She leaned over. "And look at these teeth." She made a horsey face.

"I can't quite make them out." Carlton leaned back in his chair and shifted for comfort. "But I remember them. Front two. One laps a little over the other."

"Makes me look — bucktoothed!"

"I've seen bucktoothed. Boy who was in basic with me. That boy had the teeth of a mule, which you don't. Besides, it gives you character. What kind of person has perfect teeth anyway?"

"Claudette. Maeve. *You.*"

Carlton ran his index finger over his teeth. "Yep. Sure do, come to think of it. I am, therefore, a man without character."

Alice-Ann bit her bottom lip to keep from laughing. "And my face," she continued, wondering what he might have to say about her freckles.

"What's wrong with your face?"

"You can practically play connect the dots on my face."

"Again, hyperbole. A dash of freckles across the nose only serves to make you both cute and adorable."

Alice-Ann threw her hands up and flopped against the back of the sofa. *"Cute?* Three-year-old girls are *cute* and *adorable,* Carlton. Young women almost nineteen years of age don't want to be known as . . . *cute."* She sighed. "Or adorable."

The rhythm of Carlton's breathing came slow and easy, as though he pondered something beyond Alice-Ann's ability to reason. "So what happened that day?" he finally asked.

Alice-Ann stood, walked over to the window, and peered to the side street below, then across it to the bank, where she'd clocked out a short while earlier. Late-afternoon shadows rested against it, like a blanket pulled up for sleeping. "I have to get going. Nelson will be here soon."

He chuckled. "You're not going to answer me, are you?"

She returned to the sofa. "Your mama will be up here shortly, getting supper on the table." She sniffed. "I do believe I smell lima beans cooking on the stove."

"If we're lucky, with a ham bone."

She smiled. Weakly, she knew, but at least it was a smile. "Janie Wren also wrote to Mack since he signed up and . . . Janie Wren believes he *could* have survived because some football player did."

Carlton's face grew somber. "What? She thinks he was shot down in the Pacific and . . ." He shook his head. "What? That he was picked up by the Japs?"

"I reckon." She pondered it, not as long as she had in the past few weeks, but for a moment. "I suppose it *could* have happened. I know I've — I've prayed every single night that it would be so if it could be."

Something dark and foreboding slid across his face, and his eyes — five minutes ago full of mischief and teasing — grew dark. "If that's so, Alice-Ann, you'd better pray another way."

Unexplainable fear gushed over her. "What do you mean?"

Carlton looked down. "I still can't believe they let his location get past the censors."

"What do you mean?" Alice-Ann repeated again, as though the first question had been forgotten.

"He told you they were in Emirau. The censors should have caught that." He looked at the ceiling. "This whole thing. It's just a real mess."

Alice-Ann remembered the letter. The missing sections. "They cut out part of it. I think the part about what he'd be doing there."

"They should have cut the whole blame thing."

His eyes fixed on hers until finally she repeated her question, the one whose answer she feared the most. "What did you mean about me praying the other way?"

"The Japanese, sweetheart. They're —" he paused — "not . . . *kind* to their prisoners.

"*Not kind?* Can you be specific?"

Carlton shook his head again. But this time, had she not been staring at him, she would have missed it. "No," he said. "Even if the government can't censor all of it, *I* can."

Footsteps bounded up the stairs, and a moment later, Maeve rushed into the room, her hands working her hair into a ponytail. "Hey," she said with a grin, but then her face fell. "Hey," she said again, this time drawing the word out. "What's going on in here?"

Alice-Ann stood. "Nothing." She collected

her purse from the sofa. "We were just talking about the — the war, that's all."

Maeve frowned. "You're *supposed* to be making him feel better, Alice-Ann. Reading to him and stuff like that. Not making him relive the nightmares of war."

"I'm not —"

"Wait a minute, you two," Carlton interjected. He turned his face to his sister. "First of all, Maeve, I'm feeling just fine, thanks in part to Alice-Ann."

"But I —"

"No buts, little sister. Right now I'm having a conversation with *my* friend about something important to *her.*" He turned his face toward where Alice-Ann stood planted on the oval rag rug for which she and Maeve and Claudette had helped tear material . . . back when they'd been high school girls without a care in the world. "Sweetheart, listen to me." His voice held such tenderness and caring, Alice-Ann feared she'd begin to cry. "Are you listening?"

She nodded, then whispered, "Yes."

"You pray the way God leads you. I shouldn't have said anything."

Alice-Ann stepped to the chair, leaned over, and kissed his cheek, inhaling the light scent of aftershave. "No," she added. "I'm sure there's a lot about war I don't understand." She glanced at Maeve. "I mean, how are we to understand any of it, really? We've lived our part here on the home front — the blackout curtains, the rationing, the drills . . . but what do we know of what men like Carlton and — and Mack — have seen?"

Maeve crossed the room to gather Alice-Ann in her arms. "I'm sorry, Alice-Ann. Sometimes I forget what all this has cost you, too."

Alice-Ann opened her mouth to say more but then stopped herself. What good would it do, after all? "I have to go. Really." She glanced at the cuckoo clock that ticked from a three-tiered table. "I'll have to run now to make it."

Carlton reached for her hand, and as she'd done so often lately, she willingly gave it. "Are we okay?" he asked.

"We're more than okay," she answered with a squeeze. "But I really must go."

Chapter 18

The summer of '44 proved to be one of the most sweltering Alice-Ann could recall. Rain became a long-lost relative, the kind you appreciated seeing, but hoped didn't stick around for too long. Then, once gone, rain was the kinfolk you hoped would soon return. But again, not for long.

Farmers moaned during the drought — Papa and Nelson among them — while the women met each evening at the churches for prayer meetings. The men slammed their hats into the dusty dirt; the women bent their knees and beseeched the Creator.

Alice-Ann, Aunt Bess, and Irene were no exception, which meant long hours for Alice-Ann. Not that she felt like complaining about it. Everyone in the whole of the United States put in long hours — in the factories, on the farms, in offices, at home . . . the *where* hardly mattered. And in spite of the crush of Mack's most awful

255

death — and possible involvement with another woman — pride swelled deep in Alice-Ann's bosom at being part of a county within the state of Georgia whose citizens pulled together in their hard work and faith.

Throughout the summer months, in spite of the ranting and the prayers, God continued to hold back even so much as a drop of water in answer, but — remarkably — Carlton's improvement seemed the one miracle everyone in town managed to speak of with more frequency. He'd worked diligently through the exercise regimen designed by Doc Evans, finally making his way downstairs by early August and — with the aid of a cane and Alice-Ann's arm — out the door by midway through the month.

Bynum also buzzed with a rare form of gossip. Alice-Ann, the good citizens claimed, had been the tool God used to bring Carlton back to them, nearly in full. At times, the attention felt not only unearned, but embarrassing.

"After what you did for the Hillis boy," Miss Nola Whitney said to her at the A&P one morning when she'd run down during her work break to purchase a few items for Aunt Bess, "*this* is on Mr. Whitney and me."

Alice-Ann continued to extend the ration

stamps in her hand. "Oh, but I don't expect —"

Miss Nola shook her head adamantly. "No, ma'am," she said, her voice firm. "I won't take your stamps. It's no good here today. You'll just have to save them for later."

Alice-Ann sighed, wondering if it would be any good tomorrow. Or the days after. In the past few weeks, she'd been given free admission to a matinee, received a year's subscription to the local paper, and been nearly accosted on the sidewalk by Esther Lewen, who informed her that she could come into Lewen's Department Store at *any* time and pick out a new outfit, no charge. "Accessories, too," she'd said.

"But, Miss Nola . . ." Alice-Ann's eyes grew wide and she hoped the grocery store owner could see her true feelings on the subject. "I didn't *do* anything that anyone else wouldn't have or couldn't have done."

Miss Nola snapped a paper bag open and began filling it with the unpurchased items. "Really, now? And just how many folks went to see our Carlton every day? Reading to him after long hours at work?" She slid the bag over the counter toward Alice-Ann. "And I know you had plenty to do once you got home. Bess told me how you always help out in the house and how you work with your daddy on Saturdays. I don't know how you've done it, Alice-Ann, but you are a fine example to us all."

Alice-Ann scooped the bag into her arms. "Well . . . all right. But just this once, Miss Nola." She took a few steps backward to the front door, which — like most storefront doors in the middle of the heat wave — had been left open. "Because, really . . . I didn't do anything *that* special."

"You were the mouth of the good Lord, is what you were, Alice-Ann." She nodded her chin once to affirm her statement.

Her words caused Alice-Ann to pause. "What do you mean?"

"Don't you see? The good Lord Jesus called you, Alice-Ann. He needed someone to go over and give that young man a reason to keep going. And you? You gave him friendship."

She'd never considered — not for a moment — that she'd done anything because of a "calling," the same term her pastor had used.

"You were *called* by the Lord to help that young man," he'd told her one Sunday between the Sunday school hour and the church service. Even then, she'd opened her mouth to protest, then clamped it shut. If Aunt Bess caught wind of her remotely arguing with Reverend Parker . . . *well.* God might have spared Jonah from the belly of the whale, but Aunt Bess wouldn't be so generous.

Still . . . could it be? Could God's calling be as simple as being a friend to someone in need? Even when it seemed pleasant and not at all difficult? Wasn't a "calling" like what she'd read about in their church's missionary report? Selling all her worldly goods and moving to faraway, ungodly places?

The truth was, she'd done what she'd done because she'd always *liked* Carlton. He'd been an "older brother" to her — unlike Mack, who'd held her heart in his hand. Even now, she felt an easy kinship with him. Their talk, light at times. Confidential at others.

Such as that Saturday the twelfth, during a short walk around the corner to Cooper Street, down to the first block of residential houses, when he'd given her the details of how he'd been injured. That he was the furthest thing from a hero.

"I got in the way, is what I did," he said, his chin near his chest. "That's the one thing they reiterated when we were learning cinematography."

They walked slowly, her on the inside of the sidewalk, him keeping pace with his cane. He wore dark sunglasses — he said his eyes were still sensitive to the light — so she couldn't read what lay beneath them. But his left hand held on to her right forearm and it squeezed as he spoke.

"Cinematography," she repeated. "Such a big word."

"Don't get in the way of the tanks." Carlton's voice mimicked a low-speaking figure of authority. "Don't get in the way of the soldiers with guns. Don't get in the way . . . *don't get in the way.*" He paused, bringing her to a stop as well. She shifted, bringing her hands to his forearm, holding on to him for a change, and felt the flexing of muscles growing stronger every day.

Carlton began walking again and she fell into step beside him. "So you got in the way?"

"Yeah." He turned his face toward her, then back to the sidewalk, which — as they got closer to the tiny shotgun houses on the edge of town — became edged with weedy grass between the slabs.

Out of an old childhood habit, she attempted to stay off the cracks.

"Don't tell anyone," he said. His voice lay quiet. Sad. "Okay, doodlebug?"

"I won't," she said.

"I don't know what they think really happened over there. My dad especially. Mama . . . she doesn't ask." He smiled a half smile. "You know mamas."

"Not really, no."

He stopped again and looked at her. "Oh, Alice-Ann. I didn't mean . . ."

She shook her head and smiled at him. "It's okay. I shouldn't have said — I've got Aunt Bess. She's been like a mama to me all these years."

"Your mama," he said, looking at her. "I remember her as being something real special."

"She was." From what she could remember.

"Like mother, like daughter."

Heat rushed to her face. "Now don't you start," she muttered.

He looked over his shoulder. "It's getting warm," he said.

"Warm?" she laughed. "It's downright sweltering out here."

"Ready to head back?"

"Are you?" she asked.

He nodded. "Cooper Street is downhill from the store. But —" He turned and she did too. "Uphill on the way home."

Alice-Ann giggled lightly. "Makes sense."

He looked down at her — him being a head taller than she, even on the days she wore heels — and grinned. "Remember the day Nelson and I taught you and Maeve how to ride bicycles on this hill?"

Did she ever. She had skinned knees for a week, something Aunt Bess and Papa had nearly *skinned* Nelson over. "Papa said if you boys wanted to show me and Maeve how to ride bikes, you should have done it out at the farm, where we had soft sand for concrete."

"Soft sand for con— ?" He laughed. "Yeah, I remember he gave me and Nelson a good talking to that next week."

They neared the corner. "But we learned how to ride, didn't we?"

"Yes, ma'am, you did."

A welcome breeze came from a passing vehicle. Balmy, but welcome.

"A couple of bloody knees never hurt anyone."

"No, ma'am. I reckon not."

They rounded the bend and came to the true beginning of town. "Tired?" she asked.

He shrugged. "I think I could make it across the street to the soda shop for a root beer float."

The thought made her taste buds dance. "Sounds good to me."

He stopped, propped his cane against the glass pane of the five-and-dime, and patted his front pants pocket. "I've got a pocketful of change, so we're good."

"Trust me, your dime isn't worth a nickel," Alice-Ann noted.

Carlton stuck his head in the door of the store to call out to his mother. "Heading over to the soda shop."

Mrs. Hillis hurried to the door. "You're not too tired?"

Carlton blushed. "No, Mama. I'm good."

She turned her attention to Alice-Ann. "Don't let him get too tired."

"I won't."

"Or overheated."

"No, ma'am."

Carlton took a step away from his mother. "Come on, Alice-Ann."

Alice-Ann smiled at the worried face of his mother, hoping to ease her concerns. But if she'd been successful, Mrs. Hillis's face showed no trace of it.

Every few yards they stopped, mainly so that Carlton could speak to the townspeople who were running their Saturday errands. Those who wished him well. Who wanted to slap him on the back or pat his cheek. Those who wanted to let him know they were proud of him or were praying for him.

Still.

Now, knowing what she knew, Alice-Ann

was able to read the expression on Carlton's face. She understood the depth of what he must have been through those months of rehabilitation, and her heart twisted around itself.

The police chief — Herbert Monaghan — happened to come out of the A&P at the same time as they reached the crosswalk. "Hold up there," he called, then all but trotted out into the street, stopping traffic so they could cross.

"This is getting embarrassing," Carlton mumbled to her, though he thanked Chief Monaghan kindly after they reached the other side of Main Street.

"Nothing's too good for you, Carlton," he said, rolling his beefy shoulder. "Or you, Miss Branch."

Carlton patted her hand. "Or you, Miss Branch," he teased, low enough that only she could hear.

"Everyone acts like *I'm* some sort of hero."

He shuffled to a stop. Pulled the sunglasses to the tip of his nose and blinked at her over the dark rim as his right side leaned heavily on the cane. "You are."

Alice-Ann shook her head. "I'm not, really."

He took several breaths through his nostrils, his chest rising and falling evenly. "You have no idea, do you?"

Alice-Ann tilted her head. "What?"

"You're very special, Alice-Ann."

"So everyone keeps telling me. But honestly, Carlton. I've *enjoyed* talking with you and reading to you. I've —" She rested her fingertips against the hollow of her throat, but she couldn't go on. Not out in front of the soda shop. Not with the heat rising off the sidewalk, curling around their feet, even under the shade of the still awnings.

"You've . . . ?"

She looked at the soda shop window, the specials painted in large white letters on it, along with Coca-Cola war-bonds posters. "Let's go inside. Get something to drink. I'm parched."

"And then you'll tell me? Promise?"

She nodded, knowing she would. Because if there was one person Alice-Ann knew she could confide in during these days, it was Carlton Hillis.

Inside, after several minutes of backslapping and welcoming, they found a quiet booth near the back. Ernie brought two root beer floats to the table and then, unexpectedly, took a seat next to Carlton. He hunched his shoulders and turned his face to Maeve's older brother. "Hey, Carlton, I need to ask you something real quick before my dad starts yelling at me to get back behind the counter."

Carlton slid his glass closer to the edge of the table and pulled the tall spoon from the rich goodness of its contents. "What's that?"

Ernie exchanged a glance between Alice-Ann and Carlton. "You two going to the wedding?"

The wedding. Other than Carlton's healing, which was miraculous, and the lack of rain, Claudette's upcoming nuptials had practically been the only thing folks talked about. By now, everyone knew the two lovebirds were completely lost in each other, anxiously anticipating the wedding day, disregarding Miss Nell's insistence that they wait until the war's end.

Of course the bride had asked Maeve and Alice-Ann to be her bridesmaids, and they'd been happy to oblige. Aunt Bess had promised to sew the dresses for the two of them, plus one for Claudette's favorite cousin, Beulah, who hailed from Statesboro. September would bring teas and bridal showers throughout with a late-month wedding planned for what Claudette insisted would be a perfect autumn day.

"You mean together?" Carlton now asked, bringing a spoonful of ice cream to his mouth.

Ernie blushed as heat spread across Alice-Ann's cheeks. "I'm a bridesmaid," she said quickly, then wished she'd kept her mouth closed or full of root beer. She reached for a straw from the tabletop holder and stuck it into her glass. "What I mean to say is —" she raised her eyes to Carlton, who grinned in her direction — "I *have* to be there." Alice-Ann sighed as she brought her lips to the tip of the straw.

"I'll be there too," Carlton said. "My *sister* is a bridesmaid as well."

If his words hadn't held such mirth, Alice-Ann would have kicked both him and Ernie under the table.

"The reason I ask . . ." Ernie's shoulders hunched a little higher. "Carlton, I'm wanting to — I mean, after the right period of time — I'm wanting to ask Maeve."

Carlton sat up so straight and so suddenly, Alice-Ann feared his spine would snap. "To the wedding? I assumed you'd be her date, Ern." He jabbed at the ice cream, mushing it into the root beer.

A new shade of red dashed across his face. "Uh, no. What I mean is — I want to ask her to —" his voice lowered a notch — "to marry me."

Carlton released the spoon and it stood at attention, albeit briefly, before easing to the side of the glass. "Excuse me?"

"But I need to know what your father will think about it."

Alice-Ann willed her own lips back together as she studied Carlton's face.

"Never mind what her *father* has to say," he answered. "Right now, you'd better be more worried about her big brother."

Genuine shock registered on Ernie's face and he straightened. "What? You don't like me? But I thought you *liked* me. I thought we were pals."

"I do like you, Ern," Carlton said. "I just don't know if I'm ready for my baby sister to get married."

"But — but — we're in *love.*"

His words slid over Alice-Ann. Gently, at first. Then as a painful grip.

Maeve and Ernie were in love. Maeve had never told her. Sure, the two had been sweet on each other and dated since high school, but — *in love?* Why hadn't Maeve confided in her?

First Claudette. Then Maeve. And Mack — her one true love — at the bottom of the ocean.

Alice-Ann pushed her root beer float an inch away from her.

"Bob's your uncle," she whispered aloud, not meaning to.

"Whatcha say, Alice-Ann?" Ernie said. "I don't have an uncle named Bob."

Carlton smiled at her and her thoughts returned to the conversation at hand. "It's a British saying," he told Ernie. "It means 'and that's that.' " He looked across the soda shop to the counter. "Your pop is glaring at you, Ern. You'd best get back to work."

Ernie slid out of the booth, his focus remaining on Carlton. "But will you at least think about it?" he asked.

Carlton winked at Alice-Ann, letting her know he'd been stringing poor Ernie along all the while. "I'll think about it," he said. He looked up at Ernie. "I suspect you'd best come up with a plan, though, boy. You can't work behind that counter the rest of your life and expect to support my sister in the way she deserves."

Alice-Ann followed Carlton's gaze to Ernie, who saluted the hometown hero. "Yes, sir," he said, snapping his heels together, then turning on them.

Carlton shook his head slowly. "Bob's your uncle, huh? I can't believe you remembered that."

Alice-Ann grabbed the spoon in her glass and made the same slicing motions Carlton had a few moments before. "I remember," she said.

Carlton pulled a straw from the holder. "Now, about that promise you made on the sidewalk . . ."

CHAPTER 19

"Maeve came to the bank after you returned from Europe. She asked me to come see you. To read to you. But you know all that, I'm sure."

"I do know, yes. She told me." Carlton picked up his glass and took a sip of frothy root beer. "If I remember correctly, you came over that first day." He raised a brow. "Oh, let's see . . . about the same time as Betty Jo came over."

Alice-Ann pursed her lips. "Yes. Betty Jo."

He raised a finger. "Betty Jo, who, from what I've heard, is dating —"

"Milton Hawkins," they said together.

Carlton scratched at his neck. "The grammar school principal."

"He's a nice enough man," she said, swallowing back her own displeasure at the thought.

He raised the straw in his glass to his lips. "Old enough to be her father."

Alice-Ann shook her head and giggled. "Uncle, maybe."

"It's creepy."

She rested her elbow on the table, her chin on the pad of her hand. "Jealous?"

He returned the glass to the table, where it thunked. "Not even remotely." Carlton rested against the back of his seat. "I'm actually glad I found out what she was made of." He shook his head. "She didn't even stick around to see if I'd recover or not."

No, she hadn't, and the thought of the hurt Carlton must have felt pinched at her own feelings. "Well," Alice-Ann said with a grin, "she was always flighty."

His eyes met hers and held — something Alice-Ann found he seemed to be good at, especially since losing his sight and regaining it. As though he'd learned something while blind about studying people, about looking into their eyes to see the true meaning of their words, the depths of their emotions. Their true emotions.

"Thank you for that," he said. Then, leaning in, he added, "Now, back to *your* — what shall we call it? — devotion to me."

Devotion. Maybe she had been devoted to him. But then again, maybe he'd — "I really didn't think about it much," she said. "I mean, about the reading to you. About coming over. It seemed the right thing to do and so I — I did." She sighed. "Then, when we heard about Mack, I — I didn't want to come back."

His brow furrowed. "Well, this is a fine how-do-you-do. Why ever not?"

Alice-Ann shrugged. "I don't know. I guess I felt that . . . if Mack was dead, then what was the point? But then Nancy made me feel just awful about it."

He shot her a half smile as if he wasn't sure whether her words made him happy or concerned. "Good ole Nancy. So how'd she manage that? This guilt?"

"I . . . Remember the cottage I told you about? The one next door to where she and Harry live?"

"I do. You promised to take me there — which you *haven't,* by the way — if I promised to work hard on learning to walk again — which I *have,* by the way."

Alice-Ann waved a hand at him. "Stop changing the subject." She sighed. "I said I would and I will — but I didn't say *when.*"

Carlton laughed. "Oh. Good point. Continue on, then."

She bit back a smile. "Well, Nancy said I cared more about — or had more compassion for — that old house than I did for a human being. That she couldn't understand how the same person could be so concerned about one and ignore the other." She shrugged again. "Or something like that." Alice-Ann shoveled ice cream into her mouth as Carlton shook his head in mirth. "But the truth is, Carlton, when I went back to see you, when I filled my hours, really, with making sure you were doing well, and I wasn't spending all my time lamenting over losing Mack, I — well, in many ways you did as much for me as I did for you."

He reached across the table and took her hand. She thought to jerk it away — the last thing she needed was the folks in town thinking she and Carlton Hillis had a different kind of relationship than friendship. But she didn't. She allowed his to rest over hers, protectively. "Thank you for that," he said when he finally spoke.

"For what?"

"For telling me the truth. For trusting me with it."

"You've — in many ways, Carlton, you've become my best friend."

He sat back again, his face registering surprise. "Even more so than Maeve?"

"Well . . . I tell Maeve things I could never tell — I mean —"

"Me? There are things you could never tell me?"

274

"Of course."

"Because I'm a man?"

She nodded.

"But lately," she confided, "I find myself telling you things I'd never think to tell Maeve. Not because I can't trust her, but more that I'm not sure she'd find any of it at all . . . *interesting.*"

"Like what?"

She finished off the float before she answered. "You know. About world events. Politics. The camp over in Bulloch and all that and how — even though I feel kinda bad for them — not being able to go home, you know — they sure have made our lives a lot easier." She shuddered to think what might have happened had Adler not been at the farm the day Nelson and Irene's baby had been born. "I can tell you that they're not *all* bad, and you don't judge me. You understand, I think, what they've come to mean to us."

"I don't think Maeve would understand," Alice-Ann continued, "when I say that Aunt Bess really enjoys feeding them and that Papa likes hearing what the English-speaking ones have to say and that, during lunchtime sitting out under the pecan trees, they teach Irene lullabies from their country so she can sing them to the baby."

"They've been good for the farmers, for sure. And you can bet we're treating them better than the Nazis treat our boys."

"I think you're right. One of them told Papa they get paid fifty cents a day in credits, and with the credits they can buy things at the camp, like special treats and tobacco. And Papa also says they're good workers. Not afraid to put in the hours."

Carlton's eyes scanned the restaurant before coming back to her. "I'd be willing to bet that before the war most of 'em were just hardworking boys like Nelson and me."

"And Mack," she blurted, somewhat surprised he hadn't included his friend.

He laughed. "Oh, come on, Alice-Ann. Mack never worked a hard day in his life."

Her skin prickled and she slid her hand out from under his. "What do you mean by that remark, Carlton Hillis?"

He glanced at where their hands had been, then pulled his back. "Look, I loved the boy like a brother. But he enjoyed being — I don't know — *Mack*. He didn't want to go to college, although I think he would have after the war, just to continue whatever party he thought might be happening there. He didn't want to take over his father's work at the pharmacy. If you asked him about his plans for the future, he usually

276

made some off-the-wall comment about living in the present. Gee, Alice-Ann, I'm not even sure Mack *knew* what he wanted to do or be when *or if* he ever grew up."

Alice-Ann's heart tore in half, one part knowing that what Carlton said was truth; the other wanting to defend the dead. "He said — when he wrote — that he liked flying. Liked the way it made him feel. I kinda thought he would continue with that after the war. When he came home. Maybe."

Carlton studied her for a long minute before asking, "Do you still think he's alive?"

Alice-Ann shook her head before considering the question, which surprised her. "No. Not me, I don't guess. It's Janie Wren who thinks he's still alive."

"But she gave you hope, didn't she?"

Janie had. Yes. But Carlton had just as quickly dashed it. "Maybe. For a minute. But then you said — well, you know what you said."

"Yeah. I know." He sighed, the air laced with regret. "I'm getting tired."

"We'd better head back then. I don't want to get on the wrong side of your mama."

"No, ma'am, you do *not.*"

She started to slide out of the booth, but he reached for her hand again.

"Alice-Ann," he said, his eyes gazing into hers in that way he had. "Thank you."

"You've already thanked me, Carlton."

"No. Thank you for saying I'm your best friend. That means a lot to me. Really."

"Oh. Well. Okay."

"I guess you're my best friend, too, if grown men are allowed to be best friends with their kid sister's girlfriend."

"Even if she's a clunky-looking girl like me?"

He shot her a half grin, this one full of tenderness. "Even if she's a clunky-looking, *beautiful* young woman . . . like you."

Alice-Ann glanced around, mainly for something to do other than to continue looking into Carlton's eyes, which held something new now . . . something she'd never seen before, at least not aimed at her. She spotted Ernie, wiping down the counter in wide circular motions. Alice-Ann smiled, thinking of his asking Carlton before asking Mr. Hillis's permission to propose marriage.

When she looked back at Carlton, she found him studying Ernie as well. "She's not a kid anymore, Carlton," she said with a smile, drawing his attention back to her. "She's a grown woman. Ready for love and, apparently, marriage."

"Yes, ma'am, she is," he said, his voice

soft and gracious. "Question is . . . what does that make you, doodlebug?"

What did that make her, indeed?

Her two best friends — Claudette and Maeve — both either heading down the aisle or about to become engaged. Nelson and Irene, new parents. Even Papa and Aunt Bess seemed to have found their places in life, in spite of the world's circumstances. Papa clucked around the farm like a rooster in a henhouse all protective over his flock, and Aunt Bess practically glowed, what with having so many new mouths to feed.

"I tried out Mama's pear salad on the prisoners," she said one afternoon, as though she'd had Bynum's finest ladies out for tea. "They really seemed to like it, especially that Adler. Boy, he sure can put some groceries away."

Now, sitting across the bench seat from Nelson, Alice-Ann shook her head, pondering the question again.

"What does that make you, doodlebug?"
She sighed.

"Nelson?" Alice-Ann eyed her brother. His wrist rested against the top of the steering wheel, and with his wide-brimmed hat pulled low over his eyes, he looked every bit

279

as handsome as Mr. Henry Fonda in *The Grapes of Wrath.*

"Hmm?" Nelson kept his watch on the road, never once breaking to look over at her.

"If I ask you a question, will you answer me honestly?"

With that, he looked, pursing his lips before turning back. "Whatcha got going on inside that head of yours, Alice-Ann?"

"Do you think I'm — you know — pretty?"

Nelson applied his foot to the brake as he shifted the truck into a lower gear, then turned the steering wheel hard to the left. "What in the world?"

Her shoulders slumped. "I know. I'm not." A large insect flew into the cab — she had no idea what kind and didn't bother to ask — and she batted it back out.

Nelson increased speed, shifted the truck back into a higher gear, and shook his head. "Alice-Ann, what kind of fool question is that to ask your own brother?"

Alice-Ann shoved her arms across her middle. "I'm only asking for honesty. I'd think that of all the people in the world, you'd be honest with me."

"Why don't you ask questions like that to Aunt Bess or Pop?"

She shifted in the seat, felt the sweat along the backs of her thighs slide between her skin and the simple, A-shaped cotton skirt she'd so diligently picked out that morning. "Because Aunt Bess will remind me that folks say I look an awful lot like her — which may or may not be a compliment, I'm not sure — and Papa will tell me I'm the prettiest girl he knows, which we both know is a lie only a father could say to his daughter and get away with it."

Nelson chuckled. "Yeah. You're right about that."

She waited. When he continued to stare out the bug- and dust-sprayed windshield, she cleared her throat. "Well?"

"Honestly?"

No, lie to me . . . like Carlton did earlier. Because surely he had. "Yes."

"No, I wouldn't call you *pretty.*"

She frowned. "I didn't think so."

He smiled at her to soften the blow. "You have a beautiful spirit, though."

Alice-Ann cocked a brow. "You're just saying that because you're my brother."

"No, I'm not. I mean it. Seriously. Irene's even said so. And so has Aunt Bess and Papa —"

"And Carlton."

Nelson's smile became a grin. "He did,

281

did he? Ole Carlton told you that?"

"Well, he said I'm beautiful — and I quote — 'in my own right.' And today he said I was a beautiful, clunky-looking girl." She looked out the windshield. Beyond them, across the horizon, a lightning show began — flashes of bright light she recalled her mama saying was God turning his porch lights off and on. Telling folks to come on inside.

Maybe, oh, maybe it would rain.

Nelson shifted the gears again to take the final turn up the long driveway. "Is Carlton sweet on you, Alice-Ann?"

"Sweet on me?" The very thought. "For pity's sake, don't go startin' rumors."

He laughed heartily. "Oh, good heavenly day. You and Carlton? I guess I'd better have a talk with the boy."

Alice-Ann jabbed him with her index finger. "Oh no, you don't. And he's *not* sweet on me. We're just good friends."

"Uh-huh."

This time, she punched him with her fist. "I mean it, Nelson." Alice-Ann wondered if her face had turned pure scarlet or merely a nice pale shade of red. "I will *kill* you if you keep this up." He laughed harder. "I will personally beat you black-and-blue."

Nelson threw his head back. "Ha! With

what army?"

She shoved her arms together again as their home came into view. "Hush."

The truck bounded along the ruts until Nelson brought it to a stop, turned off the engine, and then turned to face her. "Listen to me, little sister."

Alice-Ann kept her face straight ahead.

"Are you listening?"

"No."

He chuckled. "I'm just giving you a hard time." He grabbed a strand of her untamed hair and tugged. "Where'd all this come from? Seriously."

Now she turned to face him. A mosquito buzzed around her ear and she swatted, then cranked the window up. "Claudette's getting married and — don't tell anyone, please — but Ernie is going to ask Maeve as soon as Claudette and Johnny tie the knot and . . ." A small lump formed in her throat. *And Mack is dead, unless you listen to the likes of Janie Wren . . . and I don't even know if he wrote to her in the same confidential way as he wrote to me and . . .*

"And?"

"And well . . . I guess sometimes I wonder if there will ever be someone for a girl like me. Someone who obviously missed the formation line when God handed out good

283

looks and grace and charm and all.”

“Ah, I see.” Nelson rolled up the driver’s window. “Alice-Ann, you’re still young. And when the war is over and the boys come back home . . . Well, don’t rush it. You know, because you think the pickings are slim or something.”

She tipped her chin toward her chest, felt the tears stinging the backs of her eyes, then raised her chin to look at her brother. “Is it awful of me to *not* want to end up like Aunt Bess? I mean, I love you, Nelson, and I adore that baby of yours, and Irene and I are getting along okay, but I don’t want to think I might end up one day being your housekeeper or something.”

He laughed again, low and easy. “I don’t think there’s much chance of that happening.” He pulled on the handle and popped the door with his shoulder to open it.

She did the same, then slid out of the cab, where the cooler — if only by two degrees — air wrapped around her like a wool blanket. They walked to the front of the truck, where he slung his arm across her shoulder and pulled her to himself, strong and protective. “Are you going to be okay? Really, now?”

Who knew? “Yeah.”

“Good to hear.” They took a few more

steps, his arm still lying heavy on her shoulders. "Meanwhile, little sis," he said, stepping away from her and smiling, "don't rule out ole Carlton —"

"Nelson!"

" 'Cause he ain't a bad catch. You know, as far as city boys go."

CHAPTER 20

As ifNelson ribbing her about Carlton were not enough, she dreamed of him that night.

They walked along Main Street, him without his cane, toward Nancy and Harry's bungalow-style home, next to the cottage Alice-Ann had so often through the years thought to be one of the most adorable she'd ever seen.

In spite of the fact that it needed work.

And had been the scene of a mythological murder.

As they walked, they spoke to each other about deep and important things. In her sleep, Alice-Ann couldn't make out the words but rather felt the truth of them inside her spirit. They laughed easily, often poking fun without being hurtful. In the dream, Alice-Ann had been in a deep and caring friendship with Carlton her whole life, rather than only the few months since his return to Bynum. She couldn't manage to remember life before him and couldn't imagine a future life without him.

They neared the cottage, and as always, Alice-Ann paid attention to her feet in an effort to keep them off the horizontal cracks in the sidewalk. *Step on a crack,* she said, slipping her hand into Carlton's and linking their fingers, *break your mother's back.*

A scream caught her unaware and she jerked. Carlton stopped, his body rigid, his arm coming around her protectively. *It's the murderer,* he said. *Stay with me and you'll be safe.*

Alice-Ann looked up at him sharply. *You said it was all campfire stories . . .*

Stories come from somewhere, Alice-Ann, he said, the focus of his eyes never leaving the house. *Most of the time there is a layer of truth in there, if you just look hard enough.*

She followed his gaze, molding herself into him as she'd seen Irene do with Nelson. The front door burst open and a man staggered out, then turned toward them.

Mack!

He stood straight. He waved and she waved back, thinking to run to him and to thank God as she did so that he was alive indeed. But Carlton's firm grip held her in place. *Stay with me, Alice-Ann. Stay with me and you'll be safe.*

I told you. The voice came from behind. *I told you, Alice-Ann.*

Alice-Ann and Carlton turned to see Janie Wren standing there, looking like Miss America, her hair perfectly coiffed, her makeup expertly in place as though she were a cover girl in one of the magazines next to the counter at MacKay's.

I told you, she continued, *that he was still alive. Just like Tom Harmon. He's a war hero, our Mack. Such a dashing war hero.*

Alice-Ann looked again at Mack, who remained on the porch, waving. *Alice-Ann,* he called. *Don't be afraid of me, Alice-Ann. It was all just a story . . . about the murder . . . and the war . . . and the airplane.*

But even as he said the words, the vision of him faded. Desperate, she pulled herself free of Carlton. *Mack . . . I'm coming. Stay right there. Don't leave me. Not again, Mack! Not —*

Stay with me, Alice-Ann, Carlton continued to beg, rushing to catch up to her and grabbing at her arm. *Stay with me and be safe.*

Such a dashing war hero, Janie repeated. *So handsome and brave. Just like Tom Harmon.*

Alice-Ann struggled free of Carlton,

rushed toward the cottage, and turned her head to look back at Janie and Carlton, then again to Mack, who grew fainter as she drew closer. She stopped. *Mack, no! Don't leave me again!*

Oh no . . . Janie's voice caught her attention, and again she turned to see the young woman pointing at Alice-Ann's feet. *You stepped on a crack . . .*

Alice-Ann looked down. She wore the shoes Aunt Bess had purchased for her sixteenth birthday party. Had she been wearing them before? She didn't think so.

Not that it mattered.

She'd stepped on the crack.

Alice-Ann woke with a start, sitting straight up. Sweat drenched her face, her back, and the sheets around her. She glanced at the open window, where the oscillating fan rested on the sill, rotating slowly, and into the gray darkness beyond. With the blackout shades pulled to just above the top of the fan, the room lay in shadows.

She blinked. The scent of rain lingered in the air. She pushed the damp sheets from her body, swung her legs over the edge of the mattress, and pattered to the window, where she sat on the floor and peered out. Light from the full moon had managed to break through the thick clouds rolling over its face, casting veiled light over the farm.

A memory tickled her. She and Mack, standing on the long driveway. Her, all of sixteen. Him, so handsome and about to leave Bynum. Leave to fight for his country. He had encouraged her to sing the song her mother had taught her, and she had.

" 'Moon, moon,' " she now whispered the words, speaking rather than singing. " 'So full and round. Moon, moon . . . don't fall down. Stay where you are, right by that star, until moon, moon . . . my love is found.' " She squeezed her eyes together. *"Mack . . ."*

Alice-Ann tucked her feet under her as she switched off the fan, then set it on the floor. For a moment she thought of going downstairs to sit in her mama's chair, then changed her mind. These days, so much as a creak in the house would wake Papa and he'd wonder if she'd lost her mind. So instead she stuck her face as close to the screen as possible and sniffed. The promise of rain blended with the smell of dust and dirt, of tobacco and corn and peanuts. "Oh, Father, please," she prayed. "We need rain."

And what better day for it than on a Sunday.

Growing warm again, she turned the fan back on, adjusting it so that it stopped oscillating and stayed pointed on her. Still wet from sweating in her sleep, her skin turned to gooseflesh. She shifted, pressed her back against the wall, then stretched her legs, pointed her toes, felt the pull along the backs of her legs, and counted the number of breaths she took.

Seven . . . eight . . . nine . . .

"Is he alive?" she whispered, hoping God could hear her over the prayers of the millions she knew had to be lifted to him at that very moment. Especially with the war affecting the entire world. "Is that why I dreamed about Mack? Because you're trying to tell me he's still alive?"

Alice-Ann rested her head against the floral-papered wall and felt the edge of the windowsill dig into her temple. She tilted her chin upward, waiting for the tears she knew would inevitably fall.

Then, as though God had both heard and answered, the thought skipped across her mind — interrupting all thoughts of Mack — that she'd also dreamed of Carlton.

Stay with me . . . , he'd begged her.

She shook her head. The whole thing was silly. She wasn't *with* Carlton, so how could she possibly *stay* with him?

But then, why had she dreamed such a thing?

"Nelson," she said. "I should box his ears." She would, too, if he weren't bigger and older than her.

Surely he'd been the culprit. All this nonsense talk about her and Carlton Hillis. About giving him a chance.

Carlton, of all people. Her . . . well, the man who had become her best friend, really.

Alice-Ann stood, carefully returned the fan to the windowsill, then thought better of it. What with so much time passing without even a sprinkle, *should* it rain, it would no doubt be a gully washer. The last thing she needed was water in an electric fan. *That* would certainly be the cherry on her ice cream sundae.

She crossed the room slowly to keep from stubbing a toe, picked up the chair at her desk and carried it near the window, cautious not to place it too close. After setting the fan on the seat, she ambled back to bed, felt the mattress rock beneath her, and lay back, pushing the sheet to the edge with her feet. A ragged breath caught in her chest and she sighed.

Alice-Ann closed her eyes, willing herself to return to sleep. To hopefully wake to the sound of rain splattering against the house. *Carlton Hillis.*

The name brought an unexpected smile

to her lips. She sighed one more time, then slipped into a new dream.

The rain didn't let up for days. Thunder rolled with only a little lightning to accompany it. But water fell by the buckets in large drops that, at first, kicked up the dry earth, then muddied it.

By the fourth day, Papa had gone from praising God to muttering under his breath again about devastation to the crops. The long driveway to the main road had all but washed away, keeping Alice-Ann home. Without a phone, she'd been unable to call Mister Dooley, but she had an idea he knew where she was and why.

She missed being at work. She missed the smell of it — the aroma of marble and number 2 pencils, of ink and coffee and Mister Dooley's cigars. She wanted to talk with Nancy. To share small talk between customers. She even missed the customers, most of whom provided fodder for the talk with Nancy as long as Miss Portia didn't catch them at it.

And Alice-Ann ached — literally ached — to see Carlton again. She hardly meant to. In fact, she spent most of Tuesday and a good part of Wednesday morning talking herself out of such nonsense. Convincing herself that in her days stuck at the farm he had probably not missed her, not one iota. She even read over a few of Mack's letters in an effort to stop all the wild imaginings swirling around in her head. But when they only brought a sense of impending doom — holding and rereading letters written by a dead man — she retrieved the few Carlton had written to her from Europe, only to find herself laughing at his words and his sense of humor.

Not to mention his timing.

To make matters nearly unbearable during those long, wet days, Little Mack, as they'd taken to calling the baby, had become fussy and inconsolable.

"He's not any happier than his old grandpa," Papa said, rising from his chair at the kitchen table, where he'd just finished off a glass of sweet iced tea. "Here, Irene. Give 'im to me and you go on upstairs and see what Nelson's up to." He took the child from Irene, who sighed in relief before leaving the kitchen.

Alice-Ann shook her head in wonder as her father and his grandson headed out the screen door. She imagined they shuffled to a back porch rocker, where somehow he managed to soothe the child to silence. Or maybe the sound of rain against the tin roof had simply drowned the little tyke out.

"Come on, Alice," Aunt Bess said, drawing her from her misery at the kitchen table to where her aunt stood at the counter, arms crossed over a faded bib apron. One hand held a wooden spoon, probably the same one she used to threaten her niece and nephew countless times in their younger, more mischievous days. "I got some berries that are in need of a good pie to come home to."

Alice-Ann smiled as she pushed herself up from the table.

Aunt Bess dropped her arms from the roll across her middle. "Land sakes, you act like you're sixty instead of twenty."

Alice-Ann stood upright. "What do you mean?" she asked, sliding the chair under the table.

"The way you practically hoisted yourself up. Like an old woman with the rheumatiz."

Alice-Ann laughed. "You're right. I suppose I just have a lot on my mind these days, and I'm letting it wear me down."

"Now, don't you worry any about the money you're not making stuck out here these last few days."

Alice-Ann nodded. "I admit it's been on my mind." Not as much as Mack and Carlton, but wondering how she'd make up for the money she was losing had hovered around her thoughts. She smiled. "But I'm sure making a pie will help. What do you need me to do first?"

"Go into the pantry and get me my baking tins."

"Yes, ma'am."

She crossed the linoleum floor that nearly sparkled after Aunt Bess's most recent attack, complete with mop and a bucket of hot water and vinegar, earlier that morning. The strong aroma of the mixture lingered, wrestling near the door with the stink of farm animals and earth unleashed by days of rain.

Alice-Ann paused on the way to the pantry, listening to the gentle voice of her father as he spoke to his only grandchild. She tilted her head, pondering as to whether or not she could remember hearing him talk to her in such a tone when she'd been a little girl.

She could not, and as much as that fact hurt, Little Mack had quieted, and for that she was grateful.

"And when you get old enough, we'll get you out there about this time of the year and you can help us bag those peanuts."

Alice-Ann leaned closer to the screen,

wanting to hear more. Wishing, for the briefest of moments, that she could crawl onto her father's lap — an act she had no real memory of — and be an unobtrusive member of the conversation. "Now, some of the peanuts we sell and some we keep. We'll bring the ones we keep up to the house and Aunt Bess will wash 'em good and then she'll boil 'em."

Alice-Ann smiled, thinking of the days she'd helped Papa and Nelson pull peanuts. How she'd assisted Aunt Bess in the kitchen later. How the whole family watched in anticipation as Papa took a spoon, scooped a peanut out of the simmering salty water, cracked it open, and tested it for the right texture. "Another few minutes," he'd say, time and again, until — finally — "Yep. Just right. Let's eat."

"And you ain't lived," he continued between the pattering raindrops, "until you've had some boiled peanuts, salted just right. Let me just go ahead and school you right now . . ."

"What in the world are you listening to out there?" Aunt Bess's question caused her to turn. To step away from the door for fear of being found out as an eavesdropper.

She shook her head. "Papa's talking about being a peanut farmer," she whispered.

"And Little Mack is so quiet, I guess he's considering it."

Aunt Bess grinned. "Little boy's got ambition. I can tell that already."

Alice-Ann sighed as she started again for the pantry.

"Which is a good sight more than his namesake," Aunt Bess finished.

Alice-Ann stopped and turned. "What do you mean?" she asked, crossing the room for her aunt's answer. The last thing she needed was a conversation about Mack broadcast to the porch or up the stairs.

Aunt Bess had exchanged the wooden spoon for a small paring knife. Two small Fiesta bowls — one filled with unsliced strawberries, the other holding a few that had been quartered — graced the counter in front of her. Aunt Bess reached for another berry, expertly jabbed the top of the knife along the hull, edging around it until it was plucked away from the berry. "Boyd MacKay was a fine-looking young man and I know he was your brother's best friend . . ." She quartered the berry into the second bowl. "And I also know you thought the world of him." She reached for another berry and repeated her actions. "But I was always smart enough to know that he would have let the world take care of him if he could have rather than the other way around."

Hot breath caught in Alice-Ann's throat. "Aunt Bess," she managed. "I can't believe you'd say that."

Aunt Bess waved the paring knife in her direction, keeping it at a safe distance. "I'm not trying to speak ill of the dead. So don't go putting words or meanings into my mouth."

"I'm —"

"I'm only saying —" another berry fell by fourths into the bowl, joining the others in a mass of shimmering red — "even his own mama said they were worried he'd never grab hold of enough ambition to go to school and, hopefully, take over his daddy's apothecary one day."

Alice-Ann crossed her arms. "What if he didn't *want* to take over his daddy's *apothecary*? What if he wanted . . . something more?"

Aunt Bess reached for the sugar tin, scooped a tablespoon-size amount with the wooden spoon she'd held earlier, and sprinkled the granules over the berries. "Like what?" Her brow cocked. "And would you like to tell me what do you know about Boyd all of a sudden?"

Heat rose from her toes, settling in her

belly. "Well . . . I mean . . . nothing really. I
—"

Aunt Bess slid the sugar tin a few inches
away, picked up the paring knife, and
resumed hulling. "You what?"

"He — uh —" She looked down at her
feet, then up again to the confused expression on her aunt's face. Why not simply say
what she knew? It no longer mattered
anyway. So what if they'd corresponded?
Even if word got out — not that she imagined Aunt Bess falling into gossip — the
rumors couldn't be any worse than what
probably had begun to mill around about
her and Carlton. "Well, he seemed pretty
excited about going into the Army Air
Corps. Maybe he — maybe he would have
continued flying or — or serving — if . . ."

Aunt Bess dropped the knife on the counter and wiped her hands on her bib apron.
"Oh, dear." She pulled Alice-Ann into her
arms. "You're right, of course, and I can see
that this has upset you."

Alice-Ann took a deep breath, felt it quake
in her chest, then released it with a furrow-
ing of her brow. When the expected tears
burning the backs of her eyes didn't come,
she pulled back from her aunt's embrace
but refused to meet her eyes. "I think he
would have made a good pilot, don't you? I

mean, after the war."

She felt Aunt Bess's stare, knew the woman studied her for any telltale signs of hidden emotions. Aunt Bess had always been able to read her, so Alice-Ann turned toward the pantry. The last thing she needed, especially *now,* was for her aunt to know the truth.

"I suppose he would have," Aunt Bess said softly.

"I'll get the tins now," Alice-Ann said, then set about doing just that.

CHAPTER 21

Alice-Ann missed the entire week of work. Monday through Friday. No work and that meant no pay.

By Saturday morning, after the sun had borne down with cool intensity on Bynum's fields for all of the previous day, Nelson announced at the breakfast table that he believed he could get the truck down the driveway and into town and back.

"Seems awful dangerous to me," Aunt Bess said. She speared a sausage link from a blue-and-white Currier and Ives platter and dropped it onto her plate.

"Dangerous or not," Nelson countered, taking the platter from their aunt, "I've got to. I need to see if any of the prisoners are in town, ready to work." He passed the platter to Irene, who passed it on to Papa.

Irene couldn't abide eating pork, especially after helping feed the pigs in the sty. "How am I to know which one I'm eating?" she

302

once asked, her nose drawn into a wrinkle.

And Aunt Bess — always quick with a comeback — had supplied the answer. "I don't see you feeling the same about the cows."

Not that Irene fed the cattle. And not that she *wanted* to feed the pigs. But she'd signed on as a farmer's wife when she married Nelson and — one way or the other — Aunt Bess and Papa seemed determined to make her into one.

"Can I ride along?" Alice-Ann asked as Papa extended the platter to her. She took it, speared the last piece of meat, and dropped it to her plate.

"Going to see our boy?" Papa asked. "I imagine you've missed seeing him this week."

Alice-Ann's mouth dropped open, and she shot her father her best what-are-you-talking-about? stare. "We're *friends,* Papa."

"Could do worse," he said, reaching toward Irene for the matching Currier and Ives serving bowl filled with fluffy scrambled eggs. The spoon clanked against the china as he scooped a dollop onto his plate. "Can't do much better, in fact."

She blinked several times, then looked at Nelson again. "So? Can I? Hitch a ride?"

"All right by me."

Alice-Ann sought permission from her father and aunt. "Do either of you need me for anything here?"

Little Mack's cries came from upstairs, and Irene slid her chair away from the table. "The prince has returned from dreamland," she said, then left the room to retrieve her son.

"I'm sure I can make do without you," Aunt Bess said. "I'm sure you've about gone stir-crazy out here all week."

"It's not that —"

"I think," Papa added, "whether she wants to admit it or not, she misses Carlton."

Outwardly, Alice-Ann groaned, but inwardly, she admitted — at least to herself — that Papa's words held a modicum of truth. She *had* missed Carlton. She'd missed their chats. The way he teased her. She missed — well, everything about him. Even the scent of him. The way he smiled and made her smile in return. Without even trying.

"Papa," she said, keeping her voice steady, "do you or do you not need me here on the farm today?"

Papa shook his head. "No, I reckon not."

"Then I can go?"

"I don't see why not."

304

"What's on your mind today?" Carlton asked as they stepped off the curb and onto Cooper Street.

Alice-Ann slipped her hand into the crook of his arm as they crossed the street to the sidewalk stretching in front of the bank. "What makes you think I have something on my mind?"

He stared down at her, their steps slow and methodical, his cane tapping in a familiar rhythm, before answering. "You have that look about you."

She bit back a smile. "And what look is that?"

He chuckled low in his throat. "Just a look I've come to recognize."

A sigh escaped between her lips. "Okay, Sherlock."

Carlton placed his hand on hers. She flinched — she knew she did — not because she found his touch unpleasant. In fact, the opposite. If he noticed, he didn't indicate it. "Does that make you Watson?"

Alice-Ann chose not to answer. Instead, she asked, "Do you feel like walking all the way down to the house next to Nancy and Harry's? The one I promised to show you?"

This time he laughed heartily. "Oh no," he said when he'd sobered. "You'll not get away with it that easy. Tell me what's on your mind, Watson."

With a shrug of her shoulders, she said, "I think Papa is an anomaly."

Carlton stopped. He looked at her as she gazed at him. His hair seemed less groomed than usual, what with the sunlight skipping off the strands and then finding a place to dance in his eyes, which today — in spite of the brightness — were unshaded. In fact, a casualness lay over him like an old coat, as though their special friendship had settled between the two of them, and they'd lost the need for impressions. "An anomaly?"

"Yeah. You know. Someone who is one thing one minute and then in the next minute he's completely different."

Carlton resumed their walk, bringing her with him. "I know what an anomaly is."

She squared her shoulders. Kept her focus on the cane, which — in her observation — seemed to be less of a support and more of a crutch. "Oh. The way you said it . . ."

"Why is your father an anomaly? And *this* I have to hear."

"What do you mean?"

"If ever a man was the Rock of Gibraltar, it's *your* father." They stopped at the next curb, both looking toward the only traffic light in town to gauge if it was a good idea to cross. "Look at us," he added. "We made it all the way past the bank and the post office without a single soul stopping to rave about my service to our country or yours to me."

Alice-Ann glanced behind them as butterflies skipped along the walls of her stomach. *Hers to him.*

Other than the two of them, the sidewalk stood empty. "Well, Carlton," she said, turning back to him and willing the butterflies to cease their nonsense. "Today is Saturday, so the post office and the bank are closed."

"True. Light's red. Let's cross."

They kept the same pace as before — slow and easy. When they reached the opposite curb, Alice-Ann answered with "I don't ever remember my father being playful with me."

Again, he peered at her. "Go on."

"I remember him and Nelson playing ball in the front yard."

"Daddy told me once that there was no better sportsman than your daddy back in their school days. And of course, I remember him throwing the ball around with Mack and me in the cool autumn evenings, after coming back from grinding corn over at the mill."

"Yeah, well . . . I mostly remember him leaving *me* to Aunt Bess."

"Seems natural."

"Some days — since the war — he's been as tight as a twisted rubber band, ready to snap."

"Can't blame a farmer for that. Not these days. Not *any* days, really."

Her fingers flexed against the flesh of his lower arm, where tiny beads of sweat broke through, and her gaze shot down the sidewalk. Old oaks and magnolia trees with thick green leaves kept it shaded, for which she was grateful. Carlton didn't need to get too warm, especially as they were embarking on a longer walk than usual.

"I know," she said. "But lately he's been — *teasing* — when he talks to me. And not too long ago, he shared with me about — well, about when he dated Mama. He never talks about Mama. Or at least so rarely it doesn't really count."

Carlton walked in silence for several moments, his cane's clicking drowned out now by the songs of cicadas rising from the trees. Occasionally he waved to folks working in their front lawns, picking up sticks and moss knocked to the ground by the previous week's storm. Usually they called only to him, but some of them greeted her as well.

Otherwise, Alice-Ann kept her eyes on the sidewalk, counting the cracks, careful not to step on them, all the while wondering what people really thought of her and Carlton walking along together. Especially with her hand looped into the crook of his arm.

Yet, more than anything, she couldn't get over the feeling that she didn't really mind what they thought. Not a bit.

Carlton stopped, raised his chin slightly, and said, "Is that it?"

"Well, yeah, I guess so."

"You guess so? You don't know?"

Alice-Ann pulled her hand from his arm and planted both hands on her hips. "Well, Carlton Hillis, what more do you want me to say? Papa is suddenly becoming friendly in his old age and I, for one, find it creepy. Well, maybe not creepy, but at the very least unnerving."

His brow furrowed, and then as understanding dawned, he laughed. "No, silly girl. I mean . . ." He pointed across the street with the end of his cane. "Is *that* the house?"

The cottage she'd so often dreamed of stood silent and alone. Forlorn, almost. A square box with three columns instead of four, and a front porch that appeared nearly as deep as it was wide. "Oh. Yes. That's it."

"Not many cars out today. What do you

say we take a chance and jaywalk?"

She nodded and they crossed the street together, walking a little faster than they had up until then. "I think," she said when they reached the other side, "that you're not *really* using that cane for support so much anymore."

Carlton glanced from the cane to her and back to the cane again. "You may be right. But I think that it's better to have it and not need it than to need it and not have it."

"Makes sense."

He looked at the house again. "So this was the place of the gruesome murder." He made a dramatic "woo-oooh" sound and widened his eyes.

Alice-Ann punched his arm. "Stop it."

"All right, all right. Seriously, it could use some paint."

They climbed the three cement steps from the sidewalk to the walkway cutting the lawn into two patches of dark-green weeds. "And the lawn could use some reseeding," she added.

They stopped at the base of the front porch steps. Carlton used his cane to test them. "And some new boards here."

"I'm going up," Alice-Ann said as she studied the splintered wood.

"Up where?"

"To the porch."

"Careful, now."

She took the first step, turned, and looked at him. "Coming with me? Or are you going to let a little rotten wood frighten you?"

Carlton's lips formed a round O as he shook his head. "Oh, young lady," he said. "You may not know it, but I've met the enemy, and it ain't some two-by-fours in need of replacing."

She giggled as she jogged up the remaining steps, hoping none of them collapsed beneath her — *how embarrassing would that be?* — and turned to look down at him. "Oh, really?"

Carlton took each step carefully, his cane steady against the boards until he made it to the porch. "Glad you could join me," Alice-Ann teased, then crossed to the picture window on the right side of the porch, cupped her hands around her face, and peered into the house. "This is the living room," she said. Her eyes swept both the emptiness and the details. "Come over here and look at the woodwork, Carlton. Look at the gingerbread accents in the corners of the door leading to that room there. I think it's the dining room."

Carlton stood beside her, imitating her stance. "Nice. And nice crown molding and

311

baseboards," he said. "And only about an inch of dust on the floorboards."

"That's probably not all that's on the floors," she added with a frown.

"Come," he said, stepping away from her and walking over to the smaller window on the left side of the front door.

She joined him and studied the glass as she came closer. A hairline crack ran diagonally across the top right corner. "This window would need fixing."

"Yes'm."

They looked in as they had before — hands cupped, faces against the pane. "I think this is the front bedroom," she observed.

"Kinda small."

Alice-Ann smiled. Compared to the tiny box he called his bedroom, the room was palatial, but she elected not to say anything. Since Carlton had been able to get out of bed, she'd not been in the intimacy of his room, and it felt awkward now talking about such things. "Well," she said, her breath fogging the glass, "the whole house is small."

"A cottage, really," he said.

Alice-Ann pulled her face away from her hands to look at him. "You remember," she whispered.

He studied her without answering and she

did the same, noting the tiny dimple in his chin. The crinkles around his eyes. The fullness of his lips.

Oh . . .

"I remember," he said, and her eyes came back to his.

She struggled to find her voice as she faced him fully. "How — how did you remember?"

He shifted the cane from his right hand to the left, then raised a finger to tap the tip of her nose. "I remember pretty much everything you say."

"You do?" Her voice squeaked, and inwardly, she cringed.

Carlton leaned forward. His lips — those full lips she'd noticed only a moment ago as though she'd seen them for the first time in her life — brushed against her cheek, found her ear, and sent tiny gooseflesh down her arms. "I do," he whispered. "Miss Alice-Ann."

CHAPTER 22

They returned on the same side of the street as the cottage. The methodical thump of Carlton's cane kept its rhythm, but everything else in Alice-Ann's world seemed out of whack.

Carlton Hillis had brushed her cheek with his lips, his touch sending shivers along her skin, and his whisper in her ear igniting something she could no longer deny.

Carlton had become more than a friend. He'd become what she'd hoped and prayed Mack would one day be — someone she could not imagine another day without.

The previous week had been difficult — torturous, somehow — and now she understood why. She'd missed him more than she'd been willing to admit, least of all to herself. And only minutes before, standing on the front porch, peering through the windows of the house, she'd gotten a sense that they'd done more than look at molding and dust as they discussed home repairs and restorations.

Had they gotten a glimpse into their future?

"You're awfully quiet," he said, drawing her back to the sidewalk. As before — as always — her arm was looped with his, her hand resting on his warm skin. "Still thinking about your daddy being an anomaly?"

"No," she said, keeping her eyes forward, not daring to look at him. To do so would reveal everything to him all at once, and she knew it. He'd learned to read her so easily, even when she tried to keep her emotions and expressions at bay. But now . . .

"Did I — did I cross a line back there?" The words were strung with tension. "Because if I did —"

"No," she answered quickly. Maybe too quickly.

Carlton's hand found hers, their fingers linking awkwardly. "I'm not going to lie."

She looked at him. "About what?"

"How I feel."

"About what?" she repeated, knowing full well the answer.

"You."

Alice-Ann swallowed. "How *do* you feel? About me?"

"I've come to treasure you, Alice-Ann."

He stopped walking as they neared the curb on the edge of town. A few men gathered across the street in front of the feed and seed store. They wore wide-brimmed straw hats and dug their hands into the side pockets of their bib overalls. A few of them glanced their way, waved, and Carlton waved back.

"Good to see you out and about," Chuck Eastman, an onion farmer who raised his primary crop on the other side of the county from Alice-Ann's family farm, called out.

"Thank you, sir," Carlton called back.

"Alice-Ann, how's your daddy?"

"He's fine, Mister Chuck."

"Good. Good. Tell 'im I said hey."

He turned and the men resumed their conversation.

Carlton looked at her and smiled reassuringly. "Thing is, I know you still care for Mack." His eyes traveled the length of her left arm and rested on the charm bracelet, which still wrapped her wrist with an unfulfilled promise. "And that you probably never think about me the same way you thought about him."

Alice-Ann blinked as she crossed her arms, as if doing so would hide the past and the gift to a sixteen-year-old on her special night. She looked down and studied the

316

shine of his shoes and the light dust covering hers. She could wipe them down every day, but with the windows perpetually open and the sand and dirt stirred up by life on a farm, she could never really keep them clean. "I —" she started.

"Don't say anything, Alice-Ann. I don't expect you to say anything." He turned, drew her hand back into the crook of his arm, and said, "Let's cross."

She followed along beside him, her emotions as jumbled as she'd ever known them. When they reached the other side and had passed the men outside the feed and seed, Carlton cleared his throat and said, "Did I ever tell you about Berry Gentry?"

She shook her head. "No, you never told me."

"Well, I met Berry in school. He came from a farm over in Tattnall County."

Alice-Ann glanced up. "Oh?"

"He told me that back in May of '40, the *Savannah Evening Press* casually informed everyone within a five-county radius that the government would be taking their land 'by purchase or condemnation' — a vast area of — and I quote — 'crackerland.' Next thing they knew, the United States purchased — and he told that with his tongue in his cheek — such a chunk of his daddy's land that the old gentleman farmer had a stroke and died."

Alice-Ann stopped. They'd come to a shaded park bench near the town's courthouse. The need to sit nearly overwhelmed her. "Can we?" she asked, pointing to it.

"Of course," he said.

Once they'd settled and a few more people had spoken to them, a midafternoon breeze managed to find them. Alice-Ann encouraged him to continue. "So his daddy died?"

"You can imagine, right?" He leaned over, resting his elbows on his knees and linking his fingers. "All these people — Berry said over fifteen hundred families and more than six thousand people — lost their land before they had a chance to say boo. Their homes. Everything they'd worked so hard for. Gone." He snapped his fingers. "Just like that. Houses demolished and crops plowed under. And all for much less than the land was worth. Berry said his daddy had just built a tenant house on their farm that cost him more than Washington gave him for the whole kit and caboodle."

She shifted to face him. "But why? I don't understand."

"The government took the land so they could build Camp Stewart, which became one of the most vital facilities we have when it comes to this war, even though right now it's pretty much emptied out with nearly all the boys off in Europe."

She tried to imagine it — having the government knock on their door, offer them a piddling amount of money, and then ordering them off their land whether they took the money or not. She pictured Papa, gun in hand, screaming at the men from Washington. Nelson beside him. Aunt Bess, Irene and the baby, and herself, all standing behind the men. Yet, in the end, they would have been forced off, probably carried off in handcuffs had they argued too long — like the families from those counties closer to Savannah. "And so why is it that you're telling me this story now?"

Carlton reached for her hand, then sandwiched it between his. "Since this war came to our soil, everyone in this country has lost something dear to them, Alice-Ann. Families have lost loved ones. Farmers in five counties not a stone's throw from here have lost their livelihood, their land, their homes — some of them never fully recovering. Or like Berry's daddy, just up and dying." He shook his head like an old dog. "And to some degree, I think we've all lost our innocence." His eyes found hers and he gave her a half smile. "The things I saw. The things I photographed. I know I have."

"Me too," she said. Because it was true. Every bit of it. Since that day in December — the day that should have been the most special for her, and the subsequent night when she told Mack how she really felt about him — nothing in life had been the same.

"And some folks," he continued, his voice filled with understanding, "some folks like yourself have lost dreams."

She blinked, willing the tears that wanted to surface to stay at bay.

"Dreams of what could have been and should have been and might have been . . . all that."

Alice-Ann swallowed. Her throat had become parched and she wished, more than anything, that they could somehow find their way to the soda shop and she could drown her sorrows and her thirst in a tall glass of Coke. "I know," she managed to say. "I know what you're saying." She glanced over his shoulder. The Saturday afternoon matinee had finished and a steady stream of moviegoers exited into the sunlight, their eyes blinking furiously as they shielded them with their hands.

He followed her gaze, then turned back.

"I'm sure Maeve and Ernie will spot us soon."

"They went to see the show?"

"Didn't you know?"

She shook her head and realization struck. How odd that she'd gone to the Hillises' home and not even asked about Maeve. Where she was or what she was doing. In fact, in the past few weeks, she and Maeve had hardly exchanged more than a few kind words. Nothing more. No secrets. No giggles. No lunches.

"Before they find us," he added quickly, "them or anyone else for that matter, let me say — let me ask you — for one simple favor."

Alice-Ann nodded. "Okay. Sure."

Their eyes locked. "Give me a chance, Alice-Ann."

Her heartbeat quickened. "A chance?"

"Mmm. Will you allow me to be your escort to the wedding next month?"

Her escort. Did he mean . . . "A date?" This was a first, being asked out by a man.

"If you want to call it that." He smiled. "I'd like to call it that."

She raised her chin. "You're right."

Now his brow furrowed and she leaned back, pressing herself against the warmth of the bench. "About what?"

"Here come Maeve and Ernie." Alice-Ann grinned at him.

He hunched his shoulders. "Then answer me quick," he said, returning her smile.

Alice-Ann leaned forward, hoping Maeve couldn't read her lips, which quivered as she smiled more broadly. "Yes-you-can-be-my-escort."

After dinner — after Irene and Aunt Bess and Alice-Ann had finished washing the dishes and putting them away, and Papa and Nelson had pulled down the blackout shades around the house — Alice-Ann said her good nights and then trudged up the stairs.

A strange sort of exhaustion threatened to overtake her, and she feared if she did not make it to bed soon, it would succeed. Hearing footsteps behind her, she turned to see Aunt Bess only a few stairs below her. "Going off to bed so soon?"

Alice-Ann forced a smile. "Tomorrow is church. And I'm a little tired."

Aunt Bess took another step and Alice-Ann turned, continued upward, then stepped over the threshold of her bedroom. Aunt Bess followed her in. "Tell me something, Alice," she said, crossing the room to the bed. She reached for the embroidered throw pillow that rested in the center, tossed it to a nearby chair and then pulled the quilt back, folding it neatly as she went.

Alice-Ann moved to the vanity, picked up her brush, and worked her mass of hair into a ponytail. Her eyes met Aunt Bess's in the mirror's reflection. "What's that, Aunt Bess?"

The older woman sighed as she sat on the end of the bed. "Tell me what's on your mind this evening."

Alice-Ann turned. "What do you mean?"

"Now listen, because I don't have a lot of time to play games. I know you. And I know when you've got something going on up there in that head of yours. Something's changed since earlier today."

Alice-Ann frowned as she laid the brush back on the vanity. Talking to Aunt Bess about things would be nice, she knew. But once the cat was out of the bag — as the old saying went — there would be no putting it back in. To explain, to truly explain, how she felt about Carlton's question earlier that day — not to mention her answer — would also mean opening up about how she had felt about Mack.

Still felt about Mack.

But would Aunt Bess offer a sympathetic ear, or would she toss back her gray-haired head and laugh at her?

Alice-Ann pulled her nightgown from under the pillow. "I — uh . . ."

Aunt Bess swiveled to look at her. "My guess is that it has something to do with the Hillis boy."

"He's hardly a boy."

"Aha."

Alice-Ann sat near the bed pillow, crumpled her gown in her hands as though it were an unnecessary piece of paper, and sighed. "Oh, Aunt Bess . . ." She shook her head. "I honestly don't know what to do."

Aunt Bess pressed her palm into the mattress and leaned over. "Do you have feelings for him?"

Alice-Ann nodded. Oh yes. She did. But there was Mack to think of . . . How could she possibly have been in love with Mack as much as she'd thought if Carlton had so easily turned her heart toward him? Not fully, of course, but the shifting had clearly begun.

"I do," she admitted, "but there's — there's an issue."

"Mm-hmm." Aunt Bess leaned back and raised a brow. "And does this issue have anything to do with a certain young man who was shot down in the Pacific?"

Alice-Ann's breath caught in her throat as

her fingers relaxed around the cotton gown. "How did you — ? Did Irene say something?" Or had Aunt Bess read her expression earlier in the week?

"Irene didn't have to, darlin'. I don't think you've removed that bracelet once in all these years. Why, even your daddy's recognized that it's some sort of window into your heart."

"Papa?" Blood rushed from Alice-Ann's head all the way to her toes. She pressed the gown into her face and moaned. "I'm never going downstairs again as long as I live."

Aunt Bess chuckled as she stood, walked around the foot of the bed, and then sat again in front of her niece. "You think you know my brother, but believe me, I know him a tad better than you."

Alice-Ann looked up. "I can't believe he's never said anything. After all, Mack was so much older."

"No more so than this boy Carlton." She winked.

"True."

"I think," Aunt Bess added, patting Alice-Ann's hand, "he figured that by the time the war was over, Boyd MacKay would either no longer occupy your thoughts or —" She stopped short.

325

"Or he'd be dead?" The question came as a whisper.

"No," Aunt Bess answered matter-of-factly. "Not at all. None of us wanted that, even if we didn't think Mack would be the best choice for you in the long run."

"But I don't understand. Why not?"

"He was a good boy — I'm not saying he wasn't — but he had no gumption." Aunt Bess nodded once. "And gumption is what the man who carries you away from all this is going to need, I'd say. At least, that's what your papa wants."

"Papa wants me to leave?"

"Hardly. But if he thought you'd be happy as a farmer's wife, he'd've mentioned that poor ole Pete James more often. Your daddy knows, Alice —" Aunt Bess cupped Alice-Ann's cheek with her hand — "he knows you're a smart one. Too smart for picking peas and canning vegetables the rest of your life. Why, just look how well you've done at the bank since high school."

Alice-Ann chuckled. "It's not that hard. And there's nothing wrong with being a farmer's wife. I'd be proud as punch."

Aunt Bess stood and the bed jiggled as her weight left it. "Don't sell yourself short, Miss Priss." She leaned over and offered a gentle hug. "And don't," she continued as she straightened, "sell that young Mr. Hillis short either. That's all I came up here to say."

Alice-Ann smiled. "Carlton wants to escort me to the wedding."

Aunt Bess walked to the door, then turned and looked back at Alice-Ann. "If you've got the good sense God gave your daddy's best mule out there in the barn, you said yes."

"I said yes."

Aunt Bess slapped the doorframe. "Good enough, then. Get some sleep. Tomorrow's a new day."

"Yes, ma'am."

Aunt Bess closed the door behind herself. After a few moments, Alice-Ann stood, walked to the closet, and retrieved the box of letters she'd kept hidden.

Though now she couldn't quite understand why. If everyone had known — if everyone had read her emotions like yesterday's *Savannah Morning News* — she might as well have declared her feelings in a loud voice. Loud enough for the whole world to hear.

But she hadn't. She and Mack had written to each other in secrecy and she'd worn the bracelet like a blouse, as though *not* wearing it was odd rather than vice versa.

Now, however. Now she knew they knew. And now Mack was dead and Carlton was alive and he grew in her heart. Now . . .

Alice-Ann unclasped the bracelet. Her heart clenched as the cold weight of it slipped away. She thought to put it on again, then stopped herself. No. The time had come.

The time had come.

She laid Mack's gift next to his letters, then returned them all to the hiding place on the shelf.

CHAPTER 23

The rest of August went by in a blur, the news from around the world coming rapidly. The US and the Allies surrounded the Germans in the Falaise Pocket of France. Paris experienced the exhilaration of being liberated. The news seemed only to validate Aunt Bess's belief that the war would soon wrap up. That the boys would come home. That life would return to normal.

Each afternoon after work, Carlton met Alice-Ann and Nancy outside the bank, and together they walked the few blocks to Nancy's, said their good-byes to her, then stole another peek at the house next door. With each visit they added another "thing I would do" if the house belonged to one of them. And with each new idea came the notion that it could actually be so.

During their walks, Carlton regaled Nancy and Alice-Ann with news from the war — the liberation of Paris, the Slovak uprising, the Soviets taking Bucharest. Like Aunt Bess, he insisted the war would soon be over, that the men and women who had left Bynum to serve their country would return, and that life in their fair town would become normal once again. Sleepy and predictable on the day to day.

"But not the same," Nancy said. "Nothing is ever the same after something like this."

Carlton squeezed Alice-Ann's hand in agreement but said nothing.

What level of comfort Alice-Ann and Carlton had found with each other previously only grew in intensity and — oddly — contentment. For the most part, she relished the time they spent together, and came to rely heavily on his wisdom and companionship. She no longer worried about what people *might* think or *did* think, but she often wondered what *Carlton* had in mind. Fully in mind.

He'd asked her if he could escort her to the wedding and they walked together each day, and they'd taken in a few movies. He held her hand and she looped her arm with his. But other than a gentle peck on the cheek, he had yet to kiss her or to express to her his intentions for the future. Their future, if there was to be one.

Not that she was completely ready for either — the kiss or the intentions. After all, for most of her young life she'd imagined Mack would be the man to give her her first kiss. That he would also give her the last. That he would be the only one . . .

But that no longer was the case. Life, as Aunt Bess insisted often, continued on, in spite of the agony of loss.

Then came September. Every day brought news from the war and of liberations, which Alice-Ann and Carlton discussed as though they were history professors at the college he'd not once mentioned returning to, even after he received his honorary discharge.

Alice-Ann would remember that day the rest of her life, the way he sat on the bench outside the bank holding the envelope in one hand and the trifolded paper in the other. She joined him as she wrapped her light sweater around her to ward off the chill hanging in the air. "What do you have there?" she asked.

Without a word he showed her the letter. She read it slowly, then read it again. "Did you just get this?"

He nodded. "I stopped by the post office before coming here."

"I see. Well . . . Carlton? Did you not expect this?"

"Part of me wishes — *boy,* I know I should be there. Filming. Taking photos." He raked his teeth over his bottom lip. "But one stupid move and I'm missing it."

Before she could answer, before she could say how she felt about his desire for such adventure, Nancy came out of the bank, stopped, and — ascertaining the situation — asked if they'd prefer to be alone.

Alice-Ann looked to Carlton before answering.

"You can show her," he said.

Nancy stepped closer, took the letter, and read. Then, returning the paper to Carlton, she said, "I suppose Doc Evans made the decision not to clear you to return."

He nodded. "I told him I'm doing all right," he said, "but there's still some tingling in my legs from time to time."

Alice-Ann shifted toward him. "*Carlton . . .* you've never said."

He shrugged. "I figured it would go away eventually. I still say it will."

Nancy dropped to the bench on the other side of Carlton. "So what do you want to do then? Do you *really* want to go back to the war?"

Carlton gave her a weak smile, then looked at Alice-Ann. "Yes and no." He sighed.

She understood his confusion. In one

respect, she'd grown so accustomed to what the war meant, she worried about what would happen when it was all over. Would she get to keep her job or would she lose it to one of the boys returning? And what if — by some crazy miracle — Janie Wren had been correct about Mack? What if he — all this time — had been fighting on, unable to correspond with either of them? Maybe he was a POW, like Adler. Maybe he worked for some nice family — like hers — over there in the Pacific. "Well, I'm sorry," Alice-Ann finally declared with a shake of her head, "but I admit that, for me, this is a relief."

Nancy patted Carlton's knee. "Of course it is. But is there any reason why you can't return to school? You've already been working for your mom and dad, so now with your discharge you should be all right to go back."

Alice-Ann sat straight. Carlton, returning to school? Would that also mean him leaving Bynum? Leaving her? The thought worried her more than the wondering if Mack had survived.

"I'm sure your husband would tell me to finish up if I asked him what he thought," Carlton said.

"Harry would indeed." Nancy stood.

"Speaking of whom, I'd best get home." She gave them a quizzical look. "Are you two walking today?"

Alice-Ann hoped not. She had things she wanted to say to Carlton. Things she didn't dare leave to chance. Or a later time.

Carlton shook his head. "I think I'll go on back home and talk to Daddy about this."

"Good idea," Nancy said. "Alice-Ann, I'll see you tomorrow."

Alice-Ann smiled up at her friend, grateful for her way of seeing things so logically, even when everything around her fell apart. "Thank you. See you then."

After Nancy left them, Alice-Ann scooted closer to Carlton. "Do you want me to walk back to the five-and-dime with you? Maybe I can visit with Maeve while you talk to your daddy."

He leaned over, kissed her cheek as he'd done so many times before. But this time his lips lingered and he inhaled as if he were breathing her in. "Maeve's gone off somewhere with Claudette."

Alice-Ann sighed. "We've got the tea this Saturday. They're probably out shopping for whatever Claudette imagines she needs to make the day complete."

Carlton smiled at her, but the smile didn't reach his eyes. "Baby doll, I'm going to walk on home." He started to stand, but Alice-Ann grabbed his hands.

"Carlton, what do *you* want to do?"

His brow furrowed. "Can I tell you a secret?" he asked.

The memory of his sharing a secret with her at her sixteenth birthday party swept over her. He'd been so ready to marry Betty Jo back then, but she had foolishly cast him aside after his return from Europe. "Of course."

"I really *liked* taking photographs. And filming the war." He hunched over. "I was good at it. Truly good at it." He opened his mouth as though he were going to say more, then closed it again.

"No. Please don't shut me out." She couldn't bear it if he did. "What were you going to say?"

He winced, then admitted, "I think I would have made an okay teacher, you know? But when that camera was in my hand . . ." He held out his hand, palm up and cupped. "I realized I had the ability to see the world in a way that maybe not everyone can. And that I can share what I see with others. I used to wonder, as I was filming or shooting pictures, who on the other side of the world might see my work and learn something they otherwise wouldn't

335

have known. Kind of like I was bringing the reality of war home."

Alice-Ann pictured him, walking around in the wardrobe of a soldier, helmet on his head, camera in his hand, and a gun slung over his shoulder. He shot with one and only carried the other, although he knew how to use both. A boy could hardly grow up in Georgia and not know how to shoot a gun. "So do you want to do something with the camera? I mean, now?"

"I think . . ." He folded the letter and slid it back into the envelope. "I think I'd like to try my hand at photojournalism."

"What's that?"

He grinned at her as his face came to life. She knew that look, the one that said, "I'm about to teach you something." If Carlton loved anything at all — whether he wanted to be a schoolteacher or not — it was sharing with others what he knew. "Have you ever heard of Frank Luther Mott?"

She shook her head no.

"We learned about him when we were in training. He's a professor at a college — in Iowa I think, or maybe it was Missouri — who coined the term. It means . . ." Carlton tucked the letter into the pocket of his cotton shirt. "It's taking what photographers do and what writers do and putting them together so that the pictures tell a story."

"Which is what you did for the war effort."

"Yes."

"And that's what you want to do?"

"Yes. I thought maybe I should go see Mr. Dibble over at the paper. See if he might have some ideas or thoughts."

Alice-Ann wrapped her arms around his shoulders and squeezed. "I think that's a wonderful idea."

He drew back, surprised. "Do you?"

She nodded. "I do." And she did, as long as it meant he'd stay in town. At least for a while.

"And who knows? Maybe one day I'll be good enough to go to work for Mr. Henry Luce."

"I've never heard of him."

"*Time* magazine?"

"In New York?"

Carlton's eyes widened. "You never know where life will take you."

"*Life.* Now *that's* a magazine I know."

Carlton leaned back against the wrought iron of the bench. "Good one, Alice-Ann. But do you know who owns it?"

"Henry Luce?"

He tapped the tip of her nose. "You're a pretty smart cookie."

Warmth spread through her. She'd not known, of course. She'd only made a partially informed guess. But she enjoyed the conversation too much to tell him otherwise.

He smiled. "Well, then." He shifted. "I still need to talk to Daddy. Poor Maeve is dying for me to work more hours so she can work fewer." He laughed. "She used to want to go to school, but now all she wants is for Ernie to propose so she'll be next to walk down the aisle."

"She still doesn't know? That Ernie is planning to propose after Claudette's wedding?"

Carlton shook his head. "No, but old Ern has already talked to Daddy."

Alice-Ann bopped his chest with her fist. "You didn't tell me that."

He grinned as he leaned his face closer to hers. "You think I tell you *everything,* Alice-Ann Branch?"

The familiar butterflies fluttered from her stomach to her heart and back again. "No," she whispered. "Not everything."

Breath audibly caught in his chest as he drew back. "Actually, there is something I need to tell you. No . . . something I *want* to tell you."

"What's that?"

Carlton looked over her shoulder.

"There's Nelson," he said.

Alice-Ann turned. Sure enough, her brother's truck — its bed loaded with prisoners and one gun-toting guard — rumbled up the street. "His timing is impeccable." She looked at Carlton. "Tell me. Quickly."

But instead of answering, he stood, extended his hand for hers, and helped her to stand. "Nah-uh. I'm saving this for another day."

By the time the wedding day arrived — after weeks of showers and teas and gown fittings and even more global news — Alice-Ann had come to the conclusion that her beau — if she could call him that — was capable of two things: one, keeping secrets, and two, self-control. They'd long ago stopped pretending they were not seeing each other — something which brought Alice-Ann both comfort and unease. Comfort in knowing that a homely girl such as herself *could* land a good-looking man. Unease in wondering if folks around Bynum were asking how in the world such a common girl — good as she was known to be to her aunt and her daddy and to the children over at the church — could have the local hero interested in her.

The local hero.

Carlton had yet to set the citizens straight on how he'd been injured and she wondered if he ever would. The one time she questioned him about it, he only offered a shrug and a mumbled "Sweep it under the rug, Alice-Ann. You and I know. That's all that matters."

One of the benefits of everyone knowing and accepting them as a couple was that the two of them, along with Maeve and Ernie, had gone out a few times. Maeve, of course, had jumped completely over the moon at the thought of her brother and her best friend dating. She'd already practically married them and given them children who would, naturally, play with the children she and Ernie were bound to have.

Not that Alice-Ann and Carlton were discussing marriage. For pity's sake, he'd not even kissed her yet.

Finally the twenty-third of September came. Claudette's big day. And if it was a big day for Claudette, it was twice as monumental for her mother, Miss Zilda, who, as though she had become completely unaware that a war was going on and that the rest of the country had buckled under the financial weight of it, spared no expense when it came to decorating the sanctuary of the downtown Methodist church. "The last time I saw so many flowers," Alice-Ann whispered to Maeve as they stood together in the vestibule waiting for their cue to walk down the aisle, "was at old Miss Gloria Baker's funeral back when we were in eighth grade."

Maeve twisted around to whisper, "It took this long for enough flowers to grow back, I suppose, so Claudette could have her wedding."

They grinned at each other as the organ music changed to the rehearsed tune for their entry into the church. Alice-Ann waited for Maeve to take the determined number of steps before she followed behind her. Because Aunt Bess had always said watching the face of the bridegroom was the best part of any wedding ceremony, she clutched her nosegay and kept her focus on Johnny's expectant face. Then, as his dark-brown eyes met hers, Alice-Ann smiled at the man she hardly knew but who had captured Claudette's heart from the first time she'd seen him.

Like Mack captured yours.

The thought came from nowhere and she stumbled at the intrusion of it. A man's hand reached out to steady her, and when she turned to say thank you, she realized it was Carlton who'd come to her rescue.

"You okay?" he mouthed.

Alice-Ann nodded and returned to the timed pace of the bridesmaid, reached the front and stood to the right of Maeve, then turned slightly to watch Claudette's cousin Beulah march the rest of the way forward. The swinging double doors the three had walked through only moments before closed until the bridal march began. Alice-Ann stole another look at Johnny and then allowed her eyes to roam the congregation until she found Carlton again. His eyes were on her, and with a look that told her he knew she'd sought him out, he winked.

A mixture of warmth and guilt spread over her.

Beulah took her place next to Alice-Ann. The music changed again and the congregation rose in honor of the bride, who now stood framed in the doorway, her hand lain gently on her father's forearm. Behind the elegant veil, her face shone with the glow of a woman in love. Even Alice-Ann could see the purity of the emotion, uncomplicated by anything or anyone else. Whatever life had in store for Claudette and Johnny — good or bad — didn't matter at that moment. The only thing on her mind — Alice-Ann knew — was that her future as Mrs. Johnny Dailey would begin in a few moments and that their love would prove bigger than any hardship or sorrow. Nothing would stand in the way of it. Nothing.

Until death did them part.

Death. Alice-Ann swallowed over the knot in her throat. More than anything she wanted to be done with her feelings for Mack, yet they came up at the most inopportune time. Except for too many years nursing a schoolgirl crush, she couldn't imagine why. Other than the sign-off on his letters — *"Love ya"* — he'd never promised her any deep emotion, never professed undying adoration for her or even hinted at a life together.

But then again, neither had Carlton.

What if Mack's death was not enough for Carlton? What if he waited for something else? Something more? Although what, she couldn't imagine. The letters perhaps — the ones that had come to his home, addressed to his sister but meant for her. The ones she had confided to him about, even discussing many of the contents. Maybe Carlton waited for her to take them out of their hiding place and show them to him rather than only talk about them.

No, that would be silly. Carlton Hillis wasn't the kind of man who'd read another man's letters penned to his girl, even if she hadn't been his girl at the time.

Maybe . . . perhaps . . . he waited for her to say she'd destroyed them. Not that she had. She couldn't. These were letters from Mack. He was dead and they were precious to her. Every stroke of the pen. Every dot of the i's and cross of the t's.

Surely he wouldn't expect her to throw them away.

A flurry of movement next to her drew her attention back to the room and to the nearly pungent scent of too many flowers. The organist pressed down on the keys as Claudette and Johnny broke apart from their first kiss as man and wife. Alice-Ann blinked several times to clear the cobwebs as she inhaled a tad too deeply.

Good heavens. Thinking about Mack, she'd missed the wedding.

CHAPTER 24

As a bridesmaid, Alice-Ann had to be at the church early, but as a guest, she could stay late.

After Claudette and Johnny had dashed into his automobile and driven away from the church and toward the city limits sign and then on to Savannah for a few days' honeymoon, Carlton lightly touched her elbow and said, "Want to go inside for another slice of cake?"

She nodded. "That sounds good."

"I was thinking," Carlton said as they walked into the social hall, "that maybe afterward I could drive you home."

Alice-Ann looked up and smiled. "Sounds fine by me." An idea struck her. "How about we wrap a couple of pieces in one of the napkins and take them with us? I'll make us some coffee when we get to the farm."

"I have an even better idea." Carlton turned her toward him and he bent close to her ear. So close, in fact, that his words sent shivers down her arms. So close that she blushed at the thought of so many people standing around the room, watching them. "Why don't we put the coffee in a thermos and have a picnic out under one of the pecan trees in your yard?"

She stepped back, trying to put enough space between her and the intimacy of him. "That might be fun."

An hour later, after they'd managed to slip away from the still-mingling crowd and had driven out to the farm, and after Alice-Ann had made a pot of coffee and poured it into her father's thermos, the two stepped out on the porch, down the wooden steps, and made their way to the small grove of pecan trees that stood directly before the farmland started.

Carlton had secured a blanket from an upstairs closet while Alice-Ann arranged their picnic in one of Aunt Bess's baskets. He carried one while she toted the other — him still in his suit and her still in the tea-length gown Aunt Bess had worked so diligently on. Reaching a place he deemed perfect, he spread the blanket on the ground for the two of them.

"Wonder how much longer before your family gets home," he mused, looking toward the house as she poured the coffee into two everyday cups she'd also placed in the basket.

"Should be fairly soon." She handed the first cup to him and waited as he dug into the basket for the cake. "The last thing Papa likes to do is socialize too long." Having poured her own coffee, she twisted the top onto the thermos.

Carlton's chuckle came from low in his chest. "Yours and mine both."

"But probably Aunt Bess is making him stay. She'll say something like 'I hardly ever get off the farm, Emmitt. The least you can do is stick around while I socialize.'"

This time Carlton laughed heartily as he crossed his legs as if to get comfortable.

"Does that bother you?" she asked.

"What? Your father not being here?"

"No." She pointed. "Your legs crossed like that."

"Only a little. Not enough to complain."

Alice-Ann found two plates in the basket and set the slices of cake on top of them. She frowned. "I forgot forks."

Carlton waggled his brows as he picked up his piece of cake between his fingers and took a bite. "Who need forks?" he asked around it.

She laughed. "Who indeed?" She repeated

his actions, then moaned. "Oh, I love cake."

"I love *you.*"

For a moment she thought the moist treat had been sucked down her throat without giving her a chance to swallow. Then she realized it remained on her tongue and she gulped. *"Carlton."*

He scooted closer. "I do. I can't help it. I do."

Alice-Ann willed herself to breathe as she placed the plate next to her. "What — what do you mean *you can't help it?*"

He licked his lips for the remaining icing, then tossed the plate and what was left of his cake off to the side. "I know I shouldn't. I know — *I know* — you've not fully gotten over how you felt about Mack —"

"No." She breathed out the lie. "That's not true."

His fingertips lightly grazed her knee. "Come on, doodlebug. If we can't be honest with each other, how are we going to build a future?"

A future . . . Carlton Hillis wanted to build a future with her. *With her.*

Alice-Ann looked toward the house, praying Aunt Bess or Papa wouldn't make a sudden appearance.

Or — *great grannies!* — Nelson. That

would surely be all she needed at this moment.

"Say something," Carlton implored and she turned to face him again.

"I — I love you too." At least she thought she did. Surely she did. What wasn't to love, for crying out loud? He was handsome. Smart. Kind. He loved God.

And he was alive . . .

Carlton scooted closer, so close that her legs, which she'd tucked under herself, ended up nestled between his knees. "Do you?" His hands reached for her face and slid along her jawline until her cheeks rested against his palms. "Because that's what I've wanted to say to you since that day outside the bank." His eyes met hers — oh, blessed mercy, they were so tender — and he smiled. "But I didn't want to rush you."

Alice-Ann tried to shake her head but she couldn't. His grip was too secure — too gentle — too everything Hollywood, California, and Bynum, Georgia, all at once. "How could you say that?"

He blinked. "What?"

"The last thing you've done is *rush* me, Carlton. You've never even — I mean — you've never even —"

"Kissed you?" His voice teased, and if she'd had the wherewithal, she would have punched him. Punched him and ruined the moment. Punched him hard and clung to him and pressed her face against his chest if only to draw the air from his lungs.

Instead, she nodded.

"Oh, doodlebug," he mumbled, bringing her lips closer to his, "I'm about to remedy that right now."

The kiss was everything she'd ever imagined it would be — could be — in spite of not being with the one she'd dreamed of sharing it with for so long. She closed her eyes and breathed in, felt the magic of his lips on hers. The soft moistness. The light pressure that became more arduous as the moments went on. And when she thought she'd pass completely out from dizziness, he released her, found her eyes with his, and said, "Say it again. Please say it again."

"I love you," she breathed.

His forehead pressed against hers. "Put my name on the end of it. Please."

If her heart grew any warmer, it could have baked a pound cake.

"I love you, Carlton Hillis."

Carlton stayed for dinner that night, which couldn't have made Papa any happier or more excited if he'd been dining with President Roosevelt himself.

Papa asked him questions about registering for service, about basic training, about Europe, and about his decision to carry a camera as well as a gun.

Carlton, who sat next to Alice-Ann and across from Nelson, grinned as he plopped mashed potatoes onto his plate. "Well, sir, you don't exactly *volunteer* for some things. You know, Uncle Sam tells you where he wants you and you go."

Papa jabbed his fork in the air — tines down — twice. "But I bet you were good at what you did."

"I'd like to think so," he said as he passed the bowl to Alice-Ann.

"Papa," Alice-Ann added, "Carlton has been working toward doing something further with his life using his skills with photography."

"Like what?" Aunt Bess asked, her tone bossier than usual. "What kind of living can a man make with a camera?"

"You'd be surprised, Miss Branch. A man can do well with a camera if he knows what he's doing with it."

Aunt Bess waved a hand at him. "Call me Aunt Bess," she said as though he and Alice-Ann were engaged all of a sudden.

He smiled and Alice-Ann felt heat rush to her cheeks. "Thank you, ma'am," he said;

then Carlton turned to look at Papa. "As you probably already know, sir, I've been working a few hours a week for Mr. Dibble at the paper. It's not much right now, but I think if I continue like I have, the job will become full-time. See, I know enough about a camera to get me by, but I need help with the journalism part." He glanced around the table. "Miss LuAnn is quite talented when it comes to the pen, so . . ."

"So . . . ," Irene said slowly, "is she — what — *training* you how to write?"

Carlton blushed. "As best she can." He dug his fork under the hill of potatoes on his plate and brought it halfway to his mouth. "You either have a talent for writing or you don't." The fork disappeared between his lips and he swallowed, his Adam's apple bobbing. "Some of it, Miss LuAnn says, can be learned. But if you don't have the ability, there's no point in wasting your time."

Aunt Bess bustled in her seat. "I can hear LuAnn saying that as easily as I hear my own voice." Aunt Bess had always found LuAnn Dibble a little too full of herself, not that she would ever say so publicly and especially with her losing one of her children in the war. "But I'm sure if she's kept you around for any length of time, she must see some modicum of talent in your quill."

" 'A modicum of talent in your quill,' "
Nelson repeated, and they all laughed at the
archaic reference.

Carlton cleared his throat and his face
relaxed. "Thank you for that, Aunt Bess.
And thank you again for allowing me to call
you 'Aunt Bess.' Makes me feel like I'm a
part of the family."

"You practically are," Irene purred and
Alice-Ann shot her a look. One she hoped
Irene recognized as a stop-it-right-now look.

"Didn't Claudette look absolutely beautiful this afternoon?" Alice-Ann asked, hoping for a change in subject.

"Wouldn't know," Carlton said before
anyone else had a chance to answer. "I was
too busy looking at a certain bridesmaid."

"Well, now," Aunt Bess said, her words
clipped as though she, like the rest of them,
had been taken completely off guard. "I
didn't see that one coming."

Nelson shook his head. "Oh, Alice-Ann,"
he said through his chuckle. "Who would
have thought my little sister would have the
hometown hero falling so hard?"

Carlton angled his fork to cut into a slice
of tomato. "Nelson, you've got that right.
The hometown hero has fallen indeed and
fallen hard." He cut a sideward glance to
Alice-Ann's father. "I hope that's all right

with you, sir."

Papa raised his glass of iced tea. "Not only is it all right," he said with a nod, "but I welcome the words at this table."

Alice-Ann walked Carlton to his car, their fingers woven together and their palms pressed against each other. "Supper was good," he said. "I'm grateful for the invite."

Alice-Ann chuckled. "I think Papa would rather have *you* at his table than me."

He stopped, turned her toward him, and peered down at her. His eyes were so intense she almost didn't recognize them. "Don't underestimate your father's love for you. He may not be an overly affectionate man — I don't know many who are — but his wanting the best for you shows how much he cares. How much he loves you."

She smiled and, warmed by his words, felt her knees go weak. "Thank you for that."

When they reached the car, Carlton leaned against it, crossing his legs at the ankles, and scooted her to stand directly in front of him. A flash of remembrance darted through her thoughts — she and Mack leaning against his truck on that cold December night in 1941. She'd been so young then. So childish. Now, she knew, she stood before a man she could love for the rest of her life, nearly without reservation, as a grown woman. No longer a teenage girl hoping to be kissed. Now she *had* been kissed.

The first . . . the last . . . the only.

"What are you thinking about?" Carlton asked, reaching for her other hand, which she gladly gave.

Alice-Ann positioned her feet on the sides of his, hoped she looked ladylike enough, and said, "You ask me that a lot. What I'm thinking about . . ."

"What you're thinking about matters to me. You're not only one of the smartest girls I've ever known, you keep *me* thinking. And when a —" he dipped his head toward her — "war hero comes home wounded, he has to keep his brain thinking. Otherwise, with what he's seen, he'll go absolutely stark-raving mad." He straightened. "Ever hear of shell shock?"

"No."

He shrugged. "Let's talk about *that* later. Tell me what you're thinking about."

Heat tingled in her toes. "Honestly?"

"I wouldn't have it any other way."

"I'm thinking that you're the first boy to ever kiss me and I hope you'll be the last."

Carlton cocked his head. "You're not going to up and die on me tonight, are you?"

She pulled one hand free to swat at his shoulder, which made him laugh. He stood straight, drew her to him, and wrapped her in his arms.

Alice-Ann sighed. "Well, if I did die tonight, this would be a good place."

He chuckled, kissed the top of her head, and said, "Alice-Ann, I'm going to be honest with you."

She took a step back, sought his eyes — which she now completely recognized — and blinked. "I wouldn't have it any other way," she said, repeating his words.

But he didn't grin at her as she expected. Instead, he swallowed so hard she could hear the gulp. "I've got a plan."

"I'm listening."

"And I hope — no, I pray — every single night, I pray — you'll go along with it."

Her stomach fluttered and she wished she hadn't eaten so much cake in the day. "All right."

"I plan to keep on working for Mr. Dibble. I plan to keep learning under Miss LuAnn and I plan to take my work hours from ten a week to whatever they'll allow me to do." His words came so quickly that Alice-Ann had a difficult time keeping up with them. "With what I'm getting from Uncle Sam when this war is over, I plan to buy that

cottage next to Nancy and Harry —"

A tiny gasp escaped from between her lips.

"Hold on," he said. "Just hear me out."

Alice-Ann nodded.

"I plan to buy it, fix it up just like you want it. It won't be the Hearst mansion, but it'll be everything you wanted and then some. And when I'm done, I plan to carry you over the threshold of it. Whenever you're ready, though. I'm not rushing you and I don't want to frighten you." He paused as she pressed her hand against her chest. "Because you look so scared I'm surprised you've not run all the way back to the front porch."

"I — I — Carlton, you've waited until today to kiss me and not a few hours later you tell me you want to — wait, are you saying you want to *marry* me?"

His fingertips brushed along her cheekbones and found their way into her tangle of hair. The pads of his hands pressed against her ears, blocking out all sound but the blood rushing through her veins and he squeezed as he brought her lips to his. Briefly. Sweetly. Then he relaxed, and as li[fe] eased back into her hearing, he said, "I ca[n]not imagine anyone on the face of t[he] planet I'd rather spend my life with th[an] you, Alice-Ann Branch. No one — and [I]

mean *no one* — has ever made me feel like you do."

"Not even Betty Jo?"

"Betty Jo couldn't come close to you."

"But she's so — so *pretty.*"

"What is it my mama always says? Pretty is as pretty does."

Alice-Ann nodded, her face still held gently between his palms. "Aunt Bess says that too."

"Besides that, you're the most beautiful woman I've ever known. Inside and out."

"You only say that because you love me."

He kissed her again, and this time the kiss was deep and full. Much more than she'd experienced earlier and way more than she imagined. Even Rhett Butler hadn't kissed Scarlett O'Hara quite so passionately.

Had he?

"I say that because it's true," he added when they came up for air. "Now, Miss Branch. Don't leave me wondering if I've frightened you away for all eternity or if I've convinced you to spend it with me. What do you say? Will you marry me?"

CHAPTER 25

"You'll have to talk to Papa."

His mouth fell open. Had he not expected her to say yes? "And if Papa gives me the okay?"

Alice-Ann pressed her lips together; Carlton's taste remained on them. She nodded. "Yes, Carlton Hillis. I'll marry you."

Carlton wrapped his arms around her waist and he lifted her, twirling her in the thick night air, leaving her head spinning. When he stopped whooping and turning, he set her gently on her feet. It took a moment before she regained her footing, and Carlton leaned against his car once she had. "Okay," he said between breaths. "Apparently I've got to get into shape if I'm going to get that house back to rights."

Alice-Ann slid her arms around his shoulders and laid her head against the strength of his chest. "A cottage, really," she said.

He kissed the top of her head. "Yes,

ma'am. Whatever you say."

"I love you, Carlton."

"Oh." His voice quivered and he exhaled slowly. "I wish you knew how happy that makes me."

She tilted her head to look at him, her heartbeat happily tap-tap-tapping along. Light from a half-moon fell between the branches and leaves of the trees, casting a warm glow over his face. Dear Lord, he was so handsome. What in the world did he want with a girl like her? "Does it?"

"More than I can say. I love you so much, Alice-Ann. You're everything and then some to me."

Her head returned to his chest and she waited. Listened. Around her the cicadas sang as they did each and every night, while beneath her right ear Carlton's heart beat a new tune. One she'd never heard before — the rhythm of love.

Carlton planned to arrive at the farm after church for Sunday dinner the next day.

Alice-Ann stood in the foyer, expectantly. She glanced at her watch, then out the front window as he slammed the car door shut. "Papa," she said, turning toward the living room, where her father and brother had settled in to listen to a few afternoon shows on the Zenith and read the newspaper.

"What is it, Alice-Ann?" He flipped a page of the *Savannah Morning News.*

"Carlton's here."

Papa folded the paper, cast it to his feet, and stood.

Nelson, who held the sports section, turned his face toward the front door. "What's he doing here again?"

"Nelson," Alice-Ann exclaimed.

Her brother laughed. "I only mean to say that it's unusual."

Irene's footsteps tapped lightly on the staircase as she came down, having put the baby — plump and sleepy from lunch — down for his afternoon nap. "What's unusual?" she asked.

Nelson met her at the base of the stairs. "Carlton is here again."

She stopped three stairs up. "Oh, really?" Her grin in Alice-Ann's direction only served to frustrate the intended target.

"He wants to talk to you, Papa," Alice-Ann said, looking at her father.

Papa adjusted his trousers around his hips. "Does he now."

Aunt Bess entered the foyer as Carlton knocked on the door. "Oh, dear," Alice-Ann said, sorry that her entire family stood nearby as though they lay in wait. She waved her hands at them. "Shoo. Shoo. All of you."

They returned to the living room as she slowly made her way to the door, placed her hand on the doorknob, and twisted. She inhaled deeply upon seeing him. Gracious, but he was handsome!

Carlton still wore his church clothes. "Don't you look spiffy," she said.

He stepped over the threshold, looked beyond her to the living room, where, Alice-Ann prayed, the rest of the family had not gathered only to stare holes in them, then gave her a light kiss on the cheek. "So do you."

She looked down. "I'm wearing a house-dress, Carlton." Aunt Bess had always insisted they change from their Sunday-go-to-meeting clothes "lest you drop anything on them during Sunday dinner."

His eyes captured hers. "Still, you're beautiful."

Alice-Ann thanked him with her eyes. "Papa is in the living room."

"I know. I got my vision back, remember?"

She swatted him as she closed the door.

"Come on in; come on in," Papa said, rising as though he'd only then noticed they had a visitor.

"Good afternoon, sir." Carlton greeted

him, hand extended for a shake. He exchanged another with Nelson.

"How ya doin', boy?" Nelson asked him.

"Not bad," Carlton answered. He smiled at Aunt Bess and Irene. "Ladies."

"What brings you out our way?" Papa asked.

"I — uh — I'd like to have a word with you, if you don't mind." He glanced at Alice-Ann.

Papa nodded. "Man to man?"

"Yes, sir."

Papa nodded again. "Thought that might be the case." He jutted his chin toward the foyer. "Care to take a walk outside?"

Carlton exhaled. "Yes, sir. That'd be fine."

Alice-Ann wondered which of her family members held the trophy for "most excited" about her upcoming nuptials, although a formal date hadn't been set.

Aunt Bess had already started fluttering around, talking about cake recipes and dress patterns. "We can't do it up like Claudette's parents, but we'll do it up just fine," she told Alice-Ann on Sunday evening.

Alice-Ann assured her she didn't want or need it "done up" like Claudette's wedding.

Papa was pleased as punch. Over supper on Sunday night, he regaled the family with a play-by-play of Carlton's request for "my daughter's hand in marriage. A real gentleman, our boy Carlton is."

Nelson shook his head a number of times, saying, "My little sister is marrying Carlton Hillis, and Carlton Hillis is buying her the little house on Main Street. Who would have ever thought it?" Leaving Alice-Ann to wonder if his comment had to do with the age difference or the fact that he thought Carlton too "uptown" for her. Then again, *he'd* married "uptown."

Irene cornered her that night in her bedroom, asking her if she was sure about this.

"I am," Alice-Ann told her. "I love him."

Irene, who sat on the bed near the headboard, nuzzled her son, who lay sleeping in her arms. "Does this mean you've put childhood notions where they belong?"

Alice-Ann swallowed as she sat at the foot. "You mean about Mack?"

"Mm-hmm."

The pain cut deep, but she told the sorrow to stay put. "I'll always have a special place in my heart for Mack," Alice-Ann confided. "But Mack is dead. I've accepted that. Carlton is a good man. A *fine* man. And — somehow — it's like . . ." She shrugged. How could she honestly and truthfully relay her feelings about Carlton?

"Like you've been with him your whole life? And even if there's another who could have easily swayed you, you're wrapped in the notion that Carlton always was and always will be?"

Alice-Ann breathed out the relief she felt. Irene *did* understand. "Yes. How did you know?"

"I felt the same about Nelson when —" She brought her words to a halt.

"When?" Alice-Ann coaxed.

Irene's blush covered her face and chest. She blinked once, long and slow. "When I fell in love with your brother. When I *knew* it was him and no one else. Could never be anyone else."

Understanding washed over Alice-Ann. "There had been someone else?"

Irene nodded. "I often wondered if you knew."

Alice-Ann shook her head. "How would I know?"

"Because it was —" Irene swallowed in discomfort. "Because at one time I thought — I mean . . . You don't know about Mack and me?"

The room spun and Alice-Ann placed her hand on the mattress to steady herself. "What are you talking about, Irene?"

"Before Nelson and me — shortly before — Mack and I went out a few times."

How could she have never known that? And why hadn't it come up before? Not once, even nearly three years ago when Irene had teased about her feelings for Mack had she let on that — "You were in love with Mack?"

Irene drew Little Mack closer. "I thought so. But after — well, one afternoon Mack was supposed to pick me up and take me somewhere. I don't even remember where, to tell you the truth."

Could it possibly matter? "And?"

"He didn't show. He sent your brother instead while he played a game of softball with his buddies." She shook her head. "That was Mack for you. He'd always rather play games than live life."

Alice-Ann sighed. "I get so tired of people saying that."

Irene shrugged. "It's true. He is what he is — or rather what he was." She tilted her head. "I'm so sorry about Mack and, well, sometimes — if I'm being honest — I wonder if his carefree attitude cost him his life in the end."

A tiny bubble of indignation rose inside her. "That's a horrible thing to say."

"I know. But it's true. Nelson and I have

talked about it. We both loved him dearly —
one way or the other — but we at least
could admit the kind of man he was."

Alice-Ann didn't want to talk about
Mack's lack of responsibility anymore.
Somehow it didn't seem right. "So then
what happened?"

Irene laughed. "I was so mad. *That* much
I remember. Mack and I had only gone out
maybe three or four times, and as far as I
was concerned, nothing and nobody should
have come first over me." She smiled, and
in spite of being somewhat put out with her,
Alice-Ann marveled at how lovely her sister-
in-law truly was. Between her and Nelson's
good looks, Little Mack had no choice but
to grow up a heartbreaker. "Anyway, Nelson
took me to a matinee to make up for it.
Afterward we went to the soda shop and
then we went down to Brower's Pond and
went fishing."

"Nelson took you fishing?"

She laughed lightly again, then looked at
her son to make certain she'd not disturbed
his slumber. "I caught three fish before he
even got his hook baited."

Try hard as she might not to, Alice-Ann
laughed along with her. She couldn't imagine a girl outfishing her brother.

"By the time Nelson took me home, I'd

declared the date to be the best I'd ever been on. The next day I marched down to the drugstore, told Boyd MacKay he'd just messed up the best thing that had ever come into his life, and marched right out." Irene kissed the tip of the baby's nose. "Everyone thinks we named the baby after Mack because . . . well . . . but really, we credit Mack for bringing us together." She sighed as she raised her large eyes to Alice-Ann's. "I guess in a way, you can do the same. *If you really mean it.*"

Alice-Ann remained silent for a moment. Yes, she meant it, but the notion that finding Carlton came at the price of losing Mack — and Mack losing his life — was too much to think on. And certainly too much to be happy about. "I mean it," she finally said.

"Good. Because marriage isn't all hugs and kisses. There are tough times, too."

"What do you mean? I've never heard you and Nelson say cross words to each other."

Irene stood. "That's just it. You've never heard." She moistened her lips with the tip of her tongue. "One of these days that brother of yours is going to build me *my* dream house. I'm so miffed you'll get yours before I get mine."

"Sorry," Alice-Ann said, though she really

wasn't. If there was one thing she could say for Irene, it was that she had it plenty good in life. A dream house would require her to do *all* the cooking and cleaning.

Irene surprised her then by leaning over and kissing her cheek. "No, you're not. And neither would I be if the shoes were reversed." She straightened. "But thank you for that, anyway."

CHAPTER 26

Carlton surprised her the following Friday evening with three gifts.

They sat on the front porch swing of the farmhouse, blessedly alone. After Aunt Bess had fed them well and Papa had taken a walk outside to smoke a rare cigarette while Nelson and Irene went to town to take in a picture show, she and Carlton glided nearly without effort in the swing. In the silence between them, interrupted only by the squeaking of the chains, Alice-Ann wondered if her brother and Irene ever argued during those long drives to town and back. Or did they — as she would were it Carlton and her — pull down some dusty field road to kiss and make up? To make things better, were they living with Carlton's parents and not in a place of their own?

Oh, *the cottage* . . . Within six months, Carlton said, he'd have the house ready for them to move into. Maybe sooner, he added, planting a kiss to the tip of her nose to seal the promise.

Papa made his way up the front porch steps just then.

"Did you enjoy your walk, sir?" Carlton asked.

Papa nodded as he shoved his hands deep into his pockets. "Sometimes a man just needs to think a bit."

"To sort things out?"

"It's the mark of a real man, son," Papa answered with a slight smile. "When life comes at you fast, take a little walk and have a little talk with the good Lord. He'll straighten things out for you."

Carlton grinned. "I'll remember that, sir."

Papa sighed. "Well, then . . . I 'spect I should go inside and help Bess out."

Alice-Ann shook her head as he entered the house, the screen door slamming behind him. Her father hadn't helped his sister out once in all the years they'd lived under this roof as a family.

Carlton turned to her. "Now that we're alone and not likely to be interrupted any time soon, I have a few surprises for you," he said.

"You do?"

He bounded out of the swing, nearly sending her feet over shoulders. "Sorry," he said, steadying her. Then he laughed and she did too. "I'll be right back."

If he'd been excited about getting out of the swing, he sure seemed to take his time walking to his car and back. But when he finally emerged from the shadows and back into the sunlight and then under the shade of the porch, he held two envelopes — one pale pink and shaped like a greeting card, the other a long white business envelope — and a small box wrapped in thick white paper.

"What's this?" she asked.

Carlton returned to the swing and sat next to her again. "An early birthday gift."

She smiled. "Way early."

"First things first," he said, extending the pink envelope. "Open this one."

Alice-Ann took it from his hands. "Obviously a greeting card."

"Don't get sassy on me."

She slid closer to him. Their hips touched, sending electric pulses through her body. "Open it now?"

"Please."

Alice-Ann used her fingernail to pop open the seal, then pulled out the card. She held it up, the face of the card toward him. "It's really a birthday card."

Carlton answered with a grin. "Read it."

" 'Happy birthday to the one I love . . .' "
She tilted her head and eyed him. "Aww."

"Read."

She opened the card. " 'Roses may be red, and violets may be blue, but they'll never be as beautiful as —' " Alice-Ann took a deep breath. Pressed her hand against her chest. " 'As beautiful as you.' "

He kissed her cheek, then whispered, "It's true." He kept his face close to her ear and she felt the warmth of his breath there.

Alice-Ann batted her eyes to keep from crying. "I love you, Carlton."

"I love you too."

She giggled. "No, silly. That's what it says right there."

He straightened and looked at where her finger pointed to his signature. "So it does." He took the card from her. "That's not all it says." Carlton opened the card fully and handed it back to her. *"Reeeeead,"* he encouraged.

" 'Dear Alice-Ann, I'm now a full-time employee at the newspaper.' " She gasped as she dropped the card and threw her arms around him. "Oh, Carlton!"

His laughter shook his chest, pressed against hers, bringing it up and down with his. "Happy?"

"Yes. So happy for you."

He kissed her lightly. "For us."

Alice-Ann nodded. "For us."

He reached for the second envelope. "Now open this."

She retrieved a thick stack of papers with too many words and numbers for her to comprehend at first glance. "What is this?" She flipped to the back page, saw Mister Dooley's signature next to Carlton's, then looked up for an explanation.

"Remember the other day when Nancy took you to the soda shop for lunch?"

"Of course. It was only three days ago and we were late getting back. Mister Dooley and Miss Portia didn't even fuss, which, by the way, I still find a little strange."

"She was actually keeping you out of the way." He pointed to the papers. "That's a house loan, Alice-Ann. I bought the cottage for you."

Alice-Ann opened her mouth to speak — what she'd say, she had no idea — but only an *eek* came out.

"Cat got your tongue?"

Alice-Ann nodded.

"I'll start on the renovations this week, working some nights and weekends." He cocked a brow. "I'll expect some help."

She nodded again, happiness welling up inside her. The two of them, working side by side in the house she'd loved for so long. She'd scrub the floors while Carlton tore out old boards and replaced them. And she'd paint the walls while he took care of the trim.

Carlton wrapped his arms around her and laid his forehead against hers. "I bet you want to kiss me right now, don't you?"

She giggled. "Yes, but if I kissed you as hard as I want to, Aunt Bess and Papa would be out here faster than that song you hear from the Zenith ends."

"Hmm . . . what *is* the name of that song?" he teased.

"You know good and well what it is. 'People Will Say We're in Love.' "

"Gotta appreciate Bing." He turned his face toward the open door and windows, looking for signs of life inside, then turned back. "Kiss me," he said, "and kiss me well so I can give you the third gift."

Alice-Ann did as she was told, her head swirling from sheer happiness. What had she ever done to deserve such joy? Such love? Or a man such as Carlton? What goodness had she shared with the world to earn a man who would work at a job he wanted, to live in a house she'd dreamed of?

Whatever it had been . . .

They broke apart. "Doodlebug," he said,

his voice hoarse. Then he cleared his throat and offered her the small, wrapped box. As the heat in her cheeks rushed back to where it had come from — wherever that was — she tore into the paper to find a black box. She lifted the top slowly.

"Carlton . . ."

He took the ring from a nest of cotton and held it toward her with shaking fingers. "May I?"

She lifted her left hand, felt the cold metal of yellow, white, and rose gold that had been carved into tiny flowers and vines encircling a cluster of diamonds. "This was my great-grandmother's."

"It's amazing."

"You're amazing." He cupped her face with his hand and she rested in it. "I love you so much, Alice-Ann."

Alice-Ann closed her eyes, allowing the tears to slip between her lashes. She nodded. "So happy," she whispered. "I'm so, so happy."

"I promise you," he whispered back, "I'll do everything in my power to make sure you're always this happy."

She nodded again.

This was good. This was enough.

"I'm worried," Alice-Ann admitted to Aunt

Bess that evening as they washed the dishes and put them away.

"About?"

"Well . . . the wedding, for one thing."

Aunt Bess pulled her hands out of the soapy water, flung some of the suds back into the sink, and then reached for the drying cloth in Alice-Ann's hands to finish the job off. "What about it?"

Alice-Ann peered into the sink. "Are we done?"

"Except for your papa's coffee cup, which he's still got in the living room. Now, talk to me, Alice. Where's your worrying coming from?"

Alice-Ann wiped down the last pan and walked it to the cabinet where Aunt Bess stored it. "For one, it's going to cost money. And right now Papa doesn't have any to spare. None of us do." Unless, of course, your daddy happened to be a doctor. Although even by Claudette's standards — if she were honest — the September wedding hadn't been what it might have been without the war.

Aunt Bess poured herself a cup of coffee and set it on the table. "Join me?"

Alice-Ann nodded.

"I've been thinking about this too," Aunt Bess said as she poured another cup.

Alice-Ann took cream out of the Frigid-aire. "You have?"

"I was thinking we could have the service at the church, of course." She set about preparing her coffee the way she liked it and Alice-Ann did the same. "Then we'd all come back here. I'll bake the cake. Have some little finger sandwiches. Some cheese straws. Make my punch you always liked so much."

Alice-Ann wrapped her fingers around the warmth of the cup as she stared into it. Without raising her head, she asked, "What about my dress, Aunt Bess? Because I know we can't afford to buy one like Claudette wore." And she didn't dare ask about the one in the hope chest, the one she'd always *hoped* to wear. She understood now that losing someone to war carried the deepest pain, and she loved Aunt Bess too much to ask her to open the old — possibly unhealed — wound. "Maybe you could make mine as well as the bridesmaids'?" Who, of course, would be Claudette and Maeve.

"Oh, Alice . . ."

Alice-Ann looked up. Sadness settled in her aunt's eyes, but then, before Alice-Ann had a chance to say how sorry she felt for causing such emotion, Aunt Bess brightened. "I think I can do you one better than

378

that." She stood. "Come on to my bedroom with me."

Leaving cups of coffee behind, Alice-Ann followed her aunt to the bedroom she rarely walked into, for no other reason than that she felt Aunt Bess deserved some level of privacy.

Aunt Bess had never been one for anything froufrou, and her room exemplified that. Plain white walls boasted only a few family photos, along with — over the narrow bed — a framed embroidered sampler displaying a tin watering can filled with pansies that her own mother had stitched. Alice-Ann had heard Aunt Bess say, time and again, that aside from her Bible, the handwork was the most valuable thing to her heart.

At the foot of the bed sat the simple hope chest, filled with treasures Alice-Ann never thought to plunder through. Aunt Bess headed straight for it, and when she'd knelt down to unlatch it, she said, "Close the door behind you, Alice."

Alice-Ann did so, then joined her aunt on the floor, her knees pressed into the worn braided rug that covered most of the room's hardwood floor. She peered inside the cedar-scented trove, her eyes widening at the collection of yellowed letters tied off with ribbon, the silver-framed photographs, two silver candlesticks, an old mink wrap, and a long white box covering the bottom of the chest.

Aunt Bess busied herself removing the items on top, handing each one to her niece, mumbling things like "This was your great-aunt Sybil's, who I never cared much for . . ." or "When I'm dead, be sure to read these letters if you *really* want something to cry about."

"Aunt Bess —"

"Here we go," Aunt Bess declared, pulling the box from its confines. She laid it on the floor between them and ceremoniously pulled the top away. "Here we go."

Alice-Ann fell back on her feet, her mouth gaping open, her breath escaping her. Her aunt dared to expose the old wound. Somehow, in time, she'd healed past the pain of losing her beloved. Enough, now, to personally share the dress she'd intended to wear. "*Aunt Bess* . . . it's — it's simply . . ."

Aunt Bess plucked the wedding dress up by the sheer, lacy bell-shaped sleeves, drawing it out as she stood.

Alice-Ann's eyes traveled up, past the tiers of creamy satin to the deep V-neck swathed in lace. "It's like something out of *Gatsby*," she whispered. To speak any other way would have seemed irreverent.

"As you know, it was mine," Aunt Bess said, holding it up to her shoulders. "Clearly," she stated, looking down, "I was a lot thinner back then."

Alice-Ann stood. "Do you want to talk about it, Aunt Bess?"

"I know what you think," Aunt Bess said matter-of-factly. "That my fiancé died in the war." She draped the dress across the end of her bed.

"He *didn't*?"

Aunt Bess returned to the hope chest and busied herself replacing the items she'd laid on the floor. "No."

"But I thought . . ." She fingered the hemline of the wedding gown, wondering now if she *should* wear it, lovely though it was.

Her aunt sighed into the chest. "His name was Paul. Paul Trenton Pearson." She closed the lid. "He was a handsome young man. The handsomest. Blond hair. Eyes as blue as a summer sky after an afternoon rain. I'd never seen anything like them before." Her eyes met Alice-Ann's. "Nor since."

Alice-Ann eased herself onto the bed beside the dress. She slid her fingertips beneath the lace of the sleeve and marveled at the translucence. "I don't understand . . ."

"He was handsome, all right, but he —"
She walked to the occasional chair near the
open window framed by sheers, overlooking
the fields on the south side of the property.
Alice-Ann remained silent as Aunt Bess
took a moment to get comfortable, both
with herself and her story. "He took to the
bottle, I'm afraid."

Alice-Ann tried to imagine Aunt Bess with
anyone who drank. Or swore. Or even
smoked cigarettes. She couldn't. "Before
the war?"

"No. He . . . Let me go back a little, if
you will." She took a breath. "Paul and his
family didn't live *here.* In Bynum. He and
his people came from Collins."

"Then how'd you meet him?"

Aunt Bess gave a half smile. "A church
social. His daddy was a preacher over there
and once a month Mama and Daddy would
pack us all up and we'd go for Sunday night
sings." Her head bobbed. "Mama's first
cousin went to church there and we'd make
a whole day of it. Spend the night." She
sighed. "Oh, those were wonderful times,
Alice."

Alice-Ann nodded. She adored it when
Oak Grove sponsored sings. Seemed that
everyone from every country church in the

county came to stand together, hymnals spread wide. Piano ivories danced under the fast fingers of one pianist or another as the congregants bellowed songs like "The Sweet By and By" and "Onward, Christian Soldiers."

"We started keeping company, as we used to say," Aunt Bess continued. "We'd always sit together at the sings, and as time went on, about once a month he'd come here to visit on a Sunday afternoon." She nodded once and tilted her head. "Then . . ."

"The war."

"Paul came of age in 1916, and of course, he enlisted. Rode a horse from Collins to here and asked me to marry him. Said he wanted to make it official before he went off. But I wanted to wait." Sadness settled in Aunt Bess's eyes. "He was gone two years." Her sigh fell across her lap. "It seemed to be forever back then, but it wasn't long when you think about it. Still, the war had done its deed."

"But he came home?"

"Back to Collins. Daddy and Mama drove me there to welcome him back." She smiled again and Alice-Ann knew Aunt Bess recollected a memory she'd not share with her niece. "We went off, the two of us . . ." She raised her eyes. "I told him about how

383

Mama had already made my dress — that one there — and about all the ideas I had dreamed up for the two of us while he'd been gone."

"So then why — ?"

"That's when he pulled a bottle from his coat pocket. Had the audacity to offer me a swig." Her eyes became hooded again. "I tried, Alice. Over the next weeks and months, I did all I knew to do to talk him out of it." She waved a hand. "And it wasn't just that he took a nip now and then. Paul — Paul couldn't seem to stop once he got started and then he — he seemed to become someone else. Right down to his language." She winced. "And most importantly, he didn't seem to feel the same about God anymore. Of all the things the war had done to him, that was the worst."

At least Carlton had returned with his faith intact. In fact, he was about as close to perfect as she'd ever imagined a godly man to be. "So you ended it?"

"I ended it." She shook her head as the words fell away.

"How did you end it?"

"I stayed up with Mama half that night, talking things out. She said the decision was mine, but then she asked me a question I still think about to this day."

"Which was?"

"She said, 'Bessy, can you see yourself with him for the rest of your life?' And then as she left my bedroom, she turned to me and said, 'You know, hon, you can't choose who you fall in love with, but you can choose who you marry.' "

"That's . . . profound."

"Mama's always been a smart old bird."

Alice-Ann nodded, thinking of the grandmother who now lived in Screven County with her widowed sister. She hadn't seen her in a while and she'd have to remedy that. Make sure she knew that her granddaughter was getting married. "Did you pray about it?"

She smiled fully. "That's what I did the other half of the night. Between Mama's words and God's reassurance that I'd be all right . . . He laid a verse from the Good Book on my heart. 'The troubles of my heart are enlarged: O bring thou me out of my distresses.' " She nodded. "And he did. The next day I took the ring back to Paul." She harrumphed. "He didn't even beg. Said I was being childish and that he'd always thought I'd be the mother of his children instead of *one* of them."

Alice-Ann pulled her hand from under the lace. "That had to have been difficult."

"One of the hardest things I ever lived through. Back then, Alice, a woman didn't have a whole lot of options other than getting married."

Alice-Ann understood.

"I was scared, I don't mind telling you," Aunt Bess continued. "Scared of what my future would look like. Scared of never finding another man to love me." Her brows shot up. "I guess you know how that turned out."

Alice-Ann felt her shoulders sink. "Oh, Aunt Bess. I'm so sorry."

"I put the dress away, and that was that. I left Bynum, went to live with Aunt Sybil over in Sylvania, and helped her with her growing family. Then your mama got sick and your daddy needed me and . . . well, you know the rest of the story."

Alice-Ann shook her head in an attempt to get the pieces to fall into place. "Aunt Bess, why have I always heard that your fiancé died in the war?"

Aunt Bess stopped rocking, stood, and walked to the bed. "I never said he died. I said I'd lost him to the war." She brought her fingers under Alice-Ann's chin as she smiled. "And I did. If it hadn't been for that war . . . well, who knows but the good Lord."

"Do you know what happened to him?"

She chuckled. "Oh, he married. Had a houseful of young'uns."

"Oh, Aunt Bess . . ."

"What's done is done."

"Did you ever — do you ever regret it?"

"No, ma'am. Marriage and a houseful of children doesn't always equal a good life. In fact, I have no idea if he's happy or not or if he ever got himself straightened out. I *hope* so. I honestly hope the best for him and his." She pursed her lips. "What kind of a Christian woman would I be otherwise?"

Alice-Ann stood and wrapped her arms around her aunt. The older woman's soft flesh brought comfort like a fully fluffed pillow at the end of a long day. "You're the *best* Christian woman, Aunt Bess."

Aunt Bess hugged her back, then released her. "Now, Alice," she said, the strength returning to her voice, "I'd appreciate it if you didn't talk of this in town."

"Of course not."

"Well then." She looked back at the dress. "Why don't you try it on," she said, bossy as ever. "And let's give this lovely frock a purpose, shall we?"

CHAPTER 27

During her lunch hour on Tuesday, Alice-Ann dashed down Main Street to Mac-Kay's Pharmacy in search of Janie Wren. She sighed a light breath of relief at finding her stocking ladies' handkerchiefs in the middle of the store. Only a few patrons milled about, one or two of them offering Alice-Ann their congratulations.

"Janie," she said as she reached her.

Janie turned, smiled a deep-red-lipstick-against-white-teeth smile, and said, "Oh, Alice-Ann. I've heard your news." She gave Alice-Ann a brief hug. "I'm so happy for you."

"Thank you," Alice-Ann returned. "I'm actually here for your help."

"Mine?" She raised perfectly shaped brows. "You want *my* help?"

"Mmm. Remember when I came in and got the hand lotion?"

"The Jergens. Sure." She looked toward

the aisle where they'd stood not so very long ago.

Alice-Ann summoned the courage she needed to fulfill her mission. "I'm hoping — praying, nearly — that you can help . . . with this." She pulled at a strand of her hair.

The look on Janie's face was like that of a kid on Christmas morning. "Can I? Oh, honey," she exclaimed, waving her hands in a "go on" fashion. "With the right conditioners I can have you looking like Veronica Lake. You know, before she cut her hair for the cause." Janie turned. "Follow me."

Alice-Ann stayed close on her heels until they reached hair products. "See this?" Janie asked, holding up a bottle of milky liquid. "This is what you need." She reached for another bottle. "First shampoo with this. Lather. Rinse. Repeat. Oh, and use cold water, not hot, when you rinse." She handed the bottle to Alice-Ann, who wrapped the fingers of her right hand around it.

"Got it."

"Then follow up with this. Put it on, work it in all the way to the roots, and then wait for five minutes."

"Five minutes." Alice-Ann reached for the bottle with her left hand, exposing her ring, which Janie spied right off.

"Dear heavens. It's stunning," she said,

turning Alice-Ann's hand for a better look.

"It was Carlton's great-grandmother's. And I'm wearing a beautiful wedding dress from the 1920s that's — that belonged to a family member. It's — it's amazing. Truly lovely."

And it was. The dress had fit her perfectly, and even though Aunt Bess had seemed intent on remaking the dress for a more modern look, Alice-Ann's insistence otherwise won the argument.

For once.

Janie shook her head and breathed in slowly. "My, my. You are so lucky, Alice-Ann. You know, I had always hoped — that maybe when Mack came back . . ."

Alice-Ann prickled at the thought, then chastised herself for such a notion. She was in love with Carlton Hillis. If Janie Wren wanted to imagine herself in Boyd Mac-Kay's arms, that was fine with her. Or at least it should be.

No. It was fine. Completely.

"Alice-Ann?"

Alice-Ann shook her head, aware of Janie's expectant look. "Yes?"

"Can I — may I — would you like to look at some makeup? I can — I mean, I could make you look real pretty for Carlton." She blushed a perfect shade of pink. "Not that you aren't pretty already —"

While Alice-Ann knew she could have been — and maybe should have been — insulted, the genuine tone in Janie's voice told her that her old school chum meant well. "I'd like that. And don't worry, I'm not offended." After all, she was smart enough to know beauty had not been stamped on her at birth.

Janie brightened. "We just got some new cosmetics in from DuBarry. Did you ever try their emblem reds?" She shook her head. "No, I'd say you'd look best in a nice peach or pink."

Alice-Ann had no idea either way. "Other than Claudette's wedding, I've never even worn lipstick."

Janie planted her fists on her curvaceous hips. "Say, why didn't you ask Claudette or Maeve to help you with this?"

Because they're naturally beautiful, which I'm not nor ever can be. And you, Janie, are put together like an advertisement for — what did you call it? — DuBarry, which is the best I can hope for.

"You know so much more than they do, Janie. You know, about things like this."

Janie beamed even brighter. "I suppose I do," she said, then turned. "Come with me, Alice-Ann. Carlton Hillis won't believe his eyes when he sees you again."

Long minutes later, as Alice-Ann paid for her purchases, she summoned all her bravado to ask Janie how the MacKays seemed to be getting along.

Janie leaned slightly over the counter and pressed her slender fingers, nails lacquered in red polish, into the wood, and said, "Some days better than others. Miss Myrtle has a lot of what Mister Lance refers to as her spells. Mister Lance, God love him, is simply a paragon of strength, though at times he becomes melancholy too."

Paragon. Alice-Ann chastised herself as quickly as the amazement came to her that Janie knew what *paragon* meant.

"I guess that's the way men are." Papa sure fit that bill.

Janie's perfectly coiffed hair swayed as she shook her head. "Far less emotional than women. *We* carry our hearts on our sleeves."

Alice-Ann swallowed. "Do you — do you mind if I ask — do you still believe Mack is alive somewhere?" She looked out the window as if she expected him to be standing on the sidewalk. "Out there?" She returned her eyes to Janie, who shrugged.

"I do," she mumbled. "But I'm alone in that. My mother says I've lost my everloving mind." She shrugged again as she gave Alice-Ann the change from her purchases, a few coins she'd held in her hand until they'd grown warm. "Maybe I have. I sit in my room every night, reading his letters over and over. I close my eyes and imagine the day I hear he's alive and my mother finally leaves me alone about it."

Janie still read Mack's letters. Well, wasn't that just a kick in the pants!

It had been a while since Alice-Ann had done the same, not that she would share that with Janie. Or that they were still in her closet, of course, tied off with a red ribbon.

One she'd once worn in her hair.

Alice-Ann washed her hair that evening, followed with the conditioner, which she left in as instructed, then wrapped her head in a towel while she experimented with her new makeup. It took several applications and face scrubbings to get it where she didn't come off looking like some clown from the circus. Satisfied, she washed her face again, then removed the towel, rinsed a final time, and — with a wide-toothed comb — pulled her hair free of nearly all the curls.

Before she'd left the drugstore, Janie showed her how to rag-roll her hair for softer curls, which she did, then went to bed.

"Good land of the living," Aunt Bess said the next morning when she came down for breakfast. "Why, Brother, I don't know who this is at my kitchen table." She stood at the counter with a dishcloth in her hand, ready to wrap it around a steaming bowl of grits.

Her father opened his mouth to say something, then closed it.

Alice-Ann sat with relief at the table — at least Nelson and Irene hadn't come down yet.

"What's all that on your face?"

"It's makeup." She tossed her loose curls as she looked up. "What do you think?"

Aunt Bess placed the grits on the table between them, then patted Alice-Ann's hand. "I think you're real pretty, Alice. Then again, I always did."

"I just hope Carlton likes it," Alice-Ann mumbled.

"Likes what?" Nelson asked, entering the room. He stopped short when she turned slightly to face him. "Good heavens."

"I'm an engaged woman now," Alice-Ann said in her own defense. "Time I stopped looking like some dopey little girl."

Nelson pulled out a chair opposite her and plopped into it. "Well, all right then," he said, though his brow formed a deep V. "What do you think Carlton will say?"

Alice-Ann shrugged. "I guess I'll find out later today."

Carlton was as stunned as everyone else she came into contact with that day. She met him after work — as always on Wednesdays, they wrapped up at noon — in their usual place outside the bank, Nancy beside her. But his shock was only momentary. He glanced around as though he expected someone else to walk out the door behind them. Finally he said, "Nancy, where's Alice-Ann?"

Alice-Ann swatted at him. "Didn't I tell you," she said to Nancy, "that he would say exactly that?"

Later, when they were alone in their new home, making a quick list of the supplies they'd need just to clean it up enough to figure on the repairs, Carlton paused to say, "I hope you don't think I need you to do all that." He waved his hand around her head and face.

She frowned. "You don't like it?"

"Oh no. I like it just fine. I only hope you didn't do it for me. Because, honestly, Alice-Ann, you're perfect just like you are." He smiled. "Or *were*."

She stared at her feet. "I wanted you to like it."

He chuckled and wrapped her in his arms

and rocked her left to right and back again. "Silly girl. I *do*. I promise." He tilted her face up to meet his. "But you," he said, planting a kiss on her lips, "are —" he kissed her nose — "already perfect." He pressed his lips against hers again, then deepened the kiss.

She broke away from him. "I thought we said we wouldn't hug or kiss when we were alone in here together."

He hunched his shoulders and pretended to sag toward the floor. "You're right," he said, straightening. "We will honor God and —"

"He will honor us." She glanced at her watch. "Carlton, I have to catch the bus and you have to get back to work."

Carlton walked her to the bus stop, kissed her forehead, and told her he'd see her at church that evening.

"Really?" she asked. "You're coming to church with me instead of with your family in town?"

"We're engaged now," he said, pulling her left hand into his right and running his thumb over the ring. "I think we should worship together. And I know how much your church means to you. What with your work with the kids and all." One brow cocked. "And I figure if you want to keep going to Oak Grove, even after we marry and move into *our home,* that'll be fine with me."

Of course this was what she wanted. To think of the two of them, along with the children they'd one day have, worshiping alongside Papa and Aunt Bess, Nelson and Irene and Little Mack . . . what more could she hope for?

"Thank you, Carlton." She hugged him good and hard, then boarded the bus and took her usual seat.

During the ride, Alice-Ann looked out the window, watching her world go by, all the while dreaming of the day she would become Mrs. Carlton Hillis. They'd not yet set a date and — with Ernie still working up the nerve to ask Maeve — she wanted to wait to find out what her best friend's plans were first.

"Alice-Ann," Ben called out to her.

Startled, she looked forward to see his eyes in the long mirror glaring back at her. "Yes?"

"Is that Josephine James sitting in her car at the end of your driveway?"

Alice-Ann slid to another seat for a better look. "It sure looks like it. Wonder who she's waiting on."

Ben slowed the bus to a stop. "From the

way she's climbing out of the car, I'd say *you.*"

With a friendly good-bye to Ben, Alice-Ann stepped out. Miss Josephine stood near the passenger door of her car, which she held open. "Hurry *up,* Alice-Ann," she exclaimed over the squeaking of the bus's gears and rumbling of the engine as it moved along.

"What is it, Miss Josephine? Has something happened to Papa?"

"No, child. Get in." She motioned toward the door, but Alice-Ann refused to budge.

"Aunt Bess? Or Nelson or . . . *Miss Josephine,* what is it?"

"It's the American Red Cross, Alice-Ann. They've been calling for you over at my house."

"The American Red Cross?" Alice-Ann took a step closer. "For me?"

Miss Josephine looked as though she might burst any moment. "I'm not supposed to tell you, but I can't help myself." She fluttered, then said, "It's Boyd Mac-Kay, Alice-Ann. He's alive over at a hospital on Pearl Harbor. Now get in, hon. He's a-wantin' to talk to ya!"

CHAPTER 28

A thousand questions raced through her mind between the end of the road and the Jameses' slick, black telephone, which rested on a bench-style table in the hallway near the kitchen at the back of the house.

No. Not a thousand. A thousand and one.

As soon as they reached the phone — the echoes of their heels on the hardwood floors fading around them — Miss Josephine snatched up the handpiece, rammed her finger into the 0, and wound it all the way to the right.

Alice-Ann bounced on the balls of her feet, waiting.

"Carriebeth?" Miss Josephine all but shouted to the operator. "Get me the American Red Cross. . . . *Yes . . . yes . . .* Oh, for crying out loud, Carriebeth, the same ones that called here earlier." She opened her mouth to say something more, clamped it shut, then reopened it. "And don't you dare forget your oath, Carriebeth. Not a word. Not a single word . . . Well, all right then."

"What'd she say?" Alice-Ann asked, taking a step closer to hook her sweater and purse on the arm of the telephone bench.

Miss Josephine slapped her hand over the mouthpiece. "She reminded me that she's never been one to gossip and if I knew half the secrets in this town she knew, I'd — *Yes.* This is Josephine James. . . . Yes, I do. She's right here."

The older woman pushed the handset toward her, but Alice-Ann reached for her sweater instead. The temperature had suddenly dropped. "Let me just . . ." She shoved her arms in, pulled it tight around her, and sat before taking the phone, placing it to her ear, and sinking to the bench's chair. "Hello?"

"Alice-Ann Branch?" the voice asked over crackling and static.

"Yes. Yes, ma'am. I'm Alice-Ann Branch."

"Hold please."

Alice-Ann looked up at Miss Josephine's anxious face and wondered if it mirrored her own. "They asked me to hold."

Miss Josephine had come out of her sweater now and she wrung it in her hands like it was an old dishrag. "Thank the good Lord my George is down to the gristmill.

This would only bring back the pain of losing our Pete."

Alice-Ann's heart sank, knowing it wouldn't matter if Mister George heard about Mack's sudden return from the dead now or later. The grief of every family in Bynum that had lost a loved one would return with this news. They'd wish and wonder. They'd pray and curse.

If God had spared Boyd MacKay, why hadn't he spared — ?

"Alice-Ann?"

Alice-Ann sucked in her breath. From half a world away and in spite of the line noise, Mack's voice was exactly that — Mack's. "Mack?" she said, her voice no more than a whispered prayer. "Mack, is that really you?"

He laughed easily, then coughed a few times as though the laughter had taken everything out of him. "Sorry. Hey, I just found out . . ."

She pressed the phone closer to her ear, reaching up to pull off the clip-on pearl earrings like those that had once belonged to her mother. The ones her father had given Alice-Ann on her eighteenth birthday. "Found out?"

He chuckled, coughed again, and said, "I didn't know I was dead until I ran into George Junior."

"George James?"

"My boy?" Miss Josephine pressed her fists and sweater between ample bosoms.

Alice-Ann held up a hand but nodded.

"I saw him last night in the mess hall. My first trip down there since I got here."

Alice-Ann grabbed the bottom of the handpiece with her left hand. The one-thousand-and-first question leapt from her heart and into her mouth. "Mack, *where have you been?*"

Miss Josephine shifted in front of her. "And why did he call you and not his mama? That's what I want to know."

Oh, dear Gussie . . .

"Recuperating on a torpedo tube the first couple of months and then here in the hospital after that." He coughed again, the sound of it almost lost within the line static. "Listen, Alice-Ann, they aren't going to let me talk long. I still get tired pretty easily and —"

"Mack, what about your parents? Why didn't you call your parents?"

"The government men . . . decided to send someone from Camp Stewart to see them. You know, to help prepare . . . before I call home. Should be there sometime . . . today. Before church services begin tonight, I imagine. May already . . . there."

"They heard by *telegram* that you'd died, Mack."

"I know, Alice-Ann. That's the way it's done. I — I don't have . . . control — I didn't know. But I wanted to . . . you. I wanted you to hear it from me." He paused. "Alice-Ann, the thought of . . . waiting for me at home . . . I — I lost your letters. I'm sorry. But in my mind, since I got shot down, I reread them a hundred . . . or more. And I realized . . ."

The static grew in intensity, so much so that it ate the rest of his words.

"Mack?" Crackling met her cry. *"Mack?"* she called out again. But the line had gone quiet. Alice-Ann replaced the handpiece, shuddered, then looked up at Miss Josephine, whose mouth hung open like an old man's while sleeping on a hot afternoon. "We lost — we lost connection."

Miss Josephine grasped her hand and pulled her up. "Come on, Alice-Ann. Let's have some hot tea and you can tell me everything he said." She all but dragged Alice-Ann into the kitchen. "And don't leave out a single word."

"I —"

"And tell me, what did he say about my boy?" She grabbed the teakettle and filled it with water. Alice-Ann gripped the back of one of the kitchen chairs and squeezed.

How would she — could she — possibly answer Miss Josephine's questions? No matter what she said, surely by this time tomorrow everyone in Bynum would know that Mack had called the Jameses' farmhouse and had asked specifically for Alice-Ann Branch.

Everyone. Including . . . "Carlton," she sighed the name.

Miss Josephine turned from the stove. "What's that?"

"Nothing." She pulled the chair out and eased herself down. "He said he saw George Junior in the mess hall. George told him, apparently, that he had been declared dead." She shrugged. "That's all I know, Miss Josephine."

The older woman joined her at the table while they waited for the water to heat up. "But why did he call you, hon?" she asked. "Why not his mama and daddy? They've been so upset — and I know from experience what *that's* like — at losing him. And him their only —" She dabbed at her eyes, where tears pooled along the lashes.

"Miss Josephine." Alice-Ann reached across the table for her hands, folding them into her own. "They're sending someone from Camp Stewart today to tell the Mac-

Kays. They may already be there, he said."

Miss Josephine sighed a shaky breath. "That's the right thing to do. They should do that for every — every mother. And father. But I guess that would be too much to ask." Her eyes darted back and forth along the pattern of the tablecloth — a collection of red-and-yellow flowers strung together by green vines and leaves. "Too many of our boys have died. They'd be too busy sending out men to deliver the bad — the news."

"I wrote to Mack," Alice-Ann interjected thoughtlessly, because she didn't know what to say about words spoken from her older neighbor's anguished heart. "I wrote him a lot. Before. He was Nelson's best friend, you know, and I — I thought it would be nice." She shrugged again, hoping she appeared as casual about writing to him as she would have been about writing to Nelson, had he gone off to war. "You know, to keep him informed about Bynum and all that was going on here and — and — I guess that's why he called . . . me."

Miss Josephine nodded as the teakettle whistled. "Well, I reckon that makes sense," she said, standing. Then, as though it really did, she asked, "Milk or lemon?"

■ ■ ■ ■

No one mentioned her new hairdo or the cosmetics she wore at church that evening. Rather, the entire congregation buzzed about the news — which had managed to reach all of Bynum by the time Wednesday night prayer meeting started.

Boyd MacKay had been shot down in Japanese-infested waters. He'd held on to a piece of wreckage for hours in clear view of an enemy ship. Miraculously, no one had spotted him. He'd kept his face down, he said, and prayed without ceasing. Then, a miracle. An American submarine located him. They'd had to wait until dark to surface. To bring him on board. And there — while Bynum had buried another "son" — he'd spent time recuperating.

The only two, by Alice-Ann's estimation, who didn't mention Mack's return from the dead, were herself and Carlton, who managed not to say much at all. Period.

Aunt Bess said three words to her before they walked through the front doors of the church. "Admit to nothing."

"Meaning?"

She shook her head. Papa mumbled, "What's done is done, Alice-Ann. You've made the right choice."

And of course she knew she had. She loved Carlton. With her whole heart.

But she had loved Mack, too. Or at least she thought she had.

Then again . . . maybe what she'd felt for him had been nothing more than childhood infatuation. But how would she know? How *could* she know? She had so little to compare it to.

As the preacher spoke briefly of God's great provision — Him the giver of life *and* death *and* life beyond the grave — Alice-Ann replayed her conversation with Mack in her mind. Most especially what he'd said as their call had been disconnected.

"I — I lost your letters. I'm sorry. But in my mind, since I got shot down, I reread them a hundred . . . or more. And I realized . . ."

"Realized what?" she whispered from the pew where she sat between Aunt Bess and Carlton, whose shoulder pressed into hers as a constant reminder of his presence. Of his devotion to her. Of his love.

He thought she was beautiful. He'd bought her the cottage. He'd placed — she fingered the center stone — his great-grandmother's ring on her finger.

Feeling his eyes on her movement, she cast him a sideward glance. He smiled.

Mouthed, "Realized what?"

Had she spoken out loud? "Nothing," she mouthed back, then looked down. He'd placed his hand, palm side up, to rest between their legs. An invitation she willingly took. The warmth of flesh upon flesh gave her the security she needed. The ability to keep going.

If she could just get through this hour, she told herself. This prayer meeting with all the gossip sure to fill up the social time afterward. She could go home. Go to her room. Climb in her bed.

And there she would cry.

After prayer meeting, Carlton asked Papa for permission to drive her home and he gave it.

Part of her wished he had said no. The other part thanked him.

Carlton said nothing between the church and the car. Nothing as he opened the passenger's door for her. Nothing as he started the car and pointed it toward home, the blackout hoods over the headlights casting scarce light onto the road ahead. Only after they'd pulled away from the church and the shadows of the night enveloped them did he clear his throat. "I guess we may as well talk about this. Get it all out in the open."

She could have asked what he meant. She could have pretended Boyd MacKay's resurrection meant nothing to her. But that would have been the game of a child, which she no longer was.

"I don't know what to say," she mumbled.

His fingers flexed on the steering wheel. "What did *he* say?"

"How — how did you know?"

"That he called you?"

Alice-Ann gripped the strap of her purse with vigor. "Yes."

"Your father caught me outside the church before we went in."

"Oh." Papa always hung around outside with the other farmers. They'd talk about crops and weather and harvesting until someone finally stuck their head out and said, "Preacher's in."

"Well?" Carlton's voice held a new edge, one she'd never heard before.

"Why are you mad at *me,* Carlton?"

"I'm not mad at you, Alice-Ann."

"You sure sound it." Like his, her own voice had gone up an octave.

"Well, you tell me then. How would you be feeling right now?"

"If?"

Carlton passed the driveway to the farm.

"Where are we going? You told Papa you

were driving me home."

"We need time to — we *have* to talk about this."

"Papa will tan your hide, Carlton Reed Hillis, if you don't take me right home. You know what he'll think." Not to mention the fit Aunt Bess would have.

His face jerked toward hers, and in a tiny flash of light, she saw anger. No, not anger. Something more. Something different. She saw *fear.* But not of her father or even of Aunt Bess. Carlton was afraid of something else.

"I think your father will understand," he said with a swallow.

"You're afraid," she said as if she'd suddenly been granted all understanding.

Carlton slowed the car and eased it to one of the access roads along the back of their farm. When he shut the engine off, he turned to her, laying his arm against the back of the seat. "Wouldn't you be?"

"Yes."

His eyes sought hers, holding them, pleading with them as his fingertips caressed her cheek. "Do I have reason to be?" he asked, his voice once again the one she knew so well.

I don't know . . . "No." She shook her head. "Carlton, no . . ." She took his left hand in both of hers. "I love you," she said, because it was true. She was sure of it.

He sighed deeply, filling the car with his breath, warm and minty as always. "Alice-Ann . . ." He shifted again to capture both of her hands with his, then brought her left up and kissed the ring. "I love you so much." His gaze rested on their circle of promise. Their belief in a forever vow. "I couldn't bear losing you."

"You're not going to lose me," she said, tilting and ducking her head to press her lips against his. Quickly, so as not to start something she'd regret, what with them sitting in a car, alone, on a stretch of dirt hidden by crops and shadows. "I promise."

And she meant it.

She was sure of it.

Chapter 29

The next day, Alice-Ann and Carlton filled their time with working at their respective jobs, then meeting at the cottage, ready to roll up their sleeves and, as Carlton said, "get the house clean and ourselves filthy."

Alice-Ann brought a change of clothes — an old shirt of Papa's and a pair of overalls she cuffed to her knees — to the bank along with a small box of cleaning supplies and some cast-off rags. Carlton had purchased items from his parents' five-and-dime — a broom, two mops ("This job will take more than one," he told her. "And I have a feeling the first mop and maybe even the second is gonna be thrown in the trash."), a bucket, and three sponges ("Mama said you'd appreciate these."). His mother dropped by that afternoon with a large pitcher of tea and four matching glasses — all of which she said came from the store and all of which she said would "go nicely in your new home."

Then she kissed Alice-Ann on the cheek and, tearfully, thanked her for loving her boy.

Words Alice-Ann was sure had been heartfelt but only made her feel worse than she already did.

If not worse, ill at ease.

Maeve had come to the house as well, arriving shortly after her mother left as though they'd timed their comings and goings, and toting a small bag filled with — of all things — four rolls of Scott toilet tissue and two bars of Palmolive beauty soap. "Doctors *prove* two out of three women can have beautiful skin in fourteen days," she mimicked as she pulled it out of the bag and handed it to Alice-Ann.

"What?" Alice-Ann asked, her eyes looking from the soap to her friend. She laughed. "I don't know what that means."

"That's what the ad says. You know, the one Mama and Daddy have down at the store in the beauty bar products. Not *soap,* mind you. *Beauty bar.*"

Alice-Ann sniffed the soap wrapped in green paper and sealed with a black band. "Well, it smells fine, but I'm sure I'll be the third woman."

Maeve crossed her arms. "Don't put

yourself down, Alice-Ann." She glanced toward where Carlton had busied himself cleaning the front bedroom while Alice-Ann tackled the kitchen, which alone would take days. Maybe even weeks. "Look," she continued, bringing her attention back to Alice-Ann. "My brother would kill me if he knew I was telling you this, but . . ." She sighed. "He's really, *really* worried about you and Mack."

Alice-Ann returned the soap to the bag her friend still held, then took the sack and placed it on the grimy kitchen counter Carlton had previously declared "unsalvageable."

But Alice-Ann had begged for a chance to try, and he'd acquiesced.

"There *is* no Mack and me," she said, keeping her voice low. "There never was." She looked back at Maeve. "Not really, anyway." Alice-Ann reached to the top of her head, where she'd tied off a bandanna, and pulled. "I'm getting a headache from this thing. I always do."

Maeve swatted her hands away and untied it. "You've got it too tight, silly girl." She kept her attention on fixing the problem but continued speaking. "You always *did.* Look . . . I know you, Alice-Ann. The problem, as I see it, is that you never really

414

got *over* Mack. You loved him and he died, so there's no *real* end to the story." She blinked. "There you go," she said, stepping back.

Alice-Ann touched the knot. "Gracious. That's much better. Thank you."

"The bigger problem is that he didn't really die, did he?" Maeve's eyes narrowed. "You know everyone in town is wondering why he called you."

"How do they even know? Miss Josephine isn't the gossipy kind and Miss Carriebeth would lose her job if she told."

Maeve cocked a brow. "But Mister George has always been a talker. And don't get me started on what Janie Wren has been saying."

Alice-Ann leaned against the countertop and lower cabinets. "Why? What's she been saying?"

"I have come to the conclusion that Janie has a thing for him." She blinked. "I mean, for Mack. Not Mister George."

"I already knew that, Maeve. About her feelings for Mack."

"You did? And you didn't *tell* me?"

No. She hadn't. There'd been so many things she hadn't shared with Maeve since the day she started walking from the bank to the five-and-dime to read to Carlton.

From that day on, somehow, Maeve's brother had taken his sister's place as her best friend. And in time, more than best friend. "Mack was writing to her, too. So . . . you see?"

"No. I don't see. What should I see?"

"He clearly wasn't in love with *me*, Maeve, if he was writing to Janie as well."

Maeve pursed her lips, breathing in and out a few times before shaking her head and saying, "But he didn't *call* Janie, now, did he?"

By Sunday's church service the whole town had been made aware that Mack would soon return to Georgia — specifically to a hospital over in Savannah — to recuperate fully. His injuries, according to his father, were so extensive they made Carlton's look like a boo-boo fit only for a Band-Aid. Not that Mister Lance said so, but the insinuation remained all the same.

Carlton commented little about it, and Alice-Ann worked hard to pretend she held no interest other than as the sister of one of Mack's best friends and the fiancée of his other.

Early Monday morning Maeve blew into the bank like a brisk October wind, her hair flying behind her, and her upper body tightly wrapped in a cream-colored sweater. Her feet skidded across the sparkling terrazzo floor, sending screeches echoing through the cavernous room.

When she reached Alice-Ann, she shoved her left hand under the window, dipping it into the brass plate where checks and cash were passed daily. "He proposed — he proposed — he proposed," she said between breaths.

Alice-Ann looked to Nancy, who had risen up on her tiptoes to inspect the tiny diamond that twinkled beneath the low-hanging overhead lights. It looked like the farthest star in the sky, but Alice-Ann knew that to Maeve, it rivaled the Rock of Gibraltar.

"Hold on," Alice-Ann said. "I'll come around."

Void of bank customers at that moment, Nancy joined her, followed by Miss Portia. Mister Dooley stretched in his seat as though he might be remotely interested, then settled back to his paperwork with a grunt.

The three women clucked around Maeve, whose hand lay in Alice-Ann's. "Well, I say it's about time," Alice-Ann said, her grin hurting her cheeks.

"You've dated a long time, haven't you,"

Nancy said, more as a comment than a question.

Maeve nodded. "Since high school." She blushed, the rose in her cheeks making her prettier than usual. "We didn't get serious until after — after we got involved in the war."

Mister Dooley cleared his throat from across the room. "Never understood why that young man didn't go off with the rest of 'em."

Maeve turned. "He tried, Mister Dooley," she said, raising her voice to meet the expanse of the room. "But they said his asthma was too bad for him to be of any use."

"Poor Ernie and his asthma," Alice-Ann said. "Kept him out of sports in school and kept him out of the war."

Maeve looked back at her. "Ernie thought he could beat the system, but he couldn't convince the Army that being able to breathe without drowning in your own lungs wasn't altogether necessary."

"You know," Mister Dooley called out again, "over twenty million of our boys in this great United States of America have been drafted." He raised bushy brows. "Did you know that?"

"Douglas Reddick," Miss Portia interjected with a turn, "what in tarnation does that have to do with the price of cotton at the market?"

"Why nothing, Portia," he said. "I just happened to be reading an article about it this morning. Said that out of the twenty million drafted, half got sent home for one reason or another."

"Well, I reckon Ernie was one of them, Mister Dooley," Maeve said, pulling her hand out of Alice-Ann's.

"Twenty percent of that fifty was because they couldn't read," the banker shot back. "Ernie can read, can't he?"

Alice-Ann bit her lip to keep from laughing.

"Oh, heavenly mercy," Miss Portia breathed out, then gave Maeve an uncustomary hug. Nancy and Alice-Ann blinked at each other as she said, "Congratulations, dear. I'm going back to my desk." She started toward the area of the bank where her desk stood near Mister Dooley's. "Doo," she said, "of course that boy can read. He went to school right here in Bynum, didn't he? Studied under Nancy's husband, didn't he?"

Alice-Ann shook her head as Nancy and Maeve giggled, then mumbled, "I think something is going on between Mister

Dooley and Miss Portia."

Nancy wrinkled her nose as the front door opened. "Customer," she said. "I'll take him, Alice-Ann."

"Let me walk you outside," Alice-Ann said to Maeve.

"Good," Maeve whispered. "I wanted to tell you something else but I didn't want the others to hear."

"Wait," Alice-Ann whispered back, knowing how easily a voice traveled within the bank.

They stepped outside into the warm sunshine. A half block away, trees that boasted green leaves in spring and summer now stood with their limbs half-naked, a blanket of yellow and red and orange wrapped along their jutting roots.

"Mack's daddy came into the store this morning to tell us that Mack will arrive in Savannah by Friday."

Alice-Ann studied the sidewalk. "Friday."

"I thought you should know."

She looked up. "Does Carlton know?"

Maeve shook her head. "Not that I know of. He was at work when Mister Lance came in."

Alice-Ann sighed. "They must be beside themselves."

"They're turning the store over to Janie to

run for the whole day by herself. Mister Lance said they'd go over Thursday afternoon and spend the night with Miss Myrtle's sister, who lives over there with her family."

Mack. Mack would be back on Georgia soil by the end of the week. Mack, whom she'd thought she'd never see again. Not that she would any time soon. Unlike going to the five-and-dime to see and read to Carlton, there was no logical reason for her to go traipsing off to Savannah to visit. She was an engaged woman now. She had Carlton's feelings to think of.

"I — I lost your letters." The words played in her memory. *"I'm sorry. But in my mind, since I got shot down, I reread them a hundred . . . or more. And I realized . . ."*

What? What had he realized? What had he tried to say? "Um . . . I gotta —" Alice-Ann thumbed toward the bank's door — "I really need to get back inside before I lose my job."

Maeve rolled her eyes. "Like that's going to happen, Alice-Ann Branch soon-to-be-Hillis." Her face sobered and her eyes showed concern. "It *is* going to be Hillis, isn't it?" Maeve's voice seemed to come from the other end of a long tunnel.

"Of course," she said. Then, remembering to smile, she grabbed Maeve's hands and added, "Of *course,* Maeve. Now that you're engaged to Ernie, Carlton and I can make our plans. I can't *wait* to be his wife. Sincerely." She gave her friend a hug — more to steady herself than anything else — and whispered, "Congratulations. Promise me we'll talk dates soon."

Maeve kissed her cheek. "We will," she said, her voice full of certainty.

But her eyes, Alice-Ann thought later, had held enough doubt for the both of them.

That afternoon she and Carlton worked alongside each other, stripping faded and dusty wallpaper from a back bedroom. With an aluminum bucket filled with sudsy water between them, they silently dipped the sponges Carlton's mother had sent the previous week, then soaked the walls, wetting the paper enough for it to buckle. Alice-Ann pulled, her fingers red and icy cold. Occasionally Carlton pulled a wide-edged scraper from the back pocket of his dungarees for the more stubborn pieces.

When they'd cleared a sizable strip, Carlton shoved the hand tool back into his pocket and groaned. "Thank the good Lord the former owners only papered this wall once."

Alice-Ann held up her wet hands, the nails

chipped in too many places. "Look," she said, feigning a pout. "I'll have to cut them down to the nubs tonight."

Carlton wiped his hands by rubbing them on his pant legs, then took hers in his, cupping them. He blew warm breath in, which managed to soothe the iciness there but sent shivers everywhere else. "Poor baby," he crooned, which made her laugh.

She pulled her hands free. "It'll all be worth it in the end."

Carlton took a step back to survey their progress, or lack thereof. "I was thinking either a pale yellow or green paint for this room."

Alice-Ann cocked her head. "Really?" In all honesty, she hadn't thought that far.

His blush ran from the V of his long-sleeved shirt — which he'd rolled up to his elbows — to his ears. "You know . . . baby colors."

She *really* hadn't thought that far.

Alice-Ann shook her head. "I think pale green or yellow would be nice," she said, looking at the wall, then back to him. "But *not* for that reason." His eyes grew large, so she added, "Not right now, anyway."

Carlton started toward her and she put her hand up. "Get back to work, you."

His bottom lip protruded in an overdramatic pout before he chuckled and resumed the painstaking task. After a few minutes, he cleared his throat and said, "Did you hear the big news?"

Alice-Ann's spine tingled. "About Mack?" she asked, as though the news were not big at all.

"Mack?" He dropped his hand and stared at her.

She blinked several times. "He's coming to Savannah. To a hospital there. I don't know where exactly — Maeve didn't say."

"Maeve?"

"I mean, it could be Candler *or* St. Joseph's. She didn't say. She *did* say that his parents are going over on Thursday to spend the night with Miss Myrtle's sister. They're leaving the store in the hands of Janie Wren." Alice-Ann shrugged. "I'm sure she'll do just fine there by herself." His face remained stonelike, and for a second, Alice-Ann forgot to breathe. "I take it that's not what you meant when you said 'big news.' "

"I was talking about the news out of Europe."

Alice-Ann turned back to the wall, worked her torn fingernail under a strip of the paper, and then pulled. "No, I haven't heard. What's happened?"

Peripherally, Alice-Ann saw him rest his

hands on his hips and felt his eyes continuing to stare at her, his face unchanging. She turned. "What happened in Europe?"

"When is he coming?"

What was the use, really? "Friday."

He chewed on his bottom lip. "Do you want to go?"

"No. No, of course not." She swallowed as her brow furrowed. "Why would I want to go?"

"You were in love with him, remember?"

Were. She had been. Yes.

Alice-Ann returned to pulling on wallpaper, wishing she could, as simply, peel back the layers of time. Or at least eradicate everything that had happened in the last five minutes.

Or the last five years.

"I wasn't," she said. "Not really."

Carlton took a step toward her and leaned his shoulder against the half-papered wall. "Look at me."

She shook her head, keeping her focus on what was left of the floral pattern, the large once-pristine moonflower nestled in a bed of now-faded green leaves. "Carlton, please . . ."

"Alice-Ann."

She cut a sideward glance. "Carlton," she whispered, begging. "I don't . . ." Tears formed and pooled before spilling down her cheeks.

"Come here," he said, gathering her into his arms, where she sobbed openly as he smoothed her hair and kissed the top of her head.

Why had he done this? Why? To make her cry? To force some kind of confession out of her?

Okay, then. Yes, she wanted to see Mack. Of course she did. He had been an important part of her childhood. Of her growing up from little girl to young woman. But he wasn't — he hadn't been —

"Since I got shot down, I reread them a hundred . . . or more. And I realized . . ."

His voice seemed to echo in the room, drawing her back to the question she'd asked more times than she could count over the past few days: What? What had he realized? That he loved her? That she was his one true love as he had been hers?

Carlton reached into one of his pant pockets and removed a handkerchief, his initials stitched perfectly with silky blue thread in one corner. "Here you go," he said, his voice tender enough, but still inquiring. Still raising the question she knew they both wanted the answer to.

If she wasn't still in love with Mack, why

was she crying so hard?

Alice-Ann blew her nose, then reached up and wrapped her arms around the neck of the man who thought her to be so beautiful. The one who had kissed her first. The one who had placed a ring of promise on her finger. She had to make him see . . . to understand how she felt. About him. Only him.

"Carlton," she whispered, then pressed her lips against the cool skin of his neck, continuing around his throat as he tilted his head back, and feeling his Adam's apple quiver as she kissed him there.

When his hands came around her forearms and he pushed her away, she stumbled, blinking.

"I thought we weren't going to do that," he said. "Remember?"

She dropped her face into her hands. "I only wanted . . ."

The sound of his picking up the bucket caused her to look at him again. He was halfway out of the room. "I think we need to go, Alice-Ann," he said, his voice firm but unsure.

"I only wanted to prove to you that it's *you* I love, Carlton. *You.*"

He stopped at the door leading into the tiny patch of a room that served as throughway. His shoulders sagged and he spoke without turning. "Prove it to who, Alice-Ann?" He didn't wait for an answer. "Me? Or *you*?"

Chapter 30

He drove her home as expected, saying nothing as she occasionally wept in the seat beside him. She knew full well that she'd be questioned by Aunt Bess and perhaps even Papa when she walked in, her eyes puffy and red, her face blotchy, and her lips downturned. Still, she couldn't stop the tears, gratefully devoid of sobs.

The dam, she reckoned, hadn't yet burst, but a crack had formed in the structure. Trickles of water eased through, uncontrolled but not yet wild.

That one night after church — after the news had been repeated time and again and had caused such a stir in Bynum — she'd thought she would make her way to her room, crawl into bed, push her face into her pillow, and cry. Oddly enough, she had not. She told herself she'd been too stunned for tears quite yet. And while she forced herself to stay away from Mack's letters so well-hidden in her closet, a headache formed and finally swayed her to close her eyes and find the respite provided by sleep.

Maybe, she told herself as Carlton's car bounced along the driveway leading home, if she had cried *then,* if she'd made herself cry by pinching her skin until tears formed — she'd heard that those beautiful Hollywood actresses did this so as to cry on cue — maybe then, she wouldn't be blubbering now.

No. Not so. Because in all honesty, Alice-Ann wasn't completely sure if her heartache came from Mack's return — complete with Carlton's attitude about the whole thing (*Father God, why wasn't he at least happy to hear his best friend is alive?*) — or because of her flagrant behavior with Carlton earlier. She'd never done anything like that before, obviously. Hardly knew what she was doing when she did it. She'd only wanted Carlton to know that she loved him.

She was sure of it.

Carlton parked the car yards from the front door, shoved the gearshift to park, and turned to her. She turned her wet face to his, wondering what she must look like. If the compassion she saw in his eyes was any indication, she looked a fright.

He reached over and fingered her hair

with one hand. He removed the handkerchief from where he'd earlier stuffed it into his shirt pocket. "Shhh," he cooed. "I didn't mean to make you cry, sweetheart. I didn't . . ."

She peered through wet lashes. "I *do* love you, Carlton. *You.*"

While his eyes had softened, the wit and humor she'd grown to expect still hadn't returned. "I know you do. And I love you. We just — we just have to get through this, that's all."

"Carlton?"

"Hmm?"

"Can I ask you a question?"

"Anything. Anytime."

"Are you — at least a little — *happy* that Mack is alive?"

"What?" he asked, the question coming out in a puff of air. His hand hovered near her cheek, now dry and pulled tight. "Of course I'm happy. He was one of my best friends."

"Then *what* is it? Why does it seem like everything has changed?"

Carlton chewed on his lip and shook his head. For a moment, Alice-Ann thought she saw his own tears forming. But then, just as quickly, he blinked them away. "I loved him — *love* him — like a brother. I just —

431

there's just the —"

"What? Talk to me, Carlton. We were *friends* before we fell in love, remember?"

She waited, but he said nothing. He seemed to search for the answer. And not just any old answer either. She could see the determination in his eyes as they darted back and forth. He wanted the correct answer, for sure. Alice-Ann leaned her face against his hand, hoping he understood the gesture.

Take your time. I'll wait.

He turned it, cupping her cheek, and his thumb brushed against it.

"I only want — I *don't* want you to have any regrets, doodlebug," he whispered.

"I won't have any regrets, Carlton. I promise you that."

He leaned over and kissed her tenderly on the lips.

The first . . . the last . . . the only.

Keeping her eyes closed, Alice-Ann shook her head to rid it of the thought, of anything that might remind her of its origins. She felt his stare and opened her eyes to find his. Compassion had been replaced with need, the same she'd felt earlier.

"I'd better go inside." She opened the door before she impulsively begged him to put the car back in drive and to take her away from all of it. Bynum and everyone in it. Mack's return. People wondering why Mack had called her but no one coming right out and demanding an answer. She considered pleading with him to take her away from the farmhouse, where a stack of letters stamped by censors and wrapped in a red ribbon lay hidden in her closet.

Take me somewhere . . . to a place where only you and I exist and this horrible war never happened, Carlton. . . .

"Aunt Bess will be out on the front porch in no time if I don't hurry up." She forced a smile to cover for the quiver in her words. "They hold supper until I get home. Not to mention, you know how she feels about men and women parked in cars."

He grinned and she saw his wit and humor had returned. "No. Tell me."

Alice-Ann swatted at him. "I'll see you tomorrow," she said, sliding out.

"Alice-Ann," he called after her. She ducked her head to peer back inside, her hand resting on the frame of the door near the window. "If you *want* to go see him, I'll understand."

She did, but she didn't. "Let's cross that bridge when we come to it," she said. "Right now, I need to get inside." Alice-Ann blinked. "Can you tell I've been crying?"

Carlton pretended to study her. "Tell them you broke a fingernail on the wallpaper and it hurt."

She stretched her fingers toward him. "That's not even made up, sadly." She straightened and started to shut the door, then thought better of it. "I know. I'll tell them you smashed my thumb with a hammer."

He laughed easily as he started the car. "My best to your folks, doodlebug."

"And mine to yours," she said, then slammed the door.

Alice-Ann entered the kitchen, fully prepared to answer any questions her family might have about her red-rimmed eyes. But instead of the entire family, she found only Irene and Aunt Bess, who balanced Little Mack on one hip. Both seemed intent on getting supper on the table, barely noticing Alice-Ann's entrance.

"Where are Nelson and Papa?" she asked.

"Bella didn't come home with the other cows," Aunt Bess said, turning to her. "Grab that bowl of creamed corn, Alice, and put it on the table."

Irene was clad in one of Aunt Bess's bib aprons with its sash wrapped twice around her tiny waist. "What's going on with you?"

she asked.

Alice-Ann took the bowl of corn to the table. "Just tired." She diverted her attention to Aunt Bess. "Do they think Bella is out in the fields giving birth?"

Aunt Bess placed Little Mack in his high chair, then stuffed small pillows around him to keep him upright. "There you go, little one," she said. Then, to Alice-Ann, "Seems so."

"Is she wearing her bell?" Alice-Ann asked, sitting. For as long as she could remember, her father had tied a large bell around the cows and heifers about to calve. That way, he said, when they went out in the fields during the day but didn't return at dusk, he could find them.

"Far as I know," Aunt Bess said, sitting in the chair next to Little Mack. She studied Alice-Ann for a moment. "Are you all right?"

"Just tired," she repeated. "Shall I say grace in Papa's absence?"

Aunt Bess nodded, her hand on the baby's, who cooed in response. "Shush now," Aunt Bess said to him, her voice warm and loving. "Time to thank the good Lord for his bounty."

Alice-Ann repeated the prayer she'd heard her father pray since she was old enough to understand the act. "Give us thankful hearts for these and all our many blessings. In Christ's name. Amen."

"Amen," Aunt Bess and Irene chimed; then they started the ritual of passing the food.

Alice-Ann glanced out the shadeless window. "Do you think I should change my clothes and see if I can find them?"

"I do not," Aunt Bess answered.

"But a cow calving in the fields is never easy work," Alice-Ann said. "They might need an extra hand."

"Adler is with them," Irene said as she extended a bowl of yellow crookneck squash toward her.

"Oh," Alice-Ann said, taking the bowl. "He sure is going to be missed around here when the war is over, isn't he?"

"If it ever is," Irene mumbled.

"Nonsense," Aunt Bess harrumphed. "They all come to an end eventually. Now then, Alice, I'm thinking that if you're so tired you've been crying — and don't tell me you haven't — then maybe you and Carlton shouldn't be working so hard on the house at the end of a long workday."

"When would you suggest, Aunt Bess?" she asked, reaching for a platter of fried chicken. The aroma of grease and flour stirred her stomach, and it rumbled in anticipation. "Saturdays are out. We're at harvest time now. Papa and Nelson are going to need me here, no matter how many Adlers we have. I can't do any of it on Sundays. After work is really our only time."

Aunt Bess and Irene exchanged glances. Somehow, Alice-Ann figured, during their hours together in the house, Aunt Bess had managed to domesticate the young Mrs. Branch. "I think we can do without you here on the farm, Alice-Ann," Irene said. "After all, your life will soon be with Carlton. We may as well get used to that."

Alice-Ann frowned as she picked up the chicken leg. She rested it between the fingers of both hands before taking a bite, the juices of it wetting her lips and dancing on her tongue. "Aunt Bess," she said as she chewed and swallowed, "your fried chicken can make the worst day ever into the best day ever." She shot Irene a look. "And I have *no* idea who you are."

The three women laughed lightly and Little Mack stretched his chubby legs and kicked. "See?" Alice-Ann said. "Even Little Mack thinks this is too funny for words."

When supper was over and the men still hadn't returned from the fields, Alice-Ann insisted on walking out to see if she could find them.

"You'll do no such thing," Aunt Bess ordered. "You're exhausted. Now march yourself up those stairs, get your bath, and go to bed."

Irene pulled her son from his high chair. "I'll put Little Mack in his playpen, Aunt Bess," she said, "then come back in and help with the dishes." She walked to Alice-Ann and placed her hand on her arm. "Get on," she whispered. "I've got this."

Alice-Ann blinked. "*Thank* you, Irene."

"Pull the shades while you're in there," Aunt Bess called as the two younger women walked into the hallway and parted at the stairs.

"Thank you again," Alice-Ann said, now nearly too tired to trudge up the stairs.

Irene looked at her knowingly. "I'll check in on you in a little while," she said.

Alice-Ann nodded, hoping she'd be asleep before Irene made it up the stairs.

Only a few minutes later, she emerged from the steamy bathroom, clad in her nightgown and her skin still glistening from the bath and Jergens she'd slathered on. Unsure if Irene was upstairs and hoping she was still with Aunt Bess in the kitchen — maybe enjoying a cup of coffee as they waited on Nelson and Papa — she tiptoed into her room, pulled the blackout shade, fumbled her way to the bedside table, and turned on the small lamp resting on top of one of Aunt Bess's crocheted doilies. She pulled the pillow up to the headboard, then sat on the bed, pressing her back against the feathery down and feeling it flatten. She stretched her legs, crossing them at the ankles, and stared straight ahead at the closet door, shut tight and taunting. Inside, on the bottom shelf, tucked under one of her straw field hats and held together by a red ribbon, were Mack's letters. She could read them, she knew, and try to remember those she'd sent back to him. Search for any clue as to what Mack had tried to say to her during their call a few days earlier.

"And I realized . . ."

Had the realization been that he'd fallen in love with her? Or maybe with the memory of her? She'd offered him nothing, really, except the promises written between lines of correspondence.

Alice-Ann's eyes eased from the blankness of the closet door to the one separating her room from the rest of the house. There, hanging on a brass hook — Aunt Bess's wedding gown. *Her* wedding gown. The one she'd wear on the day she pledged the rest of her life to Carlton.

Her left hand stretched without provocation and her right found it, the fingertips grabbing the ring, warm and cold at the same time against her flesh.

"If you want to go see him, I'll understand."

Perhaps she should. After all, she needed to be the one to tell him about her and Carlton. Certainly before —

She sucked in her breath. What if Mack said something to his parents about his realization? If, that was, it had to do with loving her. With wanting to build a life with her. What if they told him that she and Carlton were engaged? Would it affect his healing? Cause a medical upset? Could he — ?

A light tap at the door startled her. Before she could respond, it opened and Irene stuck her head in. "Still awake?"

Alice-Ann nodded. What choice did she have?

Irene stepped in and shut the door behind her. She carried her Bible in one hand, raised it as she crossed the room, and hugged it to her chest. "Can I share something with you?"

"Sure."

Her sister-in-law pointed to the side of the bed. "Do you mind?"

Alice-Ann scooted over a notch.

Irene sat with a foot tucked under the

crook of her other leg. She placed the Bible on the bed, laid her hand on it like she was about to take an oath, and straightened her back. "Do you remember me telling you about the day Nelson took me to the movies and then to the soda shop and then fishing?"

"Of course I do."

Irene took in a deep breath that she exhaled slowly through her nearly perfect lips. "Well, what I didn't tell you is that I really struggled that night. After Nelson took me home."

"In what way?"

Irene smiled, revealing perfect teeth. The kind Alice-Ann always hoped to have but never could. "Never mind the fishing that Nelson and me did. Boyd MacKay was *the* catch, don't you know?"

Oh, she knew.

"I don't know any girl in town who ever went out with him more than twice."

"What about Annabeth Sowell?"

"Annabeth Sowell?" Irene's nose crinkled the way it did when she ate a sour apple.

"He brought her to my twelfth birthday party."

"Oh yeah. I remember that now. They did go out. I think your party was their *last* date. It was nothing serious."

"But he *kissed* her," Alice-Ann blurted, then felt the heat of how she'd come to such knowledge warm her chest. She blinked. "I followed them."

"Mack *loved* to kiss. Any girl, Alice-Ann. Don't fool yourself and don't be foolish."

Well, not *any* girl. He hadn't kissed *her*. Then again, the last time they'd seen each other, he'd been an adult man and she'd been a fresh-faced sixteen-year-old. In her mind, all grown-up and ready. To him, a child. "He kissed you?"

Her sister-in-law raised her brow. "Well and often. Believe me. I *thought* I was special. After all, we'd gone out more than his proverbial two times."

Alice-Ann uncrossed her ankles and shifted higher against the headboard. "Carlton didn't kiss me until the day of Claudette's wedding. The same day he asked me to marry him."

"That's because Carlton Hillis is a fine man, Alice-Ann." She leaned closer. "A true and godly man. And don't try to fool me. I *know* why you were crying. Nelson and I lay in the bed the other night talking about it for the longest time. He's worried about you and so am I. We *all* know how you felt about Mack, but Mack —"

"That day when he called, before we got

442

disconnected, Mack was trying to tell me that he realized —" she started, then stopped.

"Realized what? That he's in love with you?" She asked the question with such ridicule, Alice-Ann knew Irene's feelings on the subject.

How could she tell Irene that she wasn't sure? If only she knew what he'd meant to say. That he loved her? Or that he realized he couldn't take her — a still-innocent, young woman by his way of thinking — away from the farm, only to ruin her life? Or maybe had Mack come to realize the truth . . . *about himself?*

There really was only one way to find out.

CHAPTER 31

"What's the Bible for?" Alice-Ann asked.

Irene moved her hand from its leathery cover, pulled it to her lap, and opened it. "The night after my date with Nelson, I was so torn. I *really* liked him," she said, smiling as she looked up at Alice-Ann. "But Mack was . . ."

"The catch."

Irene nodded. "Mm-hmm." She turned a few of the nearly see-through pages. "That night, I told my mother — who was *certain* Mack would be the man to sweep me away and marry me, in spite of his ne'er-do-well attitudes and lack of ambition — that I felt confused. I *thought* I'd been falling in love with Mack. Maybe I *was* in love with him —"

"Even after only a few dates?"

Irene cocked a brow. "*This* from the woman who fell in love with the idea of him? With a man who wrote her letters but didn't have the wherewithal to mail them to her house?"

"How did you — ?"

She chuckled. "Oh, Alice-Ann. You think you're as mysterious as one of those Alfred Hitchcock movies."

Alice-Ann frowned at such a reference. "Never mind all that." She nodded toward the Bible. "Keep on with your story."

"That night, my mother told *me* a story." Her eyes widened. "Seems once upon a time, a long time ago, she had to make a decision between two men. Both who swore their undying love for her and both who she could see herself with. But like Aunt Bess once told me, 'You can't help who you fall in love with, but you can help who you marry.' "

"She told me that too," Alice-Ann said, wondering if her aunt had told Irene the full story or only part of it.

Irene's eyes lit up. "Mama chose Daddy, of course. I asked her if she ever wondered if she'd made the right decision."

"What'd she say?"

"That of course. Every so often when Daddy acted like a horse's patoot, she'd wonder. But then she'd look at Frank and me and all the blessings God had given her — including Daddy — and she knew she had. 'Life,' she said, 'doesn't always seem fair. But when we trust God with our decisions, it all turns out all right.' "

"That's true."

"Her mother — my grandmother — gave her this Scripture verse."

Alice-Ann leaned over for a closer look as Irene turned the book toward her and pointed with an unpolished, neatly trimmed nail. "Psalm 25, verse 17. 'The troubles . . .' "

" 'The troubles of my heart are enlarged,' " Alice-Ann took over. " 'O bring thou me out of my distresses.' " Alice-Ann looked up. These were the same words Aunt Bess had given her. *How good you are, Lord. How exact in your measure of truth to your children . . .*

"I prayed those words all night, but the truth of it was — I was trying to bring *myself* out of my distresses. I was trying to be the one who figured it all out. Finally I told God that *he* should be the one to figure it out. I mean, isn't that what the verse says?"

Alice-Ann read the verse again, this time silently. "So what happened after that?"

"The next morning, Nelson showed up with the fish." She laughed so fully, Alice-Ann laughed with her. "He'd cleaned them, kept them on ice, and brought them to my mother, wrapped in a newspaper. Said we could have them for supper."

Alice-Ann could picture the scene. Irene's mother was a nice enough woman, but she was completely citified. Trying to picture her cleaning fish was like picturing that new Hollywood actor, Guy Madison, as a girl. "I doubt she knew the treasure Nelson handed to her."

"Mother had Magnolia fry them up for supper that night. And no. Mother had *no* idea. For a boy — a man — like Nelson, bringing over a mess of fish was tantamount to bringing a rare pearl after an oyster dig." She took in a breath and sighed into the memory. "I knew right then that I'd found my true love, even so early on. Me," she said, pointing to her chest, "a girl who didn't know a cow from a heifer. Or a laying hen from a meat hen."

Alice-Ann chuckled. "Well, that's true."

"I chose the ultimate farm boy over a man my mother was certain would one day come into his own, go to school, and take over his father's *apothecary,* she called it."

Alice-Ann leaned back, bringing the Bible with her. "Do you think I should pray this?"

"Don't you?" Irene asked quietly. Then she stood and started toward the door. "I'll leave you to it," she said. "I need to go check on the baby."

"Irene?" Alice-Ann said as her sister-in-law's hand touched the doorknob.

Irene turned.

"You know, I wasn't so sure about you before. Back when you first married Nelson. I *wanted* you to like me and I *wanted* to like you, but —"

"I took some getting used to?"

Alice-Ann smiled to soften the blow. "Yes, you did."

Irene looked around the room. "All this took some getting used to for me as well. Some days I wondered if I'd made a mistake. It has taken a lot of faith — faith I didn't know I had until I needed it — to survive our first years of marriage in the midst of this war." She raised her brow so quickly, Alice-Ann almost missed the movement. "No doubt, there will be times, Alice-Ann, when you will wonder the same, war or not. But in the end, you'll know that you wouldn't have changed a thing." She smiled as she opened the door, then looked down at her hands. "Dear Gussie, that aunt of yours is going to turn me into a farmer's wife if it kills her." She held her hands up, nails toward Alice-Ann. "Remember when I had soft, pink hands?"

"I remember." She hadn't liked her sister-in-law so much then. But she'd changed. Maybe the war had changed her. Maybe marriage or motherhood. Or maybe God had taken his sweet time turning Irene into the woman he wanted her to be.

Irene turned her ear toward the door. "The men are back. Wonder if we have a new calf."

"Probably. They wouldn't have come back if we didn't."

"I'll go see. Make sure Nelson's getting something to eat."

As if Aunt Bess would let him go hungry.

"Irene?" Alice-Ann called again.

Irene stopped, this time in the hallway. "Yeah?"

"I'm glad you chose Nelson."

Irene smiled as she leaned into the room, her hand resting against the outside door-frame. "Well, what girl can resist a farm boy bringing her mama a mess of fish?"

Unlike Maeve two days earlier, on Wednesday — twenty minutes before noon — Claudette Dailey waltzed in like fog on cat's feet. Gliding across the room in a blue-and-brown wool suit, her heels clicking on the terrazzo, she held her chin high, if for no other reason than to support the snazzy hat tilted just so on the right side of her head.

Claudette walked with one arm crooked. A brown leather purse swung from it in rhythm with her steps. She smiled broadly, red lipstick accentuating her full lips, and as she neared the tellers' windows, she put on a show of removing her gloves, then scrunched them in one hand.

"Good morning, Mrs. Dailey," Alice-Ann teased.

"Good morning, yourself," she returned easily, grinning at the reference to her new last name. "Gracious, I heard you'd started froufrouing yourself up, but I had no idea . . ." Claudette tilted her head in observation. "Still, I think love has added a glow that a tube of red lipstick or a pot of rouge cannot." She turned to Nancy. "Don't you agree, Mrs. Thorpe?"

Alice-Ann watched, bemused, as Nancy bit back a smile. "Absolutely. Tell us, Claudette, how is life treating you?"

Claudette placed her hands on the marble counter and leaned in between the two with a sigh. "If life got any better, why . . . I just couldn't *stand* it."

"I take it marriage agrees with you then?" Nancy asked.

Claudette blushed appropriately. "It's marvelous." She peered sideways at Alice-Ann. "Just you wait, Alice-Ann. You'll positively bask in the glow."

Alice-Ann peered over Claudette's shoulder to meet Miss Portia's frown. A customer — any customer — coming in this close to locking the doors for the day never set well with Miss Portia. Make it one who seemed bent on dillydallying and her displeasure only intensified.

Alice-Ann cleared her throat and asked, "How can we help you today, Mrs. Dailey?"

"My husband has sent me to pick up a couple of counter checks." She popped the silver clasps on her purse, reached in, and pulled out a folded piece of paper. "Who should I give this to?"

"I can help you," Alice-Ann said.

Claudette slid the paper into the brass tray, which Alice-Ann retrieved, unfolded, and she read the numbers. As she prepared the first counter check, Claudette leaned in again and said, "I guess you've heard about Maeve and Ernie."

Alice-Ann nodded but didn't look up. "About time, I'd say."

"And what about you?" She stretched and peered through the glass separating them. "Is that your ring?"

Alice-Ann raised her eyes and held up her hand briefly. Pride swelled inside her as she said, "It was Carlton's great-grandmother's."

"It's beautiful. And just like Carlton to be so traditional." She patted her hair, pulled tight into a chignon behind her left ear.

Alice-Ann wasn't sure if her old friend's words were a cut or a compliment, but she chose to believe the latter. "Here you go, Claudette," she said, sliding the counter checks into the tray and toward their recipient.

Claudette took them, dropped them into her purse, and snapped it shut with flair. "I'm so happy for you, Alice-Ann," she said, then looked over at Nancy and smiled. "I would have never believed it — back when we were little girls oohing and aahing over Maeve's cute older brother and his friend Boyd MacKay." She winked at Alice-Ann, who felt tiny fingers of discomfort crawling into her belly. "Not to mention how Maeve and I used to go on and on over Nelson."

Alice-Ann frowned. "You did not."

"Oh, we most assuredly did," she countered with a giggle. "All boys that much older than us were fair game, including your adorable brother. Not that she would have *ever* breathed a word, but Maeve had such a massive crush, much like you did with —" She stopped short, and Alice-Ann widened her eyes in warning.

If Nancy had ever suspected her feelings for Mack, she'd never said. Certainly Alice-Ann hadn't come close to discussing them with her. That topic had always felt reserved for her and Maeve and Claudette. And then . . . just her and Maeve.

And then, only her and Carlton. The thought brought a smile to her lips.

Claudette pulled her gloves onto her slender hands, adjusting the fingers as she added, "Seriously, Alice-Ann." Her face softened. "You've made the right choice, saying you'd marry Carlton." She presented the briefest of smiles, then turned and started across the room. Halfway to the door, she threw up a hand and said, "Have a nice day, Miss Portia. Mister Dooley."

Once Alice-Ann remembered to breathe, she looked over at Nancy, who shook her head in wonder. "Land sakes, that girl."

"Girl nothing. She's a full-fledged married woman now." She forced a smile as she reminded herself that once upon a time, not so long ago, Claudette had been her confidante. A best friend. One-third of an all-girl Three Musketeers band of innocents.

Nancy opened her drawer. "Marriage is no excuse for *that*." She pulled out a stack of dollar bills as she added, "I don't know about you, but I'm ready to close out and go home." She retrieved her stack of fives and placed them next to the singles. "Are you going to the house to work? Want to walk together?"

Alice-Ann had opened her drawer as well and began their afternoon ritual. "I — uh — I actually need to make a quick stop at the drugstore before they close for the day."

"Oh?"

"Pick up a couple of items."

Nancy began her count. "I see," she said, keying in her total for the ones and then entering the figure on the tally sheet.

Alice-Ann did the same, avoiding eye contact with her coworker. The last thing she needed was a rumor. Besides, it seemed perfectly natural to walk across the street. To pick up a few items. Some cotton balls. Maybe some Epsom salts.

And she would. Aunt Bess had mentioned a few days earlier they were getting low.

If she were lucky — really lucky — she'd catch Janie Wren alone and see if they could have a little talk.

By the time Alice-Ann made it close enough to MacKay's Pharmacy, Janie was exiting the front door, wearing a light overcoat and carrying her purse. Not seeing Alice-Ann as she approached, she started up the sidewalk toward the south end of town, where she lived with her parents.

"Janie?" Alice-Ann called, hoping her voice carried over the light downtown traffic.

Janie turned. The easy smile she offered faded as soon as she recognized the woman behind the voice. "Oh. It's you."

Alice-Ann closed the gap between them. "Why do you say it like that?"

Janie crossed her arms. "Because, that's why. Why didn't you tell me Mack had a thing for you?"

"Mack?" Alice-Ann feigned ignorance, but even to her own ears, she did a poor job of it.

Janie's flawlessly painted lips opened, forming a tiny O as she shook her head. "Don't give me that, Alice-Ann. Everyone in town knows Mack called you. The Army sent men to see his mama and daddy. But *you*? You, he actually picked up the phone and called before anyone else."

"I had no control over that, Janie."

"Do you know Mister Lance and Miss Myrtle waited a whole day before they heard their son's voice? I don't suggest you come into the store any time soon, Alice-Ann. Miss Myrtle is so put out with you, she told me it was best she not have to say anything at all to you just yet." Janie nodded once as though that were that. "Miss Myrtle said she doesn't want to lose her good standing with Jesus and miss out on going to heaven."

Alice-Ann could hardly imagine Miss Myrtle saying anything at all to her or anyone else that might kick her out of God's hereafter. "Janie, that's why I wanted to talk to you. To see you. I just — I've been so busy — Carlton and I — getting the house ready and —"

"And you engaged to Carlton Hillis, no less." Janie pivoted and started walking again.

Alice-Ann managed to catch up to her, to walk shoulder to shoulder in hopes of continuing their conversation. "Janie, can we go to Tucker's? Can I buy you a soda or — ?" She didn't have enough money for a meal. Not for herself, much less the two of them.

Janie stopped, her lips forming the O again. "And take a chance of being seen? Take a chance on losing my job?" She continued, reaching the curb and hurrying across the street.

This time, when Alice-Ann caught up to Janie, she reached for her arm, hoping to stop her. "Please, Janie. Please allow me to talk to you for five minutes. That's all I'm asking for. Five little minutes."

They stood in front of the Methodist church, the one Claudette and Johnny had exchanged their vows in only a few weeks earlier. The one she'd stumbled in as she walked down the aisle, only to be steadied by the man who proposed marriage to her before the day came to an end. "Can we please just sit on the steps there?"

Janie looked at the long, narrow brick steps, then back to Alice-Ann.

"Please?"

"Five minutes," Janie said, halfway to the imposing church building. She sat, tucking her coat under her, and Alice-Ann did the same.

"Yes," Alice-Ann began right away, not wanting to waste any time. "Yes, I wrote to Mack while he was away, and yes, he wrote to me."

"Well, why didn't you tell me? That day when I went on and on about writing to him and believing he was alive?"

Alice-Ann shrugged. "It didn't seem important at the time," she said, the half-truth nearly stumbling on her tongue. "The Army said he was dead and —" Oh, how could she possibly explain it to someone she hardly knew? "It just didn't seem important at the time."

"You said that." She sighed so deeply that her shoulders dropped an inch. "Alice-Ann, you came in and you let me help you with your makeup and your body lotions —"

"I wanted to look nice for Carlton."

A look of mild fear cast a shadow over Janie's face. "Not Mack?"

"Mack was dead. Remember?"

Janie dropped her face as her hands came together in her lap. Alice-Ann reached for them, wrapping them with her own, feeling the chill within them. "Janie, I had no idea Mack was writing to you. Or you to him. Back when we wrote to each other, I mean. Before the plane crash. He's been — he's been a friend to me since I was a little girl. He and Nelson were best friends since I was knee-high to a grasshopper."

Janie looked at her but said nothing.

"I hurried over to the — I walked over to tell you that — I know people are talking about Mack calling me and everyone is wondering why . . ."

"And I realized . . ."

The words blew in on the autumn breeze skipping along the sidewalk stretched in front of the church. Alice-Ann shivered and drew her hands away from Janie's in hopes she hadn't sensed it.

"It makes no sense, Alice-Ann."

Alice-Ann felt her brow furrow. "No. No, it doesn't."

"Are you . . . ? Do you plan to go see him? In Savannah? At the hospital?"

"If you want to go see him, I'll understand."

"I don't — no." She pressed her lips together.

"Maybe you should."

Alice-Ann straightened her back. "Why do you say that?"

"Don't you want to know *why* he called you? Everybody else does. Don't you?"

"The troubles of my heart are enlarged: O bring thou me out of my distresses."

Alice-Ann turned her face back toward town. The one with the cracks in the sidewalks she'd avoided stepping on since the day Maeve had taught her the childish chant. The one with the inset titles at storefront doorways, and window displays she could practically predict as the seasons changed each year. Her eyes rested on the five-and-dime, then traveled up to the four windows along the second floor. The Hillises' home.

Carlton's home.

At least for a little while longer. Once they were married, his home would be with her, and hers with him. Once they were married . . .

And what then? Would she spend a lifetime wondering what Mack had wanted to say to her? Years of wondering if he had meant to declare his love for her . . . or his need to keep their relationship as it had always been? Fully platonic. Big brother. Little sister.

She turned back to Janie. "I do," she said, the honesty of it hitting her like a grenade in her chest.

Resolution pooled in Janie's eyes. "Then I think you should go, Alice-Ann."

Alice-Ann did too. She had to, really. She had to see him. Speak to him. Ask him what he'd meant to say to her. She understood that now.

But how would she explain that to Carlton?

CHAPTER 32

During her lunch hour on Friday, Alice-Ann hurried down Cooper Street to the bus depot to inquire about fares for the following Monday. She'd already asked Miss Portia for the day off and factored in how much her paycheck would be cut.

When she arrived at the depot, she stepped inside the tiny front room, where oak-stained bench seats rested between narrow floor-to-ceiling windows. Along one wall stood the counter, and behind it old Mr. Melson — a square-faced man with too-long white hair and a thick mustache that looked like lamb's wool — busied himself. Without looking up, he said, "Can-I-halp-ya?"

"Hello, Mr. Melson," Alice-Ann said, presenting a smile she hoped didn't appear fake.

"How're ya doing yourself, little missy?" he asked.

She rested her purse on the countertop and opened it. "I'm inquiring about buses to Statesboro on Monday."

"Whatcha got goin' on over there?"

Absolutely nothing, not that Mr. Melson needed to know that. Statesboro was completely out of the way, but if she were going to be discreet in her mission, she'd need to take extra precautions.

"I have — I need to go see someone concerning wedding plans."

"I see," the man droned. "First bus leaves at six."

Six in the morning. She'd never make it to town by then. "And the next?"

"Eight thirty. That's the last one for the morning."

Alice-Ann could make that. "And for the return?"

"Got a three o'clock and a six. That's it."

Alice-Ann studied the chart hanging behind Mr. Melson. Cities and fares were clearly noted. It would cost her sixteen cents both ways — plus what it cost to get from Statesboro to Savannah — which was money she hated to spend but couldn't afford to spare.

She opened her purse and slid two coins across the counter. "I'd like a ticket for the eight thirty and a return for the —" She paused. If she left Bynum at eight thirty, she could hopefully get to Savannah by midmorning. She hadn't been to the city in years, but if she remembered correctly, it would take her a while to get another bus to the hospital. If she factored in time talking to Mack — she promised herself no more than a half hour at most, maybe forty-five minutes — then back to the bus depot, then back to Statesboro, she *might* make it by three.

But what if she didn't? "I — uh — can I purchase that ticket once I'm there?"

"You sure can." Along with her change, he handed her a ticket printed with date, time, and location.

"Thank you, Mr. Melson," she said.

On her way back to the bank, Alice-Ann determined that she'd tell Carlton that evening as they worked on the house. With every step up the slight incline of the sidewalk, she prayed, asking God for Carlton to understand. That he might even want to go with her, if he could get the time off.

Although, if she were honest with herself, that was the last thing she wanted. She needed to talk to Mack. Alone.

By Monday, Mack would know the truth, she reckoned. His mother or father — or both — would have told him. They might even tell him that, while she had become engaged to the first and only man to ever kiss her, Janie Wren had worked alongside them, day in and day out, believing in miracles.

Miracles Alice-Ann hadn't figured on.

Or possibly hadn't believed in. Though surely, as a Christian, she should.

She'd never thought of Janie as a woman of faith — not that she saw her as loose or without moral fiber. But the Wrens weren't churchgoing people. Although, if she remembered correctly, she'd seen Janie occasionally at the youth programs she and Maeve used to attend at Maeve's church.

Had she misjudged her?

A gust of wind caught her unaware, forcing her to duck her head and place a hand on her hat to keep it from blowing into the street. When it died down, she looked up again, only to notice how gray the sky had become.

A moment later, she stepped into the alley behind the bank, surprised to see Carlton at the employee entrance. He looked sporting, dressed for work and donning an overcoat, his fedora pulled low on his forehead. He leaned with his shoulders pressed into the white brick wall, one leg straight, the other bent, the foot resting against the brick.

"Hey," she said.

He straightened, pushed his hat back, and smiled. "Hey, yourself. I hoped I'd catch you coming back this way."

Alice-Ann stepped up to him and raised her windblown face for a kiss. He obliged before saying, "Where'd you go?"

She shrugged. "Just for a walk. I — I'll tell you more about it later. Tonight."

Carlton groaned. "That's why I'm here. Mr. Dibble is sending me to Savannah. I leave in —" he shoved his coat sleeve up to expose his watch — "a half hour."

"Oh," she said. "What time will you be back?"

He kissed her, his lips so tender on hers, she scarcely felt them. "Not until tomorrow night."

"Oh," she said again. "So I'll see you . . . tomorrow night?"

"Probably not. I'd say not until Sunday."

Sunday . . . the day before she left for Savannah herself. That didn't give her much time for telling him *and* his coming to accept her decision that she wanted — *needed* — to see Mack. "What are you — why are you going?" Would seeing Mack become part of the itinerary? It seemed only right, but she hoped not. Not until she could —

"A lot happening, doodlebug. The US

Navy has admitted colored women into the reserves. Not to mention some other stuff we're hearing. Stuff going on in the Philippines right now, even as we stand here shivering."

"And you're going to Savannah because . . . ?"

"Mr. Dibble says it's time I see how the big boys do it. Says he thinks I can bring some of that knowledge back to Bynum." Carlton looked about to burst with both pride and expectation.

"I can see you're excited," she said.

He held his thumb and index finger an inch apart. "Only about this much," he said, expanding the space between them.

Alice-Ann laughed. "Then I guess I'll see you at church on Sunday?"

She'd tell him then. After service. She'd invite him to Sunday dinner at the house, and with his stomach full, they'd take a walk in the pecan groves and she'd tell him then.

He kissed her a third time, this kiss holding more urgency and love. "I'll miss you."

Alice-Ann hugged him, burying her face in his chest and inhaling his freshly washed and ironed shirt blending with the familiar scent of him. "Not nearly as much as I'll miss you," she said.

■ ■ ■ ■

By late Sunday afternoon, when Carlton hadn't shown up at the house, Alice-Ann decided to dash over to the Jameses' house and ask to use their phone.

"What's so all-fired important that you need to run over there?" her father asked from his favorite Sunday afternoon spot: in his chair, near the radio.

She glanced at her watch. "I thought Carlton would be here by now. He said he'd be back from Savannah today and — I — well, I really need to talk to him."

Papa stuck his pipe between his teeth and nodded.

"Alice," Aunt Bess said from Mama's old chair, where she tatted lace onto the collar of one of Alice-Ann's Sunday-go-to-meeting blouses. One she hoped Alice-Ann could wear on her honeymoon, wherever that might be. She and Carlton hadn't gotten that far in their plans.

"Yes, ma'am?"

"Take Josephine and George a couple slices of the pie, will ya? They both love my apple pie."

"Yes, ma'am."

Alice-Ann started out of the room, then

stopped long enough to look at her father. "You know, Papa, if you'd get a phone out here, I wouldn't have to keep running over to the Jameses' every time I need to make a phone call."

Papa raised his brow. "It's a gossip box, if you ask me."

Alice-Ann laughed. "We have electricity. We have indoor plumbing. But we don't have a telephone. If you blink long enough, Papa, it'll be 1945. Time to join the rest of the world and get a telephone."

"Tell you what you do," he said, pulling the pipe away from his lips. "Tell that young man you'll be marrying soon to make sure he puts a phone in that house he bought you. Then you can call all the people you want, all day long."

Alice-Ann rolled her eyes, smiling so he wouldn't think her disrespectful.

"And who would she call?" Aunt Bess bustled as she directed the question to her brother. "Can't call me. Can't call you."

In answer, Papa leaned over and turned up the Zenith.

Discussion over.

Maeve answered when Alice-Ann called the Hillis home. "Oh, Alice-Ann," she said, nearly breathless. "Ernie and I just got back from seeing *Arsenic and Old Lace*. You should have come into town and gone with us. It was *wonderful*. And of course, Cary Grant was —"

"Maeve? Is Carlton home from Savannah yet?"

"Oh. I don't even know." She giggled like a schoolgirl. "Hold on. Let me ask Mama."

Alice-Ann waited until Maeve returned. "Mama said he telephoned about a half hour ago and said they won't come back until tomorrow sometime. He said if you called to let you know he'd meet you at the cottage after you get off from work."

Alice-Ann swallowed, the sound of it echoing in the high-ceilinged hallway. She glanced toward the front of the house, where Mr. and Mrs. James were enjoying a cup of coffee along with their slices of Aunt Bess's apple pie.

What would she do? What *could* she do? She had purchased the ticket already; she'd have to go. But what if Carlton returned to Bynum and went to the bank first?

"Alice-Ann?" Maeve's voice called from the other end of the line.

"Yes. Maeve — I — thank you. Tell your mother that — tell her if Carlton calls again . . ." Tell him *what* exactly? That she wouldn't be at work the next day? That she was taking a bus to Statesboro and then to

469

Savannah and then another one to the hospital? That she was going to see the man she had, at one time, thought to be her one true love? To ask him how he felt about her? Because if he were still in love with her . . . Well, what would she do then?

She hadn't thought that far ahead.

"Yes?" Maeve asked. "If Carlton calls?"

"Tell him I love him."

Maeve giggled. "I still can't believe you and my brother . . . Just think. If I hadn't gone to the bank that day and asked you to come over. To read to him. Just think how different this story would have turned out."

"Yes," Alice-Ann said, hoping her voice sounded as though she were equally as pleased. "Just think."

With gas restrictions and the government determining the miles per hour at only thirty-five, the trip to Statesboro took longer than Alice-Ann had anticipated. She had to chase down the bus to Savannah as it pulled away from the curb, slapping her hand against the side of it.

Fortunately, the bus driver had been kind enough to stop for her. Had he not, she would have been forced to return to Bynum, her mission unsuccessful. Waiting for the next bus wouldn't have gotten her to

Savannah with enough time to find the hospital, see Mack, and return home.

As she endured the more than two-hour trip — before the war, it would have taken half that time — she contemplated seeing Mack again. Would he look as broken and bruised as Carlton had? Maybe not. After all, he'd had more time to recuperate.

Alice-Ann looked down at her gloved hands, seeing the imprint of her engagement ring beneath the stretched material of her gray gloves. Should she turn it inward so it didn't make such an impression?

No. It was bad enough she had made the choice to go see Mack without telling a single soul in Bynum — not even Carlton. She wasn't about to try to figure things out with Mack by beginning with a lie.

Figure things out with Mack.

The thought was ridiculous. Because really, what was there to figure out? She was making this trip to tell him about her and Carlton. To let him know where things stood.

No. That wasn't true. She was going because, as Janie had said, she wanted to know why he had called her. Her, of all people. And she wanted to know what he'd come to realize.

I've come to realize I love you, Alice-Ann.

The words came to her, riding on the voice of Cary Grant. She blinked as she gazed out the pristine bus window and wondered where such a thought had come from. Mack wouldn't say something as idiotic as that. Especially considering that by now, surely, his parents had told him about her and Carlton.

But what if they hadn't? What if they didn't consider him well enough to be told?

She'd heard that the MacKays were to return on Sunday. By now they'd shared with everyone they came into contact with — Janie included — about how Mack looked. About how long he'd have to be in the hospital. Everyone would know the details.

Everyone but her.

But she'd know soon enough.

CHAPTER 33

The wall clock over the front desk read 12:55 when Alice-Ann stepped into the cool interior of the hospital. She quickly calculated that, if she could find Mack and get out of the hospital by two or two thirty, she could catch the three thirty bus heading from Savannah to Bynum. That would put her into Bynum at five thirty. Six o'clock at the latest.

She'd simply *have* to bypass Statesboro altogether. If Mr. Melson saw her getting off the Savannah bus and started rumors, so be it. Carlton would already be at the house by the time she arrived. He'd already know she hadn't been at work. He'd already be — well, furious.

Furious and hurt.

"May I help you?" the woman behind the desk asked.

Alice-Ann wet her lips with her tongue and tasted the lipstick Janie Wren had sold her. "I, uh — I'm here to see Mack — I'm sorry. Boyd MacKay."

The woman — all business and no smiles — looked down at her register. *"M-c or M-a-c?"*

"M-a-c."

"Here he is," she said, pointing at one of the thick blue lines.

Alice-Ann read it easily. Working with numbers over the past few years had made it possible for her to read digits from every direction.

Four-zero-one.

"I'm sorry," the woman said then, looking up. "Are you family?"

Alice-Ann opened her mouth to lie, then thought better of it. After all, she'd come here because — she believed — God would deliver her from her distresses. She surely didn't want to complicate matters by falling out from under God's grace umbrella.

"No," she said. "I'm an old friend. I came all the way from Bynum to see him."

The woman pursed her unpainted lips. "I'm sorry, dear. He's in a restricted area. You have to be family to see Mr. MacKay."

"Oh. Well, then. I understand. That being the rules and all, but — I came *all the way* from Bynum."

A shake of the head said it all. "I'm afraid

we have a few people behind you who need my attention."

Alice-Ann glanced over her shoulder to see two men and two women. "I'm sorry," she said to them. Then, back to the woman, she asked, "I won't keep you, but is there a restroom somewhere?"

The woman finally graced her with a smile. "Just over there," she said, directing Alice-Ann to the left side of the box-shaped entryway.

And blessedly away from eyeshot.

Alice-Ann thanked the woman again, said, "Excuse me," and made her way quickly into the tiny restroom, where she closed the door and peered into the oval mirror above the sink.

She prayed out loud as she opened her purse and removed her comb. "Okay, Lord. We made it this far. And I figure if you can get the Hebrew children all the way from Egypt to the Promised Land — albeit in forty years — you can get me from this bathroom to the fourth floor."

After removing her hat — the only one she owned that perfectly matched the emerald-green skirt and long-sleeved jacket she'd chosen to wear — she ran the comb through her hair, which was silky smooth thanks to Janie Wren and the potions she'd sold to her.

Janie . . .

"I'm just going to go up there and see how he is," Alice-Ann continued speaking out loud, her voice barely above a whisper. She dropped the comb back into her purse, then took out the tiny tube of seaside coral lipstick and applied a new coat across her drying lips.

She wished she had something to drink. And eat, though she wasn't altogether sure she could stomach food right then.

After she finished in the restroom, she opened the door slowly and, leaning, peered out. The hospital's official gestapo — from the looks of things Germany had *nothing* on St. Joseph's — remained at the desk, now speaking to a rather intimidating-looking man who wore a thick gray coat and wide-brimmed fedora.

Alice-Ann eased out without closing the door fully, then slid along the wall until she was completely out of sight. Within a minute she located a stairwell and, turning the doorknob, found it open for use.

She hurried up the stairs, gasping for breath by the time she reached the fourth floor. She inhaled deeply, pressing against the flat of her stomach, then exhaled slowly. " 'The troubles of my heart are enlarged: O bring thou me out of my distresses,' " she said aloud. "Help me, Lord. Let there be no one to stop me as I look for room 401." Alice-Ann placed her hand on the round brass knob. "Oh. And help me *find* room 401."

She eased the door open, unsure where she'd be exactly, knowing it could be anywhere from near the patients' rooms to the broom closet. But she smiled as she stepped into the hallway, room 406 directly across from her, room 404 to the immediate right. She was in the vicinity of Mack's room. She had to be.

Alice-Ann grasped her purse strap in both hands and turned, keeping her steps purposeful and her expression as though she belonged on this floor as much as the nurses she spotted farther down the hall. Nurses who, gratefully, did not even notice her.

The door to room 401 sat half-open. She tapped on it with a still-gloved knuckle.

"Come in," Mack's voice — clearly Mack's voice — called from inside.

She pushed the door slowly, spying Mack sitting up in a typical hospital room, in an ordinary hospital bed. White wrought-iron headboard and footboard. No elaborate carvings on any of the posts. The walls were white and unadorned, like the sheets and blankets. The only spray of color was in the light blue of Mack's pajamas, the dark shock of his hair, and the wine-colored cover of the book he held between his hands.

"Well, I wish you'd look at who just walked in this room," he said, his eyes round with surprise. He closed the book and placed it on the bedside table to his right.

"Hi," she said from the doorway, too scared really to go farther in.

But he waved her in nonetheless. "How in the world did you — did you *drive* here?"

"Me?" She laughed nervously. "I don't have a car." Nor did she know how to drive. She could steer a tractor up and down rows of crops till the cows came home. But drive a car? No. "I took the bus."

"Close the door. If they find out I have a visitor, they'll run you out on a rail."

She closed the door quietly behind her, then took a few more steps in, her hands continuing to grip the purse strap. "I know," she said finally. "I had to sneak up." She glanced out the single window, peering through the venetian blinds at the dying green of the grass outside and what little she could make out of the city beyond that.

Mack laughed. "Gracious goodness. Look at you, Alice-Ann Branch. By golly, you did it. You grew up on me."

Heat rushed to her cheeks and she wondered if, along with the rouge she'd applied that morning, she might look a little like a clown. "What about you?" she said. "You don't look half as bad as —" She'd almost said, "As Carlton did" but stopped herself. "As I expected you would."

And he didn't.

"You should have seen me a few months back. But now most of the remaining damage is on the inside," he said. "I'm here because they're worried about things like blood clots and other nonsensical things like that."

Alice-Ann took a step forward. "That's hardly nonsensical, Carl—" She shook her head. "Mack."

He blinked several times, mischief playing in his eyes. "Did you almost call me Carlton?"

This was it. This was the moment she would be able to tell him that yes, she had almost called him Carlton. And why? Because she and Carlton were engaged and she said her fiancé's name several times a day, so almost calling another man by Carlton's name was a natural slipup. And oh, my! Where has the time gone?

But instead, she waved her right hand in the air and said, "Slip of the tongue. You've heard about Carlton, I assume? About his injuries and . . . ?"

He patted the side of the bed. "Come sit. We've got a lot to talk about, Alice-Ann, and right now Carlton Hillis — much as I love the ole boy — is way at the bottom of the list."

Alice-Ann spotted a chair in the corner of the room. "Maybe I should sit over —"

"Don't be silly." He patted the side of the bed again. "Come on now. It's not like we're strangers. Give a soldier a break. After all, I've made it back from death's door. The least you can do is sit next to me and hold my hand."

Alice-Ann started toward the side of the bed closest to her, then thought better of it. *If* he reached for her hand, it would be her left he held. And he'd possibly feel the ring. Or see the impression of it. Or even worse, remove her glove and have it staring him in the face.

She walked to the other side of the bed and eased down, sitting near the slight bend of his knees. Close enough to be civil, but far enough away to be proper. Sure enough, he reached for her right hand, turning it over in both of his. "Look at you," he repeated. "Wearing grown-up gloves, no less."

She squeezed his hand in the hope of making him stop teasing her, and he did. "What do the doctors say, Mack? When can you come home?"

"Home? Hmm." He chuckled. "No. As soon as the doctors release me from here, I'll go to the Camp Stewart hospital and then, when the good docs release me from *there,* I'll rejoin what's left of my squad."

"Mack . . ."

"I know, sweetheart. But this is war. I got beat up, yeah, but not as bad as — well, I hear ole Carlton — since you brought him up — got it worse than me."

She wasn't altogether sure, not having seen Mack in the beginning. "He was blind for a while. He couldn't walk. He's okay now, though. Except for some minor problems with his legs from time to time."

Knowing Carlton, more often than he let on.

"Yeah. My parents told me. Gosh. Can't imagine what it was like for him."

"He got an honorable discharge. Couldn't *you* get an honorable discharge too?"

"Not if they give me a choice. My plan is to return and make the military my career, Alice-Ann. Even if they only put me behind a desk, I'm going back."

"You seem determined."

"I am."

"Can you — do you mind telling me — what happened?"

He squeezed her hand, then released it. She eased it back into her lap, joining it with the left, which she kept turned palm side up.

"I'll be honest with you, Alice-Ann. I've never been so scared in my life."

"When you were in the water?"

"Then too. But when I saw those Japanese planes coming at us." His eyes darkened as though hooded by the memory. "I knew we were done for. There were more of them than there were of us."

"What kind?"

"What do you mean?"

"What kind of planes were the Japanese flying? Fighter? Bomber? Reconnaissance?"

Mack chuckled, and the dark mood lifted. "How do you know about such things?"

Because Carlton and I read about it. Talk about it. She shrugged. "I just know."

He leaned over a little. "Well, I'll be honest. I don't know. Those little details are gone. But I'll assume fighter, all things considered."

No doubt about it. Really. "So then what happened? I mean, as best as you can recall?"

His brow furrowed. "I don't remember, exactly. I remember seeing them coming at us. I remember yelling something to my men, but I honestly don't even remember what. I know there was a lot of screaming over the noise of the engines. Screaming from out of my mouth *and* in my ear." He paused, looked toward the door, then back at her. "I remember hearing my name, but I don't know who screamed it exactly. Like . . . like . . . ." His lips pinched. "Like this is it, you know? Like we're going down and we're dying and this is the last thing we're ever going to see. Ever going to hear." He took a deep breath and it shuddered in release.

"Mack . . . Don't keep going if you don't want —"

"I don't remember the explosion. I can almost put my finger on the feeling of falling, though. You know?"

She nodded, although she had no idea what he meant. She could imagine, but she didn't know.

"Next thing I can fully remember is being in the water, holding on to a piece of the plane. Body parts and plane parts all around me and a Japanese ship close enough I could have spit and hit the side of it." He shook his head. "Not really, but . . . I kept

— I kept my face down. If they *did* see me, let them think I was dead, I figured."

"And then the submarine."

"Yes."

"How did you — how did you manage to get on it?"

He shook his head again and smiled. "No idea. They said when they periscoped up, they saw me and I looked right at them, so they knew there was at least one survivor. But they couldn't take a chance of surfacing until dark, so — who knows how long I was out there. I'm more surprised I didn't end up as a snack for some shark than I am that I survived the air attack."

This time, Alice-Ann reached for his hand. "I'm so sorry you had to go through all that."

He swallowed. "I'm not even sure . . . You know, Alice-Ann? I can be pretty carefree at times."

She knew. She knew, and Nelson and Irene knew, and Aunt Bess and Papa knew. Everyone knew. *No gumption,* Aunt Bess had said, igniting fury in Alice-Ann.

"So I often wonder if I did something to cause this. Did I — was I acting careless? Did I cause — those men, my brothers in this war — ?" He stopped. Looked down at his hands, then back up to her. "Do you remember me telling you about Horace?"

She had to think a moment. "The boy from Idaho?"

"Yeah. Did I cause his death? *Their* deaths? All of them?"

Alice-Ann paused before answering, her mind going over some of the things he'd said to her in his letters while factoring in the guilt she knew overwhelmed the young man who'd never committed to much of anything before December of '41. "I know you can be carefree, Mack. You said so yourself. But care*less*? No. That's not like you. Especially when lives are at stake."

He looped their hands at the thumbs, the size of his hand swallowing hers, and she felt the heat of it through her glove. "Thank you for that."

Her breath caught in her chest. "You're welcome."

They didn't speak for a moment; they only stared at each other. Sizing each other up, Alice-Ann figured. Mack looked as though he had much more to say. She knew *she* did. But where did she begin now? If she'd only taken the opportunity when she'd first entered the room to tell him that she and Carlton were engaged. Finally she straightened her shoulders and said, "Everyone in town wants to know why you called me, Mack."

He chuckled again, the skin around his eyes crinkling. "Ah, I bet they do. Good ole Bynum, Georgia."

"It's home."

"That it is."

"And what did Dorothy say about home?"

He tilted his head, confused by the reference to the L. Frank Baum novel. Never mind the movie. And never mind that Carlton would have understood without missing a beat. Carlton would have said, "There's no place like it, doodlebug." And then he would have kissed her and added, "Especially when that home is with you."

A cottage, really.

She slipped her hand from Mack's. "She said there's no place like it."

Mack nodded. "Yes, yes. Of course."

"So then? Why *did* you call me?"

"Ah-haaaa . . . ," he drawled, as if he wasn't sure he had the answer. "Well, it's like this, Alice-Ann. I told you how I reread your letters over and over in my head during those long weeks of recovery?"

Not to mention months.

"Yes."

"I realized . . ." He chuckled again, the sound of it almost painful. "I realized you

486

loved me. Really loved me. And that I —
Boyd MacKay — would be the stupidest
man alive — praise God, *alive* — if I didn't
grab you up and call you mine."

The room seemed to spin, then stop. She
had to tell him. She had to say it then and
there. Blurt it out. *I'm-engaged-to-Carlton-
Hillis.* Just like that. Quickly, in the same
way Aunt Bess removed Band-Aids from
boo-boos.

She opened her mouth to speak.

But at that very moment, the door to
room 401 opened, and in a flash, she
jumped from the bed.

CHAPTER 34

The door eased open.

A fresh-faced girl of no more than fourteen or fifteen at best stood framed within its opening. She wore a pink-bibbed skirt and white cotton blouse. "I'm sorry." Her eyes shifted from Alice-Ann to Mack and back again. "I'm Cynthia Kelly. I'm here to see if you would like anything to drink, Mr. MacKay. Juice? Coffee?"

Mack shook his head. "Thank you, Cynthia. I'm good."

"A book? Magazines? Cigarettes?"

"I'm good. Thank you."

She smiled. "All right, then. If you need anything, just ring the nurses' station and I'll come back."

"Thank you again."

The girl walked out, closing the door behind her, and Alice-Ann returned to her place on the side of the bed.

"A group of high school students up in

New Jersey started something called candy stripers for a school project," she yammered. "They made their own pinafores in red and white and went to work as volunteers in a local hospital. I read not too long ago in the Savannah paper that some of the schools here were doing the same. Of course, the American Red Cross has had —"

"Alice-Ann," Mack said, interrupting her from continuing in the blubbering trivia.

"I'm sorry. I — I read a lot."

He studied her before clearing his throat. "You and Carlton?"

And there it was. He *knew.* "You know?"

"I know." He reached for her left hand, tugged at the fingertips of her glove until it came free. He picked up her fingers and turned the ring toward him. "It's beautiful, as engagement rings go."

"It was his great-grandmother's."

Mack leaned back and silently chuckled. "Just like the boy to do something romantic like that."

Alice-Ann pulled her hand free again. "If you knew about Carlton and me, why'd you — why'd you tell me — ?"

"What?"

"That you'd realized you — ?"

"That I was in love with you?"

Was. Not *am*. Was. "No more?"

"Maybe I should have said that I *am* in love with you."

She stood. "Mack, I'm — I'm —"

"Engaged to Carlton Hillis. I know. You just said so. And my parents told me on . . . Saturday, I believe it was. Right after I told them I intended to pursue you. Talk you into going away with me to wherever service to my country might take me." He winked at her. To soften the blow? To make the whole scenario worse than it already was? "Look here," he said then. "I screwed up. I take full responsibility for it. You told me how you felt about a million times in your letters and I strung you along. I guess I really am careless."

Alice-Ann pinched her nose to keep from crying. She'd waited so long to hear these words from him. If he'd only given her some indication . . . But would it have mattered? Would their story have changed? And if so . . . how?

No. He'd been dead. At least she'd believed he had been. But Janie . . . Janie believed in the miracle, and the miracle lay in a hospital bed in front of her. "You also wrote to Janie Wren."

His brow shot up. "Ah, yes. Janie." He folded his arms over his chest. "I didn't think you two were close enough to —"

"To compare notes?" she asked, her wits about her now. "Or letters?"

He laughed hard then. "Gosh, I think I rather like the grown-up you. What a shame I'm going to miss getting to know this Alice-Ann better." He cocked his head. "Assuming, that is, you really are going through with this marriage to our boy."

"Of course I am. I happen to be very much in —" She took another step back. Looked at her feet. The sensibility of her shoes.

"You happen to be in . . . ?"

Alice-Ann looked up. "I'm in love with him, Mack."

He smiled at her. "Are you sure, Alice-Ann?" A dark brow arched, testing her. "Completely sure?"

And she smiled back. "Positive," she answered. Because she was. If ever in her life she'd been sure of anything more, she couldn't remember the time. And Mack . . . Mack had spent the last few minutes being her true friend — hers *and* Carlton's — by giving her the gift she needed to say "I do" to her one true love.

Not Mack. Not him at all. Her one true love was *Carlton.* Perhaps he always had been; she just hadn't figured it out yet.

"Thank you," she said.

He shrugged. "What'd I do?"

"You know good and well what you did."

Mack crooked a finger at her, then pointed back to the bed again. "Come give your old buddy a good-bye hug, why don't you."

She returned to her place next to him, slipped easily into his arms, and felt his squeeze. Familiar and yet new. *This* wasn't the man of her dreams. *This* was Boyd Mac-Kay, her brother's best friend. Alice-Ann drew back and Mack placed his hands on either side of her face. "Listen. I *do* love you. I always have and I always will. You've been a dear part of my life. You're special, Alice-Ann Branch." He swallowed. "And I'm not saying I wouldn't have made a halfway decent husband to you. No doubt you would have made the best wife I could have asked for. But you were never *really* mine. If you had been, you wouldn't be wearing that ring right now, ready to defend your love for him." He brought her face to his, and she closed her eyes as he kissed first one cheek, then the other. For a brief second she thought to turn her face so that their lips met. To experience his kiss at least once in her life. But as quickly as the idea came, it fled. Carlton would be the only one to have that pleasure in her lifetime . . . and she *wanted* it that way.

"Give Carlton my best?" Mack said.

She welcomed the words and kept her eyes closed as she nodded, then opened them and said, "And Nelson and Irene?"

"And my namesake, who my mother says is about the cutest baby she's ever seen since — well, since me."

Alice-Ann laughed and stood. "Good-bye, Boyd MacKay. God be with you."

Mack reached for his book on the bedside table. "Good-bye, Mrs. Hillis. May God be with you, too. Both of you."

She walked to the door, ready to return to Bynum. Ready to tell Carlton everything. All of it.

"Alice-Ann?"

She turned. He'd already opened the book, but his eyes — dark blue and glistening — were still on her. "Yes, sir?"

"If Carlton does anything foolish — let's say, he loses his mind and decides you're not the girl for him — I'm only a letter away."

"He won't."

"I'm just saying —"

Amused by it all, she turned back toward the door, then looked at Mack again. "You know, Janie Wren is a pretty good catch. Maybe even better than me."

"Better than you? How can that be?"

"Well, for one thing, she never gave up hope. She always believed . . ."

Mack nodded. "I know. Daddy told me. And I'll be sure to keep that in mind."

"Will you?"

He saluted her. "I will, ma'am."

"*Will* you?"

His face sobered as though the realization of Janie's devotion only that moment became a reality. "I will. I promise."

Alice-Ann smiled, confident in his vow. "Thank you, Mack. I truly believe you won't regret it."

His dark brow shot up. "I believe you may be right, Alice-Ann." He grinned. "I'll make sure Mama and Daddy bring her with them this weekend."

She opened the door with a smile and stepped back into the hallway, closing the door behind her. Only then did she look at her watch. "Oh *no* . . . ," she said, then hurried to the stairwell.

Alice-Ann knew that it would take an enormous amount of luck — if she believed in such things — to make it to the depot in time to catch the three o'clock for Bynum. A bus she'd already purchased the ticket for. So instead of tossing up hope, she prayed, begging God for one more favor. *You brought me out of my distresses,* she prayed silently. *Now please bring me out of Savannah and to Bynum before —*

Before what? Before Carlton found out? Before he worried about her whereabouts and went next door to see Nancy, asking what time they'd gotten off work? Before he learned the truth? That she'd gone to Savannah without telling him first?

She burst into the depot and rushed over to the ticket counter, which was blessedly unoccupied on her side. "Oh, please tell me I'm not too late for the bus to Bynum," she said to the man on the other side.

He pointed out the window. "Boarding now. Ran a little late today."

Alice-Ann looked up. "Thank you, God," she said, then patted the cold marble countertop as she looked again at the man. "And thank *you.*"

She darted out a side door and to the bus. She hurried up the three steps, handed the driver her ticket, and then plopped into a seat.

"Alice-Ann?"

She turned. Out of the five or six people on board, she only recognized one — a girl who had graduated with the class after hers. "Oh, hey, Sandra."

495

"What are *you* doing on a bus from Savannah?" the young woman asked, making her way from her seat three rows back to the one directly behind Alice-Ann. Beneath her coat she wore a simple white blouse and a pair of slacks, and she smelled lightly of oil and grease.

"Oh, I — more to the point, what are *you* doing on a bus from Savannah to Bynum?"

"Me?" Sandra shucked out of her coat and gloves, draped the coat over the back of her seat, and dropped the gloves into her purse. "I work here."

"Really? I had no idea."

"At the shipyard. I'm a welder."

Alice-Ann couldn't have been more surprised. "I had *no* idea."

"Uh-huh. And my sister — you know Kristine?"

Only vaguely. An older sister, if she remembered correctly. "A little. Yes."

"She works over at Union Bag, but she lives with our grandmother because of the hours. I go home every day to help Mama, what with Daddy being gone."

"Your father is gone?" Alice-Ann asked as the bus jerked into gear and started out of its parking spot.

Sandra looked at her as if she had gone completely mad. "The war, Alice-Ann. Daddy's been in Europe since early on in '42."

Alice-Ann's mouth fell open. "I didn't know, Sandra." Had she been so wrapped up in her own war story that she missed the stories within her own community? "How's your mama getting along?"

Sandra's eyes pooled with tears. "It's hard. We don't hear from him for long stretches of time."

Alice-Ann knew enough about that to write her own story.

"And then we get a telegram that he's fine and missing us and can't wait to get home." She smiled weakly. "I hear you and Carlton Hillis are engaged."

Alice-Ann shifted so she could talk to Sandra without breaking her spine in half. "How is it you know that I'm engaged to Carlton and I don't know that you and your sister work in Savannah or that your father has been gone for more than two years?"

Sandra's smile grew. "Oh, that's easy. Mama's been working for the Daileys over at the inn. She's in charge of the housekeepers over there. And —"

"And Claudette keeps her informed, I'm sure."

Now Sandra laughed. "You know Claudette."

"Yes, I'm afraid I do." She wrinkled her

nose. "*What* is that smell?"

"You mean other than me?"

Alice-Ann glanced out the window. "Yes. It's coming from out there."

"*That's* Union Bag. Stinks to high heaven."

Alice-Ann looked at Sandra again. "How does your sister stand it?"

"Kristine says it smells like bacon and eggs to her."

They arrived in Bynum a little before six. Dusk had fallen as deeply as Alice-Ann's spirits. She'd had Sandra to chat with along the way — to keep her mind off the inevitable.

When they came into town, they passed the house. She saw Carlton's car parked between their house and Nancy and Harry's. She caught a glimpse of light in a side window, one at the rear of the house.

Carlton was there. By now, he probably suspected the worst.

More awful was that the worst was the truth.

When they arrived at the depot, Sandra offered Alice-Ann a lift home. "Mama picks me up every evening," she said. "You live a little out of the way, but I'm sure she won't mind."

"No, that's okay," Alice-Ann said. Then, thinking it over, she said, "But if you can drive me down to the house Carlton and I — it's on North Main Street."

Sandra's mother chatted nonstop on the way to the house. Even though Alice-Ann managed to respond a time or two, she was only vaguely aware of the conversation. She answered all of Miss Judy's questions, laughed in all the appropriate places, but as soon as they pulled in front of the house, Alice-Ann opened the back door, thanked them both, told Sandra to "not be a stranger." She all but ran into the house, closing the door behind her.

"Carlton?"

"In the back."

She hurried to the room where they'd worked so diligently on the wallpaper to find Carlton kneeling on the floor. He wore a pair of dungarees and a white undershirt, and his hair hung over his eyes. Using the claw of a hammer, he wrenched a piece of baseboard away from the wall, then threw it onto a stack of similar pieces of wood. "What are you doing?"

"Wood's rotten," he said. "Has to be replaced." He looked up at her, pushed his hair from his eyes, and then rested his hands on his knees. "Probably the same throughout the whole house. Don't know why I didn't notice it before." His voice was tense, leaving no room for doubt.

Alice-Ann started to come out of her coat but stopped. "Carlton, I —"

"How was he?"

She pressed her lips together. "He looks better than I thought he would. I mean, when it comes to injuries . . ."

"What?" His eyes narrowed. "I'm one up on him?"

Alice-Ann slipped out of her coat and dropped it to the floor in front of him, then knelt on it. She hadn't had a pair of nylons since America had gone to war, but there was no need to ruin a perfectly good hem, not to mention her knees. "Carlton, listen to me —"

"No, you listen to me, Alice-Ann. I told you that you could go see him, so I only have myself to blame." He shook his head in disbelief. "I just didn't think you'd do it without telling me."

"I was *going* to tell you. Yesterday. But you didn't come home."

He stood. Threw the hammer onto the pile of splintered baseboard, causing her to jump. To bury her face in her hands. "You're blaming *me* now?"

CHAPTER 35

Alice-Ann stood, ignoring the pain already forming in her knees. "No, Carlton. . . . *No.* You *have* to listen to me."

Carlton pinched the bridge of his nose and groaned. "Just tell me, all right? Just go ahead and tell me —" He dropped his hand and stared at her. "All this was for nothing, right?"

"All what?"

"The house?" He shot a look in the direction of her hand. "The ring I'm assuming is still under your glove?"

She pulled her glove off to display the ring. "Of course it's still here. I don't — I understand, Carlton, that you're upset that I went without telling you —"

"Even Nancy didn't know. I went to your work today. Did you know that? As soon as I got back. I wanted to surprise you. I even took you some flowers, which, by the way, look *great* on Miss Portia's desk. I *wanted* to walk back here with you." He put his hands on his hips. "Man, did I look like a fool." He spoke through clenched teeth.

Her heart burned inside her chest. Somehow, she had to defuse this. "You couldn't look like a fool even if you tried, Carlton."

"Well, they sure looked at me like I was. What kind of man doesn't know his fiancée isn't working that day?"

She took a step toward him. "The kind who left town when I was about to tell you and who didn't come back when I thought you would."

"So you *are* blaming me?"

"Of course not. Please listen to me. I didn't have a chance to tell you and I didn't tell anyone because I didn't want the rumor mill to start grinding. Maybe that was the wrong thing to do, but I didn't know what *else* to do."

"How about stay in Bynum?"

"You *said* it was okay with you if I wanted to see him. I *wanted* to see him, Carlton. I didn't want *anything* to ever stand between the two of us. You and me." Alice-Ann managed to gasp for a breath; the weight of the moment crushed her chest. "Carlton, there's *nothing* between Mack and me. If you'll just let me —"

"I guess when it's all said and done, I'll

finally be the joke of Bynum."

"Why would you — why would you become a joke?"

His eyes flashed. "He's the *real* hero, isn't he?"

And there it was. But was that his *only* concern? Or did it merely serve to complicate an already-difficult situation? She raised her hands, palms up, then let them fall dramatically to her sides. "What am I supposed to do with that? *Say* to that?"

Carlton's jaw flexed and his brow furrowed as he thumped himself in the chest, where sweat glistened on hard muscle. "Look at me, Alice-Ann."

"I am looking at you, Carlton."

"I mean take a *good* look. What do you see?" He scoffed. "I'm a hometown hero because I got hit in the head. And why did I get hit in the head? Because I didn't have the good sense to get out of the way." He pointed out the window as though Mack stood there, as he had in her dream a thousand and one nights ago. "But *him*? Mack? He's the real hero. Good ole Mack got shot down over the Pacific by enemy planes. Bobbed around in the water in eyeshot of the Japanese and managed *not* to get picked up by them but rather by an American submarine where he suffered for

weeks on end, waiting to get to a hospital."
He wiped his face with his hand. "And
then . . . *then* . . . he's laid up for another
few weeks until someone spots him in a
mess hall. And now he's come back to
Georgia for a few more weeks or months or
who knows how long and —" He stopped
himself. His voice had become unrecogniz-
able to Alice-Ann and she wondered if possibly to himself as well. He took several deep
breaths, blowing them out, then bent over
and pressed his hands against his knees as
though doing so was the only thing keeping
him up. Keeping him breathing, even.

"You make it sound like he *planned* this
to hurt you."

"Don't be ridiculous."

"Ridiculous?"

"And then you head off to Savannah to
see him —" he began, as though the other
words hadn't been spoken.

"Because —"

Carlton stood straight. "No." He shook
his head. "I don't want to hear it. I can't do
this right now."

"Do *what,* Carlton?"

He looked around the dust-filled room,
his eyes finally resting on the pile of wood
near his feet. "You've got to make up your
mind, Alice-Ann. Him or me."

■ ■ ■

She thought she had. Truly thought she had. That she would come home from Savannah — Mack had released her heart back to her . . . back to Carlton — and after telling Carlton the truth, they'd live happily ever after.

She'd thought God had delivered her from her distresses. She'd thought he'd heard her prayers.

After Carlton's ultimatum, she stumbled out of the house, her world upside down. She made it to the end of the walkway, then turned left instead of right. Right would take her to Nancy's. Or on into town, where she was sure she could find someone to take her home.

But she turned left instead because more than a ride home, she needed to walk. Needed to think. Needed to *pray.* She could always turn around and head back up the hill to town. Always find a ride later. Not that it mattered now. Nothing mattered now.

She walked between the manicured front lawns of the homes and the skinny dogwoods and azaleas — no longer in bloom — and tried to reason it all out. Her head was so full. Too full.

How could it be that in such a short period of time, she'd learned so much about the adults around her? About herself?

No life goes unscathed, that much was for sure.

She'd had no idea until she'd ridden into town with Papa about Miss Portia's onetime affection for him and how he'd loved her mother more. But her mother had died too early in life, everyone said. And Alice-Ann agreed.

Miss Portia had remained alone all of her life, never having found true love again. Or had she? Maeve seemed convinced that Miss Portia and Mister Dooley had some sort of romance going. But if that were the case, they'd never been open about it, and that — to Alice-Ann's way of thinking — was the saddest part of the story.

"If only my mother," Alice-Ann whispered into the cool night air, "if only my mother were here, she could tell me what —"

If Earlene Branch were still alive, Alice-Ann wouldn't be walking on this dark stretch of sidewalk where only a car or two passed this time of the evening. Inside these homes, families gathered around their supper tables. Or they'd all finished up. Black-out shades would soon be pulled and child-hood bedtime prayers would be prayed.

Alice-Ann didn't have her mother, no. Of course, she had Aunt Bess, who, like Miss Portia, had lost her one true love. Though in time, hers might have seen the light and turned from his wicked ways. Maybe.

She stopped walking. The house she stood in front of had a short brick wall in front. She sat upon it, feeling the cold like ice water through her bones. She'd left her coat on the floor of the house, the one that was supposed to have been hers and Carlton's, and she wished she'd thought to grab it.

She wished she'd thought to —

Alice-Ann buried her face in her hands and sobbed. Why even think this way? She felt the pool of tears against her cheeks as she realized she'd end up like Miss Portia and Aunt Bess. Alone. Her one true love had slipped through her fingers like water.

He'd given her an ultimatum. How could he have done that? How could he have been so cruel as to not at least listen to what she had to say about her visit with Mack? Was this the kind of man he really was? Impulsive and quick-tempered?

No. She'd never seen anything remotely like that in Carlton. Not in all the years she'd known him. Other than the night after church when he'd driven her home, stopping first on a dirt road between two fields.

Carlton had been afraid then.

Alice-Ann might not be the smartest girl in Bynum, but she was smart enough to know that anger didn't come riding into a person's heart on its own horse. Anger came from something else. Another emotion. And Carlton's anger had ridden in on a horse called *Fear.*

Fear of losing her. *Her.*

"I love you so much," he'd said to her that night, his words agonizing. "I couldn't bear losing you."

She sniffled as she brushed her tears away from her cheeks. Fear was something she understood now too. Losing Carlton was more than *she* could bear. To complicate matters, Carlton was afraid of being found out. That the whole town — the one that had dubbed him a hero, though he'd never sought that label — would find out the truth.

Carlton was a proud man who'd fallen into a trap. She understood that, too. Only that afternoon, when she'd had the opportunity to speak up right at the beginning of her visit with Mack, she'd chosen silence.

Sometimes not saying anything at all was more dangerous than opening your mouth.

She knew *that* much and she knew it well. She also knew that she had to fix this.

Somehow . . . she'd make him understand. *Somehow.*

Alice-Ann started back toward the house — their house — keeping her eyes as best she could on the sidewalk. The half-moon cast such a faint glow over Bynum, but she knew she could make it back if she focused. And when she got back, she'd force Carlton to listen. She'd sit on him if she had to — not that she could *ever* match his strength. But she'd at least try. She wasn't going to lose him without a solid fight.

A set of blackened headlights came down the street. Hoping not to be noticed, she looked back to her feet and kept walking, praying she blended well with the shadows. But then the car slowed and rolled to a stop against the curb next to her.

"You left your coat," Carlton said after he'd slid across the front seat and rolled down the window.

She felt her brow furrow. "Is that why you came?"

"Get in the car. You can't walk home and it's turning cold out here."

"I can find a ride, Carlton. And I'm fine, thank you."

"Get in the car, Alice-Ann." The tone of his voice told her he wasn't kidding.

Neither was she.

She got in and he scooted back behind the steering wheel and reached for the gearshift. "Wait," she said, grabbing his hand.

She moved closer as he looked first from their hands to whatever lay outside the windshield. "We can't just sit here."

"Yes, we can. If we have to, we can. Because I'll do whatever it takes, Carlton, to get your attention long enough to tell you what I think. Long enough for you to stop listening to the voices inside your own head so that you can hear mine."

He turned to look at her, his face more a blank slate than that of the man she loved and knew. "All right."

"I have one question. I'm only going to ask it once but I'm going to ask that you please answer with complete and total honesty."

"I've never lied to you, Alice-Ann. I'm not about to start now."

She raked her teeth over her lips. They'd gone dry and she was sure they no longer held even the faintest hint of seaside coral. "Are you afraid?"

"Of?"

"Losing me? You said once that you couldn't bear to lose me. Is that what you're afraid of?"

He returned his stare to whatever lay outside the windshield.

"Well?"

Carlton looked at her again. "I'll answer your question if you'll answer me one first."

"Okay."

"Honestly."

"Honestly," she affirmed.

"Were you — *are* you — in love with *Mack*? Or only with the *idea* of him?"

She smiled and her lips quivered. Oh yes. Carlton *was* afraid, and that put them on equal footing. "I was never in love with Mack, Carlton. I've only been in love once in my life — I know that now."

Because Mack helped me see it, not that I can tell you that. Not yet. Not now.

She squeezed his hand.

"I'm sorry," he whispered. He breathed out a smile. "Maybe I'm the one who should have gone for the walk."

"What do you mean?"

"Remember when your daddy said that a man needs to take a walk sometimes? Have a little talk with Jesus, as the song goes?"

Alice-Ann loved that song. "I remember." She turned his palm up. "I'm sorry, too, Carlton," she said, as she ran her fingers over it, felt the calluses that had formed over the past few weeks of working on the house.

She pressed her lips against them, and his fingertips twitched with the intake of his breath. "You are my one true love, Carlton Hillis," she said against the hard skin. "I've never been more sure of anything in my life." She looked up at him. "You see me as . . . *beautiful.* You — you know who L. Frank Baum is . . ."

He chuckled lightly. "What does L. Frank Baum have to do with anything?"

"Never mind." She chuckled. "And you make me laugh. You take me into the deepest part of your heart and you allow me to be a part of it. Your heart beats and mine finds its rhythm. I've never had that before. Before you."

He pulled his hand away from hers and brought it to the back of her head. "No," he said. His fingers wove through her hair, the tips brushing the edge of her hat. "I'm not *afraid* of losing you, Alice-Ann. I'm *terrified* of losing you. As much as you love me, multiply that by a hundred — a thousand or a million — and that's where my heart is." He shook his head and his eyes twinkled. "Who would have thought that the scrawny, freckle-faced, funny-toothed kid my sister used to hang out with and giggle like schoolgirls with —"

She swatted at him. "We *were* schoolgirls,

512

Carlton Hillis."

He kissed her, his lips lingering only a moment. She knew, to keep them safe. "But not anymore."

"No," she whispered. "Not anymore." She leaned back so as to look at him fully. "Did you know that you are the *only* man I've ever kissed?"

He leaned against the driver's door and the moonlight fell over his face. "You don't say," he said, his expression showing that he was quite pleased.

"Yep." She waited, then said, "And I want *you*, Carlton Hillis, to be the first. The last. The only."

His hands found hers again and his fingers played with the ring. For a moment, he looked more boy than man and she saw in his face the children they'd one day bring into the world. She sighed into the thought.

"I think I can arrange that," he finally said.

Alice-Ann smiled. "And you'll marry me?"

"Oh yes, ma'am, I will. If you think you can put up with me."

"Only if you promise to start taking a few walks and having a few talks . . ."

"Yes'm. I can most definitely do that."

"Then I can put up with you, all right. I'll put up with you and we'll put all this nonsense behind us. We'll have a good life.

And a God-centered marriage. And we'll have lots of children who —"

Carlton laughed. "Whoa, whoa," he said, drawing her close. She laid her head against his chest and listened for his heartbeat, strong and steady, then felt her own catch up to it. "How many children are you thinking?" he asked her, and the low rumble of bemusement rose from deep within.

"Well, I don't know. How many would *you* like to have?"

He thought a moment. "Three. Two girls and boy. The boy first, so he can look out for the girls."

"Or the girls first so they can keep the boy straight if he ever goes off course."

He kissed the top of her head. "Whatever you say, ma'am."

She nodded as the stress of the day drained out of her. "Well then, Mr. Hillis," she said, craning her neck to look at him.

He peered at her. "Yes, Mrs. Hillis," he teased.

"I only have *one* thing more to say."

"What's that, buttercup?"

She grinned, kissed the stubble along his jaw and chin, and said, "Bob's your uncle."

CHAPTER 36

Two Months Later
December 7, 1944

In November, as President Roosevelt won his fourth term, Alice-Ann and Carlton — not willing to wait for Maeve and Ernie to set a date — made a decision to marry on her birthday.

As soon as she made the announcement at work, Nancy exclaimed that "The Cottage" — as they'd come to officially call it — wouldn't be ready. "Please don't tell me you're going to live over the five-and-dime. Trust me, honey, that'll never do."

Well, that much was true. Irene living in a large farmhouse with Nelson's family was one thing. But a fairly small apartment? No. It wouldn't do.

When she asked Carlton exactly which threshold he planned to carry her over, he nodded as though the idea of living with *either* of their families was out of the question. "I know Nelson and Irene have been living there with your daddy and Aunt Bess, but it's a whole lot different when you're the groom saying good night and then heading off to bed with a man's daughter."

That was another way of looking at it. One she'd not thought of. "Then should we postpone?"

Carlton coughed dramatically. "No." Then he tugged on her earlobe and said, "Don't worry, my love. I'll figure out something."

Sure enough, before Alice-Ann's forehead could form a single worry line, Carlton paid a visit to Claudette and Johnny and secured a room for the two of them at Walker's Inn. "They're giving us a special rate," Carlton declared. "Only fifteen a week. Johnny says they usually charge three twenty-five a night, so that's a real fine deal, I think."

Alice-Ann nearly swooned at the thought of such a kindness from her old friend. And the thought of herself and Carlton in one room. Alone. And for only fifteen dollars a week.

"That's not a bad deal," Papa said when she told him. Then he winked at her. "Of course I'd've only charged you twelve."

"Papa," Alice-Ann said with a laugh, even as heat filled her.

Still, even with most folks happy for them

and thinking the Daileys had done some great thing, some of the church and the town's ladies declared the two of them were rushing. But Alice-Ann and Carlton knew the truth — they'd waited long enough. And they'd gone through so much, both alone and together.

They'd been through a war and they'd survived it, their love intact. Their love stronger than before.

With so little time to plan — and a limited budget — there'd be no fancy flowers or attendants as there had been at Claudette and Johnny's wedding. Alice-Ann and Carlton had both agreed — their love was enough. They needed only the ceremony, the love of their family and friends, and God's blessings.

The day had come and Alice-Ann, all of nineteen years old, decades older than only three years before, sat on the tiny stool in front of her vanity mirror, Irene behind her, working almost professionally with her hair.

After Irene had drawn the thick waves into a chignon in the back and left tiny wisps of curls around her face and against the nape of her neck, Aunt Bess helped her slip into the dress. The material sent goose bumps against her flesh, falling over her body like a soft, cool sheet.

No longer feeling the need to find beauty in a jar, Alice-Ann applied only a tiny bit of makeup, then stepped into the new shoes her father had purchased at Lewen's. She arched her back and squared her shoulders as she turned, then, to look in the mirror over her dresser.

"Beautiful," Aunt Bess said. "My gracious, Alice, I declare you're as pretty as your mama."

Alice-Ann shook her head. "Not quite, Aunt Bess, but thank you."

"I'll be right back," Irene said to the reflection meeting her in the mirror, then walked out of the room, leaving the door open. She returned a moment later, carrying a small wrapped box. "From Nelson and Little Mack and me."

"Oh, Irene," Alice-Ann whispered as she tore into it. Inside, a lacy blue handkerchief lay folded beneath tissue paper.

"You've got Aunt Bess's dress for something borrowed. Carlton's great-grandmother's ring for something old. The shoes for something new. We thought you needed something blue to complete the tradition."

Alice-Ann pulled the handkerchief from the box. "I'll carry it with Mama's Bible," she said, then reached over to hug her sister-in-law. "I love you, Irene," she said.

"I love you too."

Aunt Bess dabbed at her eyes. "Come on, girls. Too much of this and we won't make it to the church on time." She cleared her throat. "Or I'll turn into one large puddle and you'll be forced to mop me up."

The three women eased down the stairs, where they were met by the men of the family. Nelson grinned as he always did, then said, "Look at you . . ."

But Papa . . . Papa's eyes grew misty. Then he cleared his throat and mumbled, "We better get a move on."

Alice-Ann kissed his cheek. "And you most of all, Scarecrow."

He cleared his throat again. "I don't know what that means, Alice-Ann, but I'm sure it's something."

She brought her eyes to his. "It means I'm going to miss being your little girl, Papa."

He huffed. "You'll *always* be my little girl, Alice-Ann. Call yourself Branch or Hillis, but you'll always be my baby." He shook his head. "And you're so beautiful. . . . I wish your mama . . ."

"She'll be there in spirit, Brother," Aunt Bess said quickly. "Now, I do believe Alice-Ann has a groom waitin' and I see no reason to keep him like that."

Alice-Ann took in a deep breath. "Papa, do you have Mama's Bible?"

"It's in the truck."

She nodded. "Then it's time to go, I reckon."

A half hour later, her fingers worked the material of her father's suit coat as he stepped beside her, the two of them marching down the aisle of Oak Grove Baptist Church, where the scents of years gone by and furniture polish on old pews wafted around them.

Alice-Ann had no need to look down. No need to worry about cracks in the sidewalk or even in her life. Her eyes focused on those of her groom, who'd smiled at her when she'd first stepped toward him, but whose face now broke apart in a wide grin.

She grinned back at him. She couldn't help it. He made her so happy. So very, very happy. When she and Papa finally reached him, she sighed in relief, and even though she wanted desperately to slide into her groom's arms, she stared straight ahead.

"Who gives this woman to this man?" her pastor asked.

"I do," Papa said. The scent of his tobacco washed over her as he kissed her cheek, and she closed her eyes, not wanting to miss even that moment of this day.

Her father turned her toward Carlton, who mouthed, "Hey, doodlebug."

She giggled. Blinked slowly. "Hey."

"Do you," Reverend Parker continued and she looked briefly at him, then turned back to her groom, "Carlton Alexander Hillis, take Alice-Ann Branch as your wedded wife . . . ?"

Carlton cocked a brow and Alice-Ann bit her bottom lip, hoping she didn't smear the lipstick.

"To have and to hold . . . ?"

He nodded. Mouthed, "So beautiful."

Alice-Ann felt the blush rush from her toes.

". . . to love and to cherish, till death parts you, according to God's holy ordinance?"

"I do," Carlton said.

Reverend Parker repeated the vows for Alice-Ann, and her eyes never left Carlton's.

"I do," she said when her time had come to make the vow.

"Then by the power vested in me, I pronounce you to be Mr. and Mrs. Carlton Hillis."

Alice-Ann and Carlton turned to look at him.

"You may kiss your bride, Mr. Hillis," the pastor said with a sly smile.

Again they looked at each other and she stepped into his arms, strong and protective. "I love you," Carlton whispered, then pressed his lips against hers.

"And I love you," she said against them after the kiss ended.

His embrace grew possessive and secure. "Truly?" he teased.

Alice-Ann sighed. He was so very, very her one true love. "Truly," she said, and he kissed her again.

A NOTE FROM THE AUTHOR

"How much of you is in this story?"

I hear that question a lot. Truth is, there's a little bit of the author in every novel. But it's not always *our* story. Ideas often come from the moments in our lives. They also come from the moments in the lives of others.

We cannot help it. We hear something — we novelists — and suddenly a story forms. The words *what if* somehow get mingled in with that little tidbit of story, and away we go. And so it was, many years ago, when an older couple who lived next door to my husband and me invited us in for Christmas cookies and tea. As they showed us around their warm and lovely home, I happened to notice a Purple Heart, framed in a shadow box. I asked about it, and . . . well, I got a story. A few years later, I heard another WWII story — this one from my great-aunt, who told me she married my great-uncle shortly after he enlisted in the war and, thinking he'd be home soon, set about to make a life for the two of them. But his return didn't happen for *four years.* I couldn't imagine marrying my one true love only to have him leave for war and not return until four years later.

Years before hearing these two stories, when I was about ten years old, I sat in a Sunday school class and listened intently as my teacher said, "You can't choose whom you fall in love with, but you can choose whom you marry." Now, I have *no* idea what that had to do with the lesson (maybe that week's lesson was on Solomon . . .), but the wisdom (pardon the pun) of those words *never* left me.

So it was that when the idea for this book came to me (ironically, the title came to me first), the World War II stories folded in with the wisdom of my Sunday school teacher, and . . . I had a story. Or at least the bones of one.

I read dozens of books and watched lots of memoir-inspired videos on World War II, and I learned something significant: there's a reason that generation was called "the greatest." As I developed the story line and dug into the characters, I was also reminded that God has a plan for each of us, and if we trust him (and listen to him) with that plan *within* the days and minutes and seconds of our lives, he will never lead us down the wrong path. Or to the wrong love.

With that in mind, I sincerely hope you enjoyed the somewhat-true story of *The One True Love of Alice-Ann.* And I hope you'll let me know what you think by visiting me at my website: www.EvaMarieEversonAuthor .com.

Eva Marie Everson

DISCUSSION QUESTIONS

1. Alice-Ann struggles to accept how her outward appearance could affect her love life, fearing that she'll end up like her aunt Bess, caring for her brother and sister-in-law's family. What begins to change her attitude? Is there anything in your life that compares to Alice-Ann's journey?

2. At first, Alice-Ann has a hard time with her new city-girl sister-in-law. In what ways does she reach out to Irene, extending a hand in friendship? How does she miss the mark?

3. While Alice-Ann is convinced from a very young age that Mack is her "one true love," others who know him well seem convinced that he's not good husband material. Why are they able to see things about him to which Alice-Ann was blind? Have you ever found yourself in a situation like this?

4. How did you feel about the German

prisoner, Adler, helping to deliver Irene's baby? Does this seem like a realistic part of the story? How does it change Alice-Ann's perspective on the war?

5. When the wounded Carlton returns to Bynum, the townspeople call him a hero, a label he denies — but only privately to Alice-Ann. What prevents him from confessing the truth? Should he publicly denounce the title thrust upon him? What would the response be, do you imagine?

6. Aunt Bess tells Alice-Ann: "You can't choose who you fall in love with, but you can choose who you marry." Do you believe both parts of that statement are true? Why or why not?

7. Both Aunt Bess and Irene tell Alice-Ann that Psalm 25:17 played a significant role in helping them through difficult times. Irene even confesses that she had been trying to solve her problems herself. Describe a time in your life when you felt overwhelmed by "distresses." How did you handle it? What does this verse say to you?

8. Papa suggests that "When life comes at you fast, take a little walk and have a little talk with the good Lord. He'll straighten things out for you." How do you react when "life comes at you fast"?

9. On the way back from Savannah, Alice-

Ann runs into Sandra, a girl she went to school with, and is surprised to learn of her family's circumstances. Is Alice-Ann being fair to herself when she thinks she's been so wrapped up in her own war story that she missed the stories within her own community? What else might Alice-Ann have missed? Are there stories of others in your life that you might be missing?

10. Even up to the final chapters of the story, Alice-Ann seems to hold some doubts about her one true love. What do you think finally convinces her of the truth? When have you doubted the path God has laid out for you?

ABOUT THE AUTHOR

Eva Marie Everson is a multiple-award-winning author and speaker. She is one of the original five members of the Orlando Word Weavers critique group, an international and national group of critique chapters, and now serves as president of Word Weavers International, Inc. Her novel *Waiting for Sunrise,* which boldly approaches the topic of mental illness, was a finalist for the 2013 Christy Award for excellence in Christian fiction. Her other novels include *Five Brides, This Fine Life,* and *Things Left Unspoken.*

Eva Marie is a popular presenter at writers' conferences nationwide and serves as codirector of the Florida Christian Writers Conference and contests director for the Blue Ridge Mountains Christian Writers Conference. During the 2010–2011 school year, she was an adjunct professor at Taylor

University in Upland, Indiana. She describes it as one of the best times she ever had while working.

In 2002 and 2009, Eva Marie served as a journalist for the Israel Ministry of Tourism. Her article series, "Falling into the Bible," served as the inspiration for her book *Reflections of God's Holy Land: A Personal Journey through Israel,* coauthored with bestselling Israeli author Miriam Feinberg Vamosh. The book went on to become a finalist for the ECPA Gold Medallion award.

Born and reared in the low country of Georgia, Eva Marie is a wife, mother, and grandmother. She lives, works, and finds respite in her lakefront home in Florida. She enjoys reading, knitting, traveling, boating, and singing along with country music on the radio. She is pretty much owned by her dog, Poods.

The employees of Thorndike Press hope you have enjoyed this Large Print book. All our Thorndike, Wheeler, and Kennebec Large Print titles are designed for easy reading, and all our books are made to last. Other Thorndike Press Large Print books are available at your library, through selected bookstores, or directly from us.

For information about titles, please call:
  (800) 223-1244

or visit our website at:
  gale.com/thorndike

To share your comments, please write:
  Publisher
  Thorndike Press
  10 Water St., Suite 310
  Waterville, ME 04901